ONE SECOND AWAY

Also by Rick Mofina

IF TWO ARE DEAD
SOMEONE SAW SOMETHING
EVERYTHING SHE FEARED
HER LAST GOODBYE
SEARCH FOR HER
THEIR LAST SECRET
THE LYING HOUSE
MISSING DAUGHTER
LAST SEEN
FREE FALL
EVERY SECOND
FULL TILT
WHIRLWIND
INTO THE DARK
THEY DISAPPEARED
THE BURNING EDGE
IN DESPERATION
THE PANIC ZONE
VENGEANCE ROAD
SIX SECONDS
A PERFECT GRAVE
EVERY FEAR
THE DYING HOUR
BE MINE
NO WAY BACK
BLOOD OF OTHERS
COLD FEAR
IF ANGELS FALL
INTO THE FIRE
THE HOLLOW PLACE
REQUIEM
BEFORE SUNRISE
THE ONLY HUMAN

PRAISE FOR *ONE SECOND AWAY*

"A first-rate thriller."

—**Shari Lapena**, #1 bestselling author of *She Didn't See It Coming*

"With countless page-turning twists that take you from Toronto to Paris to Sao Paulo, you don't so much *read* ONE SECOND AWAY as you do *live* it. Rick Mofina's latest thriller is a roaring roller-coaster ride that will keep your heart pounding until the very end."

—**Ashley Tate**, #1 bestselling author of *Twenty-Seven Minutes*

PRAISE FOR RICK MOFINA

"Rick Mofina's books are edge-of-your-seat thrilling. Page-turners that don't let up."

—**Louise Penny**, #1 *New York Times* bestselling author

"Every thriller he writes [is] an adrenaline-packed ride."

—**Tess Gerritsen**, *New York Times* bestselling author

"One of the best thriller writers in the business."

—*Library Journal*

ONE SECOND AWAY

RICK MOFINA

DOUBLEDAY CANADA

PUBLISHED IN 2026 BY DOUBLEDAY CANADA

Doubleday Canada, an imprint of Penguin Random House Canada Limited,
320 Front Street West, Suite 1400,
Toronto, Ontario, M5V 3B6, Canada
penguinrandomhouse.ca

Doubleday Canada and colophon are registered trademarks of
Penguin Random House LLC.

The authorized representative in the EU for product safety and compliance is Penguin Random House Ireland, Morrison Chambers, 32 Nassau Street, Dublin, D02 YH68, Ireland, https://eu-contact.penguin.ie

Library and Archives Canada Cataloguing in Publication

Title: One second away / Rick Mofina.
Names: Mofina, Rick, author
Identifiers: Canadiana (print) 20250211858 | Canadiana (ebook) 20250211866 |
ISBN 9780385701983 (softcover) | ISBN 9780385701990 (EPUB)
Subjects: LCGFT: Thrillers (Fiction) | LCGFT: Novels.
Classification: LCC PS8626.O44 O54 2026 | DDC C813/.6—dc23

Cover and text design by Andrew Roberts
Cover images: (train) vacant, (background) Tierney / Adobe Stock
Typeset in Escrow by Arthur Dennyson Hamdani and Six Red Marbles

Printed in the United States of America

1st Printing

To the memory of my father and mother, together now.

We are healed of suffering only by experiencing it to the full.

—Marcel Proust, *The Sweet Cheat Gone*

By knowing the Mother one knows her children.

—Lao Tzu, *Tao Te Ching*, translated by John Minford

1

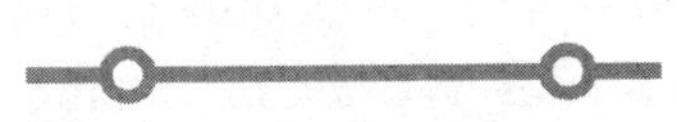

TORONTO

The jumpers were the worst. Glen Hockley had seen three suicides over his years as a subway train operator.

One woman had looked right at him in her last moments. Her face was still burned into his memory.

She'd been smiling.

That was something he had to live with.

Part of the job.

Now, as passengers shuffled on and off, Glen studied his console, then the platform mirror. All clear. Seconds later, the chime sounded.

"*Please stand clear of the doors,*" the automated voice droned.

Then:

"*Next station, Union. Union Station.*"

Union was the heart of the Toronto Transit Commission's system, known as the TTC, one of the busiest transit systems in North America. It was the afternoon rush, and Glen rubbed the back of his neck. He'd woken that morning with a bad feeling about today—likely brought on by the battles he'd been having with his teenaged son about the boy hanging out with the wrong people. Shaking his head, Glen pushed the thought aside. He'd deal with it later.

His six-car train rumbled along, trackside signals blinking green. Clear to proceed.

The Automatic Train Control system sent signals from the tracks to the control centre, relaying speed and braking instructions back to the train. With ATC, only one operator was needed to run the train, making everything more efficient.

It worked well but, whenever necessary, operators could always take control of the trains. Last week, a Line 2 operator had reported her in-cab display was flickering for several stops. She took over the cab. Control had her hold at a station, ran diagnostics, and corrected the situation. It was a bit of an odd one, Glen had thought.

Life underground suited Glen. It was unpredictable. He'd seen everything—fights, overdoses, a naked man with a chainsaw dashing down a platform with cops in pursuit. A woman had even given birth on his train. And then there were the young idiots who climbed onto the rear—subway surfers recording themselves riding to the next station for social media.

On game days, all the riders seemed pumped. Glen remembered he still had to get tickets to take his son to this weekend's doubleheader with the Jays and Yankees at the Dome. He regretted how they'd argued the last time they were together. *We'll patch things up at the game*, he thought.

His train progressed smoothly to St. Andrew, then up toward Spadina Station. Then the ATC system had a slight delay at Museum, a hiccup, which was a bit puzzling. He scanned his console. No issues. Weird.

Still, maybe I should advise Control?

Whatever it was, it seemed to correct itself as soon as it arose. Everything was good, so he continued on. At Dupont Station, light gleaming down on the earth-toned tiled walls, he slowed to a stop. Then came the cycle of chimes, doors, announcements.

Soon after, as the train left Dupont, the tunnel transitioned from a square arch to a circular tunnel. Glen had always loved this section because the streaking effect was mesmerizing, like travelling at the speed of light through space and time.

His console display flickered.

He glanced at it, then did a double take, jerking his head back.

What? Wait. This flickering isn't normal.

But as he entered a curve, the trackside signals were flashing green.

Okay, that's good. All clear. Relax.

Then, moments later, his scalp tingled, his body tensed. At the station ahead—*a train was stopped on his track.*

A horn blasted, jolting adrenaline through Glen.

His insides spasmed. His mind detonated like fireworks. He moved to override the ATC, smashing the button for his train's emergency brakes.

No time.

The stopped train ahead instantly magnified before him.

God help me!

A piercing metal squeal bled into a human scream.

2

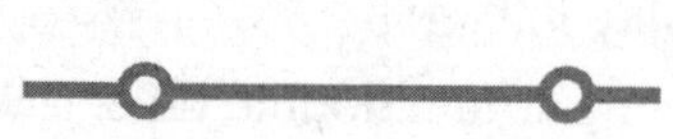

LOS ANGELES

"We're good for time."

Jessie Ward powered off her car after parking at Los Angeles International Airport.

Driving through the horseshoe had been a challenge. She was glad they'd left with time to spare and that she'd prebooked a spot. But when she turned to Dylan and patted his leg, she was pierced with doubt. *Am I doing the right thing, sending my son alone across the country again?*

She took a breath. "All set, sweetie?"

Dylan was quiet. Looking at him, she marvelled at how, not so long ago, she'd carried him in her arms—and now, suddenly, he was nine years old.

"You're going to have fun, right?"

He nodded.

"Anything you want to talk about?"

He shook his head.

"You sure?" She stroked his cheek.

He nodded, suddenly brightening. "Let's go."

Jessie smiled, got out, hefted his suitcase from the trunk, and helped him with his backpack. He'd picked it out, liking how it was dotted with a pattern of gamepads in shades of green. She adjusted his shoulder straps when he threw his arms around her, crushing her, as if it were the most important hug of his life.

"Oh, honey." She stroked his hair, the doubt returning.

"I just worry about leaving you alone, Mom."

He pulled back, his young heart so heavy it broke hers, and she cupped his face.

"Don't worry, sweetheart. It's going to be fine. Okay?"

He nodded and then they set off, walking from the garage with Jessie rolling his suitcase. She stole glances at her son. *Will this trip change him? Will he be the same boy when he returns to me?*

Several minutes later, they reached their terminal, stepping into the bustle and hum of travellers flowing through the departures area mixed with security reminders over the public address system.

They got in line for check-in with EverySky Airlines and eventually were greeted by agent Shawn Curtis, according to his badge. Jessie handed him their IDs and Dylan's travel documents.

"Thank you for flying EverySky." Shawn smiled, his keyboard clicking as he studied the paperwork and his monitor. "Ah yes, your forms look good." Shawn nodded to Dylan. "Welcome aboard, Mr. Dylan Parker Ward, aged nine, flying to New York. Or should I say, welcome back. I see you flew with us a few months ago."

"Yup." Dylan nodded.

A moment later, the printer whirred, then Shawn reached for the pages, folding and inserting them into a lanyard, then draping it over Dylan's neck. The orange plastic identification with the big letters *UM*—for "unaccompanied minor"—at the top covered much of his chest.

"Don't take this off, okay Dylan?"

"I know."

"I know, you're an old pro." Shawn smiled again before handing something to Jessie. "And here's your gate pass with the gate number and boarding time. As you know, you take Dylan through security, then report to our gate attendants."

"Yes, thank you," Jessie said.

After clearing security, they stopped at a sandwich place and Jessie bought food for Dylan's flight. When they got to their gate and the EverySky desk, another attendant checked, then returned Dylan's documents.

"You're all good to go, honey," she said. "Lindsay Bell will take care of you when it's time to board. You have lots of time."

They found seats and Dylan immediately got out his Nintendo Switch and started playing *Mario Kart*.

"Are you hungry?" Jessie asked.

Without taking his eyes from his game, Dylan shook his head. Then, struck with a thought, he stopped playing and looked up at her. "Are *you* hungry, Mom? Want some of my sandwich?"

"No thank you, sweetie." Smiling and caressing his arm, Jessie noticed the old grape juice stains on his blue-striped white running shoes.

"I should've tried cleaning those stains again."

Dylan put his bag aside, glanced down, then resumed his game. "Mom, I like it. It's like fireworks and spiderwebs."

Jessie grinned and then packed the sandwich and chips in Dylan's backpack before surveying their area, which was crowded with passengers. Near them, a white-haired man wearing a straw fedora and flowered shirt sat with a white-haired woman who was reading Danielle Steel. Nearby, a woman fanned herself with her boarding pass. Another woman, about Jessie's age, worked on her laptop while sipping an energy drink. A man with salt-and-pepper stubble, wearing dark glasses and white earphones, stared at nothing in front of him. A couple in their early twenties was close by. Jessie watched as the male half of the couple crossed his tattooed arms on his chest. His jaw clenched listening to the woman with him before she turned away and rolled her eyes.

The young couple had Jessie thinking about the turmoil in her own family—how she was in the process of divorcing Vaughn, Dylan's dad. Knowing the toll it would take on their son, flying him back and forth across the country for the second time, filled her with guilt. *Will Vaughn and I ever get back to a good place?*

She thought of her mother, residing at a seniors' centre and grappling with her declining memory. Suddenly, the burst of a preboarding announcement pulled Jessie from her thoughts.

Dylan gazed through the large window overlooking the runway and watched planes taking off. She brushed his shoulder.

"All done playing?"

"I came second last," he said with a shrug. "But I unlocked a new kart."

"Wow, that's great." Jessie thought a moment. "Let me see your watch."

She held out her open palm until he undid the green band and surrendered his smartwatch. She'd paid extra for the version with two-day battery life. It was still at 98 per cent. She opened the settings and made sure he was sharing his location with her before strapping it back on his wrist.

"All good. Now let me see your phone."

"Mom, it's okay."

"I just want to be sure, honey."

Dylan fished it from his pocket. She checked his battery level, 96 per cent. Then she went to check his messages. She tapped Vaughn's name—nothing new. Then she checked Lillian and Miller's message thread—also nothing new. *It would have been nice if his grandparents had wished him a safe flight,* she thought.

"Okay." Jessie handed the phone back. "You know you can call or text me, Dad, Grandma or Grandpa anytime. I got you Wi-Fi on the flight. You should have enough battery to last until you land. I'll be tracking you, but be sure to text me when you land, so I can stop worrying about you."

"I know, Mom. You've told me a million times already."

"I know I have, but that's my job as your mom, sweetie. Ask the attendant to help you connect to the Wi-Fi if you have trouble with it. And try to text me at least once, so I know you're okay!"

Dylan nodded, taking his phone back. Staring at the lightning bolts on the case in silence, he bit his bottom lip, something he did when he was troubled.

"What is it, hon?"

"I guess I liked it better when we all lived together."

Her heart flooded with sadness and love for him, an eruption so sudden she had to steady her voice. "I know, honey. Me too." She paused. "You know, you don't have to go, if you don't want to."

"No, I still want to go." He frowned. "I just worry about you being all alone, Mom."

Jessie smiled. "I'll be fine. I'll be busy with work and your grandma here. It's only a month, and you're going to have fun with Grandma and Grandpa, and with Dad."

"Yeah, Grandpa's taking me to a baseball game, and Grandma's going to make her apple pie. They're *so* good. And Dad said maybe we'll go to the cabin, have hotdogs and marshmallows by the fire. And go fishing! And he'll help me pick out a new baseball glove."

"There you go. See, you'll have so much fun, and the time will fly. And I want you to send me lots of pictures of your adventures. Then, when you get back, we'll drive up to Yosemite, like we planned. Sound good?"

Dylan nodded just as his phone lit up with a message.

"It's Dad!"

Jessie leaned over to read the text.

So excited to see you, buddy. Have a good trip.

Dylan responded with an emoji of a grinning face.

"See, you're having fun already." Jessie gave him a squeeze.

"Hi Dylan." Smiling and lowering herself before them was an EverySky attendant holding some documents.

"I'm Lindsay and I'll escort you to your seat now."

"Already?" Jessie said, looking at her watch. There was still time before boarding.

"You bet. Dylan gets the VIP service; one of the first to board."

Dylan got to his feet, reaching for his backpack.

"Oh . . ." Jessie's voice tremored as she stood, opening her arms, crushing him in a hug. "Oh, sweetie. I love you. Have a safe trip."

"Are you going to be okay, Mom?" Dylan looked up at her, his eyes full of concern.

Brushing the tears from her cheeks, she nodded. "We'll FaceTime a lot," she said. "I'll see you in a month."

Smiling, Lindsay looked at Dylan. "All set?" Then at Jessie. "We request that you wait here until the plane is in the air."

"Okay." Jessie touched Dylan's arm as Lindsay helped him with his backpack and suitcase. He turned and hugged his mother once more.

"I love you too, Mom." Then he and Lindsay disappeared down the jet bridge, the attendant's hand on Dylan's shoulder.

Jessie barely heard the rise of activity, the flurry of flight announcements, the queuing of other passengers that followed. When boarding ended and the gate door was closed, she stood alone at the window and watched as Dylan's plane taxied and then eventually lifted off. As it climbed and vanished up into the sky, she gave a small finger wave.

Blinking back tears, Jessie pulled out her phone and texted her ex-husband and his parents to confirm Dylan was on the way. She reminded Lillian and Miller of Dylan's flight details for picking him up at JFK in New York.

About a minute later, Lillian responded.

Thanks so much Jessie!!!

She punctuated the message with three hearts.

A few seconds later, Vaughn responded with a thumbs-up.

That's it? He can't even manage to type a few words? Jessie thought.

She swallowed and pocketed her phone without responding. Then she made her way out of the terminal.

3

SANTA MONICA

As she drove to work, Jessie tried to quiet her anxiety. *Dylan is fine. In a few hours he will be landing in New York to be with his grandparents and his father. He's going to have the best time.*

She tried set her worry aside as she reached her office, which was in an eight-storey glass and steel building. Its sweeping, curving design, fronted with a garden fountain and palms, radiated calm—the opposite of how she was feeling in that moment, she noted with some irony. In the lobby she was greeted by the security officer at the desk.

"Hello to you, Ms. Ward."

"Hey Barney."

"A bit later than usual today."

"I had things to do this morning," Jessie said, touching her ID to the access reader, until it beeped. "It'll be a half day for me today."

Barney smiled at her. "Well, you have a fine day, Ms. Ward."

"You too, Barney."

Taking the elevator to the top floor, she swiped her ID again, this time at the doors of Instinct Nine-99.

She passed along the open area of analysts, engineers and techs hunched over keyboards, studying the multiple monitors at their desks. One wall held large flat screens displaying an array of live data for security networks. Most people laboured in quiet concentration, save for the few who looked away from their work to nod to Jessie.

She headed down the hall, passing the conference room and interior offices, where she badged the access reader again to unlock the door to her office. On the wall hung an array of personal photos, along with her framed degrees from the California Institute of Technology and the Massachusetts Institute of Technology.

Her eyes lingered on the degrees for a moment longer than usual. It had taken more than blood, sweat and tears to get those two sheets of paper. No one would ever grasp the full price she'd paid.

Dropping her purse in her desk drawer, she sat at her keyboard and dual monitors. On both screens, Dylan laughed on the beach before the photo montage dissolved to her mother, looking so lovely, then to her sister, Jennifer, radiant under a floppy hat. In the moment Dylan's face returned, Jessie was struck with a pang of guilt and his words replayed in her mind.

I liked it better when we all lived together.

It tore at her heart.

So did I, honey.

Jessie's lawyer said these trips—which included the visits with Vaughn's parents—would establish a positive foundation for negotiating terms of custody between her and her ex-husband. Jessie had agreed to them but wasn't happy about it, and she had let it be known in court a few months ago. The truth, as Jessie saw it, was that Vaughn's parents had never liked her. Although they'd never stated it out loud, Jessie sensed that they thought she was too consumed by her career; that she was to blame for the destruction of her marriage to their son. But Lillian and Miller liked to overlook the facts: that Vaughn, their Harvard-grad, globe-trotting journalist son, was obsessed with his own career; that he and Jessie had grown apart, and she was no longer able to trust him.

She reached for her phone and texted Dylan:

Everything going okay, hon?

She waited a few minutes, staring at the message thread, but he didn't reply right away. Frustrated, she turned back to her computer, logging in and immediately tracking Dylan's flight. All looked good so, satisfied, she shifted to work, reviewing the list of the company's ongoing contracts, responding to messages and providing her team with instructions and suggestions.

After sending one more email, she got up and walked over to the credenza next to her desk. She opened the cupboard door and tapped in a code to unlock the small office safe that was tucked away. She removed a dark blue laptop, the polished metal as reflective as a mirror, and took it to her desk. Firing it up, she went through the multi-stage security verification, then opened a confidential file.

Using concepts and designs Jessie had developed, Instinct Nine-99 was leading the creation of a classified advanced network security system, and a deadline was coming for an interim progress report on the project. She worked for an hour before she signed out, shut down and stowed her laptop back in the safe before leaving her office.

She went down the hall to a locked interior room, its glass walls tinted. She tapped her card on the reader and entered. A man and a woman, both in their early thirties, were the only people there. At opposite sides of a long table, each worked at a keyboard in front of multiple monitors.

"Yo Jess," said Bobby Chen, who was wearing a bright tie-dyed T-shirt, his focus welded to his work.

"Hello Jessica." Sarita Singh smiled from behind her monitor.

Jessie had met Sarita, a brilliant development engineer from Bengaluru, India, at a conference in Chicago. Impressed with Sarita's presentation on new advances concerning network protection,

Jessie had offered her a position with Instinct. Bobby she'd hired right out of Stanford, where he'd been considered a rising star. Even now, three years later, he was still constantly approached by competitors. In fact, he'd recently used vacation days to make a trip to Philadelphia—for, it turned out, a job interview with a competitor that had ended in a job offer. Luckily, she'd been able to convince him to stay—although she'd had to pay him more. But Jessie had no regrets. Losing Bobby would have hurt Instinct on so many levels because, like Sarita, he knew everything about the company—and also their efforts to harness AI to develop cutting-edge technology to improve cybersecurity for their biggest client, the US government.

"How's it going, guys?" Jessie asked, shutting the door behind her. She glanced at Sarita. A couple of weeks ago, she'd flown to Baltimore for a wedding. She'd seemed happier since returning. Jessie remembered how, last year, Vaughn had come to the office to meet her for lunch. While she was getting ready to leave, she'd noticed him giving Sarita a lingering look. It had only been for a moment but long enough to make Jessie a bit uncomfortable.

"Good, so far." Bobby nudged up his dark framed glasses. "Here, have a look." He pressed a few keys, and then the large screen at the end of the room blossomed and split with a chart and a graphic that illustrated an experimental algorithm he'd been playing with.

"We've resolved a couple major bugs that were blocking progress this morning," Bobby said, "so we're feeling better."

Jessie nodded in approval. "That's terrific." Bobby and Sarita were Instinct's top engineers assigned to this contract, which meant they'd received security clearance to the nth degree. Jessie stepped closer to the screen, examining the chart.

"How are we for the next deadline?"

"We're good. A bit more coding and testing to do," Bobby said.

"We're actually ahead of schedule," Sarita said.

"Good stuff, guys." Jessie nodded at them both before leaving the room and going to the kitchen. After getting a cup of coffee, she went back to her desk—where she worked for a few hours on tasks that she punctuated with breaks to track Dylan's flight, which seemed to be on time. By afternoon, Jessie had shut down her computer and began getting ready to leave for the day. Her phone chimed with a text message from her long-time friend Dahlia Wynne:

Hi Jessie. I'm leaving Las Vegas today for LA and taking a little vacay. Got time to get together tomorrow?

Dahlia! Absolutely! Dylan left today and I've got all the time in the world. Where and when?

I'll be downtown at the Westin Bonaventure. Meet you in the main lobby at 7?

Catching up with her friend from college would be nice, Jessie thought while on the elevator. The last time they'd seen each other was at a global trade show in Miami a few months before, where they'd recalled their MIT days and swapped stories on their love lives into the night at the bar. Dahlia had told her about her recent failed engagement. *Now,* Jessie thought, *Dahlia and I can commiserate with each other. Misery loves company. And that might be just what I need now.*

Getting to her car, Jessie tracked Dylan's flight again, which still seemed to be on time. She texted him again, but there was no response.

A hint of concern rippled through her, but she swallowed hard, telling herself that everything was okay.

Dylan was in a weak service zone or engrossed in his game.

That's all.

4

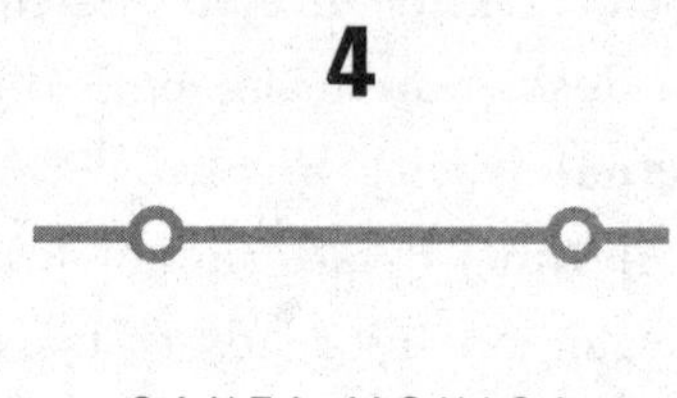

SANTA MONICA

Jessie's cottage-sized bungalow, with its red-tiled roof, stucco walls and arched doorways, stood near Santa Monica's North of Montana area.

Nearly every time she drove through her neighbourhood, she counted herself fortunate. So many of her friends had lost everything to the fires that swept through the Palisades in 2025. Her house had luckily been spared from the tragedy, and she was grateful.

When she got home, she wasn't very hungry but forced herself to finish off some cold pizza—leftovers from dinner with Dylan—then got back in the car to drive to the Palm Breeze Valley Senior Living Center.

As she walked up the path, she admired the flower beds and lush lawns, and how the trimmed trees and shrubs shaded the low-rise building. She entered the lobby and smiled at the staff, many of whom she'd gotten to know since her mother moved in a few years ago. Allie Peña was at the reception desk.

"Hello Ms. Ward," she said with a big smile.

"Hi Allie, how's she doing?" Jessie asked as she signed the log on the desk.

"Oh, your mother has had a good day so far."

Smiling her thanks, Jessie moved down the hall, where the smells of antiseptic and perfume mingled. The air carried soft conversations—voices rising with laughter as she passed a common room where a group of residents was playing cards. She moved deeper into the building, eventually approaching the open door to her mother's room.

"Hi Mom," she said as she stepped into the room. The TV droned softly in the corner.

"Oh my, Jessica," Florence said from the armchair, picking up the remote and muting the TV. "It's so good to see you!"

Jessie leaned down to hug and kiss her. Taking the chair next to Florence, Jessie searched her mother's soft grey eyes. Her cheekbones were still high, holding her beauty against the age lines lacing her face.

"How're you today, Mom?"

"I'm okay." Florence looked behind Jessie. "Did Dylan come?"

"No. He's flying to New York today to visit his other grandma and grandpa, and his dad, for a while."

Mom, we talked about it last time when Dylan was here, she wanted to add, but didn't want to raise her mother's memory issues. Instead, she reached into her tote bag. "I got you the sweater you wanted." Jessie held up a soft blue lightweight knit sweater.

"Oh, what a lovely surprise!"

Surprise? Jessie wanted to remind her mother that she'd said the air conditioning often chilled her; that she'd shown Jessie the sweater on her phone and asked her to get it for her. But, again, she decided not to open that door.

"It's a relaxed fit. I know you like that."

Touching the soft fabric to her cheek, Florence said, "Thank you." Looking around the room again, she said, "Did Vaughn come?"

Jessie hesitated. They'd been separated for almost a year. "Mom, Vaughn moved back east. We're not together anymore."

Several seconds passed, Florence blinking at Jessie before turning her attention back to the TV. She picked up the remote, unmuted the sound. It was time for *Wheel of Fortune*, her favourite show.

Smiling, Jessie studied her mother. Jessie's father had died when Jessie was a year old, leaving her mother to raise her and Jessie's older sister alone. Florence had worked as a science teacher, then become a vice principal. She was a strong, fearless and enduring woman. Jessie had always been in awe of her. Even now, watching her watching the spinning wheel, and often succeeding in solving the puzzles, Jessie could still see the defiance in her mother.

At a commercial break, Florence reached over and held Jessie's hand.

"They've had some good puzzles, Jenn."

Jenn? Jenn was her older sister, Jennifer, who'd died years ago. Jessie was silent.

Florence gave her a big smile.

"Jenn, isn't this fun?" When Jessie didn't respond, concern filled her mother's face. "Jennifer? Honey, is something wrong?"

"Mom," Jessie said gently. "I'm Jessie."

Confusion surfaced in her mother's eyes. "Jessie? But where's Jennifer? Did she come with you?"

Jessie cleared her throat. "Jenn's dead, Mom. She's been dead for a long time."

"But she was just here. Last night, talking to me."

"You were dreaming, Mom. She was in your dreams. Jenn is in heaven with Dad."

Watching her mother absorb the information, watching her heart break again, Jessie felt sadness fill her chest. She arranged the strands of her mother's white hair as the music of the game show played to the end. It was then that Sylvia, one of the centre's caregivers, came in with a small tray.

"Time for your pills, Mrs. Sheridan."

"They make me sleepy," Florence said with a frown.

"They're supposed to," Sylvia said. "Hi Jessie."

Jessie's phone vibrated. Dylan's plane had landed. Relief flooded her. *Thank goodness*, she thought as she picked up her bag and stood.

"Mom, I have to leave now," she said, gently touching her mother's face. "But I'll be back tomorrow."

"All right, dear," Florence said, patting Jessie's hand. "Thank you for the sweater."

Jessie gave her a kiss on the cheek and then said goodbye.

When Jessie got into her car, she didn't start it. Instead, she rested her head on the steering wheel. Her marriage was over. Dylan was on the other side of the country. And, bit by bit, her once-indestructible mom was slipping away.

Things are crumbling around me. She gripped the wheel, holding on for a long moment. *Don't start sobbing here in the parking lot, Jessie.*

She took a breath, collecting herself, and tried to shift her thoughts.

Dylan should be off the plane by now—in fact, he was probably with his grandparents by now. Jessie checked the app again and confirmed that his plane had arrived at JFK nearly thirty minutes ago.

She felt a flare of irritation. Lillian or Miller should've sent her a text.

Jessie was typing a message to them when her phone vibrated and started ringing. It was Lillian. *There it is*, she thought, relief rising as she answered.

"Hi Lillian."

But her mother-in-law was gasping, struggling to speak.

"Lillian, what's wrong?"

"Dylan's missing!"

5

SANTA MONICA

"How can Dylan be missing?" Panic and disbelief gripped Jessie, her voice rising to a shout. "What are you saying?"

"Somebody—" Lillian halted, swallowing her ragged breaths. "Somebody took him!"

"*Somebody took him?* What happened?" Her world was spinning; tears pricked Jessie's eyes.

"We're at JFK at the gate, we got our passes, we had his information, we went to the gate and then—!"

"Lillian, slow down!" Jessie could hear Miller in the background, his voice tense and urgent.

"Oh my God, Jessica, I don't—"

"Lillian! Stop," Jessie said. "Let me talk to Miller!"

Jessie tapped the button, switching to a video. Miller's face was white, sober with worry.

"Miller, what's happened?" Jessie scoured the background behind her father-in-law.

"Jessica, there's been a mistake. Dylan isn't here." Miller rubbed his face anxiously.

She stared at him in disbelief. "What kind of mistake? Who took him? Did you see him? Tell me what happened, from the beginning!"

"We arrived, got our passes to get him in Terminal 4 at Gate B20. It's busy here—nuts. Then we got a message from the airline saying his LA plane was now at Gate B55."

"But I didn't get a notice," Jessie said. "I would've gotten the gate change too!"

"The board hadn't been updated. We tried the B20 gate agents, but they were swamped with passengers that were about to board the plane that had just arrived."

"But *that* was Dylan's plane."

"No, his gate changed from B20 to B55. So we made the long walk to the new gate."

"And he wasn't there?" Worry churned in Jessie's stomach.

"No, he wasn't. The gate agent there said the flight arriving at B55 was a flight from Dallas, not LA. She said that the message had to be wrong."

"Hold on a sec," Jessie said. She swiped away from the video call and went to the flight tracking app. Dylan's plane was, according to the app, at JFK's Terminal 4, Gate B20. She opened another app to track the AirTag she'd put in Dylan's backpack. It showed his location as being at LAX.

LAX? No, that's wrong.

She checked the time.

Last updated two minutes ago.

She went back to the call. "Miller, did you show the agent the message you received?"

"Yes. He said it was odd but likely an error, then checked and confirmed that EverySky's flight from Los Angeles had in fact pulled into the gate they'd originally told us and was nearly done deplaning. We asked him to send a message to hold Dylan there, that we were coming." Miller ran his hand through his mussed hair. "So we walked back to the other end of the terminal, and we asked them to send a message to the attendant with Dylan."

"And?"

"It was a long walk between the gates, and the terminal was teeming with people, and with my arthritic leg and the moving walkways . . . I don't know, it had to be forty, forty-five minutes total between when we left and got back to B20."

"And Dylan wasn't there?"

Miller shook his head nervously. "No. He was gone. The plane was empty, and the staff at B20 said that Dylan was picked up by his grandparents who'd had the paperwork."

Jessie's stomach spasmed as if it had dropped to the ground as her mind whirled. *Someone else picked him up!?* She heard Lillian's wailing in the background. Without warning, she hung up and frantically called, then texted Dylan's phone.

No response.

"Fuck!" she shouted. "Dylan, pick up, please." Trying to calm her breathing, she opened the app to locate his phone.

No location found.

"Where is he?" she cried. Hands shaking, she called Miller. When he answered, she could see security and airline people huddled nearby amid the chaotic flow of travellers.

"Miller, Dylan's location isn't updating on the map. Do you think Vaughn or someone he knows got Dylan? Maybe it was a mix-up?"

Her father-in-law shook his head. "No, Vaughn's in Quebec, working on a story. He won't be back for a few more days."

Jessie gritted her teeth. "Get the police!"

"We did. They'll talk to you. Here." Miller handed his phone to someone else, and a moment later a police officer appeared.

"Who are you?" Jessie asked.

"Officer Kathy Teel, from Port Authority Police. Could you identify yourself for me?"

"Jessica Ward, Dylan Ward's mother."

"Ma'am, if you could just hold up some ID, please."

Scrambling for her wallet, Jessie found her driver's licence and held it up, and Teel took a photo of it with her own phone.

Before the officer could say anything more, Jessie burst out, "How did this happen? How could the airline just give Dylan to the wrong people? *Who took my son?*"

"We're looking into it, Ms. Ward," Teel said. "We're just trying to get more info at this stage. We understand Dylan has a phone."

"He has a phone and smartwatch," Jessie said, nodding. "I've been texting him, but he hasn't responded since I dropped him off at the airport."

"Did he have any other devices with him that we could use to track him down?"

"I put an AirTag in his backpack, but that's showing that it's still at LAX. And I was following on an airline app."

Teel frowned. "That's odd." She cleared her throat. "It appears that Dylan was collected at the gates by another couple."

Just then Jessie got a tracking notification for Dylan's smartwatch. She knew she'd get a GPS signal when he was on the ground. The app showed he was at JFK Terminal 4, near Gate B20.

How can that be? LAX or JFK. Where is he? Strangers picked him up? Nothing is making sense.

Jessie groaned as if she'd been punched in the stomach.

"Ms. Ward, we're working on it," Teel said. "We have Dylan's photo from his unaccompanied minor ID; I just need to confirm with you what he was wearing today."

Jessie's mind was racing in a million directions. The technology was misdirecting her, not working properly, confusing her. She couldn't focus. What was happening? All she wanted was to have Dylan in her arms.

"Ma'am?"

Jessie took a breath and tried to focus, then listed Dylan's blue Dodgers T-shirt, faded jeans, blue-striped white running shoes with stains, and his green backpack with the gamepads.

"Does he have physical or mental challenges?" Teel asked.

"No."

"Does he require any medications?"

"No," Jessie said impatiently. "Please, you've got to find him! What're you doing, asking me all these questions?"

"Ms. Ward, we're in the process of taking immediate action using every resource we have. We're securing entries and exits at the airport. We'll put up alerts in the airport, and we'll issue an Amber Alert here and possibly in California."

"But what about the people who took him?" Jessie pressed. "They must've shown photo ID? The airline *must* have something. Did Dylan say anything? Complain about strangers?" She dug into her purse for her hard copy of Dylan's unaccompanied minor paperwork. "I checked Dylan in at LAX with someone named Shawn Curtis, and a woman named Lindsay Bell was the EverySky attendant who escorted Dylan onto the plane. Has anyone talked to her? I put him on that plane! How could he have been taken by strangers?"

"It's all being investigated. We're working with the airline, coordinating with other agencies and reviewing security cameras." Teel looked at Jessie sympathetically. "I can assure you that we're doing everything possible to reunite Dylan with his family."

"I just can't believe this has happened!" Jessie pounded the steering wheel with her fist.

"I know this is extremely stressful. We're taking every step we need to take, I promise you. I have your information, Ms. Ward. I'll keep you updated. Passing you back now."

Teel vanished from Jessie's screen and was quickly replaced by Miller.

Jessie thought quickly. "Miller, send me the message you and Lillian received about the gate changes."

"Okay, will do."

"Have you spoken to Vaughn?"

Miller nodded. "Lillian was just talking to him . . ." He turned his head to speak to his wife. "Oh, Lillian says that he's going to call you in a moment."

"Okay, I'll wait for his call," Jessie said. "Talk soon." She hung up and closed her eyes, both hands clenched around the phone. A minute later, it rang and vibrated, and when she quickly answered, her screen bloomed with her husband's face, creased with concern.

"Jessie," Vaughn said, his voice breaking slightly. "What happened?"

"*You're asking me?* I'm in LA. This happened in New York!"

"I told you to travel with him," he said bitterly.

Biting back tears, Jessie shot back, "I don't know why you couldn't pick up our son. Instead, you had your parents, who can barely walk, go to the airport." She scowled at him. "Why are you in Canada anyway? Chasing the next all-important story, I'm sure!"

Vaughn sighed. "Okay, stop. We can't always be doing this. I'm sorry, Jess. It wasn't your fault. It wasn't anyone's fault. I'm sorry." He paused. "Right now, we need to think of Dylan."

Jessie was suddenly overcome with a pang of love for Vaughn—a flash of everything that had once been good. And she ached for them to be together, united, at this moment.

But then, like a tidal wave, she remembered what had driven them apart. Swallowing her emotions, she waved Vaughn away. "I can't do this now. I'll let you know if I hear anything."

She ended the call, dropped her phone in her lap and briefly squeezed her eyes shut, an alarm throbbing in the corner of her mind.

Then she started her car and pulled away fast.

6

SANTA MONICA

Jessie grasped the wheel, fighting to think clearly as she drove through Santa Monica. Self-recrimination stabbed at her. "Why did I let him fly alone? So someone could take him?" she muttered to herself. At a red light, she again checked to see if the location on any of Dylan's devices had updated. But there was no change.

It's as if these apps have just stopped working. She raked her hand through her hair. *Where can Dylan be?*

As soon as she was home, she was going to book a direct flight to JFK. There was no way she was going to stay on the other side of the country while Dylan was missing.

Her phone began ringing. It was Vaughn.

"Did they find Dylan?" she asked before he could speak.

"Not yet."

"Okay. Well, I'm going to fly out to New York tonight."

Vaughn paused before answering. "Listen, Jess, I think you should—" His voice crackled with static, and it sounded like he was walking quickly.

"You're breaking up, Vaughn."

"I was saying you should hold off flying to New York."

"What? Why?" She clenched her jaw. "I'm getting on the next plane to find Dylan."

"Jessie, I'm close to Montreal. I can get to JFK before you. Stay in LA. The police may need your help there."

What is wrong with him? "No, Vaughn, I need to get to New York."

"Just stay where you are for now, Jess. We need to think things through—"

Her phone sounded with a notification, and she looked at the screen on her dashboard. It was an unknown number. "Vaughn, I'm getting another call, I'll call you back."

"Have I reached Jessica Ward?" a male voice asked when she answered.

"Yes?"

"Ma'am, this is Special Agent Kirk Rutledge, FBI."

Jessie's stomach dropped. "FBI?"

"Yes. Our field office in Los Angeles has been alerted to the situation with your son in New York. We need to speak with you as soon as possible."

"Yes, go ahead," Jessie said, swallowing. "I'm just driving, but we can talk."

"We need to speak in person."

"Oh God, what is it?" Her blood pulsed. "Did you find him? Is he okay?"

"No, I'm sorry, we haven't located him. But because of his age, and other factors, we're involved in the investigation and need more information."

Jessie took a breath. "I'm a few minutes from my house."

Confirming her address, Rutledge said, "We're on Wilshire. We can be there in fifteen minutes."

At home Jessie decided to pack while she waited for the FBI to arrive. Her mind went to the AirTag in Dylan's backpack. Why was its location at LAX? Had someone taken his bag from him? But what if he'd never left Los Angeles?

But that makes no sense. I know I put him on the plane. She picked up her phone to call Vaughn and saw she had a text message. It was from an unknown number.

Hi Jessica. This is Shauna Price from the LA Times. The AP has just moved a story on an Amber Alert for your son missing from JFK in New York. We're seeking comment. We've not met but some people at the Times know your husband, Vaughn. More attention could help find Dylan.

Jessie's fears intensified. The FBI and now the press were involved, and that put everything into overdrive. Dylan was really missing. She took several quick breaths to calm herself. *More attention could help find him,* she thought.

She typed her response.

We don't know how this happened. We're praying for Dylan's safe and speedy return.

She glanced toward Dylan's room down the hall. *Will I ever see him again?* She shook her head. *Don't think like that.*

She pushed her hands through her hair, then resumed packing while her phone vibrated non-stop with messages. More people had seen the news story breaking online. Neighbours, parents of Dylan's friends, Jessie's friends—they were all in disbelief and sent words of encouragement. Dahlia even texted.

My God, Jessie! Arrived at the hotel when I saw the news about Dylan. Where are you? What can I do to help?

Jessie was responding when her doorbell rang. She rushed to the door and set her suitcase down beside it.

Special Agent Kirk Rutledge was about six feet tall and wearing a blazer over a polo shirt. He held up his FBI credentials. So did Special Agent Sydney Chavez, a young woman in a navy jacket over a white shirt. Leading them into her living room, Jessie noticed them glance at her suitcase.

Sitting on her sofa, they withdrew tablets, phones and notebooks and got straight to work.

"We're with CARD," Rutledge said, "the FBI's Child Abduction Rapid Deployment team. We're working with other law enforcement in New York to find your son Dylan."

"You think he was abducted?" Jessie asked quietly.

Rutledge held up a palm. "We're not confirming anything right now. We don't know. Has anyone claimed responsibility or reached you with any demands?"

"No, nothing."

Rutledge nodded. "First, then, we'll get a summary of events from you of what happened today."

Jessie related everything about Dylan's EverySky flight as an unaccompanied minor, including the problems she'd had with his phone and watch, the tracking app she'd used, and the details of the gate message his grandparents had received.

"Can you share all of Dylan's tech with us, including any emails or social media that he has?" Rutledge asked. "Technology can be critical in these cases."

Jessie nodded, sharing all she could.

"Some of my stuff is encrypted," Jessie said. "Because of my work."

Rutledge raised an eyebrow and made a note.

"And Dylan's online presence is pretty limited because we're strict on what he can do." She provided contact information for his friends, teachers, instructors and coaches.

"Do you know of any threats or disputes within your family or social circles that could be related to his disappearance?" Chavez asked.

"No."

"Have you received any strange or suspicious calls, messages or other communications recently?"

"No."

"Can you think of anyone who may have had a motive to take Dylan?"

Jessie considered the question, then shook her head. "No."

Chavez then asked if anyone in Dylan's family was dealing with debt, or drug or gambling addictions or issues.

"Not that I'm aware of," Jessie said.

Chavez nodded. "And Dylan had flown alone to New York before?"

"Yes," Jessie said. "Several months ago, he made the same trip on EverySky as an unaccompanied minor with no issues. At that time, he was met at Kennedy by Vaughn, his dad. On this trip, his grandparents were picking him up. He was going to stay with them for a few days, then go to be with his dad."

"Describe your background, your relationship, with Vaughn and his parents," Chavez said.

Jessie hesitated, looking at the time on her watch.

"Ms. Ward, all information relating to Dylan is relevant," Chavez said.

Jessie nodded and swallowed. "Vaughn and I met when I was at MIT and he was at Harvard. I studied computer science, he was in the journalism program. We got married, had Dylan. I worked as a software engineer before starting Instinct Nine-99, a cybersecurity company. Vaughn jumped from *The Wall Street Journal* to *The Washington Post*, then to big online outlets covering technology. He's good at what he does—connected to solid sources, always breaking tech stories. We settled in California, but Vaughn's work takes him all over the world. He was always travelling, always missing birthdays and anniversaries." Jessie blinked away those painful memories. "We grew apart. Our marriage crumbled."

"So, to be clear," Rutledge said, "you and Vaughn, who resides in New York, are separated. And Dylan lives primarily with you?"

"Yes. California is Dylan's home," Jessie said. "We want to do what's best for Dylan, but the divorce is taking time. We're working on the custody agreement, but not everyone is seeing eye to eye on things."

"How so?" Chavez asked.

Jessie shrugged. "In terms of creating a workable custody agreement and frequency of visits, that kind of thing."

Chavez wrote something in her notebook, then asked, "And how would you characterize your relationship with Vaughn's parents?"

"We've never really got along," Jessie admitted. "I always felt that they wanted Vaughn to marry a woman from the Upper East Side, someone with money. Maybe it's why they disliked me. I think they blame me for our marriage failing. I think they believe that I'm obsessed with my career."

"So, there's tension in the family?" Chavez said.

"A little."

Rutledge looked up from his notes. "You said that Instinct Nine-99 is your cybersecurity company. What do you do?"

"We look at threats to computer networks, largely for government and corporate systems."

"What does that mean?"

"We help secure them against vulnerabilities."

"Could Dylan's case have anything to do with your work?" Rutledge asked.

Jessie paused, biting her lip. "I don't know. I hope not. I don't think so, but I can't be certain." She looked into Rutledge's eyes. "Look, much of my work is highly confidential, classified even. Most people in the industry aren't aware of our contracts."

Rutledge nodded and made a note. "What about Vaughn's work? Could anyone have reason to act against him? Maybe he's digging into a dangerous story?"

"I don't know," she said. "Vaughn doesn't discuss the stories he's investigating with me. I know he's in Quebec, Canada, right now."

"And what about his parents?" Chavez asked. "Do you think they could be behind this?"

Jessie focused on the clock on the wall and considered the question. “I know we don’t get along,” she said finally, “but I can’t believe they’d do something like this. For what reason?” Shaking her head, she turned back to the agents. “No.”

“This is helpful,” Rutledge said, looking at Chavez. “Before we go, would you volunteer to allow us to take a look around your house?”

“Why?” *Why do they want to search the house?*

“Part of the investigation.”

Jessie wondered if they needed a warrant or if she needed a lawyer. But time was sweeping by, and she had nothing to hide.

“Of course.”

The agents walked through the house, recording their tour and asking the occasional question. They asked to look in the bedrooms, including Dylan’s.

When they were done, Rutledge and Chavez walked to the door. “Thank you, Ms. Ward,” Rutledge said. He nodded at Jessie’s suitcase. “Are you going somewhere?”

Jessie crossed her arms. “Yes. I’m going to New York to look for Dylan.”

Rutledge and Chavez traded glances. “What would you do there?” Rutledge asked.

“I’ll figure something out on the flight.”

He cleared his throat. “You’re free to go wherever you want, but Dylan’s grandparents are there, and your husband will arrive soon. We advise you to stay here, for now.”

“Why? You can’t just expect me to sit here and do nothing.”

“We know waiting is painful,” Chavez said. “Dylan’s disappearance could be something planned, something intentional—but it could also be a mix-up or a terrible mistake. It’s happened before. But until we can see where this goes, we don’t know what we’ve got.”

“Yes, but you can’t stop me from trying to find my son.”

7

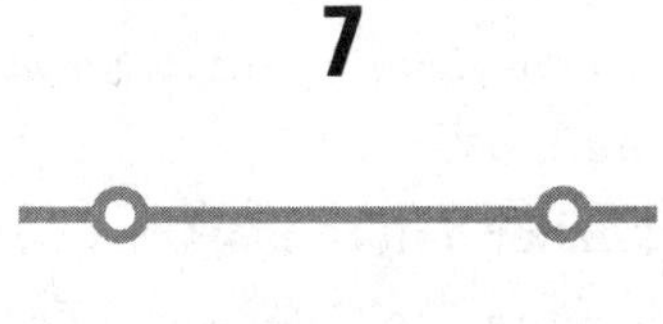

SANTA MONICA

Within minutes of the FBI leaving, Sarita arrived at Jessie's house, a laptop bag over her shoulder. "We're going to find Dylan."

Bobby trotted up the walkway behind her carrying a canvas briefcase. "We'll do whatever it takes," he said.

Jessie smiled weakly. She was lucky she had such a good team. "Thank you for this."

They'd gone to the kitchen and started setting up at the table when the doorbell rang again. It was Dahlia, phone in one hand, a tote bag in the other.

"Oh Jess," she said tearily as they hugged. "I can't believe what's happened." She pulled away and looked at Jessie. "I've come to help."

"But it's your vacation!"

"It doesn't matter. Jessie, I'm here to do whatever we need to do to find Dylan."

Hugging her again, Jessie whispered her thanks. Brushing the corners of her eyes, she then brought Dahlia into the kitchen. "This is my friend Dahlia Wynn," she said to Sarita and Bobby. "We went to MIT together, and she's going to help."

As her small team settled in at her kitchen table, Jessie glanced at her suitcase. She was torn. Should she go to New York, or should she stay in LA like Vaughn and the FBI wanted her to? The tracking tag in Dylan's backpack showed his location as LAX. What if, by some strange twist, he was still in California? *I'll stay here—but only until I know where Dylan is. Or just long enough to do what I can here to get answers.*

She held her head in her hands as if trying to suppress a nightmare. "Oh my God, where is he?" Jessie wailed.

Dahlia rushed to her side and took her hand. "It's going to be okay, Jess," she said, turning to Bobby and Sarita. "We'll find him."

Jessie drew in a shaking breath, trying to pull herself together. "Thank you for being here." She reached for her phone and began running through the key aspects and events, as she'd done with the FBI agents.

"I'll see what's up with Dylan's phone and your tracking app," Sarita said.

"Let me look at the text that sent Lillian and Miller to the wrong gate," Bobby said.

Dahlia opened her laptop, jumping in to help. "Let me see if I can get on Dylan's records with EverySky," she said.

Jessie left the kitchen for her computer. Her phone kept buzzing with messages. She quickly glanced at the screen. There was a surge of media requests, including from *The New York Times*, *Veritas Sola* and *USA Today*.

Her mind flashed to her mother. On the drive home she'd called Palm Breeze and asked that the staff keep Florence from watching the news for as long as possible. Dylan's disappearance would devastate her. Jessie blinked back tears as she sat down at the kitchen table and powered up her laptop.

"Okay," Sarita said after a few moments. "So there are a number of possible reasons why we're not getting updates. Dylan's phone and watch could be turned off, or airplane mode could be on."

"But it's strange that both phone *and* watch aren't updating," Jessie said.

"Right," Bobby said. "Maybe they were turned off, or tossed somewhere?"

"What the hell's happening?" Jessie said, slamming her palms on the table.

Sarita shook her head slowly, studying her screen. "It appears," she said, "the last known location was in LA, even after the flight took off, so maybe Dylan was separated from his bag." She looked at Jessie.

Bobby looked up from his laptop. "There was evidently an account compromise." He glanced back at the screen. "Appears they fabricated the message about the change of gate to look authentic for your in-laws, Jessie."

Jessie's eyes widened. "I can't believe this. Who'd go to these lengths to hurt our family?"

"I don't know, Jess," Dahlia said. "But looking at your EverySky records, the airline must have more info on the handoff at JFK that they're not sharing."

"We need to talk to Miller and Lillian." Jessie opened up FaceTime on her laptop and dialled Miller and Lillian's shared cell phone. She angled her laptop for the others to see as the connection was made. After a moment, his tired, anguished face filled her monitor.

"Hi Miller," Jessie said. "What's the latest?"

"We don't know," he said. "They seem to have brought in more police."

"They're still not telling us much," Lillian said, leaning into view next to her husband. Her eyes were red. "They put us in this room—this security room—"

"You're still at the airport?"

"Yes, in this room, and . . ." Lillian pressed the crumpled tissue in her fist to her eyes. "I don't have a good feeling."

"Has Vaughn arrived yet?"

"No, not yet," Lillian said. "I hope he's on his way."

"Let me call him," Jessie said. "I'll talk to you soon." She hung up and immediately video-called her estranged husband. Within seconds he was on her screen. He was in his car on a multi-lane highway.

"Vaughn," she said, her voice trembling, "where are you? Bobby, Sarita and Dahlia are here, trying to figure out what's going on."

"Hi Jess. I just left Bromont, headed to Montreal. I'll get the first plane I can to JFK," Vaughn said. "What's the latest? Any updates?"

"Well, they've put out an Amber," Jessie said.

"I saw. Anything come of it? Any leads?"

"I don't know. The *LA Times* picked it up, and they got in contact."

"Yeah, I saw the *LA Times* story online too."

"So you should be in New York in a few hours, right?"

"I think so," Vaughn said. "It's a short flight from here, but it's over an hour to get to the airport. Traffic's heavy. What are police telling you?"

"Very little," Jessie said. "Same with the FBI, who already stopped by here."

"The FBI came to the house?" Vaughn said, sounding surprised. "Oh God."

Jessie nodded. "I know. They asked me some questions, I gave them all the information I had. They did a tour of the house." She sighed. "Listen, when you get to JFK, go to Terminal 4. Find Kathy Teel with the Port Authority Police. She can put you in touch with the FBI. Your parents are also there, in a security room."

"Okay, I'll do that."

"I've sent you all of Dylan's flight stuff. Please hurry."

She ended the call and caught Bobby and Sarita staring at each other. "What is it?"

"Vaughn looked a little off," Bobby said.

"He sounded a bit off too," Sarita added.

"What do you mean?" Jessie asked, confused. She looked at Dahlia. "Do you think he looked and sounded weird?"

"He's in shock," Dahlia said. "Like all of us."

Jessie shook her head. "Nothing makes sense." Tears filled her eyes. "Oh God, I can't believe this is happening! Where the hell is he?" She massaged her temples. "The investigators must know more than they're telling me." She scrolled through her phone.

"What are you doing?" Dahlia asked.

"I'm calling the police officer from the airport," Jessie said, dialling Teel's phone number on her laptop. Seconds later, Teel answered. Behind her, Jessie could see Miller and Lillian, who were in conversation with two other officers.

"Yes, Ms. Ward?" Teel said.

"Can I get an update from you?" Jessie said. "What more can you tell me? I've spoken with the FBI. I've got friends here helping. My husband is on his way from Canada."

"I can tell you that more agencies are involved, going all out," Teel said. "Were you successful locating your son's phone or other devices?"

"No. It's possible something was hacked or manipulated. We don't know." Jessie glanced at Dahlia. "Listen, you *must* have the IDs the people who took Dylan showed at the gate." Teel was quiet. "Why didn't you release them with the alert? Did you check the security cameras? All of this should be made public!"

Teel sighed. "I'm sorry, I'm not authorized to discuss every aspect of the investigation."

"Well, who the hell is then?" Jessie shouted, startling Sarita. "We're talking about my missing son!"

The officer paused. "Can you give me a second?" The screen went dark and the audio was muffled. A moment later, Teel reappeared. "Ma'am," she said, "we can share this with you. These were the IDs used."

Jessie looked at the IDs and then at Dahlia, confused. "What?" She shook her head slowly. "I don't understand."

Lillian's and Miller's faces stared back at her from the IDs.

"This is the exact identification used by the people who took your son," Teel said.

8

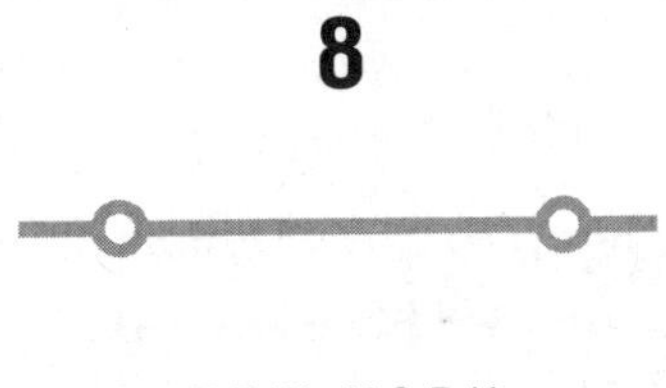

NEW YORK

Here were Lillian and Miller Ward in Terminal 4 at Gate B20.

Here they were checking their phone—then, in a sequence of video segments, starting for the far end of the terminal.

FBI Special Agent Jake Garlin studied the images on the screens mounted on the wall in the JFK office they were in. Investigators had set up a command post in the terminal's operations centre to coordinate the search for Dylan Ward.

"Run it side by side, with B20," Garlin directed the officer helping him review the terminal's security cameras.

One of the multiple screens split. A time-stamped feed showed the grandparents well along the terminal heading for Gate B55, at the same time EverySky's flight from LAX had started deplaning at Gate B20.

Among the first to leave the plane was a young flight attendant—Lindsay Bell, Garlin confirmed, checking his notes—escorting nine-year-old Dylan. Dylan was just as his mother had described: faded jeans, blue Dodgers T-shirt, blue-striped running shoes, and a green backpack with gamepads on it. Garlin watched as the child entered the preboarding area ahead of passengers emerging from the jet bridge, towing his suitcase. The young boy and his escort were then approached by two figures whose backs were to the camera, but only for a second before they vanished in a sudden jump cut.

"Just like that, he's gone from the feed," Garlin said.

Now the video showed the flight attendant without Dylan, with other EverySky attendants nearby, guiding the disembarking passengers to the flow of travellers making their way through the terminal.

"This appears to jump to after Dylan's handoff to the couple. Let's follow all the video we have from B20 in both directions," Garlin said to the officer.

Footage showed people navigating the crowded terminal, including stairs, escalators, baggage claim and the exits. But no cameras had captured Dylan or the people who took him.

Dylan was just not there.

Garlin's jaw tightened.

It's as if the video had been scrubbed, the images digitally erased. They had no photos of the suspects to circulate. JFK operations people and FBI cyber analysts working out of the Manhattan office were also examining the footage. Perhaps they'd find something, but Garlin doubted it. *This was clearly a preplanned abduction.*

Garlin thanked his colleague and then went to the closed room down the hall where Lindsay Bell, Dylan's EverySky escort, was seated.

Garlin, like all investigators, adhered to the fundamental rule that held that, until all the facts were known, no one could be ruled out. Bell was a relative rookie, having been on the job for six weeks, which was something to consider. Her background, phone and records were being scrutinized, but nothing had surfaced. Yet. Still, she was a key witness.

"Okay, Lindsay," Garlin said, sitting down across from her and looking into her red eyes. "One more time."

She clasped her hands until her knuckles whitened, and she stared down at them. "They had the proper paperwork with photo

ID—you saw it," Bell said, her voice shaking. "To me, they looked just like the grandparents."

Garlin knew that people were not infallible at matching faces accurately, especially if they were tired after a cross-country flight or under stress. Too often a slight resemblance to an official photo would be acceptable. And in this case, the suspects had had duplicated documents. They'd used the real photos of the real grandparents on their IDs. *How* they'd gotten them was under investigation.

"Describe the boy's demeanour at seeing them," Garlin said.

Bell paused. "He was reluctant at first, but he told me on the flight that he hadn't been with his grandparents in a while, six months or so. But they'd talked a lot on video calls." She thought for a moment. "I suppose that, at the gate, he seemed nervous seeing them, even resistant."

"Resistant?" Garlin asked, raising an eyebrow.

"Yeah. Kind of put off, unsure, like something wasn't right."

"What did you do about it?"

"It was a long flight, he seemed disoriented, you know? And the grandparents seemed rushed, like they needed to get going." Lindsay unclasped her hands and rubbed her face.

"It didn't raise any flags?"

She swallowed. "At the time, it appeared normal to me. I swear, they looked like their photos. They were happy to see him. He was exhausted, a bit cranky, which was normal. Then the woman handed him a little yellow computer game, which distracted him. But he was complaining a little as they left."

"Complaining?"

"Like, he said 'you look different,' then one of them said they'd lost weight, laughed it off and hurried him along." Bell brushed her eyes. "It was less than a minute and they were gone."

"Which way did they go?"

"Toward the exit."

Garlin looked down at his notes. "Your policy requires you to photograph the UM's receiving person."

"They looked just like the grandparents in the IDs."

Garlin leaned forward. "Did you take the photo as required?" He studied her.

The young woman didn't speak.

"Did you?"

"No, I didn't," she said finally.

"Why not?"

Bell pushed back. "It was a long flight. I was—I just forgot to take their picture. I messed up."

Garlin waited a few seconds before asking, "Can you recall if they touched anything?

"My pen, from when they signed the paperwork."

"We have it, and it's being processed for prints. But anything they may have discarded, tossed in the trash?"

"No." Bell buried her face in her hands. "I'm so sorry." Her voice shook. "I have a little girl of my own. I'm so sorry."

Garlin returned to the command post, where more than two dozen law enforcement officials from a range of agencies were working together in small clusters—on computers studying data or on phones or walkie-talkies—pursuing every aspect of the search. The case had been challenging for Garlin from the moment he got the call a couple of hours ago. Any case involving kids had him thinking of his two boys, and how he'd move heaven and earth to find them if they vanished like this. He rubbed his neck quickly as he glanced around.

JFK, one of the world's busiest airports, received sixty million passengers yearly, with a flight leaving almost every minute. It was a major international gateway. In the hours since Dylan had been reported missing, a number of actions had been taken, including an ongoing search of the entire airport, restrooms, concourses and food courts. Parking garages and nearby hotels were being searched by K-9 units. Public alerts had gone out. Digital signs in the airport displayed Dylan's photo and description.

But no leads yet.

"What about TSA and the airlines?" Garlin asked the agent nearest him.

"Every airline has alerted crews and onboard air marshals, with every flight, domestic and international, that departed since the child was reported missing," she said.

"Good."

Garlin considered human trafficking rings. He had people running down sex offender registries and checking intel on traffickers, in case there was a link there. He weighed other factors. Cases of children going missing at Kennedy were rare—maybe thirty or so each year. Often, in the hubbub of the airport, the children would become separated from parents and wander off. And there might be confusion with gate changes, missed flights or delays, leading them to become lost. Still, in virtually every case, the child was found and reunited with family within a couple of hours. With each passing minute, Garlin's concern deepened for Dylan.

Another reason children had gone missing at Kennedy was custody disputes.

Garlin looked through the background information on Dylan's father, Vaughn Ward. He'd graduated from Harvard and had reported for *The Wall Street Journal* and *The Washington Post*. He was now working for online publications and recognized as an authority on technology, travelling the globe breaking stories on cybersecurity issues. Vaughn had been in Canada working on a story at the time his parents were at Kennedy to pick up Dylan.

Garlin looked to the glass-walled office where Miller and Lillian Ward were still being held. They looked exhausted and distraught. Were they victims or just playing the part? Garlin knew the truth—*the full truth*—never came out in the early stages of an investigation. Often people were genuinely confused, stressed, afraid.

Or they were simply lying.

The older couple lived in Brooklyn. Miller was a retired electrical engineer. Lillian was a retired administrator with the New York Public Library and had acted in various plays as part of a seniors' community theatre group.

Garlin opened his file on Jessica Ward. Her photo stared back at him as he reviewed what the agents from Los Angeles had sent over. Jessica had degrees in computer science from Caltech and MIT, and a few years later she had co-founded Instinct Nine-99, a cybersecurity company based in Santa Monica that developed protection against threats to networks. The company had mainly classified contracts with governments and corporations.

It all went to underscore the major elements at play in Dylan's disappearance: the text misdirecting the grandparents, the people who'd used identity theft to pose as Lillian and Miller, the scrubbed video. It was a planned abduction involving a sophisticated intrusion into the security of a major airport—and, as such, Homeland and US Cyber Command had already been alerted.

But was the boy's vanishing linked to Jessica Ward's work? Or a story his father might be investigating? It was tough to say, as no ransom demands had surfaced—yet.

But this is a family with a divorce in progress, Garlin thought. Clearly there was some tension—over the custody agreement, over the marriage ending. Not to mention the undertone of animosity between Jessica and Vaughn's parents.

"Have you run a background on the mother, father, the grandparents yet?" he asked the agent nearest him.

She nodded. "Aside from some minor traffic violations—no arrests, no warrants, nothing came up."

They needed to stay on top of all the players, who were all over the place. They had the grandparents here. Vaughn was on his way to Kennedy from Canada. They were working with Santa Monica PD to keep an unseen watch on Jessica in California. And they were interviewing people with any link to them all. But in a world where technology and AI were advancing at a breathtaking pace, he couldn't rule out Jessica and Vaughn Ward. Each had the skills, and connections, to pull off something like this.

"We may have something," someone called out.

9

INDIANAPOLIS AND NEW YORK

An hour from Indianapolis, on Flight KN4414, Captain Roy King called lead attendant Dianne May into the cockpit and relayed the details of an abduction alert he'd just received from JFK.

"There are apparently false identities at play," he said. "Keep your eyes open."

May's brows furrowed as she thought. "We have two older people with a young boy onboard today." She flipped to the manifest on her clipboard and scrolled through the plane's fifty-eight passengers. "Here they are—Henry Green, aged sixty-seven, Anna Green, aged sixty-six, and Carter Green, aged eleven."

"Anything suspicious about them?"

"My son's eleven, and this boy, Carter"—she tapped the manifest—"actually looks a bit younger. And when they boarded, Carter seemed scared."

The first officer turned to her. "About what?"

"I asked if he was okay, and the man said, 'Our grandson doesn't like to fly.' I told him we'd make him comfortable, and the woman said their grandson needed to sleep." She bit her lip. "He was sleeping during our last in-flight beverage service."

"Maybe they medicated the kid," King said. "Where do we have them?"

"Assigned to row 20, seats A to C."

"Dianne, take a closer look at the information in the alert. Then go back and see if the details match," King directed. "But be inconspicuous."

Walking casually through the cabin, May pretended to be checking on the passengers. As she approached the Greens in row 20, she found the boy asleep with a pillow against the window, ball cap pushed aside on his head and covered with a blanket. The woman was in the middle seat, the man in the aisle.

"How's he doing?" May smiled.

"He's okay," Henry Green said.

"We're about an hour from landing. Can I get you anything?" May subtly scanned the seats, trying to memorize every detail.

"No thanks, we're good," the man said. He turned back to the magazine in his hands.

"Okay." May moved on, softly exhaling. She'd glimpsed the boy's backpack tucked under the seat—it was green and patterned. And she could see the collar of his blue T-shirt peeking out from under his blanket. She'd thought he was wearing white running shoes too.

She purposefully made her way back to the cockpit and described her encounter with the passengers to the captain and first officer.

"Text the air marshal," King said to the first officer. "I'll advise Indianapolis. We'll keep everything casual, routine. Let the police handle it when we touch down."

An hour later, as the plane began its descent, the suburbs and skyline of Indianapolis unfurled below. The jet touched down smoothly, and during the taxi from the runway to the gate, King made another announcement.

"Everyone, Captain King on the flight deck. Your attention, please. When we come to a full stop, everyone must remain seated. I repeat, remain seated." A few passengers groaned. "No one is permitted to leave the plane," he continued. "Law enforcement will be boarding. Please remain in your seats. We apologize for the inconvenience. Thank you."

Murmurs rippled through the cabin as the passengers reacted.

Moments after the plane halted, an attendant opened the door and six armed officers in tactical gear boarded and moved down the aisle as wide-eyed passengers watched. Heads turned and necks craned as they made their way to row 20 and the Greens.

"Please stand and place your hands behind your back," the squad commander said.

"What?" Henry Green said, confused. "No."

"Sir, please follow our instructions right now," the officer said.

"No," Anna Green said defiantly. "I'm not going anywhere."

The young boy next to her stared at the police in stunned silence.

"Sir, ma'am, do not resist, or we'll take you forcibly."

"Henry?" she pleaded. "I don't understand."

Her husband reluctantly stood, shuffled into the aisle and complied, placing his hands behind him. He was put into flex cuffs and moved out of the plane as the other passengers erupted in chatter and gasps.

The woman stood and put her arms behind her.

"This is a mistake! This is wrong," she said, tears brimming as the police cuffed her.

Carter was wailing at this point.

The commander held out his hand to the boy. "It's okay, son. Don't worry, come with us. Leave your bag, just come along now."

"What's going on?" one passenger called out.

"Hey man, what'd they do?" another asked.

The police ignored the questions, ignored the phones recording what had just happened, and led Anna and Carter Green off the plane.

The Greens were taken into the airport and immediately separated in different rooms. Henry and Anna were fingerprinted, checked for outstanding warrants. Background had them living in White Plains, New York, where Henry was employed as an accountant. Anna was a part-time real estate agent.

"Carter was visiting us and we were taking him back home to his mom and dad, our son, here in Indianapolis," Henry said during intense questioning.

In an adjoining room, Anna said that while visiting them in New York, Carter had a toothache. "He was in pain so we took him to our dentist, and she pulled it," she explained. "The dentist warned us, before we left for Indianapolis, that the air pressure from the flight might cause discomfort and prescribed medication for Carter to help on the trip."

In a third room, Carter tried not to cry, his voice slightly slurred and garbled. "Did we break the law or something?"

The Greens had no outstanding warrants. Their identities were confirmed. But before they were released, their photos and all their information were sent to the investigators at Kennedy in New York, where Jake Garlin scrutinized Carter's face on his laptop screen. Taken with other facts—Indianapolis PD's check with Carter's parents; confirmation with dentist Valerie Chalmers—it was clear: this boy was not Dylan.

Garlin kneaded his neck and looked toward the glass-walled room where they were still holding Lillian and Miller. Then, glancing at all the others working on the case, he considered the mounting investigation. They'd gone all out, using every resource and agency across greater New York and beyond.

We've got to find a piece of evidence, a lead.

He flipped to Dylan Ward's photo on his laptop.

The clock was ticking.

10

TORONTO

The faces of the people killed in the subway crash stared at Claire Brenner from her laptop during her early morning flight.

Their families and friends deserved answers. What had gone wrong?

Thankfully, it was a short haul from Ottawa to the Toronto Island Airport. It was well after sunrise when her plane landed. Claire requested an Uber and then began walking through the pedestrian tunnel to the mainland.

Waiting at the busy passenger pickup area, she checked the time. She might make it. Stepping aside for privacy, she FaceTimed her husband. Marissa, her daughter, answered, her face appearing on the screen.

"Hi Mom." She waved from the family's SUV from her school's drop-off zone. "Can we get the special tree when you get home?"

"Maybe, we'll see."

"But when, Mom?"

"We'll see, honey."

"K. Here's Dad. I gotta go." Marissa's surroundings blurred as she passed the phone to her father, got her backpack and shouted, "Love you Mom!" as she got out, slamming the door behind her.

"Love you!"

Phil appeared on the phone, the SUV's hazard lights clicking rhythmically in the background.

"Was it a good flight?"

"Yes, good. So, what do you think?"

"About the tree? Maybe it's time." Phil's eyebrows rose at a horn honk behind him.

"I'm not sure I'm ready just yet," she said. "My ride's here."

"Love you!" he said with a smile. "Have a good meeting and a safe flight home."

"Love you too," she said, getting into her Uber, a Toyota Camry. As it pulled onto the street, she thumbed her phone's screen to a picture of Max, their golden retriever. It was a month since they'd lost him to end-stage arthritis. In his final days he'd been trembling, limping in pain. Max had been with their family for pretty much all of Marissa's life.

Turning to the car window, Claire placed her grief in a corner of her heart so she could focus on the work ahead of her. "We need you attending status meetings in person, Claire," Will Walker, her director had said. "The TTC's got new information."

Twenty minutes later, she arrived at a low-rise brick building, part of the Toronto Transit Commission's Hillcrest Complex. After showing her ID, she was directed upstairs to a large meeting room, where she quickly got a cup of coffee before taking a seat at the conference table.

It was three weeks since the subway crash. Five people had been killed—a college student, a bank manager, a retired clothing retailer, a chef and train operator Glen Hockley. A ninety-six-year-old woman who'd suffered a heart attack on the stopped train prior to the crash was in hospital, in critical condition. Fifty other people were injured, some disabled for life.

The pressure on the investigators was palpable, and today's meeting was an update on developments.

"Good morning. We're all set." Larry Whitaker, with the TTC—which was co-leading the investigation with the federal Transportation Safety Board of Canada—started with a roll call of the thirty people gathered there from various agencies.

"Let's recap the events of the crash," Whitaker began. "Due to a passenger's medical emergency on Line 1 Northbound Run 123, the emergency alarm was activated. Operator John Pattel took the cab, stopping his train at St. Clair West Station, radioing the control centre, setting events in motion.

"The centre alerted all northbound Line 1 operators to take their cabs and hold at stations or stop. Trackside signals went red along the line.

"Upon studying his train's screens for his interior cameras, Pattel locked his console, left his cab carrying his handheld radio, and moved quickly down the open gangway through the train's cars to his passenger in distress. Although some passengers had already called 911, he also made a call, requesting paramedics.

"At that moment, Pattel reports that his train jolted forward with alarming force, shoved from behind with an explosive bang. He fell face-first to the floor. Passengers also fell.

"Pattel managed to get up and used his radio to alert the control centre that his train had been struck from behind, activating a full emergency response." Whitaker paused. "We have video footage recorded in the moments after the crash by passengers and Pattel." He glanced around the room. "A caution, this will be intense."

The large flatscreen at one end of the room came to life, and Claire and the other investigators turned their attention to it.

They saw images of Pattel, a bleeding gash on his temple, working at the car's control panel, getting the doors open, directing passengers out to the platform. He then moved toward the last cars, to cries for help.

The footage showed how the last car, the entire car, had been lifted in the collision and was almost touching the roof of the tunnel, crumpled like tinfoil. Mangled seats were crushed into the car's ceiling, passengers were entwined in the twisted metal, some partially pinned and dangling.

Those who could move were bleeding, sobbing, stumbling forward or jumping to the ground through side doors. Off-screen a voice could be heard shouting, "Cut power to the tracks at St. Clair West, passengers on the ground! Repeat: cut power to the tracks at St. Clair West! We have passengers on the ground! We need all first responders now! Send everything you got!"

The video then switched to a shot of the subway car that had crashed into the stopped one. Emerging from the billowing clouds of dark smoke were bleeding and soot-streaked passengers, some with torn clothing, some aiding injured victims, some on their phones as they stumbled toward the platform. The tunnel echoed with groans and shrieks for help.

Amid hissing and wisps of smoke, the camera moved to the front of the incoming train, and Claire gasped as the screen showed, in horrifying detail, how the lead car had telescoped into the stopped train's rear car, heaving it up and mashing it into the roof of the tunnel. The lead car of the struck train had crumpled under it like a crushed tin can.

The camera shot panned into the operator's cab. In the aftermath of the event, crimson rivulets webbed from the metal enmeshed with an operator's uniform, an arm and hand protruding, like a final wave.

The video ended amid a ripple of soft coughs. Whitaker allowed a moment for people to process what they'd just watched. "The cause of this accident is still a mystery," he began, "but the sparse evidence we have hints at a malfunction somewhere in the system. CCTV footage, track signals, event recorders, the train's brakes, control systems, repair and upgrade histories—everything continues to be analyzed." He looked out at the table of investigators. "The operator of the incoming train, Glen Hockley, had been hired by the TTC fourteen years ago, initially as a bus driver. He then operated streetcars before training and qualifying to operate a subway train, a position he'd held for eight years."

"And his record?" Claire asked.

"Operator Hockley's record was clean," Whitaker said. "No indication of fatigue, stress, distraction. Toxicological analysis was negative for the presence of alcohol and other drugs." He turned to Otto Colt, a lead investigator on his team, for an update.

"Using data from the event recorders, we've reconstructed the crash sequence." Colt nodded to the screen and then pressed a button on his keyboard. "We need to re-examine everything again."

The room watched as an animation appeared on the screen. "You'll see," Colt said, "the striking train, Run 115, is easing out of Dupont Station here, northbound for St. Clair West. It's operating in Automatic Train Control mode. At this point, the trackside signals were flashing green." The animation switched, and he continued. "Northbound Run 123, the train before Run 115, was stopped at the next northbound station, St. Clair West, due to a medical emergency. The control centre alerted all northbound Line 1 operators to take over their cabs and hold at stations or stop in the tunnel. Indications were that the trackside signals were a solid red. But twenty seconds after leaving Dupont, 115 had not stopped. Sixty seconds later, 115 was still proceeding to St. Clair West at normal speed, entering a curve."

Claire studied the screen. The animation showed the trackside signals as a solid red.

"The control centre's effort to communicate a stop command to the operator failed," Colt said. "And, unfortunately, the train detection and collision avoidance system failed." He then explained to the group how Run 115 was still operating in ATC at normal speed when the operator of an opposing train, Run 131, leaving St. Clair West Station southbound, had sounded its horn at 115, warning it to stop before entering the station where 123 had stopped. According to sight distance testing, 115 was coming out of a curve, allowing the operator five seconds to have a full view of the stopped train. The operator had taken over the cab and applied emergency braking. Emergency braking was functioning normally, but there was not enough time to slow the train to avoid the collision.

"Again, for the benefit of everyone," Colt said, as the reconstruction video ended, "trackside signals encompass modules and sensors on the tracks and trains to wirelessly send data on the train's location and speed to the control centre. The control centre can tell the trains when to slow down, speed up or stop." He paused. "It appears the train control system didn't detect the stopped train and told 115 the track ahead was clear."

Colt let the weight of the tragedy hang in the air.

At that moment, Len Fisher, an engineer with the provincial Ministry of Transportation, seated next to Claire, asked, "Where are we leaning on cause at this stage?"

"A combination of a fault in the control system and the operator not heeding red lights," Colt said.

Claire spoke up. "Regarding the modules—they're relatively new, installed on Lines 1 and 2 just within the last year, is that correct?"

"That's correct," Colt said.

"Have the track-level modules that transmit critical audio frequency signals been analyzed for intrusion?" Claire asked.

"That's underway," Colt said. "But intrusion is unlikely."

Claire frowned. "Why is it unlikely?"

"Being new, they were installed with the latest technology, with constant software upgrades for operations and security. We suspect the failure is somewhere else in the system because the new modules are deemed impenetrable."

"*Impenetrable?*" Claire repeated, casting a glance toward other investigators. There were people at this table from the Royal Canadian Mounted Police and the Canadian Security Intelligence Service; she knew many, and they were familiar with cybersecurity. Claire doubted they'd agree to calling a system *impenetrable.*

"I'm sorry. Who are you again?" Colt asked Claire. "Who are you with?"

She straightened in her chair. "Claire Brenner. I'm a senior cybersecurity analyst under the Communications Security Establishment in Ottawa."

"Do you have any more questions?" Colt said.

"I do. Regarding these 'impenetrable' modules—are the records correct in showing they were installed by a contracted third party, SynerRapid Systems?"

"Yes," Colt said.

"And you said these track-level modules that transmit critical audio frequency signals are being analyzed for intrusion?"

"Yes. Am I repeating myself here?" Colt said.

"By whom?" she asked, ignoring his tone.

"The contracted party, SynerRapid Systems, the same company that installed them. The company is among the best in the world."

"I'm aware." Claire looked at the notes on her screen. "Records show that within two weeks before the crash, a Line 2 operator reported that her in-cab display unexpectedly strobed for several stops, so she took over the cab. Control had her hold at a station, ran diagnostics and corrected the situation."

"Yes, that happened," Colt said.

"Can I get a readout of the report, diagnostics, everything, for that Line 2 incident?"

"We already looked at that and found the matter had been remedied. Why do you want the readout?"

"To check it against the readout for Run 115."

Colt's jawline tensed. "As I said, we looked at—"

"We'll get that for you, Ms. Brenner," Whitaker said, interrupting Colt. "Thank you. Additional review can only support our findings."

"Moving on." Colt turned back to the large screen. "We have extracted new information which could help us determine the cause. Operator Hockley survived for less than a minute after the crash and tried speaking into his radio. It was recorded. The quality has been enhanced. We'll play it now, so all of us will be hearing, for the first time, approximately ten seconds of what were his last words. Headsets everyone . . ."

11

NEW YORK

"New York City 911, do you need police, fire or medical?"

"God told me to call you."

Rosario Sanchez narrowed her eyes at her screen. The caller was near the east side of Prospect Park. She glanced at the proximity of units.

"Why did God tell you to call?"

"You know how it is, if you see something, say something. Well, I saw something and God told me to call the police."

Rosario rolled her eyes. She was ready for what was coming. In her years as an emergency operator, she'd heard it all. From "There's a UFO on the Chrysler Building" to "I just drowned my baby girls because they wouldn't stop crying."

"What is your address?" Sanchez asked.

After sharing his location on Crown Street, the caller said, "My name is Deacon, but keep the rest anonymous."

"What did you see, Deacon?"

"It's about the boy in the news, missing from the airport."

Sanchez raised her eyebrows. "What can you tell me?"

"It was yesterday. I wash dishes at JFK. I did my shift, was heading home on the train to Brooklyn. I saw this child, this white boy, on my train acting like he was upset."

Sanchez's fingers blurred on her keyboard as she took down the information. The call was also being recorded.

Deacon said: "This boy was with this white couple. A man and woman, older folks, sittin' near me. I swear that I heard this boy say, kinda soft, kinda cryin', 'I don't know you. Why are you doing this? Where are my grandma and grandpa?'"

"Anything else?" Sanchez asked as she typed.

"This boy looked kinda scared. It was odd."

"Approximately how old was the child?"

"Hard to say. Maybe like eight, even twelve. Not sure."

"Describe the two adults with him."

"White folks, older. The man had glasses and a cap, a Yankees cap. The woman had white silver hair. They were wearing the Covid masks, the boy too. And there was the boy's backpack and a suitcase with wheels. Don't recall the colours. The backpack was maybe green."

"Was there anything distinctive about the couple or the boy—tattoos, jewellery, clothes, that kind of thing?"

He described the boy's clothes, then said, "Wait. His shoes."

"What about them?"

"They was white with blue stripes, but there was something they didn't say in the news. But I notice these things. I used to work at the laundry down on Empire. We knew all about stains. The boy's shoes were stained, brown purplish, like he got juice or soda spilled on them."

Sanchez continued typing. "Did you talk to them? Did they say anything?"

"No, I was mindin' my own business, like you do on the train. But I heard the boy say those things and I thought it was strange, like maybe they were playin' a game. But them old folks was all serious, kinda shushin' the boy, saying something like, 'We're taking you to your family.'" He paused. "Oh yeah, the boy says 'I'm hungry' and the woman says they'll eat later, like to quiet him down."

"Can you remember when and where this was?"

"Well, yesterday after my shift." Deacon estimated the time, saying he'd gotten on the AirTrain at JFK to Howard Beach. "I noticed them sometime after Howard, when I got on the A. Then I transferred for Prospect. I'm not sure where they got off."

"Thanks for calling, Deacon," Sanchez said. "Let me just go over the details once more, okay?" She confirmed the caller's story.

"The news got me thinking about what I saw until finally God told me, if you see something, say something. So that's what I'm doing. I hope y'all find that boy, and God bless y'all."

Garlin took another hit of black coffee and rubbed his jaw. He'd washed up and shaved at a bathroom sink after managing two hours of sleep on a command post cot at Kennedy, where the investigation had deepened.

Yesterday's alert from Indianapolis had been a false alarm. And the breach of JFK's cameras had heightened concerns for several agencies. More resources were arriving, intensifying efforts to locate the suspects on airport security cameras and networks throughout New York City. But it was a needle-in-a-haystack operation. News coverage had led to scores of tips, and all were being pursued. But so far all had gone nowhere.

Garlin's phone rang. "Agent Garlin, FBI."

"Agent Garlin, this is Vaughn Ward, Dylan Ward's father. I'm calling for an update."

"Good morning, Mr. Ward. We're working on pulling together an update, but nothing concrete on Dylan's whereabouts yet. We're doing everything we can to find him."

"How did this happen?" Vaughn asked, static crackling.

"We're working on getting answers," Garlin said. "Where are you? Are you in New York?"

"No, not yet. I got stuck in traffic. By the time I got to the airport I'd missed the last flight out."

Garlin looked at his watch. "Why not drive directly? It's only about seven hours."

"I know, but it was very late. I had major problems at the car rental desk. I even slept at the airport. Listen, I'm flying out as soon as possible today."

"Are you flying into JFK?"

"Yes, JFK, if I can."

"We'll have someone meet you at the gate here. Give me your flight number."

"I will when I get it." Static sizzled over Vaughn's words. "I just can't believe this happened. When I think of someone taking Dylan, I just . . ." He trailed off. "Please keep me posted. I'll be there as soon as I can."

"Will do, Mr. Ward," Garlin said. "Send us your flight number ASAP."

The call ended and Garlin tapped his phone in his palm, thinking. "Helen," he said to a nearby agent. "Can you check with Customs and Border for pre-clearance screening for Vaughn Ward, the missing child's father, at Trudeau International?"

The agent nodded. "I'm on it. I'll check inbound flights from Montreal for numbers too."

Just then, Allan Novick, a senior agent and veteran of kidnapping cases, came into the room. "How's it going, Jake?" he asked.

"Lots of leads that aren't really getting us anywhere."

"You think Vaughn Ward could be behind his son's abduction with his parents' help?"

"Uncertain at this point," Garlin said. "We had no grounds to hold the grandparents and released them. We've got Nassau County sitting on their house out in Lynbrook."

"And the boy's mother?"

"We're watching her and haven't ruled her out."

"Because?"

"Because of unresolved custody issues, family tension," Garlin said. "And she has the technical skills to pull this off."

"With his background and contacts, so does her husband," Novick pointed out. "Maybe this is a planned parental abduction, with one party pitted against the other, to make one parent look irresponsible? Or to flee the country with the boy?"

"But why go to the extreme of a cyber intrusion at a major airport?"

"I've seen parents take incredible steps—allegations of abuse, stalking, bribing officials, kidnapping, you name it." Novick paused. "Let's move to expedite unsealing their divorce records in California. It could shed some light on the situation."

"We'll get working on that now," Garlin said, adding, "But Al, a security breach of this magnitude takes this to a different level."

"It could be that Jessica and Vaughn have no hand in this. It could be other forces involved," Novick said. "Maybe it's trafficking, or something tied to her work, or one of his stories. Or something else. Any history of gambling or drug debts? Any threats? Have any ransom demands?"

"Nothing like that so far," Garlin said.

"Until we know the facts, we rule out no one."

"Guys, you need to see this," NYPD detective Mario Lugano suddenly said, waving them to his screen. "A tip from a train rider. MTA followed up, grabbed security video and enhanced it."

Garlin and Novick quickly made their way to Lugano and huddled around his screen. There were images of an older white couple with a boy aged around ten. They were all wearing face masks. Garlin looked at the date stamp in the corner of the screen.

"The timeline fits," he said. "But the kid's clothes are inconsistent with the description we have." No faded jeans, no blue Dodgers T-shirt. This boy was wearing a hoodie and sweatpants. But it was common for kidnappers to change the appearance of their victim.

"Check out the shoes, Jake," Lugano said.

12

LOS ANGELES, EN ROUTE TO NEW YORK

Dylan's alive and in New York.

As Jessie's jetliner climbed from Los Angeles, the images of him on the subway train with his abductors tormented her.

Why did these monsters take him?

Several hours ago, the FBI had shown her the photos of Dylan on the subway train with his abductors.

"Oh my God, that's Dylan!" she had told Garlin. her heart bursting. "That's Dylan's body shape, his posture, the juice stains on his shoe, that's him!"

"What about the people with him?" Garlin had asked.

She studied them. "I don't recognize them at all!"

Now, begging for the plane to go faster, she asked heaven to protect Dylan. As the jet levelled, she tried texting Vaughn again, but the airline's Wi-Fi was skittish. Before boarding at LAX, she'd called his parents for an update on his location.

"He told us he was stuck for hours in traffic by a big accident on the highway near Montreal," Lillian said. "We're still waiting for him."

Jessie closed her eyes. "Are you kidding, Lillian? He's still not there?"

"He faced traffic problems and other delays. He said—"

"My God! Our son is missing! Vaughn should've driven through the night! Montreal's only a few hours from New York City!"

"He's getting a flight today," Lillian said. "Oh, Jessica, we're worried sick for Dylan, and the police are treating us like criminals, like we're involved! They questioned us for hours before they let us go home."

This isn't about you! You lost him! She'd had to bite back on her anger, and instead managed to say, "Let me know the moment you hear anything."

Now, as the plane reached cruising speed, she racked her brain trying to figure out who the suspects could be. The sighting of Dylan on the subway was a break, but if investigators knew more, they hadn't told her.

Guilt replaced her impatience, assailing her again. She should never have put Dylan on that plane alone. She should've flown with him. And when he was reported missing, she should've ignored everyone's advice that she stay in California and flown to New York immediately. Now that the subway video proved he was in New York, she would move heaven and earth to find him. No one—not the FBI, nothing—was going to stop her from flying to New York.

Before she left Santa Monica, her friends had assured her that they'd keep up their investigation while she was gone.

"We'll contact everyone we know in New York for help," Sarita promised. "We'll work on every angle."

"A full-court press," Bobby said. "We're not stopping until we get Dylan back."

"Thank you guys so much." Jessie blinked back tears. "I don't know what I'd do without you." She went into the living room to find her phone charger, Dahlia following her.

"I'm so glad we know Dylan is alive," Dahlia said, perching on the sofa. "Do you have any idea who those people who took him are, Jess?"

Jessie shook her head. "Believe me, if I did, I'd tell the FBI."

"I hate saying this, but could it be Vaughn somehow? I mean, last night you said custody talks weren't going well."

"They aren't, but I can't see him being so calculating, so cruel."

Dahlia thought for a moment. "Could it be linked to the work your company's doing?"

"No, it's secure," Jessie said. "It's all classified. No one knows about it."

"Are you sure?" Dahlia pressed.

Jessie sat next to her on the couch, put her head in her hands. "I don't—I really don't know."

"I'll reach out to my contacts, see what they're hearing. And I'll send a message to our classmates from MIT." She dropped her voice and glanced at the doorway. "You know—everyone who worked on the project."

Jessie looked at her, confused. "Professor Jackson's project? But—"

"They were the best, Jess. And let's face it, you were the superstar. They can help. You need to try everything to find Dylan."

Jessie accepted that Dahlia was right. "Okay. Thank you."

"Let me come with you to New York, Jess. I've already put my colleagues onto my project, and I can extend my vacation. I'm all yours. I can help."

Jessie hugged Dahlia. "Thank you, but no. You've already done so much."

"All right. Then I'll stay and help here."

They returned to the kitchen.

Jessie smiled at her friends. "I love you all. Thank you."

"Remember," Sarita said, "you saw Dylan in the subway video. There's hope. Hang onto it."

Bobby had driven Jessie to LAX, and as they'd pulled out of her driveway, he suggested that they stop at Instinct Nine-99 so she could get her blue work laptop.

"It might be better to have it with you," he said. "And it could be useful, depending on how things go."

"You're right. Just in case."

As soon as Bobby parked, Jessie ran into the office, pulled the laptop from the vault, then stowed it in her laptop bag.

Back in the car, Bobby said, "Listen, Jess, don't worry about the project. We're ahead of schedule on all our contracts. I'll handle anything on that front here. Our priority is Dylan. We'll get all the others in the office to help."

"I need him back. It's all that matters." Jessie looked out the window, tears blurring her vision.

Jessie glanced at her bag, stuffed under the seat in front of her and packed with her things and clothes for Dylan, for if—no, *when* she found him. She chewed on her bottom lip. *Who are those people in the subway video? Why did they take my son?*

She leaned her head back. She was blessed to have her friends helping her pursue Dylan's abductors. If anyone could determine their identities, it was them. And maybe her classmates from MIT.

MIT. Jessie looked out her window and into the clouds. Her sister Jenn had been set to go to UCLA before a drunk driver killed her. After her death, everything their mother had saved for her tuition went to Jessie's, and Jessie was determined not to squander it. She'd focused every ounce of energy into her grades and making sure she got into MIT—and when she did, she honoured her sister's memory by working harder than she'd ever worked in her life.

It paid off. A world-renowned, Nobel Laureate professor, Leonard Jackson, had chosen her to join other exceptional students on a classified research contract. During that time, Jessie learned, experimented and established the groundwork for advancing technology that would eventually help her launch her own company. It was also during that time that she'd met a charmer from Harvard named Vaughn Ward. They'd fallen in love and started their life together. And had Dylan.

She opened her personal laptop and opened up the photo app. Vaughn and a baby Dylan on the beach, her little boy gazing at the waves with his handsome daddy. Dylan on his new bicycle, proudly smiling for the camera. A family photo at the amusement park two years ago.

We were happy. So happy.

Jessie closed her eyes, resurrecting her last memory of Dylan, at LAX with the EverySky agent helping him with his backpack. Jessie heard herself telling him she loved him, touching his arm. She could feel him hugging her.

"I love you too, Mom."

Jessie's shoulders began shaking as she sobbed, covering her mouth to muffle the sound. *Please don't let that be the last time I ever see him. I'm losing my mom. I've already lost my dad, my sister. Please don't take my son.*

The last couple of days—the crucifying anguish, fear, the lack of sleep, the heartache—had taken its toll on her, and she gasped for air while trying to keep her cries quiet.

An attendant suddenly appeared. "Are you all right, honey?" Concerned, she touched Jessie's arm.

Waving her hand, Jessie nodded with a weak smile.

Both women knew she was lying.

The attendant's eyes flicked to the family photos on Jessie's laptop screen, and then she leaned closer. "I don't know what's going on," she said softly, "but I'll say a prayer for you." Her eyes held compassion. "Now, come on, it's time to put your computer away, lift your tray and check your belt. We'll be landing in New York soon."

13

NEW YORK

Adrenaline coursing through her, Jessie bumped other travellers, weaving around them, practically running along the jet bridge at JFK, towing her bag behind her.

It was now mid-afternoon in New York, and she was glancing at her phone for any messages from Vaughn when a voice called to her.

"Jessica Ward?"

She looked up, saw a man and woman in business suits. They showed her their IDs—Special Agents Jake Garlin and Helen Malone from the Federal Bureau of Investigation.

"Ms. Ward, please come with us," Malone said.

"Did you find Dylan? Is he okay?"

"We'll update you shortly. Come with us, please."

Within minutes, Jessie was sitting in a room situated between a luggage outlet and a currency exchange. She was trembling as they closed the door, deadening the bustle of the terminal. Garlin and Malone checked her identification before sitting across from her. Two men in dark blazers, badges clipped to breast pockets, stood against the wall.

Jessie looked around. *No Dylan. No Vaughn. No Miller. No Lillian.*

"Did you find him?" she asked, her voice cracking. The agents' faces were void of expression. "Is he dead? You tell me if he's dead."

Seconds passed before Garlin finally spoke. "We haven't found him yet," he said.

Jessie exhaled in frustration. "But you've got the subway video. You can track down the people who have him."

"We're working on it," Garlin said. "We need your help."

"*My* help?" Jessie asked. "Where's Vaughn? Isn't he here?"

"Some new information has come to light," Malone said. "Will you help us?"

"Yes, anything."

"First," Malone said, "we must advise you of your rights under Miranda."

Jessie froze. "My rights? I don't—"

"It's a formality."

"A formality? For what? Am I a suspect? Am I under—?" Jessie looked wildly from Garlin to Malone.

"No, but we're required to advise you of this as part of the investigation," Malone said. "Are you willing to proceed?"

Swallowing hard, Jessie nodded. She was read her rights, and she agreed to continue without a lawyer.

Malone leaned closer. "Jessica, are you involved in your son's disappearance?"

The blood drained from Jessie's face. She was silent.

"Did you not threaten to take Dylan away from his father?" Malone asked.

"No!"

Garlin withdrew from his pocket a sheet of paper.

"We've obtained transcripts from a recent custody hearing between you and your husband," he said, unfolding the paper. "You said: *You will never take Dylan from me. I'll do everything in my power to prevent that. If I have to, I can make him disappear from your life. You'll never see him again. You know I can do it.*"

Jessie closed her eyes and shook her head slowly.

"That sounds like a threat," Garlin said. "And, Ms. Ward, you have the skills to carry out a threat, the ability to manipulate texts, scrub video, employ the use of third-party players to assist you. You have the ability to orchestrate this entire operation." He let a moment pass, then continued. "Who else was aware that you were putting your son on a plane as an unaccompanied minor?"

"The airline," Jessie said quietly. "I have the documents to prove—"

"Besides the airline."

She took a breath. "Vaughn, his parents. A few co-workers and colleagues in California."

"Do you know the people with your son in the MTA video?" Garlin asked.

Jessie didn't answer.

"Our FBI cyber teams are analyzing the evidence," he continued. "At some point they'll determine who sent the message misdirecting the grandparents, and who intruded on JFK's security cameras and scrubbed the footage. Executing this abduction was a sophisticated operation. But it's something you could do. In fact, being in California when the disappearance unfolded gives you an alibi. It also shifts blame to your son's grandparents and your estranged husband. You've acknowledged tension and animosity with his family. We know these disputes can escalate, make parents take extreme actions." He leaned back in his chair, arms crossed.

"Jessica," Malone said. "You're facing a list of serious federal crimes. It could cost you everything. If you are involved, and acknowledge your role now, we can help you. So, tell us truthfully, are you involved in Dylan's abduction?"

Jessie glanced at one of the poker-faced men against the wall. "I said what I said during an emotionally heated exchange in court. Did you also look at the record for what Vaughn said?"

The agents were silent.

"If you got *my* words, you got *his* too. He said that if he didn't get the custody terms he wanted, he would do whatever he had to do. He said, quote, 'do not underestimate me.' That's what he said." The agents didn't speak and Jessie charged ahead. "Vaughn has the capability to pull this off. He can call on his friends, his sources. Most are cybersecurity experts. And his parents would help. Miller and Lillian have never liked me. And Lillian's got her theatre group with lots of friends who act."

Garlin said, "You still haven't answered our question."

Jessie's jaw tightened. "I am not involved in my son's abduction."

Garlin looked back to the men against the wall, then to Jessie.

"During divorce proceedings, didn't you accuse your husband of infidelity?" he asked.

The truth hit Jessie like a gut punch, but she looked the agent in the eye. "Yes. I accused him of infidelity."

"Accusing him of being unfaithful gives you a motive. You made the threat in court, and you have the means to carry it out."

Jessie put her face in her hands. *I cannot believe this.*

A long silence passed before Malone finally spoke. "Would you consent to volunteering your phone to us? We could seek a warrant, but if you consent, it will be faster."

Jessie's mind weighed the consequences of giving up her phone. "Why should I consent to letting you have it?"

"It could aid the investigation and is a sign of cooperation."

"I am cooperating," she said. "But I'm not giving you my phone."

"Okay," Malone said, nodding slowly. "Would you agree to submit to a polygraph?"

"A polygraph? You are wasting your time on me."

"We have to rule out all possibilities, we need—"

A knock sounded at the door, then it opened to a man with an FBI badge indicating he needed Garlin and Malone to join him outside the room.

In the small hallway, the man's face was flushed. He cleared his throat. "I'm sorry to interrupt, but we've confirmed that Vaughn Ward was not on Flight 5199 from Montreal."

Malone and Garlin looked at each other.

"Do we have a location for him?" Garlin asked.

"No. We triple-checked with our people up there—Canadian officials, airport, airlines, border people, everyone. It appears he was never in Canada at all." The agent looked at his notepad. "And get this, preliminary reports we just got from our cyber guys show that Vaughn Ward's communication to us was rerouted from an as-yet-unknown source. It means nothing originated in Canada."

"He's been misleading us," Garlin said.

14

NEW YORK

Red lights pulsed outside the brownstones of the tree-lined street in Brooklyn's Park Slope neighbourhood. Sirens echoed in the distance as heavily armed members of the NYPD's Emergency Service Unit, suited up in tactical gear, rushed to Vaughn Ward's residence.

Given the exigent circumstances encompassing the risk to life, destruction of evidence or escape of a suspect, they didn't need a warrant. They swept through the building strategically, searching for Dylan and Vaughn. Detectives canvassed residents in the building; officers searched dumpsters, alleys and rooftops. A drone scoured the vicinity, including a playground. The canine unit worked on the scent from Dylan's clothes that Jessie had brought from California. Outside, in the street, radio transmissions crackled, news crews arrived and onlookers gathered at the sealed-off outer perimeter half a block away.

Jessie was pacing at the yellow tape, trying in vain to call her husband, but there was no answer. "Dammit," she said to herself. "Where are you, Vaughn?" Scenarios were burning through her mind of what the police might discover inside the house, when she heard her name being called and turned to see Lillian and Miller working their way to her, concern carved into their faces. Her mother-in-law opened her arms, but Jessie ignored her. Seeing them for the first time since Dylan's disappearance ignited her fury as she stepped right up to them.

"What did you do?"

"Jessica," Miller said. "You don't understand."

Investigators and reporters nearby overheard Jessie's raised voice and turned, but she was undeterred. "You're involved in this!"

"No, Jessie," Miller said. "We were tricked at the airport!"

"You're helping Vaughn. Tell me, where did he take Dylan? Did he leave the country? Does he have a girlfriend helping him?" Jessie's hands were clenched into fists at her sides.

"I swear, we don't know anything," Lillian said.

Suddenly, FBI agents Garlin and Malone, along with NYPD detective Mario Lugano, approached.

"ESU found no one inside," Lugano said. "We've issued an alert to locate Vaughn's vehicle."

"Let me in to have a look," Jessie said.

Lugano shook his head. "It's a potential crime scene. We need to preserve it."

"You might miss something! Please, you could watch me!" Jessie urged. "We're losing time! Please!"

Garlin and Malone took Lugano aside to huddle with other senior officials on the scene. A few moments later, Lugano returned. "This is what will happen. The Crime Scene Unit has just arrived. After they've processed and released the residence, we'll take you in and you can have a look. But it won't be for a few hours." He pointed with his chin. "There's a hotel only two blocks from here."

Jessie nodded and watched as detectives wearing white hazmat suits, gloves and face masks entered Vaughn's building to photograph, examine and document everything, looking for any strand of evidence to aid in the search for Dylan. "Okay, I'll head there," she said.

She nodded goodbye to Vaughn's parents and then hurried to the Golden Greenwood Hotel on Fourth Avenue. She checked in and immediately secured her blue laptop in the in-room safe. Then she took a quick shower and changed into fresh clothes. She collected her bag with her personal laptop and phone, returned to Vaughn's building and waited in anguish with uniformed officers near a cluster of police vehicles.

When the Crime Scene Unit finally finished, Garlin and Lugano escorted Jessie up the front stoop and into the building. Floorboards creaked and curious neighbours emerged in doorways, gawking at Jessie. It was surreal. Two days ago, she'd put Dylan on a plane by himself. Now he was missing with the FBI accusing her of parental abduction.

But now, it was Vaughn they suspected.

She entered her ex-husband's apartment, wincing at the pungent smell of the chemicals that the CSU had used to detect blood. Black smears of fingerprint powder covered the doorframe and light switches of the entry.

She looked around the apartment, a place she'd never been. She thought Vaughn must be doing well to afford this place, a two-bedroom on one of the most desired blocks in Park Slope. The afternoon sun fingered through the wooden shutters of the bay windows to the living room, with its high ceiling. All the furniture—sofa, chairs and tables—looked like it had been repositioned and the cushions removed and examined. The fireplace mantel and the end and coffee tables were feathered with fingerprint powder.

Nothing in this room indicates Dylan was here.

Bookshelves lined the walls; the books had been removed, searched, replaced or stacked haphazardly. The framed prints and landscapes that had hung on the walls were on the floor in a corner.

With Garlin and Lugano near, taking stock and watching, she went to the kitchen and looked at the empty marble countertops, the bold tiled backsplash, new stainless-steel appliances and pendant lights over the island. All had been smudged with fingerprint powder. The double sink was empty. She opened the fridge—milk, eggs, beer, condiments. Nothing Dylan would eat. No leftover pizza or takeout. No ice cream in the freezer. She checked cabinets and drawers, the handles covered with residue. None of Dylan's cereals. No snack chips or cookies.

Garlin asked, "Anything?"

Shaking her head, she moved on to the first bedroom. The mattress had been removed and was leaning against the wall, the sheets piles in a corner. A closet had some of Vaughn's coats; a small en-suite bathroom was in disarray from the forensic process. There was no soap or shampoo in the shower. No toiletries or recently used towels. Nothing in the laundry hamper. Nothing she could link to Dylan.

The larger bedroom was Vaughn's. Its shuttered windows filtered the sunlight falling onto the king-sized bed. An eiderdown duvet and bamboo sheets were heaped on the floor beside the mattress. Clothes, thoroughly searched and analyzed, had been left dishevelled in the closet. Jackets, shirts, pants. But a number of empty hangers had her thinking.

No suitcase in the corner. When we lived together, he always kept his suitcase and bags in the corner on his side of the closet.

Opening the drawers of his dresser, it seemed depleted of underwear. The bathroom was heavy with the smells of soap and shampoo. Then something tugged at her heart as she noticed a lingering trace of the lavender scent of Eternity, Vaughn's cologne, as pleasing and short-lived as a falling star as it mixed with the chemical smells of the forensic treatments. Missing were his toothbrush and shaving kit. She stood in the bathroom thinking how nothing indicated he was living with another woman.

"Well?" Lugano stood by the doorframe.

Saying nothing, Jessie returned to the living room and the old wooden table in the corner nook that served as Vaughn's home office. The surface was covered with fingerprint powder. Still, she could see a spot where a coaster failed to cover a few faded coffee rings.

Vaughn's laptop was gone.

She turned to Garlin. "Did you find his passport, his laptop, his phone?"

He took a moment, deciding what aspects of the investigation to reveal. "None of those items have been located."

Then, looking around, she froze, her heart suddenly filling with warmth. At the desk's edge were two framed photos: one of her; next to it, a framed photo of her and Dylan. Her gaze swept over the bookshelves with worn reference books and keepsakes from his travels. All had been searched and processed for fingerprints. The camel sculpture from Kuwait, the beads from Qatar, the elephant carving from Senegal, the small drum from Jamaica. She walked to the corkboard next to the shelves.

Fixed to it with a pin and a binder clip was a pictorial calendar with scenes of the California coast. The month showed Sand Dollar Beach, which pulled her back to the happier time they'd gone there together. Jessie blinked at the memories.

"Our guys want to know what you make of these?" Lugano pointed to the notations lacing the calendar's days.

"Vaughn's old-school, always writing things down, just in case he loses computer access." Jessie stepped closer to the calendar. Scrutinizing it, deciphering his scrawl. One date had "d-line," for deadline; a week later it was "absolute d-line." Likely for an article.

Another date simply said "Dental 2pm." Her eyes moved over notes for paying various bills. Some dates had notes that he'd crossed out. Then an underlined note that said, "Dylan Mom, Dad," clearly and accurately marking Dylan's arrival. Then, several days later, a note: "Dylan, Me."

Wait.

Her attention went back to several days before Dylan's arrival date to a scrawled notation, one that was crossed through. She couldn't make it out. Dismissing it, she moved on.

A couple of days later, a note said: "Beth Cab."

She looked hard at Vaughn's notation.

"Who's Beth Cab?" Garlin asked.

As she puzzled over it, something pinged in the corner of her mind, but before she could dissect her thought, she felt her phone vibrating.

Bobby was calling.

"Jess, we've got a lead!" He was breathless with excitement when she answered. "We've got clients in New York and one just notified us. After going through their video, they picked up an image from a camera near Penn Station. I've sent it to you."

"An image?"

Her phone vibrated again, and she opened a photo of two masked people on the street—appearing to be the same people from the subway video—walking with a boy—Dylan.

It was clearly Dylan.

Jessie gasped, her hand flying to her mouth as she turned her phone to Garlin.

"Near Penn Station?" Jessie said.

"The time fits," Bobby said. "It was recorded not long after the subway video you saw. It's them!"

Jessie studied the image of Dylan on the sidewalk near Penn Station. Then she returned to looking at Vaughn's calendar notation—"Beth Cab."

The pinging resumed, growing louder as she processed the image. Then the notation, shutting her eyes to keep the thought from escaping.

"I know what this note means! It's where they took Dylan!"

15

OTTAWA

"*They were green . . .*"

Above the piercing screams, rushing air and bleating alarms, Glen Hockley's dying words flowed through Claire's headphones.

"*. . . the lights were green . . .*"

Since she'd attended the Toronto meeting yesterday and returned home to Ottawa, she'd been listening to Hockley's last words, replaying them over and over.

She even heard them in her sleep.

Last night she'd worked until 2 a.m. and was up before sunrise to take a shower, trying not to wake Phil and Marissa. She got yogurt, a banana, made black coffee, went downstairs to her basement office and resumed studying her notes and reports. After replaying the horrific crash montage, she reviewed the collection of TV news reports, encompassing the footage released by the TTC and firefighters.

Within minutes of John Pattel's report of the collision, first responders had begun arriving at the scene. News media had broadcast fragments of dispatches as the control centre continued activating emergency procedures for train services on Line 1, while alerting paramedics and firefighters that passengers were trapped in the wreckage.

Some TV reports carried the never-ending wail and yelp of sirens as waves of fire trucks, ambulances and police units converged at the station. The area had been sealed for rescue operations and investigations. Overhead, helicopters circled, broadcasting live while cutting to news crews on the ground as journalists scrambled to reach the station, interviewing survivors and questioning officials.

Searching for indications of a cause, some reporters referred to the tragic 1995 subway train collision at St. Clair West Station. And they raised a near miss in 2020 at Osgoode and other incidents of varying magnitude across the country and around the world over the years.

The footage released by officials showed how, below the surface, shifting beams from firefighters' helmet lights raked the dust clouds in an otherworldly realm. Then came the grind of high-powered saws and spreaders as crews cut through metal to free the passengers. Radio cross-talk bleated as doctors and paramedics treated, then transported each extricated passenger.

It was not shown, but Claire knew that Glen Hockley's body had been the last to be removed as the grisly work continued into the night.

The news media had kept watch, relating how the initial steps of the investigation expanded, involving a number of local, provincial and national agencies in the search for answers. The coverage indicated that it was too soon for officials to conclude if the cause was due to human error, mechanical failure, a fault in the system, a combination or something else entirely.

"Until then," one TV journalist said, "mystery envelopes this terrible crash."

Closing the videos, Claire thought. That Otto Colt was dismissing intrusion as a possibility didn't sit well with her. His working theory on the cause was twofold: a fault in the control system, and the operator didn't respond to the red lights.

But Claire didn't buy it.

Not entirely.

Not when Hockley had said with his last breath that the lights were green. And she wasn't confident that they'd determined if the module had generated accurate audio frequency signals to the track circuit.

Claire studied all the information she had until movement above her meant her family was waking up. She started breakfast for them.

"I know what kind of tree I like, Mom," Marissa said after finishing her eggs. Getting ready, she held out her phone, showing Claire a tree with dark green foliage and snow-white flowers.

"Nice, honey. Looks like a dogwood."

Phil kissed Claire, collected his toast and scrambled eggs into a sandwich, wrapped it in a napkin and grabbed his commuter mug. "Let's go, kid, we're running late." He looked at his wife. "Forgot to tell you, hon. We got a guy coming to service the furnace, could be soon. They're juggling their schedule."

"Got it."

"It's pizza night, Mom," Marissa reminded her, giving her a hug.

"Oh, right!" Claire said, kissing her daughter. "Have a good day."

After cleaning up and getting fresh coffee, Claire returned to work in a house void of the comforting padding of paws on the floor. A house now profoundly empty. But eclipsing her grief was the unbearable loss of life in the subway tragedy. She looked once more at the pictures of the people who had died with Hockley. The chef, the manager, the retiree and the student. What had gone through their minds in those horrifying last seconds?

Did the module—the impenetrable module—fail?

Tapping a pen to her chin, Claire went back to the incident two weeks before the crash. A Line 2 operator had reported her in-cab display had unexpectedly strobed for several stops.

Could the two incidents be related?

She sent a message to her engineering friend, Len Fisher, who'd sat beside her at the Toronto meeting.

Two minutes later her screen chimed, and a man in his late fifties with thick unruly white hair and black-framed glasses appeared.

"Hey Claire."

"Thanks for calling, Len. I've been thinking about the meeting yesterday. What're your thoughts on Otto Colt's theory?"

"Otto's good, but it's just a theory so far, and we do have a lot more to do. I've been thinking about the meeting yesterday and I thought you raised some good points."

Claire nodded. "What do you know? What're you thinking?"

"Between you and I?"

"You bet."

"I've sent Otto and Larry Whitaker a note cautioning that we do not overlook the direct radio alert to the operator from the control centre. That is a separate factor entirely. It would indicate a broader system failure."

"What was their response?"

"Only Larry got back to me, agreeing it has to be considered."

Claire took a moment before speaking. "I can't help thinking about the operator's last words, the modules and the report from Line 2 on the flickering console display. Maybe there's a connection. What do you think?"

"Well, our people worked with TTC and Toronto police, and we found no indication of tampering or vandalism physically on the tracks with the modules. And no deterioration or environmental erosion of the devices—they're new. Still, anything's possible and you raised some valid questions." Len removed his glasses, cleaning them with a cloth. "You requested the report for Line 2. What does it tell you?"

"Haven't got it yet," she said, adding, "And the fact Otto said the modules were impenetrable, new with constant software upgrades, raised a red flag with me."

"And you raised it with Otto."

"And he said they were being analyzed for intrusion by SynerRapid, the contractor who installed them." Her mouse and keyboard clicked as she opened the company's file. "I know they have a stellar reputation. Still, that kind of self-policing raises another red flag. I'm considering contacting them directly to observe or participate in that analysis."

"You'd be advised to first go through Otto. He's known to be territorial. I'd check with your boss."

"Thanks, Len. I have to give this more thought."

The call ended, and Claire rubbed her tired face. Feeling exhaustion settling in her bones, she stood and quickly changed into jeans and a hoodie and grabbed her phone. As she headed out the back door, she glimpsed Max's leash on the coat hook. Pushing back on her sadness, she left her house for the trail along the Ottawa River.

SynerRapid's impenetrable modules were new but underwent constant software updates. No matter how many levels of security SynerRapid Systems implements in their modules, there is always the potential for intrusion, especially with AI and advances in technology. I need to dig into my theory.

Her phone vibrated with a notification from Larry Whitaker.

Claire: Please find attached via encrypted delivery, the readout of the report and diagnostics regarding the Line 2 incident. Password to follow in a separate message.

Thanking Larry, Claire thought to herself, *This is a start.*

16

NEW YORK

The answer was there—in Vaughn's calendar note.

Beth Cab.

"It means a cabin near Bethel, in upstate New York," Jessie told the detectives.

"How do you know that?" Lugano asked.

"We used to go there, as a family." She nodded, affirming the realization. "And when I put Dylan on the plane, at LAX, he told me that Vaughn had said maybe he would to take him to the cabin. I think that's where they went." The agents were quiet, and Jessie just stared at them. "Are you listening to me?"

Garlin looked up from his phone. "How did you get this image of Dylan near Penn?"

"My company has long-time clients in the city—a couple of corporate buildings. We asked for help," Jessie said. "They reviewed exterior security and picked this up from a camera near Penn Station."

Garlin and Lugano traded glances.

"Please. I'm begging you to listen to me!" Jessie said. "Every instinct tells me the people helping Vaughn could've taken a train to Bethel from Penn Station."

"To a cabin your family stayed at in Bethel?" Lugano asked.

"Yes." Jessie pressed her palm to her head. "They were called Shady Timber Rest Cabins." She sighed and looked at Garlin. "Look, if you're not going to move on this," she said, "I will."

He held up his hand. "Hold tight. Don't go anywhere."

Garlin and Lugano emerged from the bedroom and announced that the investigation now encompassed upstate New York and Penn Station.

"The image your people got of Dylan at Penn was a good lead," Garlin said. "Working with the NYPD and MTA, we got more images of Dylan and the suspects, but they must've gone into a gap near Penn, because we lost them. They're working on tracking paths they may have taken and getting more images. We're extending the search."

"Please, you've got to get me upstate to Bethel now," Jessie said.

Garlin explained how they had to adhere to the legalities of an ongoing investigation. "We can't risk the appearance of influencing or coercing you, by taking you to a potential crime scene."

"But you let me in here," Jessie said, frustrated.

"Yes, but that was *after* this location was processed and released," Lugano said. "We've yet to discover a scene near Penn Station or upstate."

"I'm telling you, it's Bethel."

"You're free to go on your own," the NYPD detective said.

Feeling time slipping away, Jessie picked up her phone. She needed to get a rental car. "You have to keep an eye on Lillian and Miller," she said before heading out the door to the street, checking her phone for the short-term car rental service her company used.

As Jessie drove north on the Palisades Parkway in her rented Ford Escape, her heart raced.

She knew she was right. Vaughn had gone to Bethel.

"But I don't know where in Bethel," she muttered to herself.

She called Bobby in Santa Monica. "Bobby, I have a lead that Vaughn and his cohorts took Dylan upstate to Bethel, and I need help. I don't know *where* in Bethel."

"Go ahead," he said. "Got Sarita and Dahlia here, standing by."

"Can you check with every cabin, motel and resort in the Bethel area? Find out where Vaughn's booked."

"We're on it!" Bobby said. "Wait, Dahlia wants to talk to you."

"Jess," Dahlia said. "You okay?"

Jessie swallowed, taking a moment to find her voice. "I'm hanging in there. Thank you for the Penn Station video, showing me Dylan's alive. I just don't know what I'll do if—"

"It's going to be okay," Dahlia said. "Dylan is coming home."

Ending the call, Jessie flexed her knuckles, which were aching from her grip on the wheel as she accelerated well beyond the posted speed. She glanced into her rear-view mirror. A green SUV was behind her. Jessie was certain it had been trailing her since she left New York City. Was it an unmarked police vehicle assigned to follow her? That could be a sign of mistrust—or perhaps it was help.

It was late afternoon now; the miles went by until her phone chimed, signalling a new message. It was a text from Vaughn.

Stop looking. It's better this way.

Chilled to the core, she swallowed hard, staring at it until a horn honked because she'd swerved from her lane. Regaining her composure, she took a breath and dictated her response.

Better for who? What do you mean? Is he okay? Please, let's talk, Vaughn! Please!

A minute passed, then two more, with no indication he was going to answer. She sent another message.

Please. Where are you? Let's work it out. Please.

In the icy silence that followed, tears streamed down her face. Fighting to calm down, she focused on the scenery. It was years since Jessie had been to the rolling forested hills of the Catskills. Dylan had been so young when they'd stayed at Shady Timber Rest. Getting pulled into the memory, she could hear the crackle of their campfire, sparks spiralling to the stars. She could smell the toasted marshmallows and the burning wood.

She could hear their laughter.

We were a good family then.

Bethel was one of Vaughn's favourite places. Hers too. They'd hiked there, fished, loving it for its beauty and the vibe of the historic Woodstock music festival that had taken place nearby.

Her phone suddenly rang, pulling her from her daydream.

"Ripple Edge Cottages," Bobby said. "They confirmed Vaughn Ward rented a cabin at Ripple Edge Cottages."

"Thanks, Bobby." Jessie hung up and entered the name of the cabins into Google Maps. She was six miles away.

It took several minutes before she reached the lakeside office at Ripple Edge. But she didn't stop there, because beyond the entrance, along the narrow earthen road, through the trees, emergency lights flashed.

Dragging the back of her hand across her moist brow, she guided the Escape down the twisting pathway, coming upon a knot of vehicles from Sullivan County and the state police. They were parked at a cabin, lights pulsing. Two uniformed officers were cordoning off the yard with yellow tape.

Oh God.

She rolled up until the palm of a deputy sheriff stopped her.

She put the car in park and got out.

"I'm Jessica Ward. Did you find my son?"

The deputy blocked her path, not answering her.

"Is my son okay?" Jessie tried to move around him, but he wouldn't let her pass. "Let me in please!"

"Ma'am, I'm sorry, you can't go in there."

17

SANTA MONICA

Dahlia glanced up from her phone at the engineers and techs at Instinct Nine-99, who were locked in to their screens, keyboards clicking.

Bobby and Sarita were among them, immersed in the search for Dylan. They were still waiting for word from Jessie in New York on the cabin.

Returning to her phone, Dahlia's fingers flew over the keys as she continued sending pleas for help to old college friends, some of whom had gone on to work at NASA, Google, Nvidia and Apple. They had connections across the country and around the world. A few knew Vaughn from his reporting days.

One of you must've heard something about him, Dahlia thought as she scrolled. Everyone she'd contacted was heartbroken for Jess and offered support. But so far, no one had gotten back with any useful information.

Frustrated, she peered through the window of Jessie's locked office, at her paintings and framed degrees. Jessie had achieved so much in her life and career. Dahlia hadn't had a similar path. Her mother was a chemistry professor, and her father, an engineer with NASA. Their tolerance for deviations from rules, or mistakes, was razor thin. They weren't pleased she'd been accepted into MIT; they'd expected it.

Dahlia had felt pressure to succeed, to shine, there. The school was affiliated with one hundred Nobel Laureates. Some of their professors were Nobel Prize winners. The students who made it into the computer science program were overachievers.

Dahlia had been honoured when Professor Jackson, widely regarded for his research advances in technology, selected her, Jessica and a handful of other students to conduct research on a classified government-funded project to enhance cybersecurity. Professor Jackson was always complimentary of Dahlia's work, but it was Jessica's work that had eclipsed hers, impressing him above all others. Jessica was the star of the project team—and that was saying something considering some of Jackson's students were now with the military, the CIA, NSA, and the Cyber Defense Agency. Dahlia, who'd blazed her own path as a cyber expert working around the world, had reached out to those classmates too.

She remembered how working on the project had meant long hours. One time when they needed a break, she'd taken Jessie to a party with some of her Harvard friends. One of them was Vaughn. Dahlia had gone to a couple of concerts and lectures with Vaughn, who was well-known in Cambridge. But when she introduced him to Jessie, he was smitten.

Dahlia smiled at the memories.

When our hearts were young.

Eventually, Jessie and Vaughn would get married—the globe-trotting journalist and computer geek who built a cybersecurity company. And they would have a little boy, Dylan.

A picture-perfect life. But it was now shattered.

Dahlia thought of her own heartache, her recent broken engagement. "I just don't feel we'll make it in the long run," her fiancé had told her on the rainy night they'd walked in London.

Sighing, she pulled herself out of the past and checked her phone again. Nothing new, and no word from New York. She rubbed her aching temples and went to the kitchen for coffee, finding Bobby and Sarita there.

"Hey Dahlia," Bobby said.

"I keep coming back to a question," she said. "Could the abduction be connected in some way to Instinct's work?"

Exchanging a look with Bobby, Sarita said, "We've thought that too. But we've heard nothing to link it."

"All our contracts are secure," Bobby said. "I mean, right now, everything points to Vaughn, the divorce and custody."

"Right," Dahlia said.

"Still," he said, "I wonder about Vaughn's video call. The one we all saw."

"What about it?"

"He seemed a bit off, you know. He didn't sound right."

"Well, look at what he's done," Dahlia said. "And what he was trying to hide."

"Man, I'd love to take another look at the call. I wish Jess had recorded it." Bobby rubbed his chin. "There might've been a hidden recording feature that was enabled, one we don't know about. I'm gonna check the cloud and with the video conferencing platform about retention of data."

Bobby left the kitchen, and Sarita turned to Dahlia. "Why do you think this happened?"

Dahlia shook her head. "Nothing makes sense, Sarita."

"But you've known Jessica and Vaughn longer than anyone. We knew their marriage was over, but I always thought he was a nice guy."

"Right." Dahlia gave her a little nod. "He's a bit of a flirt. But we all know that."

Sarita turned her head but not before Dahlia saw the beginnings of her blush. "Sarita? You okay?"

Sarita dropped her voice. "There was one time," she said, pausing. "He gave me a look, you know, smiling that smile. It was weird."

"And?"

"That was it."

Dahlia held her gaze for a moment. "No surprise. You're pretty. And there's no denying that the man exudes charm."

"I'd heard that you went out with him in college," Sarita said, taking a sip of coffee.

Dahlia gave a mild grin. "I met him at a museum and told him I liked a piece he did on emerging technology for the *Crimson*. We went out a few times and—" Dahlia's phone vibrated, interrupting them, and she looked at the screen. "Sorry, I have to read this. It's a text from a friend, someone Jessie and I knew at MIT." She read it quickly, then said, "Oh my God!"

Sarita's eyes widened. "What is it?"

"Something about Vaughn that could change everything. I have to let Jessie know right away."

18

BETHEL AREA, UPSTATE NEW YORK

"Did you find Dylan?" Jessie was shaking, beads of sweat rising on her lip. A police deputy held her back at the edge of the cabin's property. "I'm his mother! Tell me!" Her voice exploded into the air like artillery fire ripping through the trees. Jessie's gaze burned into the sober-faced cops blocking her at the crime scene tape, until the youngest-looking of the bunch, chin bearing a red nick from shaving that morning, softened his expression.

"Ma'am," he said, clearing his throat. "He's not in the cabin, ma'am."

"Where is he then? Is Vaughn in there?" Her voice broke. "I got a message from him. I'll show you!" They didn't react. "Why is this a crime scene?"

No one spoke. The young officer looked at Jessie nervously.

"I don't see my husband's car." She looked to the cabin, then to the police vehicles. "Did you arrest him?" She held up her phone. "See? He sent me this message." She threw up her arms. "Can someone tell me what's happening?"

"Ma'am," another deputy said. "We can't speak to anything. The lead investigators should be here soon, and they'll update you."

There was a commotion at the forest edge, where a K-9 unit was active. Tail wagging, snout to the ground, a German shepherd moved along the lakeshore. Not far off, officers unpacked equipment from their van. Jessie turned to see more emergency vehicles and a couple of local news teams arriving. Groaning at the gravity of what was unfolding, she leaned back against her car as her phone vibrated with a call.

"Jess, any word?" Dahlia asked. "Did they find Dylan and Vaughn?"

"No. But Vaughn sent me a text while I was on my way here. It said, *Stop looking. It's better this way.*"

"What? What does that mean?"

"I don't know, Dahlia. I'm worried." Jessie raked her fingers through her hair.

"Where are you?"

"At Ripple Edge. Police are here. It's a crime scene, and no one will tell me anything."

"Jess, I have information."

"What is it?"

"You remember Nathan and Lisalee from school?"

"Yes, of course."

"Well, they got in touch with friends at Bloomberg and Reuters who know Vaughn." Dahlia paused. "Before I tell you, listen to me, Jess: this is just a rumour."

"Tell me."

"Vaughn applied for a foreign bureau post with a news agency."

Jessie frowned in confusion. "A foreign bureau? Where? Which agency?"

"I don't know. They're digging into it. But one thing is clear—Jess, this isn't good."

Jessie pressed her phone against her ear. "Tell me, Dahlia."

"They're pretty sure, according to the rumour, that the bureau is in a country that has no extradition with the US."

Jessie's stomach dropped, and she slid down her car's fender. *No extradition with the US?* If Vaughn fled with Dylan to a country that had no extradition treaty with the US, he couldn't be arrested and returned.

And I'd never see my son again.

"Are you still there?" Dahlia asked, concerned. "Jess, I'm so sorry. But we're chasing it down."

"Thanks for telling me, Dahlia," Jessie said. "Listen, I have to go." Ending the call, Jessie raked her hands through her hair again, losing herself in her thoughts until barking jerked her attention to the dog at the lake, followed by the whirring and buzzing of a police drone lifting off. A car pulled up next to her Escape, and Garlin and Lugano stepped out.

She stood and rushed to them. "Tell me what you know," she demanded. "No one will tell me anything."

"You were right," Lugano said. "Your husband was here."

"And we're searching for anything to help find out where he is right now," Garlin added.

"Searching for what?" She looked impatiently from one to the other as they hesitated. "Oh, don't do this now!" She gritted her teeth and took two steps into their space. "I pointed you here. I deserve to know what you're doing!"

"We're still assessing Vaughn's Brooklyn residence," Lugano said. "And we're chasing down his phone records, bank and credit cards. But it appears he's gone dark. Off the grid."

"Off the grid? No, no. He sent this to me while I was driving up." Jessie held out her phone, and the two investigators studied the text. "And a friend tipped me off to something. Apparently, Vaughn has applied for a job with a foreign bureau in a country that has no extradition treaty with the US."

"If that's true," Garlin said, "it could point to a planned international parental abduction." He got out his phone. Before stepping away, he said, "I've got to update our guys."

"What about the two people who took Dylan?" Jessie asked Lugano. "They're part of all of this."

"Still investigating," he said. "We're working to get images from the subway out of JFK and a video near Penn Station."

A news truck from a New York City station suddenly pulled up to the site, and Jessie stared as Lillian and Miller exited. Furious, she rushed to them. "Why the hell're you here?" Her outburst drew the attention of everyone around them. She didn't care. "Arrest them!" Jessie pointed at the older couple, her eyes flashing. "Arrest them now!"

"Jessica, please." Lillian was in tears. "Did they find Dylan?"

"Don't you dare ask about my son!" Jessie yelled. "You helped Vaughn with the scheme to steal Dylan and leave the country!"

"What're you saying?" Miller asked, his eyes searching Jessie's face. He looked at Garlin, Lugano and the tape cordoning the cabin. "What's happening here?"

"You got your friends to help," Jessie said. "You got two actors, theatre friends, to deceive everyone, so Vaughn could carry out his plan to take Dylan from me!"

"No, Jessica." Miller shook his head. "That's not true!"

"Liar!" Jessie stepped closer to him and pounded at his chest. "Where's Vaughn? Where did he go? Tell me! Give me back my son!" She was sobbing now, unable to stop.

Garlin and Lugano signalled for the deputies to help, and they pried Jessie from Miller and Lillian and then escorted her to the far side of a patrol car, where she was out of sight of the news cameras. A deputy stayed with her. Jessie was numb, oblivious to the chaos, to the dispatches spilling from the car's radio. The deputy offered her a bottle of water, which she declined.

Jessie took stock of her surroundings. *Please, let us find Dylan before it's too late.* Her prayers were scored by the sounds of the police dispatches, which were growing increasingly urgent, compelling Jessie to focus on them.

"*. . . the drone's got it . . . a vehicle submerged . . . rear quarter nearest the surface . . . New York tag . . . plate registered to the subject . . .*"

"No!" Jessie's scream echoed across the lake.

19

BETHEL AREA, UPSTATE NEW YORK

Air bubbled softly to the calm surface of the lake as divers worked underwater.

Jessie watched from a distance, her pulse drumming. Several yards away stood Lillian and Miller, and further along the shore, Garlin and Lugano huddled with investigators at a makeshift command post.

It was nearing dusk when the New York State Police Underwater Recovery Team arrived to begin the process of recovering Vaughn's submerged SUV. It had been identified approximately sixty feet from the edge of the lake.

No one knew how long it had been there. The initial investigations had found no signs of life.

To collect potential evidence, they'd taped off the area where they believed his vehicle had entered the water. They mapped the parameters of the dive. After assessing the car's position, its depth below the surface and the water conditions, the team assembled its equipment. They estimated that the car was at a depth of five to ten feet with its rear tilted to the surface.

The divers got into their gear, then entered the lake, communicating by radio with the surface teams, who were stationed nearby in boats and at the command post onshore.

Everyone on land was quiet as they waited for the crew to emerge. The only sound was the underwater team's radio transmissions, echoing softly in the stillness of approaching twilight.

Jessie prayed quietly, "God, please don't let them find Dylan!" She threw another quick glance back at the cabin.

Garlin and Lugano had assured her that no one had been found in the small cottage, even confirming that the canine unit had not detected Dylan's scent, but it was still being processed for evidence. Clenching her eyes shut as divers probed Vaughn's car, the same questions tormented her. Where were Dylan's abductors, and was Dylan with them? Had Vaughn been planning to relocate to another country and take Dylan with him? She shot a cold look at Lillian and Miller. Had they helped him stage everything? Give him enough time to flee the country with Dylan? Maybe he'd dumped the car to cover his tracks, to disappear?

As she stared at her in-laws, Jessie tasted the acrimony between her and Vaughn. They'd said horrible things to each other in court.

A radio transmission stopped her cold.

"*. . . we have one deceased adult male inside . . .*"

Lillian's scream reverberated across the lake as Miller held her, struggling to keep both of them on their feet. Jessie doubled over, consumed with a thousand new fears. The deputy with her attempted to comfort her, but Jessie shook him off. "*No other victims found in the vehicle,*" the transmission relayed, and Jessie nearly collapsed.

Dylan wasn't in the car.

The recovery continued, with no one knowing who the deceased male was.

Two hours later, a state trooper stood in front of a crowd of reporters. She read out the details from her phone.

"The body of an adult male has been recovered in a 2023 SUV by the New York State Police Underwater Recovery Team. The vehicle has been removed from the lake at Ripple Edge Cottages and is being transported for further processing. The body will undergo an autopsy to confirm identity and cause of death.

"This operation is part of the multi-agency investigation into the suspected abduction of Dylan Parker Ward—age nine, of Los Angeles—from JFK International Airport in New York.

"The Forensics Identification Unit is on scene here, and the State Police Underwater Recovery Team will continue search and recovery operations.

"We have no further comments at this time. For updates from us, follow the New York State Police Newsroom."

As the trooper turned away, reporters lobbed their questions.

Jessie kept her distance from Lillian and Miller, and the media. They'd declined to speak with the news people while waiting for more information.

She watched two police divers disappear into the lake.

This can't be real, she thought. *It makes no sense.*

Wiping at tears but feeling nothing, she stared at the otherworldly underwater luminescence of the scuba team's lights as they scoured the lake. Boats equipped with sonar moved slowly over the area. Drones hovered along the shore. A police helicopter, its brilliant light raking the water, conducted ever-widening search patterns.

Vaughn's words reverberated in her mind.

It's better this way.

20

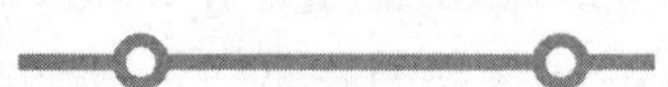

BETHEL AREA, UPSTATE NEW YORK

Jessie refused to leave the crime scene, keeping a vigil through the night. She shivered in her car, continually refreshing the news on her phone and laptop.

Exhausted, her nerves shredded raw, sleep came in snatches, punctuated with the sputter of radios and the hiss and rattle of equipment.

The police had not found Dylan, giving Jessie hope that he was safe. But her hope slipped each time she drifted into fits of sleep and dreams.

... Vaughn and Dylan, their faces aglow by the campfire at the lake ... roasting marshmallows ... Vaughn's smile ... Dylan laughing ... "This is the best time ever!" ... Vaughn's Brooklyn home ... his desk ... his work area ... the California coast ... his calendar ... Vaughn's scrawled notes ... something ... there's something ...

A gentle rap on her car window startled her awake, and her eyes squinted against the light of the dawn. It was three days since Dylan's abduction. Stiff and groggy, she lowered her window, letting in the crisp morning air and looking up at the young female deputy at her car.

"I got you hot coffee and some food." She handed Jessie a take-out cup and a paper bag. "A muffin and some fruit." She nodded toward the cabins. "In case you didn't see it last night, there's an outdoor restroom down there. Relatively clean."

Jessie looked to the lakeshore, where the search operation was ongoing. Her question didn't need to be voiced.

"Nothing yet," the deputy said. "More people are working along the shoreline. More investigators are being tasked."

"Thank you."

The food and coffee helped. Jessie scrolled for messages and news updates. Other than requests for interviews from the Associated Press, *New York Daily News*, the online news outlet *Veritas Sola* and the *Los Angeles Times*, there was nothing. She tried reaching back into her dream.

There was something there.

But it eluded her.

Not long after daybreak, near the temporary command post, Jessie glimpsed Garlin and Lugano. They were huddled with two other officers, deep in conversation. A few moments later, the small group made its way to her. She started getting out of the car, but Garlin stopped her.

"You can stay where you are, Ms. Ward."

He opened the driver's-side door, and they gathered around her.

Jessie took in the two new faces: a woman in her late thirties, in jeans and a blazer, hair pulled back in a no-nonsense ponytail; a man in his early fifties, with salt-and-pepper hair, dark framed glasses, a sport jacket and jeans.

At that moment, Jessie knew. She just knew.

"Jessica," Garlin said. "This is Bonnie Chase and Leon Deckert with the state police Bureau of Criminal Investigation."

"Jessica," Chase's voice was soft, "Leon and I are now leading this part of the investigation."

"*This part?*"

"Jessica." Chase's face was full of compassion. "We've confirmed the identity of the deceased person found in the vehicle. I'm sorry to have to tell you: it's Vaughn Ward, your husband. I'm sorry."

Jessie's eyes widened in disbelief. She pressed her fist to her mouth, stifling a shriek.

"No!"

This isn't real. This isn't happening.

Moments of her life blazed through her mind. Their wedding day; Vaughn urging her to just give one more push; Dylan's birth; her finding the messages on his phone and accusing him of an affair; him storming out of their home . . .

Now, with four grim-faced detectives scrutinizing her, an icy, crushing numbness coiled around her. "Are you certain?"

"Yes," Lugano said. "We expedited his dental records."

Staring at the lake, Jessie swallowed hard. She finally looked at the group. "What about Dylan?"

"We haven't located him, yet," Chase said, then lowered herself so that she was eye to eye with Jessie. Her eyes were green, her voice warm. "Jessica, I am so sorry, but there's more. The preliminary indications found that Vaughn's death was a homicide."

"Homicide?" She shook her head in denial. "But how?"

"We're not releasing the cause just yet."

"Did you tell Lillian and Miller?" she asked, her voice breaking.

"Yes, they've been notified. We've got them a crisis counsellor," Chase said. "Would you like us to call anyone? Arrange anything for you at this time?"

Jessie waved away the offer, her mind only on her son. "If someone murdered Vaughn, what about Dylan?" She looked to the lake. "What happened to my little boy?"

Chase turned to her partner, who'd been studying Jessie.

"We're hoping you can help us." Deckert glanced at his phone, then back to Jessie. "Our colleagues here with the FBI and NYPD have shared the last text you received from your husband." Jessie nodded. "Were there any additional messages from him?"

"No, nothing."

"Given the time you received the last text, and preliminary indications of the time of your husband's death, it appears to have been sent to you *after he was deceased*."

Jessie's eyes widened. "*After?*"

"That's correct," Deckert said. "This indicates to us that the text he sent you was fabricated, like his communications from Canada. Maybe by someone who'd cloned his account and used an untraceable burner. As you would know, it's not difficult to do that."

"What about the two people who took Dylan from the airport?"

"There's a lot of investigative work needed to locate them and recover your son. But we're losing time," Deckert said. "To help us, we'd like you to consent to giving us your phone and your laptop." Jessie followed his eyes to her laptop and phone on the passenger seat. "Volunteering those devices will aid the investigation," he continued. "Your husband's parents have given us their phone, and we're going through your husband's carrier to determine who cloned his account. Will you help by giving us your phone and laptop?"

Jessie was silent.

"Allowing our people to analyze them could help us find your son and whoever is responsible for your husband's death," Deckert added.

If she surrendered her personal laptop and phone, she knew what kinds of advanced forensic tools law enforcement would use to search them. She knew how they'd be able to extract data, even deleted data. And they would see references to Instinct's classified government work. It wasn't anything detailed, but she still felt she had to protect those contracts. It made her uneasy to just have that information easily accessed.

"Will you consent?" Deckert asked.

Jessie met his eyes. "I have to think about it."

"I see." Deckert's jawline tensed. "You could be regarded as being uncooperative, as if you're concealing something." He flipped through his notes. "I spent much of the last night reading the background on this case. I've investigated a lot of homicides and I have to tell you, Ms. Ward, I see several coincidences making for some disturbing circumstances." He raised an eyebrow, then looked at his notes again.

"It's interesting. You're a MIT grad who runs a cybersecurity company in Los Angeles. You have a custody dispute. You put your son alone on a plane. He goes missing at JFK after fake texts misdirect his grandparents. Somehow security cameras at JFK are hacked and images scrubbed. It looks like fabricated communication of some sort through burner phones from your husband. You are allowed into his Brooklyn residence. Your co-workers in California find video of the suspects near Penn Station *before the NYPD*; you lead police here. We find your husband's body. And in the last few months, you accused him of infidelity and told him, in court, and I quote, 'I can make him disappear from your life. You'll never see him again.'"

He stared at Jessie. "And now, Ms. Ward, you're reluctant to help us find your son by consenting to give us your two devices." He paused. "It raises questions, don't you think? We know divorce and custody battles can be bitter. If you really wanted to exact vengeance against a spouse you suspect of cheating, and his parents, for whom you apparently have no love—well, you'd know how to do it, like you implied in court. Let me put it this way: if you choose not to cooperate, we can get a warrant for those two devices."

Jessie's face reddened with indignation. "My son's been abducted. My husband's been murdered. And you think I'm behind this complicated scheme? If that's what you think, then arrest and charge me now."

Deckert remained poker-faced. "As I said, it's circumstantial. At this point."

Garlin nodded. "If this isn't related to custody," he said, "could it be related to a story your husband was pursuing? Or any of the work Instinct Nine-99 is doing?"

"I don't know." Jessie's anger was rising. "Anything's possible."

"Have you received any ransom demands?" Chase asked.

Jessie shook her head and shut her eyes.

"I know this is a horrible time and you've been out here all night," Deckert said. "So, think hard about giving us your devices and we'll think hard about getting a warrant." He snapped his notebook shut, turned and walked away, followed by the others.

Several moments later, Jessie got out of her car and locked it. With the investigators watching from nearby, she walked along the lakeshore, hugging herself in the cold.

Vaughn's murder had changed everything. She'd lost a huge part of her life, but she couldn't grieve. Not now. She had to find Dylan. Taking slow breaths, she pushed herself to be strong, to maintain control. Time was working against her.

She pulled out her phone and made a call.

21

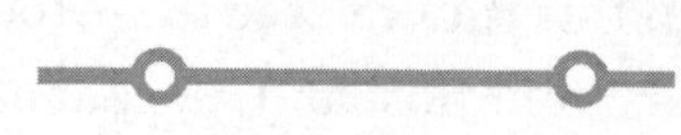

OTTAWA

The Communications Security Establishment, the national agency responsible for foreign signals intelligence, cyber operations and cybersecurity, was situated in a modern glass-walled building in a forested section of Ottawa's east end.

Claire Brenner was at her desk by 7 a.m. and had been working on her case for an hour before she glimpsed Will Walker, her director, entering his office down the hall. She gave it a few minutes before approaching his office, stopping at the open door.

Phone to his ear, he was standing, adjusting his blinds. Will was a thickset man with a short military haircut. Glancing from behind his glasses, he waved her in. "Right. Good," he said, before hanging up. "Take a seat, Claire. The TTC got you the material you requested for the Line 2 incident?"

"Yes," she said, sitting down in the chair in front of his desk.

"Go." He unbuttoned his collar, loosened his tie.

Consulting her tablet, Claire began. "So," she said, "fifteen days before the Line 1 crash, a Line 2 operator reported unexpected flickering of her in-cab display for several stops. The Line 2 train was held; they investigated, replaced a faulty component, then put the train back in service."

"What caused the flickering?"

"Well, they identified a capacitor issue in the console."

"You seem doubtful." He rubbed his chin.

"I studied the reports. The techs did a good job searching for hardware or software issues. In one memo, they hypothesized that the problem source was actually a sensor and transmitter giving inconsistent data resulting in strobing."

"Were they questioning the track-level modules, the ones installed by SynerRapid?"

"Yes, but they ruled it out."

"Why?"

"Well, they're considered impenetrable because SynerRapid used the newest AI-enhanced technology. And since the techs had already identified the flickering problem in the console, they ruled out the modules as a suspected cause."

"How does this come into play with Line 1 and the crash?"

Claire scrolled through her notes. "According to data from TTC event recorders, it's believed that not long after the Line 1 train left Dupont, heading northbound for St. Clair West Station, the Line 1 console display may have flickered, like Line 2's did. Line 1's event data indicated a fault in the seconds before the crash."

"What're Whitaker's and Otto Colt's thoughts on this similarity?"

"They saw nothing specific tying them together. And latest word is that Otto Colt is now thinking that the module failure was a hardware issue, not a frequency or software issue; that the failure, combined with the operator missing the red lights, was the cause." Claire shook her head. "But with his dying breath, the driver said the lights were green."

Will waited as Claire checked her tablet.

"About a week before the Line 2 flickering, putting it three weeks before the crash, SynerRapid launched a scheduled series of software updates for the track circuit transmitter module which puts out code-related audio frequency signals." She paused.

"Keep going."

"Well, we know software updates can be a vulnerability for intrusion."

Will nodded. "And the audio frequency signals are being analyzed for intrusion in this investigation by SynerRapid Systems—the company contracted to install them."

"Yes," she said. "We need to be part of that aspect of the investigation. To have SynerRapid Systems looking at it is self-policing. It could pose a conflict. I mean, they might not want to acknowledge a failure and be open to litigation. Or there could be other factors."

"Agreed."

"Will, I fear that the Line 2 flickering could have been a practice or early attempt at intrusion, a penetration test by a hostile entity, which resulted in a successful and tragic effort with Line 1."

Will was quiet, looking at her steadily.

"Give me a couple minutes to process this. I have to make a call. Go grab a coffee and come back."

When she returned, he was still standing, rolling up his sleeves.

"All right, SynerRapid's finished their preliminary work at the scene on the modules. Indications are the modules were not a factor."

Claire was puzzled while Will held up a finger.

"However," he said, "they've replaced the modules in the crash zone with new ones. The modules they removed will undergo further examination at their lab."

"And?"

"And you'll be participating in the analysis at SynerRapid's lab."

"I will?"

"Your flight to Chicago leaves tomorrow."

22

VIRGINIA

Approximately two months before Dylan Ward's abduction

After the crack of the bat, Carl Lasker winced watching the Yankees player send the ball arching over the Green Monster at Fenway, taking his hope and money with it.

"That one's long gone." Greg Burch turned from the big screen over the bar. "And New York takes it."

Carl sipped his beer.

"You never said how much you had on Boston," Greg said.

Carl pasted on a smile, masking his rising panic. Shrugging, he said, "Not much. How 'bout you?"

"Me? A hundred on the Yankees. But man, their pitcher was on fire. Really painting the corners."

Carl nodded the nod of a man who had lost while Greg selected a few surviving fries cooling with the remnants of his club sandwich, then changed the subject. "Hey, I got so caught up in the game I forgot to ask, how's Hannah doing?"

"Good."

"Everything all right, health-wise and all?"

"She's doing fine."

"How old is she now?"

"Seven."

"They grow so fast, don't they? And how's Vanessa?"

"All good."

"Brianna said to tell you it's our turn to have you guys over. She said a barbecue, maybe this weekend or the one after?"

"All right, I'll check with Vanessa." Carl finished his beer. "I should get going." He flagged their server for the check and reached for his wallet, but Greg stopped him.

"I got this."

"You sure?"

"I just doubled my money today. My treat, buddy."

"Thanks."

Carl had always got along with Greg. They were related by marriage, their wives being cousins. Greg was a good guy.

Walking across the parking lot, Carl took several deep breaths, processing what had happened with the game. He started his Nissan Rogue, and the rumbling of his ten-year-old SUV reminded him that the hole in his muffler was not getting smaller. Vanessa was reluctant to drive it, fearing it was unsafe. She used their new Explorer.

Pulling out from the parking lot of the bar in Fredericksburg, he headed for the 95, gripping the wheel until his knuckles whitened.

What went wrong?

Carl had run the analytics on the players and the teams so far this season. He'd examined the pitchers' stats, the stats on day games and the outcomes when the Red Sox had home field advantage. Today's bet was supposed to help him climb a little out of the hole. He replayed every precaution he'd taken. Still, the weight of how much he'd lost strained his stomach until he felt nauseous. Then came the urge to chase today's loss with a new bet to recover it. It was a dangerous option, one he wrestled with as he drove.

The Sunday afternoon traffic was good. In less than twenty minutes he'd reached Stafford, a suburb of Greater Washington.

The Explorer was parked in the driveway in front of the attached double garage of their contemporary two-storey brick house—much bigger than the little place they'd rented in Fredericksburg. Now they lived in a family neighbourhood, close to good schools and parks. But you pretty much had to drive everywhere else, and the traffic—man, the traffic—could be a challenge.

He glanced at their new SUV, thinking how they would own it after three years of low-interest payments, taken out in Vanessa's name and co-signed by her father, Marvin.

It was another headstone in the cemetery of Carl's failures.

After parking next to it, he dragged the back of his hand across his mouth.

I've got to think of something. I've got to do something.

He shifted and reached into his rear pocket for his burner, swiping through the contacts, stopping at a number and studying it for a long moment, thinking.

This might be the only way.

The squealing laughter of children playing a few doors down pulled him back to the present. He went inside fighting the fear eating at him, forcing himself to carry on like things were not as bad as they were.

The house was quiet, except for Vanessa's voice in their home office. He made his way there, finding her on the phone. She had her back to him, but he saw her computer monitor open to financial statements.

"So, tell me again what this means?" she said. "Yes . . . I understand . . . but we need . . . right . . ."

Carl's pulse picked up, and he went to the kitchen, opened the fridge, took out a container of pineapple chunks, got a fork and speared one.

"You're back."

He turned to see his wife in the doorway, a sheaf of papers in hand.

"How was the movie?" he asked. "Where's Hannah?"

"She's at Olivia's. The bank called us, Carl."

"On a Sunday?"

"Yes, on a Sunday. They're going to cancel one of our credit cards because we've missed payments. We've missed payments because we're constantly overdrawn—"

"But I thought—"

"Don't interrupt. This time we were overdrawn because we had to come up with our two-thousand-dollar co-pay for Hannah's drug therapy, which we nearly missed. I had to plead with insurance for an extension. *Again.*" She paused, waving the papers. "And we're barely chipping away at the interest on *your debt*!" She shook her head. "This has to stop, Carl."

"I know, Vanessa."

"Do you?" Her voice broke. "You went out with Greg this afternoon to a sports bar and—"

"Yes, and he said Brianna wants us—"

She thrust out the papers like a shield in battle. "Don't—just don't! So, you went out with Greg in Fredericksburg. Did you watch games at the bar?"

"Of course."

"Did you bet on a game?"

He didn't answer.

"Did. You. Bet. Carl." Her stare drilled into him for an answer.

"Yes."

Wounded, she blinked back tears. "How much? Tell me the truth!"

"I lost five hundred."

"Oh my God!" Her voice trembling, she threw the bank statements on the counter and raised her hands in surrender. "You're throwing our money out the window while I'm on the phone pleading with the bank! You promised you'd stop. You promised you would get help." She crossed her arms. "I have no choice. I'm going to my dad. *Again!*"

"Don't go to him, Vanessa, please. I'll do something. I swear."

"Empty promises, Carl." She stared at him. "Do you know how serious this is?" She didn't let him answer. "We have the mortgage, insurance, taxes, car loans, student loans, groceries, credit cards, and Hannah's drugs. I have looked at all our expenses, again and again. And you know what? We both have good jobs. With our combined salaries we could probably manage. We could live a normal life, save for retirement. Except for one thing. Your gambling debt. Your huge gambling debt of eighty-two thousand dollars with the massive interest! We are barely scratching at the principal of the loan to pay it, and you can't stop adding more. Like today, throwing five hundred away! We're in financial quicksand."

She wiped at her eyes.

"We're this close to losing everything," she said, holding up her thumb and forefinger, close together without touching. "Do you realize that if we can't make our co-pays, Hannah might not get her drug therapy? Our daughter is sick, Carl! We could lose the house. You're gambling with our lives! I can't live like this! I can't!"

She left the kitchen, storming upstairs to the bedroom. Carl could hear her sobs before she slammed the door.

He stood there, still holding the container of pineapple. He returned it to the fridge, then turned to see Hannah and Jann Horton, their neighbour, standing inside the kitchen door. Something sad fluttered across Hannah's face in the awkward silence before Jann managed to smile.

"Hi Carl, I just brought Hannah home."

Feeling his face redden, he nodded. "Thanks Jann."

"Give my best to Vanessa," she said before leaving.

Hannah went straight to the family room and turned on the TV. She settled on the couch, watching *SpongeBob SquarePants*. Carl sat next to her but was oblivious to the goings-on in Bikini Bottom. The tension in their home was thick in the air, with Carl certain he could hear the murmur of Vanessa upstairs on the phone to her father.

He looked at Hannah. “How’re you doing, honey?”

Keeping her eyes on the TV, she shrugged. “Okay, I guess.”

“Did you have fun with Olivia today?”

“Uh-huh.”

“That’s good.”

Carl’s Adam’s apple rose and fell. The truth was he hadn’t lost $500 today. He’d lost $7,000. And the $82,000 debt they were slowly paying off would inch closer to $100,000.

Wait until Vanessa learns the truth.

A degree of panic began rising in his gut, and he came to a decision, reached for his burner and texted the number.

I’m ready. I need help.

He closed his hand around his phone, knowing there was no turning back. It took less than a minute before his burner vibrated.

We’ll set up a meeting.

23

BETHEL AREA, UPSTATE NEW YORK

Walking along the lakeshore, Jessie looked at Dylan's smiling face in the photo on her phone and traced her fingers over it.

After making her call, and a decision, she returned to her car, then went to the command post. Deckert and the others ceased their conversations when she arrived.

"I wasn't thinking clearly." She handed her laptop and phone to Deckert. "I want to cooperate. I'm volunteering my devices. I made no wipes. Everything's there and open for access. No need for a warrant."

Accepting them, Deckert traded looks with the others before asking, "Who did you call?"

"My lawyer."

Deckert nodded slowly.

Jessie took in a breath and then looked out at the lake where the search was still taking place.

Chase followed her gaze. "I'm sorry. They've found nothing more. They've used sonar, gone over areas multiple times. Nothing else in there."

"And the cabin and the woods?"

"Nothing. And, we're told, nothing from preliminary processing of your husband's car. We'll be concluding operations here soon."

"What about Vaughn's apartment in Brooklyn?" Jessie asked.

“We’re done there,” Lugano said. “Analysts are examining anything they’ve collected. The residence will soon be released to his parents.”

“And the security intrusion at JFK and Vaughn’s texts are still being examined,” Garlin added. “We’re working on several fronts.”

Then Deckert said, “We need your sign-off. We’ll be keeping your property for a while.” He handed Jessie a document for her signature.

After signing the form, she took another pained look at the lake. “I’m going to return to New York.”

“We can have someone drive you,” Chase said, “like we did with your husband’s parents.”

“I prefer to go alone. I’ll be okay.”

“How can we reach you?” Garlin said. “Since we have your phone?”

“Through Instinct, or the Golden Greenwood in Brooklyn. That’s where I’m staying. I’ll get another phone and laptop tomorrow. I’ll relay my new contact info.” She handed the signed document to Deckert.

Holding her devices, he looked at Jessie until she met his eyes. “Appreciate your cooperation,” he said, tucking the signed paper into his pocket.

Jessie hadn’t had much of a social life at MIT. The workload and the hours demanded by Professor Jackson’s project were all-consuming. Then after one gruelling day, Dahlia had suggested they go to a Harvard party. “Good idea. We need the break. It’ll be good therapy,” Jessie had joked, not knowing how that party would change the course of her life.

Dahlia had pointed out Vaughn as soon as they’d arrived. Like Dahlia, a lot of women in Cambridge knew him. Not only because he wrote for *The Harvard Crimson*, but because he was charismatic, bright, disarming and possessed a kind of sexual magnetism.

Spotting them, he came over. "Who's your friend, Dahlia?" he asked, holding Jessie's gaze.

"This is Jessie. She's from California."

"California. Land of the gold rush, limitless opportunity," he said with a big smile. "And unmatched natural beauty."

Dahlia rolled her eyes. "Jessie, this is Vaughn Ward."

"And where are you from, Vaughn Ward?" Jessie asked.

"New York, New York."

"New York, strategically important and holding potential for greatness, as George Washington said to the mayor, back in the day."

"Well, well." Vaughn was taken. "Aren't you engaging."

"Aren't you."

They hit it off that night, and in the days that followed he asked her out. Somehow, she found time for coffee with him. A week later, it was burgers and a walk around the Harvard campus. She told him about losing her father, her mother raising her and her sister alone on a schoolteacher's salary, and how her sister's death had helped her get to MIT. He told her about his middle-class family, how his parents aspired for him to ascend the social ladder. He told her about his relationship with a medical device patents heiress, Sunny Vellamey, who lived on the Upper East Side, and how the relationship had thrilled his mother. How disappointed she'd been when he'd ended it before leaving for Harvard.

Jessie and Vaughan continued seeing each other, and months into their relationship Jessie finally met Vaughn's parents when they visited their son. Miller was cordial, but Lillian was cool—and Jessie soon realized why.

"Sunny still asks about you, Vaughn," Lillian remarked over dinner. Ignoring the awkward silence she'd created, she continued, "Some say your first love is *your true love*."

"And was Miller your first love?" Jessie asked.

The smile on Lillian's face melted. Miller stifled a laugh. Vaughn didn't. The subject changed, with Lillian casting a quick, dark look at Jessie.

Still, Jessie and Vaughn's love deepened. It was exciting being with him. She loved walking on campus with him. He pointed out Weld Hall, where John Reed, his idol, had once lived. Vaughn would take her to old movies, like *The Front Page* and *All the President's Men* and, of course, *Reds*. He'd recite his favourite lines to her. He was idealistic, wanting to dedicate himself to finding the truth and reporting it as a journalist.

"No matter the forces against you," he told her, "never give up, Jess."

Not long after they graduated, Vaughn was hired by *The Wall Street Journal*, and she worked as a software developer for a startup. A year or two later, they got married.

They were living their dream, both succeeding. Then they had Dylan, the light of their lives. Vaughn stepped up, changing diapers, helping with late-night feedings. He was a good dad. But he was also invested in his stories and travelling.

There were times she suspected he was unfaithful. She had no proof, but occasionally, she'd glimpse his phone over his shoulder while he read cryptic texts that said things like *keeping this between us* and *no one knows I'm doing this*. She wondered aloud who they were from, and he'd say, "Sources for a story."

But the more they both worked, and the more he was away, the more things went wrong. Over the years their arguments had got more intense. Finally, they separated, with Vaughn moving back to New York, and they began divorce proceedings and negotiations for custody.

We tore everything apart.

Jessie gripped the steering wheel, consumed by visions of Vaughn's SUV being pulled from the lake, the yellow tarp covering his corpse.

Oh God, where's Dylan?

Overcome, Jessie pulled over, stopped the car and thrust her face in her hands, shaking with heaving, convulsing sobs.

Dylan's abduction, Vaughn's murder—this was not about custody. She had been wrong to suspect Vaughn was behind this, wrong to blame Lillian and Miller.

Regaining her composure, she eased back onto the parkway. She hadn't gone far before a breath caught in her throat as she glanced in her rear-view mirror. Was that a green Chevy Tahoe in the distance behind her?

No, it couldn't be. She was being paranoid. Her lack of sleep was taking a toll. Another deep breath and she focused. Her lawyer had said that by surrendering her phone and laptop, she'd showed cooperation. But she was still on thin ice legally because she had not indicated—even when questioned at JFK—that she also possessed a second computer—the blue laptop that was locked in the safe of her Brooklyn hotel room.

Nearing New York City, she stopped at a mall in New Jersey, went to a computer store and purchased the best laptop and phone they had—and a second phone to use as a burner. In the parking lot, for good measure, she glanced around for a green Chevy Tahoe. Relieved not to see one, she got into her car and powered up her new laptop and phone. Working quickly, she activated the phone and moved her data onto it through the cloud, connecting to all the key accounts. Then she made a video call to Bobby in California, who was in the office early.

Ensuring he had Sarita and Dahlia with him, her voice shook as she relayed what had happened over the past twenty-four hours.

"It was Vaughn in the car. He was murdered."

Sarita clasped her hand to her mouth, and Bobby cursed softly, looking away.

"No!" Dahlia said.

"Dylan's still missing." Jessie steadied her voice. "They found no trace of him in the car, or lake. But I had to surrender my phone and laptop. I just got new ones."

"And your work laptop?" Bobby asked.

"I still have it." Jessie swallowed hard. "I believe in my heart Dylan is still alive, and with your help I'm going to find him."

24

NEW YORK

Jessie returned to her Brooklyn hotel by midday.

She unlocked the safe and pulled out the thin blue laptop.

Using the four-step verification process, she logged on and connected to a specialized ultra-secure communications network. She made a quick review of Instinct's most recent work. All was in order.

After logging out and locking the laptop back in the safe, she took a shower. For a few minutes, the needles of hot water soothed her strained nerves. Then she got into fresh clothes, resumed transferring data to her new phone and laptop via a secured online database, and made another call to her team in California.

"I was wrong," she said, pressing her fingers to her temples. "This wasn't carried out by Vaughn and his parents, and whoever's behind it is skilled. We know that they lured Lillian and Miller from Dylan's gate. They hacked into JFK's security. They know what they're doing."

"Have the police told you anything about the two people who took Dylan from the airport?" Dahlia asked.

"No. We know nothing about them."

"Listen," Bobby said. "I don't want to worry you, but we've got media outside the building and we're getting a lot of calls."

"You haven't made any comments, have you?" Jessie asked.

"No," Sarita said, "but the comms team has drafted a statement. Bobby will send it to you."

The email arrived and Jessie opened it.

We are shocked and saddened by the death of Vaughn Ward. He was a beloved father, husband, son, friend and colleague. We are devastated by the abduction of his son Dylan and are working with police. We ask for patience and understanding at this difficult time, and for anyone with any information to contact the FBI.

Jessie cleared her throat. "Yes, that's okay to release."

"Jessie," Bobby said, "I'm trying to get more video from the Penn Station area and anywhere else. I'm still working on getting more on that video call with Vaughn. I thought he looked odd in it, and now we know it had to be a deepfake, just like Vaughn's messages to you. I'm trying to find the origin of all his communication since Dylan's disappearance."

"Okay. And Dylan's phone still hasn't been found," Jessie said. "We can't get a signal, right Sarita?"

"Right," Sarita said. "It's probably turned off. We get nothing."

"And," Jessie said, "the AirTag isn't functioning properly, and his watch is turned off too."

"We're on top of all of it," Dahlia said. "I'm still pleading with our colleagues and friends everywhere to help us find him."

"Why did they take Dylan and . . ." Jessie's voice weakened, then was strong again. "Why take him and *kill* Vaughn? It can't be about our work. I've received no demands, no ransom calls."

"Could it be someone trying to stop a story he was working on?" Sarita asked.

Nodding, Dahlia said, "Was he getting close to exposing something someone didn't want revealed?"

"Why did he go to the cabin?" Bobby asked. "Was he lured there?" Bobby looked at Jessie through the screen. "Do we know how long he was there? How long he's been deceased? How he died?"

Clenching her eyes tight, Jessie shook her head. "I know nothing. They won't tell me anything."

"Just got a message from Kent Hurst in Washington, DC," Sarita interjected. "He wants to talk to you privately, Jessie. Now, if possible."

Jessie nodded. "Send him my information."

"Washington?" Dahlia said. "Is he with the Defense Counterintelligence and Security Agency?"

Bobby shook his head. "Not this guy. Hurst oversees the acquisition of the classified stuff we're developing. He's the client."

An hour later, Jessie's phone rang. When she answered, Kent Hurst appeared on her screen.

"Jessie, our office is very sorry to learn all you are going through. Our thoughts are with you."

"Thank you, Kent."

"Forgive me," Hurst said, "but given the situation, we've been asked to confirm that your work is secure."

"Yes." She shot a glance at the safe. "Everything is secured with me."

"Can you provide me with a visual?"

She hesitated but then got up and quickly removed the laptop from the safe.

"Here," she said. "Hold on." She went through the multi-step verification process of logging in again, then turned the screen around for Hurst to see.

"Very good, thank you."

As she was shutting the system down, Hurst steepled his hands under his chin.

"We need assurance that your ongoing work for us is secure and not related to these terrible events."

"It can't be," she said. "No one knows the nature of our work. I haven't received any demands or threats." She swallowed. "I assure you, Kent, everything is safe."

"Thank you, Jessie. You have our hearts and our support. We'll keep each other informed on the situation."

As she ended the call, Jessie dragged her hands over her face, biting back her tears.

It can't be about us. Because if it is—

She shook her head, bringing herself back.

Because if it is, then it's my fault.

25

NEW YORK

"Hello?" Miller answered, his voice hollow.

Jessie paused before speaking. "Miller, it's Jessica." She searched for the words. "I am so sorry." Her father-in-law forced a sharp intake of breath as he hefted his words to the surface. "Our son's been murdered. Our grandson's been kidnapped. The police suspected us. Because *you accused us*."

"I'm sorry," she whispered.

"We were tricked at the airport, Jessica." His voice tremored. "Tricked like two old fools."

"I know. It wasn't your fault, and I was wrong." She paused, then said, "Vaughn and I had our problems, but I will always love him."

Miller was crying now, the words tumbling from him. "Who killed him, Jessie? Why?"

Jessie waited, then asked softly, "May I speak with Lillian? Is she with you? I need to apologize to both of you."

"She's sedated and sleeping. A nurse is with her. I'll tell her you called."

"Miller, wait—"

"I'm exhausted, Jessica, I need to go now."

"Wait, please. I need your help." A few seconds passed. When she could still hear Miller breathing on the other end, she continued. "Did the police release Vaughn's home to you?"

"Yes. They gave us the keys, but we're going to have to wait until they release him to us. We've been told they need to do a full autopsy and further investigation. We don't know how long it will be . . ." He began choking on his words. "Or when we can plan his funeral."

Jessie sighed. "Miller, I need to get back into Vaughn's home."

"You can get in there in a few days," he mumbled. "Once things have settled."

"Miller," she pressed. "I have to do it now."

"Why?"

"I have to look again. There has to be something there to help us find Dylan, to find answers. Do you have the strength to go inside with me? Or I can just pick up the key from you."

A beat passed, then Miller said, "The crime scene people combed through it. You went through it with the police. What could be there?"

"I feel I missed something, and time is not on our side."

He weighed her request, then said, "I'll meet you in front of Vaughn's building in thirty minutes."

The scene in front of Vaughn's building stopped Jessie cold.

Media trucks lined the street. The sidewalk was thronged with TV crews, reporters, news photographers. Steeling herself, she continued. Cameras bobbed; microphones were thrust at her. She was captured in the lights and flashes. Questions were fired at her, all overlapping each other.

"Who do you think killed your husband?"

"Why was your son abduct—?"

"—any ransom demands—?"

"Is it connected to a story your husband—?"

"—work done by your comp—?"

Jessie stopped, held up her hand. "Please—all I can say is that we're doing all we can to find my son while we mourn his father's murder. And if anyone anywhere has information, please call the NYPD." Jessie glanced beyond the media cluster to the bystanders across the street before continuing, keeping her voice steady. "To the people who took Dylan, please, I beg you, don't hurt him. Please release my son."

When Miller arrived in a cab, she helped him through the intense glare of the news cameras. He was ashen, grief carving lines deep into his face. He looked like he'd aged a decade. Cameras flashed as Jessie hugged him and he held her close and tight, as if to keep from falling from the earth. Jessie realized that the last time they'd embraced so intensely was the day she and Vaughn were married.

"I am so sorry," she said into his ear. "For all of this."

Together they pushed through the crush of reporters.

"Please, we just need to go inside," Jessie said.

They ascended the front stoop and Miller fished the keys from his pocket, hands shaking. He unlocked the door and they made their way in, leaving the chaos outside.

Floorboards squeaking, they came to Vaughn's door, where Jessie paused. "Brace yourself," she warned. "The crime scene people moved things around."

The chemical smells, the furniture repositioned, Vaughn's belongings in disarray, fingerprint residue swirling everywhere like black clouds of doom.

Miller moved slowly from room to room, his eyes sweeping over everything. He came to Vaughn's desk and admired his framed Harvard degree, the awards and news stories that hung on the wall.

"He always wanted to be a journalist." Miller smiled at the photos of Dylan and Jessie. "And a good husband and a good dad."

"He was all of those things." Jessie touched her father-in-law's shoulder as he lowered himself into Vaughn's desk chair. With tender reverence Miller touched the areas on the desk not covered with fingerprint powder.

Taking stock of the room again, Jessie asked, "Do you know anything about him trying to get a foreign bureau posting?"

Miller looked at her. "No. I think he was happy freelancing."

"Do you know what story he was working on before . . . all of this?"

Miller shook his head. "He didn't talk to us about stories he was researching."

"That sounds like him," Jessie said. Vaughn had followed the practice of never telling anyone—not his editor, not Jessie—anything about what he was chasing until he had it nailed. He never cared about being the first to break the news; he'd rather get the whole story and get it right.

Once more, Jessie looked at his souvenirs from his travels around the world: the camel, the beads, the small drum and the elephant carving. "Miller, do you or Lillian know if he was seeing anyone?"

"I don't know, Jessie. He was private about that too. I guess it's possible."

Nodding, Jessie then moved to Vaughn's calendar, studying his handwritten notations on various dates. Her eyes landed on "Beth Cab."

"Why did he go to the lake at Bethel?" Jessie said. "Do you know why he went there before Dylan got here?"

"I'm guessing to get things ready, but I really don't know." Miller shook his head. "The detectives said they were tracking his credit and bank cards. I'm hoping that will give us some answers." Miller looked around the room, at the open drawers and dusty surfaces, and then at Jessie. "Want to know what they told us?"

He gestured around him. "That we're responsible for having this cleaned up. And the cabin, too, since he'd rented it." He covered his face with his hands. "After what we've been through—what we're going through, I—"

"It's okay," Jessie said, trying to sound calm. "We'll hire a professional service. I can get my company to handle that. Don't even think about it."

She turned back to the calendar, concentrating on the few days before Dylan's arrival and a scrawled notation that Vaughn had crossed out. When she'd first looked at it, she couldn't make it out. Studying it now, she saw it had been crossed out with red ink, but the original note was made in blue. Narrowing her eyes, she held up her phone and, using the zoom, examined Vaughn's familiar handwriting.

"Meet with?" she muttered. "'Meet with' and then a question mark? What does that mean?"

26

CHICAGO METRO AREA

Nearly halfway across the country from New York, on the fourth day of the search for Dylan, Claire Brenner arrived at the SynerRapid Systems facility near Arlington Heights, a suburb northwest of Chicago.

"Executive offices to the right with admin to the left. This way to our control room and labs," said Krista Quinn, a SynerRapid engineer and Claire's guide. She'd wasted no time ushering Claire through the new 180,000-square-foot complex, the US location of the multinational company headquartered in Europe. Constructed of recycled steel and glass, it had a clean, simple aesthetic. The glass walls rose two storeys, inviting plenty of natural light into the building.

Claire stole glimpses of Quinn, who was in her late twenties with hair pulled back in a too-tight ponytail. She wore bright red-framed glasses and had a rigid, by-the-book vibe.

"I've never been to Ottawa," Quinn said. "My sister has, says it's pretty."

"It is," Claire said as Quinn explained how at this facility, which employed eight hundred people, SynerRapid engineered a range of products, from components in EVs, to transmission and circuit switches for subway systems, to advancing technology in the grid. She pointed out various divisions, noting some were on the far side of the plant.

"Behind those doors to the left, our library. It has extensive holdings of mass transit systems and track circuit technology. Adjacent to it, compliance and testing records." They continued down a long corridor to a glassed section where Quinn used her security badge to swipe the lock on a door.

"And here we are—the control room."

The open area was lined with a wall of large screens displaying tables of track layouts. Nearby were stations and workbenches. At one end, a handful of staff was seated at a large table with a meeting in progress.

Turning to Quinn and Claire, the man leading the discussion stopped and rose to greet them.

"Dieter, this is Claire Brenner with the Communications Security Establishment's cybersecurity branch in Ottawa. Claire, this is Dieter Zurne, SynerRapid's chief engineer. He's here from our head office in Munich overseeing our role in the investigation of the Toronto crash."

Zurne, in his early sixties, with a chiselled chin, wore a white lab coat. He extended his hand.

"Ms. Brenner. Welcome." His eyes were intense, as if scanning her. His hand was firm but cool, and she was glad of a brief handshake. "Please, have a seat."

Claire joined him and the others at the table. He led a quick round of introductions of analysts and engineers. Claire took out her laptop, phone and notepad, and looked at Zurne expectedly.

"Let's bring you up to speed, Ms. Brenner. After the incident, I led our team in Toronto onsite. We joined Otto Colt's investigators studying the trackside modules." Zurne paused. "I don't recall seeing you there?"

"No, I was not there at that time."

"No anomalies were found, no irregular phenomena, malfunctions or deviations. And nothing to point to intrusion—" A suppressed snicker escaped from someone in the group. Briefly annoyed, Zurne blinked slowly, then continued. "Nothing pointing to intrusion, as was subsequently suggested by you, I believe."

"That's right," Claire said.

Zurne continued. "So, after our onsite analysis, the Toronto investigators agreed with our findings and allowed us to remove the modules in question and fly them here for further study. We replaced them with newer modules for continued operation of the Toronto system."

"And has your examination of the devices here led to any determinations?"

"We've only begun, but I am confident we'll find no indication of penetration."

Claire tilted her head. "What makes you confident?"

"Because our modules are impenetrable," he said. "They use Ethernet, nothing public-facing, and in our case they're constructed with advanced technology. Essentially, it eliminates external access and possible intrusion. Ms. Brenner, this is basic knowledge."

"Still, the modules are linked to points of potential vulnerability in the system."

Zurne didn't respond. He folded his arms, leaned back in his chair and waited for her to continue.

"The modules communicate data that ultimately feeds into the subway system's control centre and to the operator's cab, in support of Automatic Train Control," Claire went on. "They're part of that data highway, if you will, with the goal of monitoring speed, track occupancy and keeping safe distances between trains. The control centre can dispatch cautions on speed, braking or emergency stops."

Zurne nodded.

"But at some stages," Claire said, "the modules are linked to wireless signal generation, access points. And around the world, including Toronto, the transmission of data in trackside and onboard systems is becoming increasingly wireless." She paused and looked at Zurne, who nodded again. "And as with all systems, the Toronto system can receive software updates via the internet. While SynerRapid's modules use and operate locally on Ethernet, SynerRapid's upgrades are done remotely, aren't they?"

"Yes, of course." Zurne sighed. "Do you have a point here?"

"Bear with me." She turned to her laptop. "Three weeks before the crash, SynerRapid made a scheduled series of software updates for the track circuit transmitter modules. A week later, a train operator on Line 2 reported flickering in her cab console."

"Yes, we're aware," Zurne said. "And that issue was resolved."

Nodding, eyes still on her laptop, Claire continued. "Moments before the crash on Line 1, there was a flickering in the cab console, according to event recorders." She glanced at the others, then Zurne. "We know software updates can be vulnerable to intrusion."

"And?"

"And I think someone penetrated the system by exploiting a software update."

Zurne lifted his chin, and around the table a few eyebrows went up.

"I think the flickering in Line 2, which followed the software update, was a penetration test, an attempt to go deeper into the system, to take control," Claire said. "I think it succeeded weeks later, resulting in this crash."

"And did you bring evidence to share with us?"

"No. I thought it was something we could look into."

Soft coughing and throat clearing rippled around the small group. Zurne looked directly at Claire. "Tell me, what is your background?"

"I have degrees in computer science and engineering. Before joining the CSE, I was a computer system architect in the military."

"I see." Zurne tapped a finger to his chin. "While intriguing, Ms. Brenner, I'm afraid your scenario is impossible, and for several reasons. The flickering in Line 2 was a capacitor in the console, essentially akin to a faulty light bulb. It had nothing to do with your scenario."

"Yes, but—"

"But it's purely a coincidence that this happened so close to the software upgrade. Albeit, the upgrade is done remotely, but it is encrypted, and the system is heavily firewalled. As well, there are measures in place to detect and alert the control centre to any intrusion attempts. The failsafe systems work."

"Until they don't," Claire said. "Five people were killed, and fifty more injured."

A wave of tension rolled over the table.

"We know this was a horrible catastrophe," Zurne said. "But you're overlooking the human factor here. The operator ignored the trackside signals, which were red."

"With his dying breath, he said they were green, Mr. Zurne."

"Yes, and that may have been a dying wish arising from his shock and trauma."

Claire shook her head. "No. I don't think so. And to your point about the human factor. Software upgrades are created and distributed by humans. Hostile entities can penetrate a system exploiting human weakness or error. Everyone at this table knows that it's possible to find an unlocked back door."

"It is beneficial for us to debate and challenge each other until the true cause is identified," Zurne said. "But our logs concerning the software updates show no attempts at intrusion."

"Would you allow me to review them?"

He stared at her for a moment, before agreeing. “We’ll facilitate that. And we’ll be happy to have you observe our analysis here.”

But a wisp of offence lingered on his face, his smile not reaching his eyes.

27

CHICAGO METRO AREA

Later that day at SynerRapid, Claire was taken to a table where the Toronto modules had been placed. They were in various stages of dissection. Each module housed the electronics in black casing, about the size of a child's lunchbox. Extracted components were undergoing testing by engineers at individual workbenches.

"Look." Annie, an engineer, drew Claire's attention to her oscilloscope screen. "No parasitic oscillation."

Travis, another engineer, showed Claire his ongoing analysis, scratching his three-day stubble and telling her, "Not finding any cable faults."

After an hour observing, discussing and consulting data, Claire was invited for a break in SynerRapid's cafeteria.

"You must be tired?" Annie bit into her muffin. "Was your flight direct? How long was it?"

"It was direct, nearly three hours. I'm fine." Claire unwrapped an egg salad sandwich and took a bite.

"My folks took me to Ottawa once." Travis drank some Mountain Dew. "To see my aunt. You got a nice canal there."

Jill, another member of the team, was eating. "The only time I visited Canada was Toronto, for a Taylor Swift concert with my cousin. I loved the city." Then she added, "It's just so sad about the subway crash."

They fell silent for a solemn moment before Travis spoke. "You really think the system was penetrated?"

"Yes." Claire sipped her coffee. "We just need to find the evidence."

The SynerRapid workers fell silent again, and Claire studied them. They were bright people, proud of their work, and didn't take to having it questioned. Moreover, they were sensitive to the fear that not only were they linked to the tragedy, but that its cause might have originated right here, at SynerRapid, in the work they were doing.

A few hours later, Claire was sitting at a table, sending an update email to Will Walker when her inbox pinged. Krista Quinn appeared next to her. "I just sent you the logs you requested," she said. "They're encrypted. Here's the password." Quinn typed into her phone and another message pinged on Claire's laptop.

"Thanks," Claire said before putting her elbows on the desk and rubbing her eyes.

"It's been a long day for you," Quinn said. "Let's go. I'll drop you off at your hotel. It's on my way."

The drive to the DoubleTree where Claire was staying was quick. Quinn stopped in front of the entrance. "We start at seven a.m. I'll pick you up at six thirty out front here. You good with that?"

"I'm good. Thank you for this, Krista," Claire said, getting out.

She was just about to close the door when Quinn spoke again. "Claire, wait."

Claire held the door open and looked at Quinn.

"We don't believe it was us."

"I get that," Claire said. "But this is a big investigation with a lot to look at and a lot at stake."

At the snack bar in the hotel, Claire picked up a Caesar salad, a Diet Coke and banana. In her room she changed into sweatpants and a hoodie, then called Phil's phone. Marissa answered, smiling and waving.

"Hi Mom! Is Chicago fun?"

"Not seeing much of it this time," Claire admitted. "Sorry, work pulled me away just when you wanted to look into getting a dogwood tree. How're you doing, sweetie?"

"It's okay, Mom." Marissa's eyes brightened. "I got invited to Tabitha's birthday party, and it's a sleepover!"

"Oh fun."

"It's in two weeks," Phil said, his face appearing next to their daughter's. "How's it going?"

"It's going. How about over there?

"Good, except the furnace guy came. We need to replace the unit and the AC."

"Yikes! But we knew it was coming."

They talked for another half hour with Claire working slowly on her food. The call grounded her, and when it ended, she felt a surge of energy and immediately set to work on the logs for the SynerRapid software updates.

She was seeing this data for the first time. It was distinct from the TTC's report on the diagnostics from the flickering on Line 2. And it was distinct from the TTC reports on Line 1. Otto Colt appeared to be of the mind that software updates and Line 2's flickering console were unrelated to the crash, but Claire disagreed. She believed her scrutiny of SynerRapid's software logs would enable her to detect any attempts or points of intrusion.

But nothing was emerging. As time ticked by, she'd failed to find anything in the logs. Tension tightened the muscles in her shoulders and neck. She slammed her laptop shut and looked outside. The sun was sinking, but she still had some light. She pulled on her running shoes, grabbed her phone, key, wallet. Within minutes she was outside, taking in the fresh air as she jogged onto Arlington Heights Road. Trotting at a good pace, she passed gas stations, restaurants, office buildings.

As she ran, she thought of her first pass at the logs. She reminded herself how a hostile player, one that was highly skilled, could easily avoid being traced. And with advances in AI, they could mislead investigators or cover their tracks. Thereby making the logs look as if they were never there.

Stopped at a traffic light, Claire was jogging in place when her phone vibrated with a message.

She didn't recognize the number.

You were not told everything today at SynerRapid.

28

NEW YORK

The longer it took to recover a child stolen by a stranger, the greater the chances they would not be found alive.

It was now day five in the search for Dylan Ward, and with each passing moment, the likelihood of finding Dylan safe lessened even more because of the link to his father's murder.

The FBI was now the lead agency in the ever-widening, increasingly complex investigation into his disappearance. Garlin had arrived early this morning at his desk on the twenty-eighth floor of the FBI's New York headquarters in Lower Manhattan, because, in less than an hour, he would head a case-status meeting.

At 9 a.m., Garlin joined more than two dozen people settling around the table in the boardroom. The blinds were closed to the views of traffic on the Brooklyn Bridge and FDR Drive below. He did a roll call of the agencies with people in the room, and those on the line, then gave an update on the case.

"We have no evidence pointing to the death or injury of Dylan Ward. Until then, for us, he is alive. In Vaughn Ward's homicide, cause of death—which I stress is holdback, therefore not to be released—is a single gunshot fired into the back of his head at close range." Garlin glanced at the others to ensure his words were absorbed. "No weapon, or casing, recovered—only the fatal round.

New York State Police ballistics and forensics continue to process the vehicle, the cabin and the scene upstate in Sullivan County."

Investigators were working on how Vaughn Ward's time of death aligned with his bank and credit card transactions and other aspects, like his calendar notations. Vaughn Ward's laptop and phone had not been located.

"We're still working on establishing a timeline. With warrants to access service providers, our people are studying logs of calls, texts, data and, where possible, locations."

Garlin paused.

"Bear with me. Prior to departing Los Angeles, Dylan received a text from Vaughn. Vaughn also made subsequent calls and sent messages to Dylan's mother." Garlin looked around the room. "He also sent messages to his parents, and investigators at JFK, including me. All Vaughn Ward's communication I've referenced was made after his death by someone using untraceable burner phones, and masking numbers. Vaughn Ward's voice was cloned using AI."

Several people nodded; others raised their eyebrows and widened their eyes.

"Which brings us to JFK," Garlin said. "The text misdirecting Dylan Ward's grandparents to the wrong gate at Terminal 4 was also generated from an untraceable burner. We're working on the numbers used by the burners, again, with warrants to further investigate the carriers and examine records.

"Of grave concern is the fact JFK's security camera system was hacked and footage scrubbed. At this point, the perpetrators appear to have gained entry by exploiting a weak point in the airport's network and erased their trail. We have FBI and other national cybersecurity people working on this. We all agree: this is a planned, complex criminal act, by skilled players."

"Agent Garlin," a detective from New Jersey interrupted over the line. "Where are we on the two suspects?"

"I'm coming to that now."

A large screen at one end of the room came to life with a multi-coloured web mapping the New York City subway system. The screen split in half, with one side showing surveillance footage from multiple cameras.

"Everyone on the video call seeing this?"

Several voices confirmed.

"You can see by the animation on the map," Garlin said, "we track the suspects on the subway starting at Howard Beach to 23rd Street." A montage of two masked people with Dylan appeared on the screen. "We know from the NYPD, and private cameras, they surfaced at 23rd and made their way to the area near the Garden and Penn Station. We lost them there, in a gap. They may have changed appearance, gotten a ride or handed Dylan off to associates. We've alerted security for Amtrak, New Jersey Transit and Long Island Rail Road commuter trains, to get them to review footage and ticket purchases. All taxi and car services, hotels, businesses, restaurants—everything is being checked."

"They're masked," an NYPD detective said. "What're we doing to ID them?"

"They used cash for their MetroCards, so nothing there," Garlin said. "We're using facial recognition, but the masks make it challenging. We're attempting to concentrate on the eye area, a technique called periocular recognition. But with the male wearing glasses, and given both suspects are not facing the cameras at any time, even at the turnstile, it impedes capturing details."

After relating other aspects of the investigation, Leon Deckert, the New York State Police investigator leading on the homicide, jumped in.

"We have yet to rule out Jessica Ward," he said. "There was an ongoing custody dispute. Court records show she made veiled threats against her husband, who she suspected of marital betrayal."

He paused. "Jessica Ward has motive, ability, skill and the resources to do this and make it look like a cyberattack. She could've staged this, hired people, hired someone to kill her husband, intending to recover the child later."

"It seems a stretch to me," said another investigator.

"It's not," Deckert said. "The FBI looked at her for this. We've all seen people attempt every scheme you could imagine. She runs a cybersecurity company in LA."

"We can't rule out Leon's theory," Garlin said, turning to the three people sitting at one end of the table.

"Van?"

A man cleared his throat and nudged his glasses up. "Van Busfield, with CISA. From the outset we've been quietly looking into Instinct Nine-99 for any link to the case, any national security threat."

"Quietly?" Deckert repeated.

"Meaning Ms. Ward is unaware," Busfield said. "Here's what we have so far. Jessica Ward was a top student at MIT and Caltech. After graduating she developed software systems and started her own company. Most of its work involves strengthening cybersecurity at hospitals, banks, casinos, corporate networks—to defend against ransomware attacks.

"We know that Instinct Nine-99 also has classified government contracts. We're still running them down. At this point, we've not determined any link, or ransom demands, relating to the work. And we've found no contract connected in any way to security at JFK. This is where we're at, so far."

An NYPD detective spoke up. "But what about Vaughn Ward? He was an investigative reporter. I understand he looked at cyber issues around the world. Maybe someone wanted to stop him from exposing something. Do we know who he was working for, and what story he was working on, at the time of his death?"

"Not yet, only that he was freelancing," Garlin said. "With the warrants, our search of his data may yield something." He added how Ward appeared to have been a private person. They'd found no solid leads from his digital footprint on social media, or through a canvass. "But we can't rule anything out," he said. "Forces from a hostile government, organized crime, global trafficking rings. At this point we need to get solid evidence and follow—"

A phone pinged.

"Apologies," said Lieutenant Roger Barnow with the NYPD's Crime Scene Unit, which was supporting with initial fingerprint analysis. Peering over his bifocals, he read a text. "This just came in from our Latent Print Section. They've got partials from the pen used by the suspects who signed for the boy at JFK."

Murmurs of enthusiasm ripped around the room and among those on the line, with someone saying, "Now we're talking."

29

SÃO PAULO, BRAZIL

That same day, thousands of miles from the FBI's New York field office, Miguel Vita took care, ensuring his train aligned with the platform.

He checked the cameras in his cab before opening the doors for passengers to board at Bruno Covas/Mendes-Vila Natal in the far south. The station was on Line 9–Esmeralda, part of the regional commuter network webbing from the São Paulo Metro, in a system that moved millions of riders daily in one of the world's largest cities.

"Tonight will be glorious," Carlo Silva said, shouldering into a car with his father, both wearing the green and white jerseys of Palmeiras, a top-ranked São Paulo football team.

"It will be a tough match, the Rio guys are strong this season," Pedro Silva said, glad his teenaged son had found seats in the crowded car. It was a long ride, and they needed to change trains to get to Allianz Parque, the stadium in the heart of the city, for the game against Flamengo from Rio de Janeiro.

Soon after they sat down, Pedro gestured for Carlo to give up his seat to a white-haired woman with lines in her face.

"You're a kind boy," Maria Lopes said, sitting with a sigh. "I'm vising my sister at Casa de Repouso Villa Lobos. I have too many stops to stand." She patted Carlo's arm in thanks.

Sitting near was Hector Lima, heading to his shift as a building janitor. He rarely smiled because he was missing a few teeth. But as the car filled, mostly with football fans, Hector allowed a grin when they began singing.

The team songs and chants floated to the cab as Miguel, the operator, closed the doors. Estimating his load at more than one thousand passengers, he eased the train to Grajaú, the next station to the north.

Moving south on Line 9–Esmeralda, Tania Costa fought to stay awake on her train, which was packed with tired, homebound workers as it slowed into Primavera–Interlagos Station. Enduring another long daily commute from her job as a clerk at an insurance company downtown, Tania was anxious to see the drawings her daughter had made at school that day.

Practically standing over Tania, gripping the handrail, was Cesar Braz. Still wearing his uniform, Cesar—who dreamed of becoming a police officer—was a security guard at one of the corporate skyscrapers in Vila Olímpia. Now, jammed in with the other riders, Cesar, aching to sit, took in the air—a mix of music leaking from headphones, body odour and perfume. Then he picked up a new smell. Someone had food, heavy with onions, making Cesar's stomach yowl.

Up front, in the cab, operator Marco Mauro checked the platforms and the cameras, before moving the train southbound for Grajaú, the next station.

As the eight-car train gathered speed, Marco could feel the heaviness of what he estimated to be over two thousand passengers—a near-capacity load. He viewed the grassy valley, the palms, the houses of the sloping neighbourhoods as if they were sliding to embrace him.

Scanning his console, Marco reflected on his years as a train operator, how his father and uncles had driven trains. Now, accelerating on the elevated segment he looked to one side at the rooftops of the sprawling patchwork of neighbourhoods.

As his train hummed, Marco smiled at the thought of how his little boy played with toy locomotives. Yes, Marco believed the rails ran in his family's blood. Now, with the tracks clicking under him at 30 miles per hour, he scanned the graffiti of the ageing warehouses and storage buildings as they passed by.

Soon, he'd be coming up on Grajaú Station. But as he prepared to slow down, his instrument panel flashed off and on—for less than two seconds.

What's this?

His eyes widened.

On its own, the train's speed was suddenly increasing as Grajaú Station came into view.

Marco's attempt to slow the train failed.

Scalp tingling, he made another futile effort.

The train blew by the platform at 50 miles per hour.

In the cars behind Marco, confusion, anger and concern registered with the stunned passengers who'd been poised at the doors to get off at Grajaú, their voices rising.

"Hey! That's my station!"

"This is not an express!"

"We should be stopping!"

Across the city, occupying the upper floor of an office complex, was the control centre. A wall of video screens showed real-time position, speed and status for trains on illuminated maps covering the network. Closed-circuit camera feeds provided additional live monitoring so operators at workstations could scrutinize their assigned zones.

Vera Ferreira, the control operator for Line 9–Esmeralda, felt her pulse jump when she saw that a southbound train had skipped a station.

Overcrowding? An operational issue?

A station skip for non-express was rare. Without authorization, it was a safety violation. Trained to be calm and fast, she immediately radioed operator Marco Mauro.

"Train 27, this is control. Why did you skip Grajaú and increase speed? Resume normal operation."

"Control, Train 27! Our controls are malfunctioning—will not respond! Repeat, 27 southbound controls not responding!"

One second later, an alarm light on Vera's board began flashing, yanking her concentration to the switching crossover at the rail yards between Bruno Covas/Mendes-Vila Natal and Grajaú Stations.

The switch has moved to the wrong position.

Vera's heart pounded—instantly she received a tense radio call from Miguel, operator of the train heading north.

"Control, this is Train 32! What's happening? We've been diverted without notice onto the southbound track—we are proceeding north on the southbound track. Has it been cleared for us? What's going on—is this maintenance? Operational?"

The tiny hairs on the back of Vera's neck stood up as it hit her.

She had two trains on a head-on collision course!

The relentless blinking alarm light—now with a *whoop-whoop* warning chime sounding imminent danger—triggered a digital countdown clock alerting her to a collision in one minute and nineteen seconds.

Swallowing hard, Vera's fingers blurred as she initiated protocols while dispatching radio commands.

"Trains 27 and 32, activate your emergency braking now; 27 and 32, activate emergency braking now!"

The flashing lights blinked with urgency on the map on the wall, two blips approaching each other accompanied by the alarm's unyielding pinging, drawing attention from the other control operators.

"Control to Trains 27 and 32, apply maximum emergency braking now!"

Vera shot a glance to the map and her control panel, her mind white hot as the digital clock drove the time down to sixty seconds.

"Emergency! Emergency! All trains on Line 9, stop! This is an emergency. All Line 9 trains stop!"

The southbound train was moving at 51 miles per hour. In his cab, Marco clamped his jaw, attempting in vain to slow his train.

"Control, Train 27, braking procedures not responding!"

The landscape blurred by while, to the south, Miguel battled to stop his northbound train, gripping the controls, repeating braking procedures without results, the track blurring ahead.

"Control, this is Train 32, nothing is working—can you override?"

In the control centre Vera's supervisor rushed to her station.

"Vera, override the line, shut it down now!"

Gasping, with fifty seconds to go, she launched commands to kill power to the line, as she, her supervisor and others watched the blips draw nearer.

"Oh God, it's not working!" In desperation, she repeated the shutdown sequence. "It's not working!"

On Line 9, with forty seconds to impact, each train emerged in the distance as small objects that were growing.

Frantically working every control to stop his southbound train, Marco's stomach twisted as the oncoming train barrelled toward his. In the northbound train, all the saliva evaporated in Miguel's mouth as he repeated the braking measures.

Suddenly, Marco heard the hopeful sound of the power driving his southbound train groaning off. At the same time, an ear-piercing screeching arose from the brakes finally engaging on the northbound train, then came a steel-on-steel grinding from the brake being applied on the southbound train.

The deceleration jolted passengers in both trains, slamming many into each other, throwing most to the floor. Phones, bags, water bottles were sent flying amid screams as the cars vibrated and thudded.

On the tracks, sparks sprayed like fireworks from the braking wheels as each train slid, grinding to a stop within twenty feet of each other.

In the cars, people scrambled to comfort those with cuts, contusions and sprains, all to the moans and soft sobbing of some frightened passengers. No one was seriously hurt, yet none of the riders were yet aware of what had taken place.

Outside, through the acrid-smelling smoke rising from the stopped trains, Miguel Vita dragged his forearm across his sweating brow and stared from his cab at Marco Mauro, who made the sign of the cross.

30

WASHINGTON, DC

Approximately two months before Dylan Ward's abduction

Carl waited in a corner booth of the bar. The lighting was dim; the seat, patched with tape, had torn again; a half-eaten bag of chips had spilled out under the table in a puddle of something. Johnny Cash's "Ring of Fire" floated in air that smelled of beer.

It had been three days since Vanessa's blowout over his gambling. He'd told her that he was meeting someone to get help. That's all he'd said. Questions she threw at him went unanswered.

"I don't want to get into it," he'd told her. "I'm serious about fixing things. Leave your dad out of it and give me time. Please."

The bar was in a DC neighbourhood with tired-looking buildings and a sense of people who'd been forgotten, or wanted to be left alone. He liked the anonymity of the place. It had opened in the 1930s, and to this day was a "cash only" business.

While he waited, Carl pushed down his anxiety. His debt was massive. Hannah needed her treatment. They could lose the house. He could lose his job. They'd have to move in with Vanessa's family—which would confirm to his in-laws what they'd always believed about him: that he was a failure.

Carl swept a hand over his face. "How did I get here?" he muttered to himself.

As a kid, school had been a breeze. He'd always been at the top of his class, excelling in math. He'd loved computers. He could take them apart and build his own, often a better version. But he also craved the thrill of the risk of a wager. That's when he began gambling, thriving on analyzing the odds to prove himself right—always ahead, or at least breaking even. It wasn't about the money. More than anything he was addicted to the psychological thrill of living on the edge.

He'd carried his gambling to MIT, never letting it affect his work. In fact, while betting on sports, he'd excelled academically and was counted among the rising stars of computer engineering.

When he met Vanessa, her father had urged him to come and work for him. Marv wanted Carl to upgrade and operate the entire computer system—inventory, sales, online, everything—for his six electronics stores. To Carl, the family business was not much more than a chain of hardware stores. No way was he going to do that.

Carl's rejection had wounded Marv. Profoundly.

In the years that followed, Carl never succeeded in getting a position with the NSA, the CIA, Homeland, or the FBI's Cyber Division. His failures had fuelled more gambling. Occasionally he would win big. But his losses increased. His defeats underscored his deteriorating sense of self-worth. He felt left behind when he learned how well his MIT friends had done.

One was with Strategic Command. Others were advancing AI technology and working toward curing diseases. One had started a cybersecurity company. Another was an international consultant for governments and corporations on network security.

And me? I'm a lowly contractor, nearly $100,000 in debt.

And every time Vanessa went to her father for help, it proved to Marv that Carl was a loser who could not support his family.

How did I let things get away from me?

As he looked up from his despair, Carl glanced to the door just as his lifeline entered.

Rod Tate.

Carl gave him a small wave as Tate headed over to him.

They'd first met a few months ago, when Carl was at a sports bar with a group celebrating a work friend's birthday. It turned out Tate owned a small computer repair shop in the district's southeast. They'd talked about computers and sports, and later that night, with Tate observing Carl's disappointment at the outcome of a game on the TV, Carl let slip that he'd lost on what he believed was a sure bet.

"How much?" Tate had asked, taking a sip of beer.

"Three thousand."

Tate winced. "Ouch."

"That's going to hurt at home. My losses are adding up."

"Sorry to hear, man. Maybe next time things will turn around."

Two hours later, as they walked to their cars, Tate had said, casually, "Listen, I was thinking about your hit and what you said about losses adding up. I meet a lot of people, all kinds of people, at work."

Carl nodded, wondering what Tate was getting at.

"What I'm saying is, if you're ever in a jam, let me know. Maybe things can be arranged."

"Arranged?"

"To help you."

Now, four months later, Tate was sliding into Carl's booth.

"Thanks for meeting me," Carl said.

"Well, I made the offer, now I'm here."

"Okay, I need help." Carl glanced off, unable to meet Tate's eyes.

"How much help?"

He finally looked at Tate. "One hundred and fifty k."

Tate paused before answering.

"That can be arranged."

"How do we do this?"

"I know people who need the kind of help you can provide. And they're willing to pay for it."

"What kind of help are we talking about?" Carl asked.

"Information you have access to." Tate shrugged. "Are you willing to do this?"

Tate was talking about Carl's work, he realized. "There's a lot of risk."

"Yes, but you're a smart guy."

"You guarantee they'll pay?"

"For the right information, they'll pay."

Carl thought about it, accepting he had no choice.

"Okay, I'll do it."

31

NEW YORK

Jessie stepped into the elevator of the fifteen-storey office building on Avenue of the Americas in SoHo. As the doors closed, she leaned against the wall, twisting the strap of her bag. *Am I right to come here?*

She shut her eyes, unable to silence the alarm ringing in her head or block the images of the car hauled from the lake. Vaughn's murder. Dylan's abduction.

All she wanted was to see her son.

Yesterday, she'd gone to Vaughn's apartment with Miller for the second time, relieved that no media was outside. She had spent part of the day re-examining everything and talking to his neighbours, who knew little. After she'd seen Miller off in a cab, she walked back to her hotel. At one point, she thought she was being followed by a man and a woman. She figured they were press people, but she couldn't be sure because they never approached her.

She was exhausted. Who knew what was real and what wasn't?

Acting on an idea, Jessie had opened up her text messages, scrolling until she found the one from Shauna Price, the *Los Angeles Times* reporter who'd contacted her about Dylan's disappearance. *Some people at the* Times *know your husband,* she'd said.

Jessie called her to ask who Vaughn might have been freelancing for. Shauna said she'd ask around, promising to call her back. Forty-five minutes later, she did.

"Word is he might've been floating a story to *Veritas Sola* in New York. That's all we have. Hope this helps. We'll keep reporting on the case and keep you posted."

As she hung up, she thought, *Of course it's* Veritas Sola.

Veritas Sola, Latin for "truth alone," was an online news organization established in 2010. It was world-renowned for its investigative journalism, having won several Pulitzer Prizes.

It had been among the news outlets covering the story from the beginning, requesting interviews from her and Vaughn's parents. Now, Jessie had a reason to talk to them, and the editor had agreed to her request to meet.

As the elevator rose to the *Veritas Sola* offices, so did Jessie's hope of getting answers.

The door slid open, and she took a breath as a woman in her late twenties, dressed in a black turtleneck and jeans, approached her.

"Welcome, Jessica. I'm Chelsea Webber, reporter. Come this way."

They walked through a newsroom filled with staff focused on their monitors to the subdued clicking of keyboards.

"We have about forty people here," Chelsea said. "And about sixty across the country, and another seventy around the world."

Jessie was led through a cabinet-lined hallway to a large office with a desk piled with files and books, all in ordered chaos. Behind it was a man wearing a dark blazer and powder-blue shirt. A taut smile appeared behind his frameless glasses as he stood.

"This is our editor, Rich Lafont," Chelsea said. "Rich, this is Jessica Ward."

"Thank you for coming, Jessica," Lafont said. "Please, have a seat. If you don't mind, Chelsea will join us."

Jessie glanced at her. "This is just a conversation, not an interview," Jessie said. "I don't want this recorded."

"Absolutely," Lafont said. "A conversation, and nothing more without your permission."

"Then it's fine."

"Would you like coffee, tea, anything?"

"No thank you." Jessie settled into the chair in front of the desk. Chelsea sat in the one next to hers.

"Again, our condolences for your loss. We're hoping for the safe return of your son."

"Thank you."

"How can we help?" Lafont leaned back in his desk chair and stared at Jessie.

"I have some questions about Vaughn," she began. "I understand that before his death, Vaughn was freelancing for you? Can you tell me what he was working on?"

Lafont looked at Chelsea for a few seconds, then back at Jessie. "The FBI and NYPD have asked us the same questions."

"They have?" Jessie was surprised.

"Yes, they were here a couple days ago, and I'll tell you what we told them, which is that Vaughn has freelanced for us in the past. He is—*was*—one of the best journalists in the business."

His use of the past tense pierced Jessie.

"He came to me with, well, with a wisp of an idea," Lafont said.

"What was it?"

"That's just it. I don't know. He was guarded about it."

"So he didn't give you any details?"

"No, nothing. He wanted assurance first that we'd have his back once he presented his finished piece to us. You know, that we'd stand by the story."

"So you have no idea what it was about?"

"No, and believe me, I pushed him. I said, 'I have to know what the story is, Vaughn.' Still, he was protective. So I gave him the assurance—with the caveat, and Vaughn knew this, that all our stories are triple-checked before we run them." Lafont leaned forward in his chair, thinking. "Vaughn was confident he had an exclusive lead on a major revelation. He had the inside track with sources ready to expose what he described as, and I'm quoting him, 'something big and deep and even dangerous.'"

"*Dangerous?* What does that mean?" Jessie looked at Chelsea, who shrugged.

"I don't know," Lafont admitted. "It's not clear if the subject was dangerous, or revealing it was dangerous, or both. He was guarded about it."

"And now he's dead." Jessie kept in control. "What do you think about this?"

"I don't know. I have no evidence, but I believe Vaughn was far along on the story, or he wouldn't have come to us. I believe one reason he was being cagey about the piece is that he may have also been considering pitching his scoop to *The New York Times* or *The Washington Post* as well."

"But what could his story have been?"

"We have no clue. But, as you know, he reported extensively on cybersecurity issues in this country and around the world. So, it's most likely something along those lines—something I would think you're familiar with."

Jessie accepted Lafont's account as plausible, knowing how Vaughn worked. She bit her lip. For so long she had believed that all those secret messages of his meant that he was being unfaithful. *But maybe his mistress was actually his job—his pursuit of stories.*

She pushed down her guilt and looked at Lafont. "Is there anything more you can tell me?"

"Just that we never reached an agreement, or gave him the assignment. It was just a preliminary chat, but I could see it in his eyes."

"What?"

"That he believed he was onto something," Lafont said. "Jessica, I should add that in the wake of the police visiting us, our lawyers advised that we may be subject to search warrants."

Jessie was confused. "Search warrants for what?"

"Looking for leads on the case, I would think," he said. "We'll challenge them on constitutional grounds. But who knows if that would work."

He watched Jessie gaze out the window behind him.

"If I may, Jessica, with the utmost respect," he ventured, "would you agree to an interview?"

32

NEW YORK

Jessie had agreed to be interviewed by Chelsea because she believed that the story would help with her search for Dylan.

Chelsea recorded and took notes as she covered all aspects of the case, including Jessie's and Vaughn's personal histories. She listened attentively, occasionally passing Jessie a tissue. It wasn't long before Chelsea came to her last questions.

"Could the story Vaughn had been pursuing, and Dylan's abduction, be related in some way to the work your company Instinct Nine-99 has done, or is doing?"

Jessie paused, weighing her words. "The police asked me similar questions. I don't know, but I don't think so, because Vaughn had no way of knowing what our contracts concern. In fact, no one does. It's all highly confidential."

"But what if he had a source?"

Shaking her head, Jessie said, "Maybe, I'm not convinced. No one has made any demands. I don't know what to think."

Chelsea thanked her, then clicked off the recorder and closed her notebook. Blinking while debating a thought, she looked at Jessie. "I think I should tell you about the last time I saw Vaughn. It wasn't that long ago."

"Yes, please."

"We were out with a group of news friends at a bar. He'd had quite a lot to drink, but he wasn't too drunk or anything. Anyway, I don't know why, but he just opened up to me. He got talking about having second thoughts about the divorce."

Jessie was taken aback. "Second thoughts? What do you mean?"

"Like, maybe he wanted to reconcile, that he regretted the things he did and the things he said to you."

"What did he do that he regretted?"

"He didn't say, but it sounded like he'd made a mistake that he deeply regretted."

"A mistake?" Jessie was stunned. "Let me ask you: do you think he was seeing someone?"

Chelsea shook her head. "No, I don't. He seemed lonely, sad even, like he didn't want to go through with the divorce." Chelsea paused and then winced. "Please don't think I'm out of line. I thought it was something you'd want to know."

Jessie smiled at her. "I appreciate it. Thank you." She thought for a moment, then asked, "Were there any rumours about Vaughn seeking an overseas bureau posting?"

"None that I'm aware of."

Jessie nodded, then stood. "Thank you for this." They hugged, then walked down the hall toward reception, where a man in a New York Jets hoodie appeared in front of them.

"Oh, hi Derrick," Chelsea said, following his gaze to Jessie. "Um, this is Jessica Ward. Jessica, this is Derrick St. Jean. He heads our IT department."

Derrick stared intently at Jessie. "Forgive me, Ms. Ward. I don't mean to be rude, but I recognize you—I saw you were here and . . ." He looked to Chelsea, then back at Jessie. "Could I talk to you alone for a moment?"

"Derrick, I don't think so," Chelsea said. "She was just leaving."

"No, no—it's okay," Jessie said. "What is it, Derrick?"

"I'd like to talk to you in private, at my desk."

Chelsea and Jessie traded looks. "It's up to you," Chelsea said with a shrug.

"It won't take long," Derrick said.

"I'm so sorry for interrupting," Derrick said, leading Jessie down a hall. "I saw you meeting with Chelsea and Rich, and I heard about all that's happened. Sorry about that too. Here we are."

Derrick's desk was removed from the newsroom, tucked in a far corner of the office. His workstation had three monitors, a cluster of drives, jacks, cords, tools and other equipment. He rolled a swivel chair over for Jessie, then sat in his own, moving in close to his desk. His fingers raced over his keyboard.

"Why do you want to talk to me?" Jessie asked, looking around at Derrick's setup.

Derrick craned his neck, glanced down the hall, then lowered his voice.

"I saw the news, and some of the reporters here told me the FBI and NYPD detectives had been in the newsroom, and there could be warrants, you know?"

"Yes."

He turned back to his computer, his mouse clicking, his screen changing with lightning speed to various secured databases. "Vaughn was here not too long ago," Derrick said, again checking that they were alone. "He had a problem with his laptop."

Jessie's attention sharpened.

"I know Vaughn. He'd worked for us a couple times, and I helped with tech stuff before. He was a good guy."

"He was," Jessie whispered.

"Well, last time he was here, he was concerned about an issue with his laptop, and he didn't trust taking it to a shop, you know? So, he asked me to take a look."

Jessie nodded. "Okay."

"You know, being in the business you're in, how we back up everything."

She nodded as Derrick worked, clicking and typing. Vaughn had been paranoid about losing his work.

"Anyway, I fixed Vaughn's issue, but first I backed up everything and saved it, just in case his computer started acting up again."

Excitement grew in Jessie's stomach as Derrick went on.

"A lot of his stuff is encrypted, password-protected, you know?" Derrick grinned at her. "Of course you know, look at who I'm talking to. I hear your company's got some good people." He pressed a few more keys, then held up a small item. "No one has to know," he said with a wink. He placed a green USB flash drive in Jessie's palm.

"I've copied all the files from Vaughn's computer for you. Maybe it'll help."

33

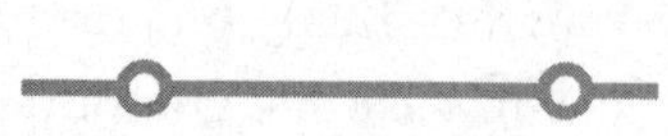

NEW YORK

Jessie left the *Veritas Sola* news offices and urged the cab driver to take the fastest route to Brooklyn.

Her head was throbbing, but she felt *hopeful.* She had Vaughn's computer files, which might give her the answers she needed.

But time is hammering against me.

Jessie then considered Chelsea's revelation—that Vaughn hadn't wanted the divorce. That he regretted what he'd done. That he wanted to reconcile.

Her hope gave way to a twinge of regret.

I should've tried harder for us. Maybe I wanted to reconcile too.

As they travelled on the upper level of the Manhattan Bridge, she looked to the Brooklyn Bridge, remembering how she and Vaughn had walked across it once on a visit. Maybe what had happened to them wasn't his fault, or hers. They'd both loved their work and had gotten caught up in it. Jessie felt a sob rising, pushed it down, took another breath and glanced at her bag.

The flash drive Derrick had given her could hold the answers.

Jessie had to move quickly.

The driver made good time to Brooklyn and soon she was around the corner from her hotel.

In her room, Jessie fired up the laptop she'd bought in New Jersey, plugged the USB drive into it and began opening Vaughn's files.

The first thing she came to broke her heart. Vaughn had saved old photos of all of them together in a folder. Jessie scrolled through the images—her and Vaughn with Dylan at the Central Park Zoo, then the three of them on the Staten Island Ferry. Here they were at Disneyland. Then on the beach in Malibu. A rare moment—a video of them together with Dylan blowing out candles on his birthday cake. Here they were at the cabin.

Happier times.

After her moment of grief, Jessie brushed her cheeks and began checking the other folders on the drive. As Derrick had cautioned, and as expected, most were encrypted. But that didn't stop her. She had to work fast because, as the staff at *Veritas Sola* had said, the FBI would seek warrants for access to Vaughn's files. With her copy, she had a head start.

Thinking quickly, she launched a proprietary app on her laptop that she had downloaded earlier. It was an advanced tool developed by Instinct Nine-99 that allowed her to override Vaughn's encrypted data's permission list and let herself in. It took a little time, but soon she was able to decrypt many of Vaughn's folders and files, gaining access to some.

Many were archived stories, drafts and research material. She scanned all of them but found nothing that, to her, appeared relevant to the situation. She then went to the folders with files that Vaughn had most recently modified. She groaned. Most of the newest ones had additional password protection. This was not going to be quick. But she wasn't giving up.

Concentrating, she went to a folder Vaughn had labelled "To Do" and tried to get into the most recently modified file. It took some time, but Jessie succeeded in bypassing the security and opened it. The file's integrity was intact and it was readable.

Shifting in her chair, she concentrated on the document, surveying what appeared to be Vaughn's random thoughts and fragments on a story he was pursuing.

Jessie's scalp prickled, not believing, or comprehending, the brief notes as she read them.

"Oh my God, what was he working on?"

"Something big and deep and even dangerous," Rich Lafont had said.

Did he uncover something that cost him his life and the abduction of our son?

Jessie scanned the file, her eyes landing on the final, cryptic notation.

No facts. No credibility. No story. Need to meet with X. Inside source.

Who is X?

Jessie thought of Vaughn's calendar on the wall of his home as realization dawned. The crossed-out note had said "Meet with ?"

Could *?* be *X*?

But who was X?

34

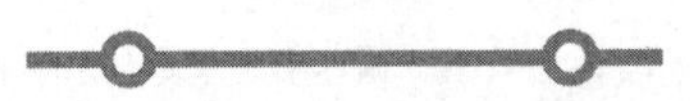

CHICAGO METRO AREA

It was late afternoon when Claire walked out of the DoubleTree past the Denny's and got onto Arlington Heights Road, following the directions of her anonymous tipster.

After receiving the first message last night, she had received another.

We need to meet. Will send details.

She still didn't know who the sender was.

Claire had spent much of today at SynerRapid, again consulting with analysts and engineers, studying the Toronto modules, the extracted components and data. By afternoon, as they'd neared completion, Dieter Zurne and Krista Quinn had taken her aside.

"Did your review of the logs reveal any anomalies?" Zurne asked.

"Nothing so far."

Zurne smiled. "That's because there was no intrusion."

But I'm not finished, Claire had thought.

Claire had told no one about the mysterious message, but she spent much of the day wondering who among SynerRapid's staff could be the one who'd secretly reached out to her using an untraceable number. No one stood out.

When the day ended, Quinn dropped Claire off at the hotel and turned to her. "Now that we've cooperated," she said, "it's assuring that you've examined our work objectively."

"There's still a long way to go in the investigation."

"Yes, but the problem was not with us."

"Thank you for everything, Krista." Claire got out of the car.

"Not at all. Have a good flight back to Canada tomorrow."

Thirty minutes later, alone in her room, Claire received a new message.

Bring your laptop / notes, walk S. on N. Arlington Heights Rd.

Claire proceeded under the I-90 overpass. Soon, on her right, she came to the edge of a huge forest known as Busse Woods. As traffic hummed in both directions, she stayed on the sidewalk that bordered the woodland, checking her instructions.

Continue until you see Northwest Point Boulevard.

When she reached it, she was guided into the forest.

Take the trail entrance. Then take the first right and stop at the first park bench. Wait there.

Claire walked along the paved trail that cut through the thick forest of tall hickory, maple and oak trees, until she reached the bench and sat. Her heart beat a little faster, not liking the idea of being alone, having been guided to this area. She saw no one on the trail in either direction. *What if this is a setup?* A breeze hissed through the treetops; the sounds of traffic faded.

Her unease was allayed when she heard soft steady thudding and even breathing as two joggers passed. Soon after, a cyclist glided in front of her in the opposite direction.

Minutes went by as she listened to birdsong.

An older man and woman nodded, smiling at Claire as they strolled along the trail.

More time passed.

She checked her phone.

No new messages.

When she looked up, she saw a lone figure approaching. It appeared to be a woman in jeans, running shoes and a hoodie with the hood drawn over a ball cap, hands in the front pocket.

The walker neared and Claire saw a flash of red hair. It was Jill, an engineer from SynerRapid.

She sat next to Claire on the bench. "You can't tell anyone about us meeting," she said. "Give me your word."

Claire took a moment before responding. "You have my word."

Jill took a breath, looked to the left and right, then got to it. "There was a vulnerability in the software update."

"There was?"

"For at least a week, maybe longer."

"But I found nothing in the logs."

Jill looked at her for a long moment. "That's because the logs were tampered with."

"How do you know?"

Jill looked off into the trees. "There was an engineer, Kyle. He was in charge of the remote software updates for the modules used in the Toronto system, and others in the US and around the world."

Claire tried to place his name. "Did I meet him?"

Jill shook her head. "He's dead."

"Oh my God."

"He was using drugs, and SynerRapid fired him. After he was let go, he hacked into his personnel file to alter his work record, to make himself look like an outstanding employee, to build a legal case." Jill took a breath before continuing. "What this meant was Kyle got into SynerRapid's systems remotely through a back door that was left wide open, undetected for at least a week. We know hackers can search for vulnerabilities with lightning speed."

"When did this happen?"

"In the time leading up to the Toronto crash, maybe two weeks."

"Does SynerRapid know this?"

"I don't know. If they did, they probably wouldn't admit it, especially to you. Maybe they think they've plugged the hole, as it were. They'd want to keep it quiet so as not to face litigation for Toronto or jeopardize global contracts," Jill said. "The thing is, because of this, the Toronto system was left wide open to intrusion. And hackers, good ones, move so fast."

After absorbing the revelation, Claire said, "Why haven't you reported this?"

Jill's cheeks flushed, emotion filling her voice. "I was the one who found Kyle, in his apartment. They say it was an accidental overdose, but—but we were dating, and I broke it off . . . I have a little girl and Kyle was not ready to be a dad." She took a long breath. "I don't know what really happened with the vulnerability—and no one knows what I've told you. I just don't want this coming back to me. I know Kyle had nothing to do with the subway incident. All he did was leave a door open, you know?"

"I'm sorry about you, and Kyle," Claire said. "He may have had nothing to do with Toronto, but what he did set things in motion. People were killed, and so many others were hurt."

"I know." Jill brushed away tears. "That's why I'm telling you. So you and your people in Canada can investigate this and find out who did it."

"Good." Claire indicated her bag. "Do you think you can look at the logs with me? I have them right here."

"Yes, I'll help you."

35

SANTA MONICA

A pall had settled over Instinct Nine-99 after Vaughn's murder, but Bobby, Sarita and Dahlia continued going flat-out in the search for Dylan.

Bobby had been able to download the recording of Vaughn's call with the group from the messaging app's cloud and was spending the day studying it. It was now clear that all of Vaughn's communication with his family had been fabricated, and Bobby was determined to confirm who was behind it. He replayed the video, staring at Vaughn. From the get-go he'd suspected something about Vaughn in this call was off. Now it was obvious that it was a deepfake—a good one, but a fake just the same.

Bobby's fingers moved over his keyboard as he contacted a Bay Area company that was among the best in analyzing and tracing deepfake videos. A chime sounded and Sally Yoon, a friend from his Stanford days, appeared on his monitor.

"Hey Bobby, I'm sorry about what happened with everything at Instinct."

"Thanks. I need a favour. I got a deepfake video. Can you find the source and keep this all on the down-low?"

"It's related to the case, right?"

"It is. And it may be crucial. I need it done, like, yesterday."

"Shoot it to me. It'll take time, but we'll make it a priority."

He sent her the video, then he downed the last of his Diet Coke. Jessie had mentioned that she had information from Vaughn's laptop, and she was hoping that she'd find a link between a story he was working on and his murder and Dylan's disappearance. But what if all of this wasn't tied to Vaughn but to Jessie, and to Instinct's work?

Jessie had a vault in her office where she kept her Instinct laptop. That computer held the most advanced concepts for the classified network security system they were developing, so Bobby was glad that Jessie had taken it with her to New York, as he'd suggested. What no one outside of Jessie, Sarita and Bobby knew was that, as a backup, he possessed half of the work; Sarita had the other half.

And Jessie had it all.

It was how they protected the details of the system they were constructing.

The white couple was in their late sixties. The man wore a ball cap and glasses, and the woman's white hair was laced with grey. They were walking on West 28th Street, along Chelsea Park, where a children's soccer game was happening. They were about a block from Penn Station.

The photo had been taken and posted by someone on social media. They'd captioned it "Frankie's goal!"—completely unaware of the older couple in the background.

Sarita leaned closer to her monitor, examining the image. The time stamp was right but there was no boy with the couple, and their clothing did not match the video from Penn Station.

She sighed. *Back to the drawing board.*

She'd created a program to scour social media posts for anything on these suspects and Dylan. She had collected all the descriptors of the suspects—then everything gleaned from posts made by tourists, cyclists, walkers, dashcams—and loaded them into the program. The program searched every social media platform using the descriptors and then kicked out possibilities to scrutinize.

Sarita clicked on another photo, one from the High Line. A couple sitting on a bench. She looked closely at the man and woman. *No, too young*, she thought, rejecting the image. She looked through other photos, quickly dismissing them. Frustrated, she leaned back in her chair and rubbed her face.

"There has to be something," she said to herself, sitting up and going back to her computer, blinking back tears.

Vaughn's dead.

She'd never tell anyone—especially not Jessie—but she had held a place for him in her heart. She remembered the time he'd smiled at her, how she felt something electric pass between them. Maybe for him it was just flirting, but for her it was more. Then when she'd learned Jessie and Vaughn were estranged and he'd moved to New York, her hope had climbed and something came over her. Alone at night, Sarita imagined Vaughn's smile, his voice, enjoying the fantasy of what her life could've been like with him.

But now he was gone.

"You okay?" Bobby stood at her desk.

Pushing her thoughts away, Sarita reached for a tissue. "It's just so sad. Vaughn is dead and Dylan is missing. I can't believe this has happened."

"I know, but we have to work through it, Sarita. For Jessie."

"Who would do this? And why?"

"That's what we've got to find out." He checked the time on his watch. "Jessie's calling soon to give us an update. Do you think you'll be okay?"

Sarita nodded as Dahlia walked past them, phone to her ear, voice low in quiet conversation, stopping at the large window overlooking the front parking lot. Ever since the case broke, Los Angeles media had kept a vigil in front of Instinct Nine-99. The number of news vans and TV satellite trucks parked out front had grown with each passing day.

"Jessie just texted," Bobby said. "She's calling in two minutes."

Dahlia, Bobby and Sarita went to a meeting room and shut the door. A moment later, Jessie appeared on the wall-mounted screen, looking tired but determined.

"This is what I've got." Her voice was strong. "Vaughn had pitched a freelance idea that was short on details to *Veritas Sola*. I met with them. The editor told me all he could, and I got Vaughn's computer files."

"What was his idea?" Dahlia asked.

"I don't know. I've only got fragments of his notes so far." She paused, collected herself, then typed. "Standby, I'll show you."

The large screen showed a page of text.

They're close to executing events around the world . . . they will serve as a message and foundation to something much bigger to follow . . .

"Whoa." Bobby sat up.

"What does that mean?" Sarita asked.

"Who's close?" Dahlia was making notes. "What events?"

"We don't know," Jessie said. "And there's this."

She shared another document.

No facts. No credibility. No story. Need to meet with X. Inside source.

"X?" Bobby asked. "Inside source to what?"

"We don't know." Jessie shook her head. "But I think the X note is tied to one he'd made on his calendar days before Dylan was to arrive at JFK. That one said 'meet with' and then a question mark. I'll send you a photo of the calendar."

"And what *events* is he talking about?" Sarita said. "What could he mean?"

"Maybe a rumour, or a conspiracy he was following?" Jessie said.

"Maybe it's tied to something like we've seen," Dahlia said. "I'm thinking of the ransomware attacks on Las Vegas casinos. Then there was the global event in the summer of 2024 arising from a defective software update."

"I got stuck at Hartsfield in Atlanta because of it," Bobby said.

"Yeah, it was massive," Sarita added. "Paralyzed airlines, hospitals, banks and government agencies around the world."

"Whatever Vaughn was chasing could've been plausible," Bobby said. "And, like we figured before, maybe he was close to exposing something someone doesn't want revealed."

Jessie nodded. "This is what he told the editor—that he was working on 'something big and deep and even dangerous.'"

"It *was* dangerous," Sarita said. "Look at all that's happened."

Everyone was quiet for a moment before Dahlia spoke. "How did you get his files, Jess?"

"I had some help," Jessie said. "We need to find out who Vaughn's mystery source is and what he was working on. I'm worried we're running out of time to find Dylan."

"Don't give up, Jess," Sarita said. "We'll find him."

When the call ended, Jessie vanished from the screen.

As Bobby and Sarita left the room, Dahlia's phone vibrated.

36

SANTA MONICA

It was a blocked number, but Dahlia answered.

"Dahlia, this is Brenda Phan."

The call catapulted her back to when they were classmates at MIT.

"Brenda, thanks for getting back to me."

"Sorry it wasn't sooner. How's Jessie? This is just horrible."

"A nightmare," Dahlia said. "We're doing all we can to find Dylan. Can you help us?"

"I'll do whatever I can."

"You're still with the CIA, right?"

Several seconds passed before Brenda answered. "We're not involved," she said.

"But you must know something. What are you hearing?"

"Just that Homeland and CISA are looking into it because of the abduction, the manipulated video, the intrusion of JFK security. But the media has speculated on this."

"What about any stories Vaughn was working on before he was murdered?"

"I'm sure they'll be taking it all into consideration."

"Have you heard anything about Instinct Nine-99? Or the contracts they're working on?"

"From my understanding, Homeland, CISA and others are monitoring her and the company, mainly because of the technology they're developing."

"It's groundbreaking," Dahlia said.

"I'm not surprised. Jessie was so brilliant at MIT. So were you. You two were geeked-out superstars on Jackson's team. I know he was really impressed by her."

"Yes, he was."

"I was so sad when I heard he'd passed away."

"Yeah, me too. He was exceptional."

"You were so fortunate to be on his team, doing research at the lab in Lexington," Brenda said.

Dahlia looked out the window at the news vans parked outside. "We were."

Brenda paused. "What did you guys do there?" she asked. "Word was that you were developing some new technology."

"It was classified government work. We actually swore an oath to secrecy. You know how that goes."

Brenda laughed. "Based on who Professor Jackson was, I do," she said. "Hey, have you contacted the others from your team?"

"I'm trying, but I've been unable to reach everyone."

Their call ended with Brenda promising to help. And Dahlia continued checking with others she knew in her network and from MIT. The news coverage of Vaughn's murder seemed to make them more agreeable to talking to her this time around. She finally reached Roseanne Wysner, who she'd recalled as soft-spoken and possessing one of the sharpest minds in the MIT group.

"It's been a long time, Dahlia," Roseanne said.

"That IT conference in Abu Dhabi two years ago, wasn't it?"

"Three."

Dahlia then moved through the niceties, steering the conversation to what mattered: asking if Roseanne, a systems analyst at the NSA, had heard anything that could help. A few seconds ticked by before Roseanne offered some information.

"I heard that there may have been chatter that Vaughn was pursuing a story related to cybersecurity."

"What about it? Jessie also picked up a similar thread. Is there anything more you can tell us?"

"Only that there was chatter. Nothing substantial. That's all I know at my level." A moment later, Roseanne added, "Did you try Carl Lasker? He was with us on the team at the lab."

"I couldn't reach him. As I recall, he was kind of introverted."

"I used to sit with him at breaks. He was wild with numbers, could solve math problems in his head. Remember the time Professor Jackson gave us a massive math problem? Carl solved it first, faster than anyone else."

"Right, yeah, he was a human machine."

"Always calculating the odds of things happening. Some of the guys told me that he'd developed a side hustle betting—and winning. Mostly on sports."

"I should talk to Carl. Where is he now?"

"Working for one of the big federal security agencies. He must've heard something. I'll check it out and get his information for you."

37

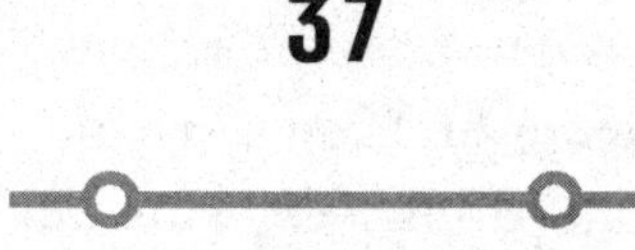

VIRGINIA

Approximately two months before Dylan Ward's abduction

Traffic was moving well northbound on the 95, flowing through the suburban Virginia woods. The calm of Chopin's Nocturnes filled Carl's SUV, and he made good time commuting from Stafford to Quantico, arriving at the Defense Counterintelligence and Security Agency, where he worked as an analyst. Among its many roles, the DCSA protected critical technology and classified information used by private companies on behalf of the Department of Defense.

After using his identification at the security gates and turnstiles, Carl settled in at his desk. In keeping with his routine, he logged into the system, checked emails and looked for updates from his colleagues and supervisors. He scanned his inbox for any relevant news until it was time for the morning meeting.

As they did every day, the group shared intel updates, went over current projects and listed priorities. Today, during the discussions, Carl kept rubbing the back of his neck and, finding it hard to swallow, sipping water as his pulse quickened.

Thankfully, no one picked up on his nervousness.

Walking back to his desk, he reassured himself. *I have to do this. I have no choice.*

"Hey, Carl, what do you think?"

He stopped and turned to Gabby, a fellow analyst.

"About?"

"The edict on working hours. You didn't seem happy about it in the meeting just now."

He shrugged. "Naw, never gave it a thought."

She gave him a once-over. "You all right?"

"I'm okay." He rubbed his leg. "This old high-school sports thing flares up from time to time."

"Ah, the price of glory days. Talk to you later." Gabby gave him a finger wave and disappeared to her workstation. Taking a breath, Carl returned to his desk, immersing himself in his work. For most of the morning he analyzed reports. All the while, he mentally checklisted every security protocol in place.

Employees were not permitted to bring any personal devices into the office. No laptops, no phones, no portable drives, no USB flash drives. No hardware was permitted. The ports for external hardware had been disabled. And the system was embedded with software to detect unauthorized data transfers to prevent copying. Surveillance cameras monitoring all staff were mounted in the ceiling to capture nearly every angle and cubicle.

Carl had replayed his plan a thousand times in his mind. It had to work.

Jackie, his colleague to the right, was away on a course for two weeks. Devon, to his left, was in hospital for minor surgery. Their desks were in a low-traffic area, which meant that, currently, Carl's zone was a ghost town. And fortunately, a previous supervisor was an advocate of having flora in the office as a mood enhancer. Several planters stood as section dividers bordering the end run of cubicles around Carl's area. The bird of paradise and the philodendron atop the divider in front and behind him thrived. He'd observed the days when office maintenance people came around with their cart to tend to them, which meant repositioning them. Which meant momentarily blocking Carl from the security cameras.

Today was a day for plant care.

Early afternoon, Carl spotted the cart across the work area making its way to him. As it neared, he focused on his screen and called up a recent classified report on emerging risks.

The plant people—an older woman nearing retirement and a younger man, both in khaki shirts, jeans and gloves—arrived to work around Carl, watering and pruning. They temporarily moved the plants so the sprawl of branches was dense enough to block the camera's view of Carl. While they worked, softly discussing movies and music, they turned away and Carl took the chance to reach into his shoe to pull out a slender burner phone.

It was a small high-quality phone he'd purchased in cash for one purpose only. At home, he'd removed the SIM card and disabled all wireless connections, ensuring it was signal-free—and now, carefully, surreptitiously, he palmed it. He made sure his monitor was cued to pages he wanted, then he slouched slightly in his chair, ensuring the bird of paradise and philodendron's big lush leaves were blocking him from the cameras and that the plant people were involved in their work. With his elbows on the armrests, positioning his hands as if paused in thought, Carl aimed the phone's camera eye, took a picture, then clicked through the report, photographing page after page.

With each photo he took, he thought of Hannah, and Vanessa, and how the walls were closing in on his life.

If I can get through it this one time, I'll be free and clear.

Carl's heartbeat surged. He could go to prison for this—the biggest gamble of his life.

It didn't take long.

When he was done, he tucked the phone back in his shoe, took a few slow breaths, then politely offered to assist the workers with moving the plants.

"You're so kind," said the woman.

38

NEW YORK

An eerie calm had descended on the deserted street of two-storey houses in the Woodhaven neighbourhood of Queens.

The NYPD's Emergency Service Unit truck was far down the block, where it served as the command post for the takedown and rescue operation.

It took time to set up. Word of police action spread fast as marked and unmarked units from the 102nd Precinct sealed the area to all traffic. Neighbouring residents in the line of fire had been quietly evacuated to safety behind police lines.

A hostage negotiator stood ready inside the command post where an ESU supervisor directed heavily armed team members to take up positions. Garlin and Lugano were near the commander and used binoculars to study the target house, the home of Robert and Nancy Cook.

It shortly after dawn on the sixth day of Dylan Ward's abduction.

The NYPD's Crime Scene Unit had recovered a partial print from the pen Dylan's abductors had used at JFK. They'd started with IAFIS, the FBI's Integrated Automated Fingerprint Identification System, then gone to state criminal record databases, which had come up empty. But the databases also included prints submitted for background checks required for certain professions. After a broader search, they got a hit on the partial, which the fingerprint analysts said was consistent for Robert Cook.

Records showed that Cook was sixty-eight years of age and a retired high school physical education teacher. Further investigation found that his wife, Nancy Cook, aged sixty-seven, was a retired bank teller whose fingerprints were also found in the databases. They both resided at the target address in Woodhaven.

Garlin glanced at his phone. The Cooks stared at him from their driver's licence photos. Identification analysts could now confirm facial recognition of the eyes from subway video images consistent with the driver's licence pictures. But the Cooks' fingerprints drove it home, making this a critical lead, bringing investigators closer to Dylan and the people who'd murdered his father. Garlin hoped the boy was inside and alive.

ESU members in body armour established a perimeter around the house, crouching under windows, pressing against its white vinyl siding. The Cooks' 2023 Jeep SUV was parked at the house; two members of the team used it as cover. Snipers were positioned at vantage points on neighbouring buildings.

Several moments passed, then the commander green-lighted the operation for a dynamic entry.

The tinkle of breaking glass sounded, followed by a loud bang, then a sizzling crackle. Then the bright sparking light from the flashbang grenades that were deployed. Within seconds, the team members rushed in through the front and rear doors.

39

NEW YORK

Jessie had spent the night at her hotel, going back and forth with her team in California trying to determine what Vaughn had been investigating before his murder. They needed to find out who his source was and how it could lead to Dylan.

Before going to bed, Jessie had called her mother. "I'm sorry I haven't been to see you, Mom," she said. "I've been away on business."

"I know," her mother said as Jessie heard the TV. "Don't worry, dear."

"How're you doing?"

"I'm fine. Honey, listen."

"Yes, Mom, what is it?" A long moment passed. Finally, her mother spoke again. "It's going to be okay, Jessica. You can visit me when you're done doing what you're doing. But it's going to be okay."

It was as though her mother was instinctively aware, through some cosmic genetic radar, of the horror she was battling. Holding her palm to her head, pushing back her anguish, Jessie said, "That's right. I love you, Mom."

As the sun rose on the sixth day of Dylan's abduction, Jessie made coffee and ate a bagel while checking the news and her email for updates. Finding nothing, she decided to get ready. She took a quick shower and was dressing when her laptop and phone pinged with a news alert. She checked it.

BREAKING NEWS: NYPD descending on Queens residence of persons of interest in JFK child abduction and murder of father: Sources

Her heart pounding, Jessie opened the alert. No additional information. She copied the bulletin into a request for the address, sending it simultaneously to Rich Lafont and Chelsea Webber at *Veritas Sola.*

As she was about to leave her hotel, her phone chimed with a response from Chelsea.

Just arrived. NYPD setting up.

Then another message with the address.

Accelerating and weaving through traffic, Jessie's cab made good time getting to Queens, then Woodhaven, rolling by shops, bakeries, restaurants, and into neighbourhoods of tightly spaced houses.

"This is as close as we can go." The cab driver nodded to the street ahead, which was blocked by a patrol car.

After paying, she got out and began running, a cold sweat emerging on her back as she scanned the scene beyond the patrol car. Everything closed off; thin lines of residents pointing, necks craned, staring far down the line of houses. The stillness of the surreal, funereal quiet chilled her.

Reality hammered at her.

It could end here!

With Vaughn's murder, a piece of Jessie's heart had been ripped away—

Now Dylan!

No! Please!

40

NEW YORK

Red-line laser lights and flashlight beams raked the haze of the house as the ESU team searched for Dylan and the Cooks. But every room was empty and everything was in order, down to the empty kitchen sink. They swept through each floor—the three bedrooms, halls and closets. They were all empty. The two bathrooms were empty, and so were the basement and attic.

They went through everything a second time before the team leader radioed his commander.

"Nobody here. Send in CSU."

Given the life-and-death circumstances and with the clock ticking, Garlin and Lugano, suited up in coveralls, face masks, gloves and boot covers, accompanied the forensic experts. Careful not to touch anything, they observed and searched for evidence to confirm if Dylan had been here.

The crime scene team photographed and video-recorded everything, noting how the beds were made, that there was little food in the fridge, that the trash was empty. Then they processed every inch of the place for fingerprints and DNA.

Lugano noticed a framed photo of a cat on the corner of a wall of the kitchen. A lower shelf space had a couple of frayed yarn balls, a dry water bowl.

"Looks like they have, or had, a cat."

"Maybe ESU scared it off," Garlin said.

"This place is pretty clean. It's like the people left for vacation," said one suited analyst.

"Or fled," Lugano added.

Garlin came to the desk. There was no computer, but there was a printer. They'd need to get warrants to access the ISP and look for any information. He studied the printer. The techs could try accessing the printing history. Next to it was a paper shredder. The shredder had a clear plastic top and Garlin could see that it had been emptied.

"Someone was being careful."

"And they recycled." The analyst with Garlin nodded at the plastic blue and green recycle bins on the floor next to the desk. Both were empty. Thinking about recycling, Garlin had an idea.

"Can you open the printer's paper storage tray and check it?"

The analyst looked at him.

"People who recycle will conserve," Garlin said. "Some will print on the clean side of used paper."

Nodding, the analyst opened the tray. Then he checked the paper, fanning it. It appeared to be blank on both sides until a few pages flashed with text.

Reading it, Garlin's eyes narrowed, and he cursed under his breath.

"I think we got something."

He pulled out his phone to take the photos himself.

41

NEW YORK

Jessie surveyed the locals, the gawkers, the news crews with cameras aimed at the distant house. Her breathing quickened at the sight of another crime scene, the yellow tape the flag of her never-ending horror. Eyes wide, she pushed through the chaos, searching for someone, anyone, with answers.

"Jessica! Over here. Jessica!" Chelsea Webber, phone and notebook in hand, waved, then ran toward her.

"Did they find him?" Jessie asked.

"I don't know. We heard that an older husband and wife live in that white house. See, the one by the blue SUV down there." Chelsea pointed. "We're hearing from sources that they may have found evidence linking them to the abduction at JFK."

"What evidence?"

"I don't know yet," Chelsea said.

"Oh God!" Jessie drove her fingers through her hair. "Is Dylan in there?"

"I don't know," Chelsea replied. "I haven't seen anyone brought out, or arrested."

Just then, Jessie saw ESU members and investigators in white coveralls pulling off face masks as they trickled from the house.

"I have to get inside!"

Attempting to duck under the yellow tape, she was stopped by a uniformed officer.

"Do not move, ma'am."

"I'm Jessica Ward. My son Dylan could be in there!"

"Keep behind the line, ma'am!"

"Please tell the detectives I'm here. Please!"

"Show me some identification."

Jessie fumbled for her driver's licence and Instinct ID, handing them to the officer. He turned and, reading from them, spoke into his radio. Listening with his earpiece, the officer waved over a uniformed cop, then lifted the tape for Jessie.

"Ma'am, come with me. Only you." Then he pointed at Chelsea. "You stay here behind the line."

The second officer and Jessie hurried down the street and straight past the house.

"Wait, where are we going?" Jessie asked, scanning the outside of the house for any sign of Dylan. "Did you find my son?"

"I don't know," the officer said, escorting her further along the block to the command post.

They neared a group of people who appeared to be residents being interviewed. Amid the uniformed and plainclothes police, Jessie spotted Garlin and Lugano.

Observing the people talking to police, Jessie read concern in their faces as they pointed and gestured while investigators took notes. Upon seeing Jessie, Lugano nudged Garlin.

Stepping away, they took her aside, but before they could reach a private spot behind the service truck, she let go with questions.

"Is Dylan in the house?"

"We're investigating," Lugano said.

"That's not an answer!" Jessie yelled. "Is he there?"

"We have not located him in the residence," Garlin said.

"Then where the hell is he?" she said. "Did you arrest the suspects? I want to speak to them."

"Ms. Ward, we're working to get answers, to determine who these people are," Garlin said. "To locate your son."

"How did you find them?"

"Our investigation led us to the people who reside here. They're strong persons of interest," Garlin said. "No one was located in the house, but this was a good break."

"We need you to get back outside the cordon," Lugano said.

"That's it? That's all you'll tell me?"

"That's all we can say for now," Lugano said.

As they began walking her back around the truck, Jessie again eyed the cluster of neighbours talking to police. Desperate, she rushed over to the group, interrupting the detectives with them.

"Help me, please!" she said. "I'm the mother of the missing boy!"

Surprised, the group looked at Jessie, recognition dawning.

"Hey, yeah, I saw you on the news," one man said.

"Tell me what you know about the people in that house."

"Ms. Ward, don't talk to these people." Lugano caught up to her. "We have to get their statements. Let us do our job."

Ignoring him, she pleaded with the neighbours. "Please, tell me what you know."

"Ms. Ward," Garlin said, "I have to warn you, do not obstruct us."

She met the sympathetic eyes of one woman, who looked at the man beside her.

"Nobody knew much. They were odd," the man said.

"What do you mean by 'odd'?"

"Kept to themselves. Spouting strange conspiracies."

"They were kinda spiritual," the woman said. "Some people said that, years ago, they—"

“That’s enough,” Lugano said. “Ms. Ward, we need to get you outside the cordon.”

“Wait! No!” Jessie said. “What do they mean about strange conspiracies?”

Lugano and Garlin didn’t answer, leaving Jessie back outside the tape.

The investigators traded a glance as they walked back to the command post discussing the paper found in the printer—left behind, as if forgotten by someone rushing to leave.

“What do you think?” Lugano asked. “The text on that sheet was about human smuggling and international trafficking rings.”

“It’s a critical lead,” Garlin said. “And if it’s true, this case just got darker.”

42

OTTAWA

Not wanting to wake Phil and Marissa, Claire had entered the house quietly through the kitchen door. In the dim, tranquil light, the digital clock on the microwave over the stove displayed 1:46 a.m.

It had been a long travel day. Her flight, thanks to a medical issue with a crew member, had been delayed leaving O'Hare. Despite her exhaustion, though, Claire's mind was racing. Propelled by the revelation of the vulnerability in SynerRapid's software upgrades, she started making coffee. She wanted to work on the logs.

As her coffee brewed, she surveyed the family bulletin board, noticing Marissa's pictures of the dogwood tree and the invitation to Tabitha's party. Pinned next to it was a brochure for a new furnace and air-conditioner with "$14K" written and circled in ink. She sighed. She'd been away for two days and life at home was already moving on without her. She *wanted* to be home with Marissa and Phil; she *wanted* to pick out that new tree and drive her daughter to birthday parties. Then she thought of the people killed in the subway crash. Their loved ones deserved answers. She picked up her coffee and her laptop, and went downstairs to her basement office.

Concentrating on the areas Jill Bailey had pointed out to her, she started at the beginning. The software update for the Toronto track circuit modules had been installed remotely, during off-peak hours.

Got it. Check.

The logs showed no anomalies after deployment, but some minor adjustments had been made.

Okay, adjustments are routine.

The logs showed no high number of unsuccessful attempts at unauthorized access, indicative of a brute-force attack. And Claire saw no attempts to change the system settings—nothing to show a breach.

But there has to be something.

Rubbing her temples, she recalled Jill noting how the logs could be overwritten or manipulated to obscure traces of a breach.

I know that. But where was it?

Jill had suggested that by developing and using AI-assisted malware, the attacker could alter or erase evidence of the attack, even bypassing intrusion detection systems.

But we know that.

Claire needed to determine where and how it had been done to prove the case. Once more, she scrutinized the data. The answer was there; she just knew it.

It was 3:20 a.m. when she went to bed. She suddenly woke with a start a few hours later.

Sighing, she reached for her phone. Nearly seven. She looked to her right. Rumpled sheets on Phil's empty side. She went to the bathroom, pulled on her robe, then went to the kitchen, greeted by the aroma of sputtering bacon. Phil was making breakfast and talking to Marissa.

"Hi Mom!"

Marissa put down her phone and sprang from the table, wrapping Claire in a long hug. Claire then kissed Phil's cheek.

"You got in late."

"Took forever to get home."

Claire went to her suitcase by the door, unzipped a pocket and pulled out two T-shirts. One for Marissa, one for Phil, purchased at O'Hare, each bearing a stylized "ORD" graphic. It was tradition for Claire to get them T-shirts when she travelled.

"So cool! Thank you!" Marissa admired her pink shirt.

Phil's was navy. "I love it, hon, thanks."

They ate breakfast together, and while nibbling bacon and toast, Claire caught up with her family, which was nice. Then Phil and Marissa got ready and left for the day.

As Claire showered, she thought about the logs and where to look for evidence of a breach. Suddenly, she knew. She dressed quickly, typed out a message to Will, then drove to the CSE building. As she sat at her desk, Will approached.

"Got your text," he said, pointing. "The small meeting room in fifteen?"

Claire nodded, answered a few emails, then went down the hall and joined Will and her colleagues, Nita and Marc, who were also working on the Toronto case.

"Guys, Claire's got something from SynerRapid," Will said as he closed the door.

Claire opened her laptop, syncing her screen with the room's larger wall-mounted monitor. Clicking her mouse and entering commands, Claire brought up the logs and gave a quick overview of the significant points, and told them how she'd been trying to detect the intrusion.

"Did you look at the CRC functions?" Nita asked.

"I did," Claire said. "We know an attacker can modify data, right?"

"Right," Marc said. He studied the logs. "Compare the latest checksum with the original, and you should see attempts at tampering."

"But," Nita said, "they can recalculate the checksum so that changes cannot be detected."

"You guys are on the right track," Claire said. "Fortunately, SynerRapid not only provided me with the software update logs, they gave me the backup logs they'd created as well."

"Oh, then you can compare them to identify discrepancies," Nita said.

"Which I did," Claire said with a smile. "At first, I found nothing. But then—look." She tapped her mouse, and the cursor highlighted a line on the log.

"This is the backup log." Another click, and the screen split. A line was highlighted on a second log. "See? The backup log is not consistent with the more recent log. Essentially, the malware missed here."

"I see it," Marc said.

"Now look."

Claire tapped her mouse is a flurry of clicks, then several new pages emerged on the large monitor.

"Look at the logs and readouts for the flickering incident on Line 2 and for Line 1, leading up to the crash."

"There it is, for Run 115," Marc said.

Claire glanced at her boss. Will's focus was welded to the monitor.

"Are you telling us," he began, "that the cause was a sophisticated attack resulting in the attacker taking operational control of the train and successfully crashing it?"

He turned to Claire.

She swallowed hard and started nodding.

"Yes, that is what I am telling you."

43

VIRGINIA

Approximately six weeks before Dylan Ward's abduction

Carl needed this to work out.

It's nearly over.

Still, ever since he'd handed the burner phone containing the classified report to Rod Tate at his shop in DC, the weight of his actions had been pressing down on him.

"We'll stay in touch," Tate had said, handing him another burner. "After the client reviews the data, you'll receive payment in three days."

It's been three days, Carl thought, pulling onto his street. He'd checked the new burner from Tate constantly. Nothing. He'd checked his own original burner. Nothing. As their house came into view, Carl froze.

Parked in his driveway next to Vanessa's Explorer was his father-in-law's red Ram pickup.

His reflex was to keep driving. But then, suddenly, Marv was standing near the Explorer, and they made eye contact. Escape was impossible.

I've got to face him and get this over with, Carl thought, the muffler on his Rogue giving a last rattle as he parked, then stepped into the driveway.

"Hello Marv."

Marv's face was devoid of warmth. He glanced at Carl's house, then glared at Carl. Shaking his head slowly, he said, "This better be the last damned time." He pointed a finger at Carl's chest and dropped his voice to a muzzled growl. "The last time. Does your MIT brain understand?"

Carl nodded.

"Get your shit together and take care of your family." Marv held him with an icy gaze and then climbed into his truck. Carl choked down his humiliation, watching as Marv's 1500 Big Horn rolled down the street.

Soon I'll shove every penny and every word back at you.

He checked his phones again. Nothing.

Inside the house, he found Vanessa at her computer, going through bills.

"Hi," he said to her back. "Where's Hannah?"

"In her room." Vanessa didn't turn around.

"How much did he give you?" Carl asked.

She swung around in her chair to face him. "He gave *us* ten thousand dollars."

The sting of her words made his skin prickle.

"Dad said we should try again with a debt counsellor and maybe look at a second mortgage, or refinancing."

Marv's involvement sickened Carl. "We're not doing that. I said I would fix things and I have."

"Have you?" She folded her arms. "Are you getting counselling?"

"No, not yet."

"Then how are you fixing things, Carl?"

He gave her the truth, wrapping it with fabrications. "I've got something going."

"Is this another surefire betting scheme?"

"No. Freelance work for some people in DC."

She tilted her head. "What people? What kind of freelance work?"

"Computer engineering for a private company," he said. "They're trying to get ahead of a competitor. I had to sign a non-disclosure agreement because they need to protect sensitive information. But, Vanessa, the pay is really good. It will help us."

She stared at him with a measure of skepticism. "I don't know what you're up to."

"Trust me, I am seriously going to fix things."

"We're hanging on by a thread, Carl."

He opened his mouth to reassure her just as a phone vibrated in his pocket. "I should take that."

He walked into the backyard. It was his own original burner phone. He looked at it. It was a text. Payment had come through.

Relief washed over him as he accessed the numbered offshore account he'd set up, one with strict banking secrecy. He was also using privacy coins employing a stealth address and mixers, to make transactions hard to trace. Once Tate sent the currency there, Carl would cash out using an exchange. Then he'd send it pinballing through other offshore accounts. But his relief was short-lived as he then noticed the amount he'd been paid.

What the—?

He called Tate, who answered on the second ring.

"Where's my one-fifty? You sent a thousand!" Carl struggled to remain calm, glancing over his shoulder at the house.

"It was a dated draft report."

"I gave you what you asked for. Pay me, because I'm done."

"No, you're not," Tate said. "You can do better."

"I've put everything on the line," Carl said through clenched teeth. "I'm finished. Pay me."

"You'll get paid when you give us more."

"You're not listening, Tate. Pay me, or I'll—"

"*Or you'll what?* What will you do, Carl? Let me remind you that with this report you've stolen and sold us, you've broken the law. And if it was whispered to *The Washington Post*, everyone in the country would know your name."

Carl didn't speak. Tate was right.

"Pal," Tate said, "you can't undo what you've done." He chuckled. "Is it sinking in? You're on the inside. Give them something of value, they'll pay you, and then you're done."

Reality hit him like a sledgehammer. *I've been set up. I was so desperate, I was stupid.* Gripping the frame of Hannah's backyard swing set, steadying himself, he squeezed the phone.

"It shouldn't be too hard for you to obtain information of the highest sensitivity concerning advanced technology," Tate said. "Given your position and your experience."

Carl nearly snorted. *Experience.* He'd had so much promise at MIT; now he was a low-level analyst and his life was in a tailspin.

He surveyed his yard, the laughter of happy neighbours and the aroma of barbecue floating over his fence and underscoring his crisis. Suddenly, he glanced up at his home and saw Hannah at the window looking down at him. He thought of the costs of the treatments she needed, thought of Vanessa, their crushing debt and his father-in-law's disdain for him.

He was trapped in circumstances of his own making.

All of this was his fault.

"Are you ready to work with us, Carl?"

44

OTTAWA

Hours after Claire had presented her findings to her director, she was on her way to lead an emergency task force briefing.

She and her colleagues arrived at the Canadian Centre for Cyber Security, a few miles west of the CSE building. Tasked with defending Canada's cyber assets, the CCCS drew from a number of experts. The branch was housed in the upper floors of a curved ten-storey glass building along the Vanier Parkway, overlooking the Rideau River.

Claire, Nita and Marc gathered with others working on the Toronto case, including members of the RCMP's cybercrime unit, known as NC3. No one in attendance had a security clearance level lower than top secret, and many were enhanced top secret. The best of the best in the country were now focused on the attack that had left five people dead and fifty injured.

Claire stood at the table in the centre's control room.

"A quick update to follow the summary we sent out to you earlier." She relayed what she'd discovered at SynerRapid's offices and how she'd received intel about a vulnerability in the software upgrades deployed in Toronto's subway system. How it had led to a hostile intrusion through which the attackers had gained control of the train and caused the crash.

"Let's see if I've got this," Otto Colt said on the video call from Toronto. "A fired SynerRapid worker, who had been responsible for upgrading the software implemented here in the TTC, hacked into SynerRapid's system to change his personnel records? And by doing so, left the door open?"

"Correct," Claire said. "And with the logs SynerRapid provided, and guided by the whistleblower, we confirmed the vulnerability was quickly exploited by threat actors. They're constantly searching for security gaps and excel at finding them."

"This is good work," said Larry Whitaker, from the TTC.

"Our goal today is twofold," Claire continued. "Because our investigation is ongoing, everything here is classified. But first we need to alert our urban rail systems."

"It's been done," said Diane Danley, a director with the federal Transportation Safety Board. "We've issued a confidential bulletin to all the major operators across the country—Montreal, Vancouver, Calgary, Edmonton, here in Ottawa, and others. We're instructing them to monitor all software updates, scrutinize any patches, safeguard against attacks and, if necessary, remove and replace equipment."

"Thank you, Diane," Claire said. "We cannot stress enough how important it is for our transit operations to be vigilant. Clearly, the other critical aspect here is to get on the attackers' trail. It will be difficult. What they've done is overwhelming and unprecedented. They're good. They've left us few breadcrumbs." She paused. "We cannot release details because this has become a criminal investigation, and we don't want to tip our hand."

"That's right," said RCMP superintendent Daniel Massey. "We're on the path to finding these actors and bringing them to justice. Let's get going."

In the control room, amid banks of monitors and screens, experts and analysts got busy at workstations, examining SynerRapid's logs and data from the Toronto subway system.

Like surgeons, they meticulously and painstakingly looked for a lead, a clue. An identifiable signature that would take them into a netherworld teeming with malicious actors and criminal organizations.

For not only were they working to pinpoint who was behind the attack, they had to ensure it didn't happen again.

45

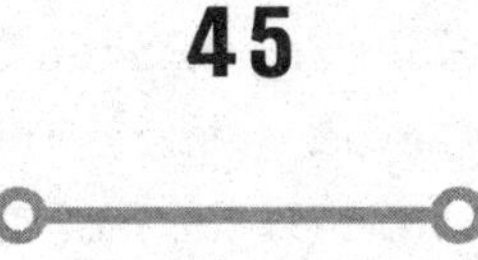

NEW YORK

"A retired phys ed teacher and a retired bank teller from Queens take a California boy from JFK. Maybe they murder his father and maybe traffick the boy," Lugano said, offering Garlin a stick of Juicy Fruit.

"There's more to this." Garlin shook his head, declining the gum. He looked at his phone and the photo of the page on human smuggling found in the printer. "We've got to keep digging."

Garlin and Lugano were following up on the statements collected by patrol in Woodhaven after yesterday morning's search of the Cooks' home. They moved from house to house, and to apartment buildings. Working with NYPD detectives and FBI agents, they were getting a clearer picture of the lives of Robert and Nancy Cook. Did they have any ties to Jessica or Vaughn Ward, or their family? Any suggestion of an affiliation with international trafficking rings? They were not in any US criminal database, and checks were also being carried out internationally.

State police were determining if the Cooks had been upstate in Bethel before or at the time of Vaughn's murder. Some warrants had been executed, but they were waiting on others. So far, investigators had determined that in the week leading up to the abduction, the Cooks had withdrawn a large amount of cash from their bank.

Beyond that point, activity on the Cooks' phones, social media, bank and credit cards had ceased.

They'd dropped off the grid.

What was most puzzling was that the Cooks seemingly had no known computer expertise—certainly nothing at the level required to hack into JFK's networks. So the FBI and NYPD cyber experts were continuing to work on that aspect of the case, to identify who was behind the hacking of the security cameras, the scrubbing of footage, the misdirection and the deepfakes.

After interviewing one neighbour, who said they'd once seen the Cooks sitting side by side at a nearby coffee shop working on a laptop, Lugano and Garlin stepped outside the house and compared notes.

"I figure the Cooks gotta be working with someone," Lugano said.

Garlin agreed. They were being sure to ask neighbours if the Cooks had any interest in any particular subjects or belonged to any groups. Nothing had emerged that might link the couple to international human trafficking. But they'd picked up pieces here and there, fragments of information, including rumours that the Cooks had been grappling with a past tragedy.

They came to the house six doors down—a neat red-framed two-storey home. They climbed the ten stairs to the door, which was answered by Ida Mahoney, a small woman in her late seventies with round glasses.

Sitting on her sofa, she offered Lugano and Garlin coffee. They declined, and she remarked on yesterday's police activity.

"They evacuated me from my house. So dramatic. I hope everything's okay." She reached down to stroke the two cats threading around her ankles. "The dark one is mine, Tony Mahoney. The light one is Marmalade. She belongs to Nancy."

"Nancy Cook?" Lugano asked.

"Yes, I'm cat-sitting for her and Bob while they're on vacation."

Garlin and Lugano glanced at each other.

"Do you have a contact number for them?" Garlin asked.

"I do. Is everything okay?" Ida looked concerned. "People are saying they're in trouble. Did they get caught up in one of those computer phone scams?"

"We're checking things out and need to talk with them," Lugano said. "Do you know if they're travelling with any children?"

"No. They don't have any kids." Ida reached for an address book and recited a phone number that the detectives quickly jotted down.

"Did they tell you where they went, or when they'd be back?" Garlin asked.

"No, they just decided to take a vacation. Which is funny, because they're retired. Anyway, Bob said they were going wherever the road took them."

"No general destination?" Lugano said.

"No." Ida shook her head.

"Their car is parked at their house," Garlin said. "Do you know how they travelled?"

"I'm not sure. Ned might know."

"Ned?"

"Ned Fletcher." She pointed with her chin. "My neighbour across the street. Used to be in the Army."

A few minutes later they were at a brick house with a bay window, and climbed the stairs to the door with a US flag above it.

A white-haired man with a buzz cut, wearing a flannel shirt and leaning on a cane, eyed them after they showed him their IDs.

"I got nothing to do with it." He adjusted his grip on his cane. "I want to cooperate, but I got nothing to do with it."

Somewhat perplexed, Garlin and Lugano followed him to his living room where he picked up a remote, switched off the TV and settled into his recliner. Garlin noticed a business card on the coffee table, catching the words "Criminal Defense Attorney." He threw a look at Lugano to point out the card.

Garlin decided to take a formal approach, informing the elderly man that it was a crime to lie to the FBI. "We'd like to record our conversation, is that all right?"

"I got nothing to hide so I'll cooperate." Fletcher sat up, leaned on his cane, then tapped the card. "But if you're here to arrest me, I'll exercise my right to shut up and call my lawyer."

Garlin set his phone to record, dictating the preliminary details.

"We respect that," Lugano said, "but what is it that you have nothing to do with?"

"I wasn't home yesterday, but I saw it's all over the news about Bob and Nancy, that they took a kid from JFK, which I don't believe by the way. I know they're a bit flaky, but taking a kid, I find that hard to swallow."

"Why would we think you had something to do with it?"

"Because they used my car."

A sudden silence quieted the room. "What do you mean, Mr. Fletcher?" Lugano asked.

"Look, Bob tells me his Jeep needs engine work and asks me if he can rent my RAV. It's new, and I don't drive it much, because my leg's getting worse. Anyway, I tell him to take it. Just pay for any service. He insists on giving me two thousand dollars in cash to use it for a few weeks." He pointed his cane to the TV. "I had no idea they were going to become like Bonnie and Clyde in my SUV."

"Mr. Fletcher, can you give us details, the VIN and plate."

"Sure, it's a white 2024 RAV4 XLE Hybrid. Plate number is . . ."

46

SÃO PAULO, BRAZIL

That same day, far from the investigations in Canada and the US, control operator Vera Ferreira touched the back of her hand to her moist brow.

Her boots crunched on the crushed stones of the tracks at the rail yards near Grajaú Station.

She was taking part in the initial probe into the near collision on Line 9–Esmeralda because it had happened in her zone. Assigned to the team of technicians and engineers analyzing the incident, she was drawing on her background studying engineering at the University of São Paulo. She had never graduated—she'd had to leave school to get a job to support her family when her father became ill—but she still possessed an enhanced understanding of signalling systems.

It was two days since two trains had come within feet of colliding head-on. Dozens of passengers had suffered minor injuries. Thankfully, no one was seriously hurt. Within hours, a preliminary analysis of Line 9's maintenance records showed that the entire affected segment had recently undergone scheduled repairs and upgrades.

Today, the group arrived with equipment and tools to continue its work, starting with the track switch—assessing the condition of the components for wear, failure and signs of external tampering.

"What is it, Vera?" Antonio, one of the engineers, had noticed that Vera had consulted her phone several times.

"There was the recent crash in Canada on the Toronto system, and I was wondering if there could be similarities."

"I get that," Antonio said. "We're aware. But it's best not to jump to anything. Toronto's still being investigated. In our business there are incidents of varying degrees around the world every day, right?"

"Yes."

"And we have incidents of varying degrees right here in São Paulo. So let's focus on our case right here."

Antonio and Vera came to a couple of technicians crouched in concentration at the rails near the crossover.

"Here we go." One of them pointed to a piece of trash lodged in the rail. "This would've prevented the switch from working properly. Likely got jammed in there after being blown about by that recent storm."

Using their gauges and other tools, they bent down, taking measurements and photographs. Other engineers physically removed the cover of the switch box. They connected cables to the control units and modules and reviewed the logs.

"Everything appears to be in order. Scheduled upgrade shows no anomalies." The engineer studied his screen. "However, there's an indication of a power outage, a temporary loss of power."

"Check the time of that outage," said a technician, her eyes locked on her own laptop. "I think it could've been a result of the storm leading up to the incident."

"Yes, it aligns," the engineer said. "And remember, there was the report of an outage at one of the substations that powers the line. The protection relays kicked in."

Vera observed and listened as the group carefully reviewed, probed and tested, then retested various aspects of the system. After a few hours, a preliminary theory had emerged.

"Our investigation is far from complete," Antonio said, "but it appears that this incident was a result of a combination of factors: storm debris lodged in the crossover causing a malfunction; a power outage with lingering effects on the remote signalling arising from module upgrades."

Antonio looked to the others for consensus. All were nodding, except Vera.

"But the trains accelerated and the operators reported their cab controls were unresponsive," she said.

"Yes, and it can be attributed to the factors we have just determined; it would be in keeping with the theory."

Vera looked to the technician who was giving a thumbs-up after completing another diagnostic test of the modules for the Automatic Block Signalling and Automatic Train Operation.

Her brows drew closer, her face tightening with uncertainty.

"Vera," Antonio said, "the failsafe systems worked. Our theory is valid."

At that moment, the frantic dispatches of the train operators replayed in her mind, amid the unyielding alarm chimes and blinking warning light at her desk.

Our controls are malfunctioning . . . nothing is working . . .

Now, standing at the track with the investigators, Vera drew in a breath and held it for a long time before exhaling.

"Could we be missing something?"

47

VIRGINIA

Approximately six weeks before Dylan Ward's abduction

At 2 a.m., Carl sat on the side of the bed, hair tousled, body tight. Unable to sleep, he glanced at Vanessa in the ambient light. She was breathing evenly. He went downstairs to the basement and his locked storage closet.

On a shelf, laptops from different eras of their lives were stacked. He never recycled them—you never knew when you might need them. He slid out one, its top covered in scarred stickers for the Patriots, Bruins, Celtics and Red Sox, reminding him of his successful sports betting systems while he was at MIT. Unwinding a power cord and finding an adapter, he fired it up. Soon he was searching old folders, his pulse racing.

I screwed up. Tate has me.

Carl had agreed to cooperate with Tate's demands earlier in the day because he had no other choice, but he'd negotiated a higher fee of $250,000. It felt right, for the level of information he was going to steal and the laws he would break.

His anxiety was carved into his face, which glowed in the light of the laptop's screen. What he needed was not entirely in the notes he'd kept while working on Professor Jackson's program. But just having the notes was illegal and could put him in prison. Even back then he'd thrived on taking risks, living on the edge.

And now he was free-falling, gambling with his family's lives.

How did I get here?

Years ago, he'd been considered one of the brightest and best. When he was among the small group of students at MIT selected by Professor Jackson for his classified government project, it had felt like the launch of an exceptional life. They'd worked at MIT's Lincoln Laboratory in Lexington, which researched and developed advanced technology for national security. They had to undergo background checks, polygraphs and sign oaths to secrecy in order to receive the security clearance. Nothing was allowed to be brought into the lab, and nothing could be taken out.

"You'll be conducting research and development for Project Gold Arrow Horizon," Professor Jackson had told the team. "You're going to hack into the most critical and secure networks with the goal of stealing data, disrupting systems or taking control."

He'd said the attempts would first be made on simulated targets, then they would move on to real-world targets in controlled exercises to stress-test responses and defences. The group would be divided into teams—half would design modes of attack, half would create modes of defence. Then the roles would be reversed. Each team was encouraged to unleash every skill, tool and concept to accomplish their goal. Jackson was aware that many on the team had won capture the flag competitions—global events that focused on the cybersecurity skills of ethical hackers.

Over the next few weeks at the lab, the attacking team launched countless cyberattacks, with the intruders pushing through known boundaries—breaking into systems showing vulnerabilities that could lead to catastrophe. At the same time, the defenders, in a see-saw battle, struggled to keep ahead of the hackers by developing incredible advance defence programs, implementing instant fixes or anticipating and shutting down attacks.

Like the others, Carl had thought the project was mind-blowing. Every individual on the team possessed superior talent, but the woman from California seemed to be a star on her own level. But in being sent into cyber war, challenging each other and testing systems, they were all gaining deeper knowledge, something that was not lost on Carl.

Using his card-counting skills he'd developed from his gambling, he employed his ability to do mental math and his heightened memory to essentially, and surreptitiously, look over his teammates' shoulders. At night, in his room on his laptop, he'd make notes of plans, codes and schemes he'd taken each day from the project.

A violation of his oath.

When Project Gold Arrow Horizon ended, Professor Jackson praised his team before disbanding it.

"Some of your achievements are remarkable," said Jackson, who years earlier had won a Nobel Prize for his work in computer engineering. "Your attacks and defences are simultaneously assuring and frightening. What some of you have shown is brilliant. Your concepts, such as the cutting-edge notion of an eternal key, may not be applicable at this time, but with the anticipated technological advances of artificial intelligence, I am confident they will become a reality."

Jackson concluded by saying that the members had shaped a cornerstone for developing, advancing and harnessing technology. He encouraged them, when going ahead in their careers, to develop and apply their ideas for the benefit of everyone on the planet.

Then Jackson had died a few years later.

Carl closed his laptop and dragged his hands over his face.

He knew that his notes from Project Gold Arrow Horizon did not hold enough to satisfy what Tate and his people had demanded.

But he also knew that some of his former colleagues who had participated in the project, who had gone off to accomplish great things, had government contracts in advancing cybersecurity.

And with his job at Quantico, he had access to those classified contracts and not all, but most, of the information related to them.

It would be a bargain at $250,000.

Now, to get his life back, all he had to do was pass it to Tate.

48

NEW YORK

Here they are. Unmasked.

The monsters who stole Dylan.

Eyes narrowing, fury reddening her face, Jessie studied the photos of Nancy and Robert Cook on her phone.

She saw similarities between Robert and Miller's weathered looks. Nancy's cheeks were like Lillian's. Yes, the Cooks could pass as the friendly neighbours next door, or anyone's grandparents, hiding behind the masks of ordinary people.

The banality of evil living on your street.

Chelsea had shared the Cooks' names and photos with Jessie after obtaining them from police sources the previous night. Jessie had then sent them to Bobby, Dahlia and Sarita in California. She'd also sent them to Miller, then called, asking if he and Lillian knew the Cooks.

"We don't know who they are," Miller said.

"Are you absolutely sure you didn't meet them somewhere?"

"Jessica, I'm telling you what we told the police: we've never seen them before."

And now, a week after Dylan's abduction, with the crime scene tape removed around the Cooks' house, Jessie returned to Woodhaven to pursue her own door-to-door investigation.

She encountered people who hadn't been home when the investigators had canvassed or when ESU had descended on the Cooks' house. With a sense of urgency, she tried showing people Dylan's picture on her phone, hoping he might've been spotted in the neighbourhood.

"I ain't interested," one woman said.

At another house, a man said, "Can't you read?" then tapped his window sticker: "No Soliciting. No Exceptions."

Others were more receptive.

"Oh my God, yes!" a girl in her twenties, with tattoos and a nose ring, told Jessie at her door. "I didn't see the boy ever. But I was home studying when all the drama happened."

"What do you know about the Cooks? Anything about their past?"

"I don't know about that. But once I was walking by their place, and the man was in the yard and said, 'Do you know there is more darkness than light in this world?' I said yeah, whatever. They were freaky."

Walking to the next house, Jessie continued shooting every fragment of information she learned to California. Someone in the neighbourhood had to know more about the Cooks.

She came upon two women in their forties. Eileen was walking a small white poodle. Her friend, April, was drinking a coffee. Within seconds of Jessie explaining and showing them Dylan's picture, they began nodding. The women had been evacuated when the police had moved on the Cooks' home and had told detectives all they knew.

"The Cooks were different," April said.

"How so?" Jessie asked.

"They were just . . . weird," Eileen said.

"Have you ever seen my son there?"

Both women shook their heads. They looked toward the Cooks' house as the poodle tugged on its leash.

"This is little odd," Eileen said. "But a year or so ago, I was walking Brandy, and then Bob was walking alone, and he just joined me and started opening up about Nancy's condition."

"What condition?"

"It seems she had a disorder where her sense of reality was off. She believed that they'd had a child that was killed as a teenager, or was kidnapped. I was stunned. Bob said that Nancy had never been pregnant, but she believed that they'd had this son, and at times it was too much for him."

Jessie felt a chill run down her spine. "Do you know if he got help for her?"

Eileen shook her head. "He never said another word. The next time I saw him it was as if he'd never spoken about it."

"You know," April said, "I'd heard that they got caught up with conspiracy groups online."

"What kind of conspiracy groups?"

April shook her head. "I'm not sure. All of this is just some neighbourhood gossip."

Jessie thought for a moment.

"Do you know if they were good with computers? Would they be able to hack into JFK security cameras?"

"No way," April said. "I mean, they're older than us and we get help from our kids. In fact, Bob asked my son, who works in IT, to help him once."

"Do you know what he needed help with?"

"Hold on, I'll ask Cameron." April turned away and made a call.

While she was connecting with her son, Jessie sent a few quick notes to California. Eileen bent down to snuggle Brandy and then looked to the Cooks' house.

"I'm so sorry for what you're going through," she said.

"Thank you."

"Okay, here's Cameron on video call." April held out her phone. "Go ahead."

On the screen, a man in his twenties waved and said, "Hello."

"Hi Cameron," Jessie said. "Do you remember what Robert Cook asked you to help him with?"

"He wanted to know what the dark web was and how to get on it."

"The dark web?"

"Yeah, strange. So I explained what it was, told him it was risky. But he still wanted to get on. So I helped him download the browser he needed. I told him how things worked and that he really needed to be careful, that it could be dangerous—lots of shady, illegal stuff."

"Did he say why he needed it?"

"Yeah, I asked him, and he just said he and his wife needed to go there for their volunteer work."

"What?" Jessie looked at Eileen and April. "Volunteer work?"

"Yeah, a bit mysterious. But that's what he said," Cameron said. "I have no idea what he and his wife were doing."

The poodle began fussing and yipping, which Jessie took as her cue to thank Cameron, April and Eileen before letting them move on. As she continued down the sidewalk, she sent another update to California. She came to the edge of a small park and sat on a bench absorbing what she'd learned. That Nancy Cook believed she had a dead son and that the couple had been on the dark web terrified her. *My poor, sweet boy.* Overwhelmed with despair, in the tranquility of the park, she broke down in tears. She prayed that Dylan was safe.

Minutes later, her phone vibrated. A video call from Bobby.

"Are you free to talk? Sarita and Dahlia are here too."

Pulling herself together, she took a quick inventory of her surroundings. She was alone. She inserted her earphones.

"Go ahead."

"We've looked at everything you've been sending us today," Bobby said. "Scoured social media for Robert and Nancy Cook of Woodhaven, Queens, using all of our resources to pinpoint their activity."

"Anything?"

"Nothing recent. We went back nearly two years," Sarita said. "Seems Nancy and Bob posted sunrises and sunsets with a hodgepodge of inspirational quotes."

"Then things changed," Bobby said. "About a year ago, they began posting about international trafficking rings and their growing concern arising from conspiracy theories."

"*Trafficking rings?*" Jessie repeated, her mind racing, marshalling all the disparate pieces of information about Nancy Cook's condition, Robert seeking help to get on the dark web, and now their posts about human trafficking. Her fears were swirling when Dahlia leaned toward the camera.

"I know this may not make sense, Jess, but could it somehow be connected to Instinct's cyber work?"

"What? But how? Why?"

"Look at the cyber elements. You have two senior citizens from Queens who not only attacked your family but had the skill, or had help, to pass as Dylan's grandparents, penetrate and manipulate JFK's security system, create deepfakes and vanish. They did all this with your family as the target."

"You think this is why they took Dylan and killed Vaughn?"

"There has to be a connection," Dahlia said. "Do you believe the Cooks did this on their own?"

"Bobby, didn't you reach out to friends about the deepfake video from Vaughn?" Jessie asked.

"Sally Yoon, an expert and good friend from Stanford, is still working on it. But she says it's complex."

"See," Dahlia said. "I think it further underscores that the Cooks aren't working alone in targeting your family or business."

"But why target *us*?" Jessie said. "Our work is secure. No one knows the details of Instinct's contracts. What do they want?"

"Maybe there's more to it," Dahlia said. "It brings us back to Vaughn and the story he was working on. Maybe he was going to expose something about trafficking? Or cyber threats?"

"Yes," Sarita said. "Remember his note said 'Need to meet with X. Inside source.'"

"Hang on," Bobby said, typing something on his laptop. "I just got into a private chat group and found other postings by the Cooks. Check this out. Saw all kinds of weird stuff."

He copied them into their group chat.

"Look."

Bobby indicated passages from the *Rubaiyat of Omar Khayyam*, T.S. Eliot, and one from Friedrich Nietzsche that said "What doesn't kill you makes you stronger."

A moment later, he said, "Here's a line from Scripture that says, 'Suffer little children, and forbid them not, to come unto me.' And look at this."

Then Bobby pointed out a post about volunteering for anti-trafficking action.

"*Volunteering*," Jessie repeated the word.

"Here's one about participating in rescue operations," Bobby said.

"Oh God," Sarita said.

Slowly Jessie's hand rose to her mouth. Vaughn's words to the editor at *Veritas Sola* rang in her ears. *Something big and deep and even dangerous.*

49

SANTA MONICA

After the call with Jessie, Dahlia returned to the office she'd been using at Instinct.

Everything they knew—the revelations about the suspects, the human trafficking angle and the JFK cyber intrusion—streaked through her mind. Then she went over all she'd done in the past few days, contacting everyone she knew in her search for the answers to Vaughn's murder and Dylan's abduction. She'd focused primarily on her fellow students from Cambridge. Most of them were from MIT. Vaughn and a few others had gone to Harvard.

She had zeroed in on Professor Jackson's team for Project Gold Arrow Horizon. There had been ten members, including herself and Jessie. She ran down the list again now. One member, Trevor-John Verse, an engineer with Signals Intelligence, had died after a fall while hiking in the Italian Alps. Over the last few days, of those left, Dahlia had reached every other team member but one.

Carl Lasker.

He was working for the Defense Counterintelligence and Security Agency, according to fellow team member Roseanne Wysner, who'd passed Dahlia his contact info.

But Carl hadn't responded.

Other members of the team had described Carl as "kind of a loner" but also "a gifted mathematician." One had said that she thought Carl was sneaky, always skulking, lurking around the opposing team during the capture-the-flag scenarios.

Dahlia remembered Professor Jackson praising Carl's skills, saying how he held such promise as a developer of cutting-edge technology. But now, Dahlia thought, with Carl apparently working as a low-level government analyst, he seemed to have fallen short of his potential.

Dahlia weighed the information.

How could anyone think this could have anything to do with Vaughn's murder and Dylan's abduction?

Those comments about him being a loner who was sneaky, and him seeming like a guy who hadn't realized his promise, continued running through her mind.

She looked at her notes.

His job was at the Defense Counterintelligence and Security Agency.

That could be it.

She reviewed the DCSA's roles and mission—and like puzzle pieces, everything fit.

Dahlia left her desk and rushed to Bobby and Sarita. "I think I'm onto something. Can you help me, guys?" They looked up from their screens. "Bear with me," she continued. "Instinct Nine-99 is working on developing advanced cybersecurity systems, correct?"

Bobby and Sarita nodded.

"But Jessie's received no ransom demands. Nothing."

"That's right," Sarita said.

"Your work's protected. It's safe. Few people know about it."

"That's right," Bobby said. "Everything's secured here, with me, with Sarita and with Jessie."

"It's set up so only Jessie can access everything at any time, even remotely from wherever she is," Sarita said.

Bobby shot her a warning look. She'd said too much.

"That's fine, that's good," Dahlia said.

"What's this about?" Bobby asked. "What're you onto?"

"Because a lot of Instinct's contracts are classified government work, you're required to go through all the intense background and security clearances, right?"

Bobby nodded.

"And you had to deal with the DCSA, the lead government agency tasked with conducting background investigations and vetting—with the goal of protecting IT systems from vulnerabilities and attacks."

"Yes," Sarita said. "The Defense Counterintelligence and Security Agency."

"Where're you headed with this?" Bobby asked.

"An MIT colleague of ours, who worked on a classified government program with us, works at the DCSA," Dahlia said.

Sarita looked at Bobby.

"What this means," Dahlia continued, "is that he has access to Instinct's sensitive information—and it's possible, just possible, that he may have been envious of all Jessie has achieved."

50

OTTAWA

Some monitors displayed topology maps with network switches, nodes and connections. Others showed logs, intrusion detection charts and graphs. Still others flowed with pages of code as experts dissected the data in the attack on the Toronto subway system.

Claire and the investigators were working late into the day at the Canadian Centre for Cyber Security, drilling down on vulnerabilities, cross-referencing information.

Racing against the clock, they were searching for the posture of the attacker, anything to indicate a unique signature that would lead to an arrest. But the hunt was complex and the trail sophisticated, because whoever was behind this attack was highly skilled.

Reviewing all the elements of the case again, Claire and her team crafted a basic primer outlining how the suspects could have taken control of a subway train. They might have used phishing emails to deceive a worker and thereby gained access to critical systems. Or they could have found vulnerabilities in the software, or anywhere along the supply chain, which was essentially what had happened here through SynerRapid's software update.

But Claire and her team had to go deeper now, to find more evidence.

Another avenue involved penetration tests to locate and exploit weaknesses, which they believed had happened with Toronto's Line 2. And above all, the attackers had needed to gain understanding of the transit system's automated process and operational network protocols.

The alert they'd sent out earlier across Canada was later released internationally. It had prompted queries from transit operators in the US, Europe, South America and Asia.

An inquiry from South America stemmed from a recent near-collision in São Paulo, but at this stage the initial investigation in Brazil was pointing to maintenance and weather-related issues. Keeping São Paulo in mind, the Canadian investigators pressed on, examining several fronts.

Some international operators had begun exchanging intelligence with Claire and her team. Everyone was aware that advances in technology had also increased security risks. Recent history showed that, globally, there had been several identified cyberattacks on transit systems. Claire and the team looked into them, some going back a few years.

In 2021, hackers affiliated with a hostile government had attempted but failed to infiltrate New York City's subway system. They had only got so far before the MTA's multi-layered security programs thwarted the attack.

A year or so earlier before the New York City hacking, equipment used by the Bay Area Rapid Transit system was probed by hackers who'd discovered back doors that were communicated to a hostile nation. It was believed that the system's weaknesses could have given attackers control over critical systems. The breach was detected, and corrective steps were taken before any disruption of the system was completed.

In 2023, in Italy, Rome's Metro was breached for three hours when criminal hackers took control of nearly all of the system's security surveillance cameras. In that same year, in Denmark, hackers exploited a contractor's software-testing process to attack Danish State Railways and force the shutdown of operations for a day. And a ransomware attack in Germany froze all display monitors on a regional rail system.

In Mexico City in 2023, hackers attacked the city's mass transit system, temporarily taking out its communications, disrupting payment systems and accessing the personal information of employees. A few years earlier, cybercriminals had attacked Philadelphia's transit system, disrupting operations and demanding a ransom to restore access. The trains were not shut down, but the attack interfered with scheduling and fare systems.

But in all the known cyberattacks on transit systems, there had never been a complete hijacking of a train. The incident in Toronto was believed to be the first.

Claire and the other investigators worked non-stop, sharing confidential details and data with their counterparts around the world. She was buoyed by the fact that the number of experts and analysts joining the hunt had grown. Glancing away from her screen to take a break and knead her neck, she noticed several analysts standing at the desk of one agent who was on a video call. She was leaning close to her screen, intensely discussing intel with a cybersecurity agent in Europe. Then, for the benefit of those near her, she nodded big nods.

"Got it." The analyst turned to the others. "We have a signature and a lead on the attackers."

51

NEW YORK

Identifying the vehicle used by Dylan Ward's kidnappers was a break in the case.

It meant investigators were gaining on Robert and Nancy Cook. But there were hurdles.

After confirming Ned Fletcher was the registered owner of the 2024 Toyota RAV4 XLE, Garlin and Lugano had given him his Miranda warning and checked his background. He was clear. He had no record. But Fletcher had refused to tell them much more. It took time, but with his attorney present, he cooperated.

Right off, investigators learned the stolen-vehicle GPS tracking service Fletcher had put in his car when he'd bought it had been disabled. This was also confirmed by the dealer. The RAV4's last known location was the Cooks' address in Woodhaven.

For Garlin and Lugano, those steps to disable tracking features further demonstrated skills and awareness on the part of the Cooks—or whoever was helping them. They expected the car would have been dumped by now, or the plates changed. Fletcher had given them additional identifying information about the car that they could hold back and use to filter tips. Above all, the lead on a vehicle accelerated the investigation.

Alerts for the SUV were submitted to NCIC, the National Crime Information Center, a central database for tracking information related to crimes. Alerts on the SUV were also submitted to the NYPD, county and state databases, including those in neighbouring states. All plate readers and toll, traffic and highway cameras were scoured, along with the CCTV at parking lots at, or near, major terminals.

The NYPD issued a new Amber Alert, and a dragnet had been cast.

At the same time, all attempts to track the Cooks digitally through their phones, any recent social media posts, and bank and credit card activity continued to hit a wall. The number they'd gotten from the cat-sitting neighbour, Ida Mahoney, was a dead end.

So, early on the morning of the eighth day of Dylan's disappearance, law enforcement officials gathered with media in the press room at NYPD headquarters at One Police Plaza in Manhattan for a news conference.

Bart Burrow, the NYPD's chief of detectives—flanked by special agents in charge of various divisions for the FBI's New York field office, and commanders from local, state and federal agencies—took the podium and got started.

"We have two strong persons of interest in the abduction of Dylan Ward from JFK airport over a week ago," he said. "Investigators with the New York Police Department, Transit, state police, JFK security, the FBI and many other agencies have been working non-stop. Today, we can bring you information that we have on the following two persons."

A large screen came to life with headshots.

"Robert Cook, aged sixty-eight, a retired high school physical education teacher. Nancy Cook, aged sixty-seven, a retired bank teller. Both New York residents, last known address in Woodhaven, Queens."

The screen split and a montage of clips from security cameras played, starting with those from the AirTrain at JFK to Howard Beach, then at other locations along the MTA system. In the images, the Cooks and Dylan were wearing face masks. Images were enlarged to focus on Dylan's jeans, his blue-striped running shoes with stains and his green backpack with a pattern of gamepads.

"Our investigation shows that upon his flight's arrival at JFK from Los Angeles, Dylan was abducted by two people posing as his grandparents. These two people are our persons of interest."

Another image showed the couple with Dylan on a street in Manhattan.

"They were last seen on the day of the abduction near Penn Station. And, in a key lead, we believe they are using this vehicle with the New York licence plate shown here."

Images of a white 2024 RAV4 XLE Hybrid appeared on the screen. A kidnapping poster issued by the FBI appeared, along with the NYPD's updated Amber Alert.

"We're posting and circulating all of today's images and information. Right now, we're asking for the public's help. If you have any information, call the Crime Stoppers tip line. There is a reward. Now we'll take a few questions. Please identify yourself and your outlet."

Burrow pointed to the first hand up.

"Kevin Aubin, *New York Post*. Is the murder of the boy's father upstate in Bethel related to the kidnapping?"

Burrow nodded. "We're looking into any possible connection." He pointed to another raised hand.

"Celeste Brown, NBC. Early in the case there was speculation online that this tragedy arose from a custody dispute with family members involved. Have you ruled them out now?"

"Until the homicide and abduction have been cleared, nothing and no one has been ruled out," Burrow said.

"But you have two persons of interest?" the reporter pressed.

"Yes," Burrow said. "We have two persons of interest and a vehicle. However, we have yet to determine whether they are connected to other people, other entities or linked to anything." He looked out at the reporters. "Yes, you."

"Ben McShane, *Daily News*. Chief Burrow, have you ruled out the Cooks for Vaughn Ward's murder?"

"As I already stated, until we find who is responsible for each act, nothing is ruled out."

"A follow," McShane said. "Are the Cooks connected to the Ward family?"

"All part of our investigation," Burrow said, pointing to the next hand.

"Juan Hernandez, CBS. Can you comment on speculation that Vaughn Ward's death and his son's kidnapping may be linked to a story he was working on? That this was an attempt to silence him?"

"We're looking at everything," Burrow said.

"Dianna Stanton, *New York Times*. Chief Burrow, can you confirm that the security camera system at JFK was breached as part of Dylan Ward's abduction?"

Burrow glanced to the other officials, then said, "We're looking into everything as part of our investigation."

"Sir, that's not a denial."

"We're looking into everything."

"Still on this subject," Stanton said, "Dylan Ward's mother has a cybersecurity company based in California. Considering the possibility JFK's cybersecurity was breached, have you ruled out any links to the mother's business?"

"Nothing has been ruled out."

"Evan Greene, Fox. Chief Burrow, can you comment on the speculation that the Cooks have links to trafficking rings?"

"No, we're not going to comment on speculation."

"Eloise Sanchez, Associated Press. Chief Burrow and the FBI people, have there been any ransom demands?"

"We can't speak to that," Burrow said.

"Another question. Do you have a working theory on the case?"

"We're following the evidence and the facts," Burrow said.

"Do you have any indication that Dylan Ward has been harmed or killed?"

"No. Aside from his abduction, we have no indication that he's been hurt. We have every reason to believe he is alive."

52

NEW YORK

"*We have every reason to believe he is alive . . .*"

Jessie's hand flew to her mouth watching the livestream of the NYPD's press conference on her phone. She was unable to make it on time because she was stuck in traffic due to a crash on FDR Drive.

As her cab inched along the parkway, her anxiety revved, tormenting her. She seized on the words of the NYPD's chief of detectives in a futile effort to remain calm.

When she finally arrived at One Police Plaza, she talked, then demanded, her way into the press room. But the briefing had ended. A few news people lingered in pairs and trios having side conversations with officials.

Spotting Lugano and Garlin, she went to them.

"Ms. Ward," Garlin said. "We'll talk over here." They took her out of earshot of the reporters and were joined by Bonnie Chase and Leon Deckert, the state police investigators she'd met at the lake.

"We looked for you before this started," Lugano said.

"Got stuck in traffic, so I streamed it," Jessie said. "Are you closer to finding Dylan?"

"The Cooks and the vehicle are solid breaks," Garlin said.

"What about the Cooks' interest in trafficking rings?"

"We're investigating," Garlin said.

"You keep telling me that!" Jessie's voice rose. "After all I've lost, all I'm going through, this is what you tell me?"

"We have to protect the integrity of the investigation in order to prosecute those who are guilty," Lugano said.

Jessie looked at Chase and Deckert.

Deckert said, "Ms. Ward, did you know the Cooks? Or have any relationship with them?"

She was taken aback. "Why ask me that? Of course not. They're complete strangers!" She shook her head, her voice cracking, "Jesus!"

"We know this is hard." Lugano's tone was soft. "But we are making progress with this new information."

"I can't do this." Fighting tears, she walked away.

Jessie hadn't gone far before a few lingering reporters approached her. The lights of two cameras came on.

"Can you give us a statement today, Jessica?" One reporter extended a microphone. Two others recorded with their phones.

"It's been eight days now," Jessie said, "and to the people who know where my son is, I beg you, please don't hurt him. Please let Dylan go."

"Do you know why Dylan was taken? Is it related to your husband's journalistic investigations? Is it related to your company's work?"

"No, I don't know."

"Have you received any communication from the kidnappers?"

"No, none."

"If your son should see this news coverage, what would you say to him?"

Jessie paused, emotion rising as she looked into the camera and spoke. "I love you, Dylan. Be brave. I will find you." Her chin crumpled, but she stayed in control. She held up her hand. "Thank you."

She stepped away and into the restroom to collect herself. As she washed her hands, she met a stranger in the mirror, a woman whose cheeks were sunken, her mouth drawn in. This was the toll the horror and exhaustion had taken.

But she didn't care.

Her eyes were fierce.

She ran a hand over her face. She wasn't going to stop looking for Dylan. Coming out of the bathroom, the hall was deserted but for two people talking at the far end. She recognized one as Chelsea, the reporter from *Veritas Sola*. Jessie watched as she typed on her phone, then read a response and typed again. A few seconds later, when she looked up, she spotted Jessie and made her way over.

"Jessica, hi," Chelsea said. "How are you holding up?"

Jessie shook her head. "No one will tell me anything."

Looking around, ensuring they were alone, Chelsea dropped her voice. "I have some information."

Eyes widening slightly, Jessie listened.

"I have a lead near Bethel."

Jessie gut tightened. "Where Vaughn was killed?"

"Yes, this may be a lead to a source Vaughn was going to meet before he was murdered. I'm driving up there now."

"I'm coming with you."

53

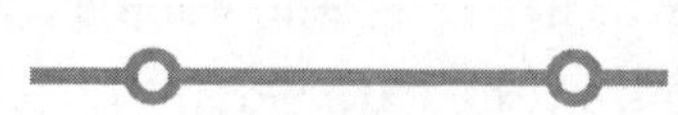

VIRGINIA

"Get upstairs, Hannah, and brush your teeth. Jodi's mom is on her way!" Vanessa finished packing Hannah's lunchbox and looked at the clock. The carpool would be here in a few minutes.

She turned on the TV to check the weather just as her husband returned from his morning run, his T-shirt damp on his chest and armpits.

"Good run?" Vanessa said, keeping her attention on the TV.

"Yeah." Carl, still breathing hard, got water from the fridge.

"A storm's coming this afternoon," Vanessa said, studying the forecast, confirming Hannah would need her raincoat. A commercial came on, advertising a sports gambling site. Vanessa picked up the remote and said, "We don't need to watch that."

Ignoring the comment, Carl turned to head upstairs. "I'm hitting the shower."

Vanessa was about to change the channel but froze when the morning show returned with a breaking news chyron at the bottom of the screen and a sober-faced anchor.

"*We're back, and we're going to take you live now to New York City, to join a news conference in progress, with updates on the case of the California boy abducted at JFK and his father's murder in upstate New York.*"

"I heard about this." Vanessa increased the volume.

"Me too." Carl stopped to watch, his curiosity morphing into concern.

It was nearly two months since he'd passed classified data to Rod Tate—who, satisfied with the highly sensitive information, had initiated payments. So far Carl had received $35,000 in installments, a few thousand at a time. More was coming, but the payments had been stalled, making him anxious. Because it was still far short of the $250,000 he'd negotiated.

To date, he'd given most of the $35,000 to Vanessa, which she'd accepted with suspicion.

"This is a lot of money, Carl. Swear to me you're not gambling."

"I swear I'm not gambling on sports. This is from the freelance job I told you about."

In the last few weeks, with the influx of cash, Carl's life, and that of his family, had improved. They'd made payments for Hannah's drug therapy, caught up on bills and chipped away at Carl's gambling debt. Not only did it keep Vanessa and her father out of Carl's face, he'd also gotten the muffler repaired on his SUV.

And because he couldn't stop himself, he'd placed a few bets on the side. Not on sports, but on the death dates of ageing celebrities. He'd kept his wagers small, because the huge gamble he'd taken with his life was paying off.

Or so Carl thought. Until now.

He swallowed hard, his Adam's apple moving up and down as Jessica Ward appeared in his living room pleading for her son.

"*. . . to the people who know where my son is, I beg you, please don't hurt him . . .*"

Vanessa looked at him, shaking her head. "Dear Lord. That poor mother. Do you know her? They're saying she went to MIT."

He just stared at the TV, rooted where he stood.

"Carl? Do you know her?"

Snapping out of his daze, he shook his head. "Come on, Vanessa. How would I know her?"

"Well, they said she was an MIT grad, an expert in computer engineering and has a computer security business. It's possible."

"I don't know her," he lied, a crease emerging on his forehead.

Vanessa looked at him. "Are you okay?"

"I'm trying to remember. A lot of people went to MIT, a lot of different subjects and disciplines."

"It's such a terrible story."

"It is," he said.

He'd first learned of Jessica's story when it surfaced online more than a week ago. He was initially concerned until reports suggested it was a case of parental abduction, that Jessie and her ex-husband were fighting over custody. But day after day, more facts about the boy's disappearance had come to light, and more and more MIT classmates had reached out to him. They'd asked if he knew anything to help Jessica, which escalated his worry. Carl hadn't responded to a single message.

But Dahlia Wynn was relentless.

Carl had never liked her. She gave off a strange vibe—always eyeballing him, always watching everyone. He'd always wondered what her deal was. So he didn't answer her messages.

On the TV, two photos appeared—Robert and Nancy Cook, the persons of interest in the disappearance of Dylan Ward. Fear coursed through Carl. Long before the abduction, he had sold to Tate material that included his old MIT notes from Project Gold Arrow Horizon, including some detailed concepts. But the sweetener was data from the Defense Counterintelligence and Security Agency on classified contracts from a range of companies doing business for the government, including those for Instinct Nine-99.

Jessica Ward's company.

Consumed with his own troubles, Carl had never thought ahead. Never thought this thing through. He'd never considered what could happen once he sold the information to Tate. He had been so desperate. But now, watching the news, reality dawned on him. *They may have used the information I gave them to get to Jessica Ward and her family.*

"Law enforcement officials say they are confident that they are close to locating Dylan Ward," the news anchor was saying.

Carl swallowed. Were they connecting the dots? Could they connect anything to him?

"It's so awful," Vanessa said, turning the TV off. "I can't even imagine something like this happening to us—if someone took Hannah."

"I don't want to think about it," Carl said, as his phone vibrated.

He pulled it out of his pocket and looked at the screen.

Another text from Dahlia.

54

SANTA MONICA

Running on a few hours of sleep, Dahlia had arrived early at Instinct Nine-99.

In the elevator, she looked at her phone. No response from Carl Lasker. She'd texted him an hour ago, but he still hadn't replied. She took a breath. It wasn't just that he hadn't been in touch; other factors were giving rise to her apprehension.

Bobby and Sarita were already at the office and had just finished meeting with team members who had worked late in their round-the-clock search for Dylan. As she made her way over to them, she noticed people gathering in the boardroom.

"What's going on?" Dahlia asked Sarita, nodding toward the boardroom.

"The NYPD just held a press conference about Dylan. It's replaying on CNN's news cycle," Sarita said, with Dahlia following her to the meeting room where Bobby had cued a video up the big screen.

They watched the replay as officials gave an update on the case. Some Instinct people were taking notes. Then Jessica appeared, making an anguished plea for Dylan's return. Soft sighs and groans floated around the room.

Sarita said, "She's going through hell."

"She really is," Dahlia said, shaking her head. "How much is she supposed to suffer?"

The news conference ended, and Bobby turned to those at the table. "The new leads give us more to work on too."

"Let's see if the Cooks are connected to Carl Lasker in the Washington, DC, area," Dahlia said.

"Why? Who's he?" Sarita asked.

"The guy Jessie and I knew at MIT that I told you about."

"Hold on." Bobby's eyes were on a new message he'd received. "It's Jess. She's with a reporter from the news conference chasing a lead. She says she'll tell us more when she can." He put his phone down and looked at Dahlia. "So, Carl Lasker," he said, "the guy at DCSA. What about him?"

"At MIT Jessie and I were on a small team chosen to work on a classified government research project. Carl was also—"

Dahlia's phone vibrated, and she glanced at it.

"I don't believe it—it's him. It's Carl," she said. "Of all the people I reached out to, Carl was the only one who didn't answer. He finally responds!" She read his text aloud. "*Been busy. Sorry. Terrible what's happened to Jessica. Wish I could help.*"

She looked at Bobby and Sarita.

"He *wishes* he could help?" Bobby said. "He'd have access to a lot of data. Wouldn't he know if the DCSA was concerned on any level after the abduction and murder?"

"I'll push him." Biting her bottom lip, Dahlia typed a response.

You can help! Aren't you with DCSA with access to her company's contracts and information?

"What else can you tell us about him?" Sarita asked.

Dahlia thought for a moment. "Carl was, well, an outlier. He was a brilliant super-achiever but something of a loner." Her phone buzzed, and after reading his response, she held her phone out to the others.

"I'm not aware of anything. And if I were, I couldn't discuss it," Sarita read.

"Wow," Bobby said. "Sounds like a brush-off."

"Seriously." Sarita pursed her lips. "If Jessie's a former college friend, wouldn't he want to help in some way?"

"What is it with him?" Bobby asked.

Dahlia shook her head. "I remember that he could do huge math problems in his head and was pretty good at analysis and calculating odds. He got into betting on sports. But from what I and others recall from our work on the project, Carl was regarded as, well, sneaky."

"Sneaky?" Sarita said.

"He seemed to lurk, spy on the work of others, that sort of thing."

"And now, working at the Defense Counterintelligence and Security Agency, Carl conceivably, potentially, has access to Instinct's classified info," Sarita said.

"Conceivably," Dahlia said. "While I can't confirm it, I have a bad feeling about him."

"He's seemed kind of evasive, cryptic, even cold with his responses," Sarita said, "considering how you and Jessie knew him."

"I don't trust him," Dahlia said.

55

BETHEL AREA, UPSTATE NEW YORK

"Covering this story, we cast a wide net."

Chelsea Webber was at the wheel explaining how she'd gotten her lead on Vaughn's murder as they drove along the parkway with Jessie's pulse pounding.

"Anyone can DM *Veritas Sola* through our social media," Chelsea said, passing a slow-moving semi. "A woman working at a restaurant near Bethel contacted me saying she knows something about Vaughn."

"What could she know?"

Chelsea shook her head. "She'll only talk in person and won't talk to the police, which could mean anything. Restaurant workers see and hear a lot. Let's see what she knows."

Jessie agreed, gazing at the forests as the miles rolled by.

Eight days.

Eight days since Dylan's abduction, Jessie's nerves tingled as she gripped her phone. She sent a message to the Palm Breeze, asking the staff to let her mother know she was still away on business and that everything was okay, wincing at not being able to tell her mother the truth.

It's better this way.

She turned to the window, remembering the last time she'd travelled this road with Vaughn and Dylan, and how much they'd laughed during the drive. Her heart ached, and she heard her son's words in her ear again.

I liked it better when we all lived together.

A surge of guilt washed over her. She'd loved Vaughn—she didn't think she'd ever stopped loving him. For a time, they had been so happy.

We should have tried harder.

Suddenly visions of Vaughn's car being pulled from the lake came to her, and she closed her eyes. She had to find out what had happened. She had to find out who X was.

The rhythmic clicking of the turn signal brought Jessie back to the present as they neared the beautiful Bethel area.

"We made good time." Chelsea consulted the GPS system on the display screen of the news outlet's Jeep. She nodded ahead to a building and a roadside sign: "Four Jays Motel & Diner."

"Here we go," Chelsea said as she parked the car and turned off the engine.

A bell above the door rang as they entered and were greeted by the aroma of coffee and fried food. The song "Mr. Tambourine Man" floated from the music system.

"Sit anywhere you like," said a woman wiping the counter. "I'll be right with you."

The dining room was a fair size with a few customers here and there. Chelsea scanned it before leading them to a somewhat private booth. A moment after they were seated, the woman—"Lottie," according to her name tag—appeared with laminated menus.

"Just coffee," Chelsea said, turning to Jessie.

"Coffee's fine."

"Alrighty." Lottie took the menus from the table.

"Excuse me." Chelsea kept her voice low. "We're supposed to meet Rose—she says she works here. Rose Sanger?"

"Rose?" Lottie nodded, glancing at a woman sitting alone in the far corner booth. "I'll send her over."

A minute later, Rose was at their table, sitting next to Jessie. She was in her thirties, with shoulder-length, softly layered hair. She wore a printed top, fitted jeans and thick-soled sneakers.

"Which one of you is the reporter?"

Chelsea lifted a few fingers.

"Show me your ID."

Chelsea's eyebrows climbed slightly before she got her *Veritas Sola* ID out of her wallet.

Nodding at it, Rose turned to Jessie. "Are you a cop?"

"No."

"Who are you? Wait!" She narrowed her eyes. "You're the mom, the wife. I saw you on the news." Rose looked around, satisfied no customers were nearby. "Sorry to get fired up, but listen, here's the thing: my husband is in prison. He was set up. I won't go into it. He'll be out in six months. If I'm talking to police, it looks bad. You understand?"

"Totally," Chelsea said. "Thanks."

Lottie returned and set down two coffees.

"Want anything, Rose?"

"I'm good," Rose said.

"Ladies?" Lottie asked.

"I don't think so," Jessie said, shaking her head.

Once they were alone again, Jessie asked Rose what information she had.

"Your husband was here. I served him."

"When?"

Working it out from work shifts and prison visits, Rose landed on a date several days before Jessie had put Dylan on the plane to JFK.

Jessie swiped through her phone for a photo of Vaughn. She held it out. “Are you sure it was him?”

“One hundred per cent. Listen, it was crazy up here when they hoisted his car out of the lake. There was all the news with his picture, talk about how he was some hotshot reporter. I knew it was him. I served him right here”—she stabbed the table with her finger—“before he was found dead.”

Jessie winced at her words, and Rose touched Jessie’s shoulder.

“Sorry.” Rose blinked fast, looked away.

“May I record this conversation?” Chelsea said.

Rose shook her head.

“Can I take notes?”

“Okay, but you cannot use my name.” Rose looked at both women. “I’m not a bad person. I want to help. I read how any piece of information can help, so I want to help.”

“What do you remember?” Chelsea said.

Rose paused, as if replaying the scene in her mind. “He was in that booth in the corner for the longest time.” She nodded toward the window. “He was alone. He seemed anxious and kept looking outside like he was expecting someone.”

Jessie held up photos of the Cooks. “These people?”

“No.”

Jessie quickly swiped to photos of Vaughn’s parents.

Rose shook her head again. “No, what I mean is I didn’t see him meet anyone.”

“That’s it? That’s all you have to tell us?” Chelsea said.

“Well, see, all he had was coffee, and whenever I came round, I would overhear him on his phone saying things like ‘Where are you?’ Things like that.”

“Did he say a name?”

Rose shrugged. “Didn’t hear one, and he was concentrating on his computer.”

"Did you notice anything, any details on his screen?" Chelsea asked.

Thinking hard, Rose slowly shook her head. "No, no . . . Wait, hold on. I saw a word in larger type. I think about an insect or something. Maybe it was a spider. I don't know."

Chelsea glanced at Jessie, who shrugged, puzzled.

"All I remember is that he seemed stressed and like he was waiting for someone."

"Did he meet anyone outside when he left?" Chelsea asked.

"I don't know, because my shift was ending, so I settled up with him. He paid cash and was still here when I left."

Jessie suddenly had a thought.

"Who might have served him after you left?" she asked.

Rose turned to the counter, where Lottie was slicing portions of pie. "Lottie."

Rose got up and went over to her. They talked briefly, with Lottie looking at the women a few times. She followed Rose back to the table.

"Go ahead, tell them," Rose said. "It's okay."

"Well, yeah." Lottie glanced to the empty corner booth where Vaughn had been seated. "I got him coffee. I think maybe someone did come in and sit with him."

"Was it a man or a woman?" Jessie said. "Can you describe them?"

"No, he kind of waved me off, like they didn't want to be bothered. Besides, I really don't remember much on account of this big family group came in. It was someone's birthday. I got pretty busy."

"A birthday?" Chelsea asked.

"Yeah, for a little girl—with presents, cake and everything. Marleen Warton's daughter. Marleen used to work here."

"Where did they sit?" Chelsea asked.

Lottie pointed to tables not all that far from Vaughn's booth.

"People take photos and videos at these things. Did Marleen's group do that?" Chelsea asked.

"For sure, lots."

Chelsea and Jessie looked at the tables and the angle to where Vaughn had been sitting with his mystery guest.

"Is there any chance we could get Marleen Warton and her family to share the videos they took so we could look at the background?" Jessie asked.

Lottie looked at Rose, then said, "I can find out."

56

SÃO PAULO, BRAZIL

At the public square, in the shade of the palms near the Fountain of Wishes, Vera Ferreira studied her phone.

Lips pursed, her body tense, she had to know how two loaded trains had come within seconds of colliding.

So many people would've been killed, if not for God's grace.

It had happened on Vera's line, on her watch, and she needed to know why. She opened a document on her phone that outlined previous incidents in the system.

Could there be a link to the near crash?

About six years ago, a Line 7 train had skipped one station due to a signalling issue, but was stopped safely without injuries. A couple of years later, two trains on the Line 15–Prata monorail collided head-on at low speeds. It had happened during early morning marshalling, and the trains were empty. One driver received minor injuries. Again, signalling was a factor. More recently, a train had derailed after intense rain triggered a mudslide near a tunnel. No passengers were aboard, and there were no serious injuries.

Over the years, there had been other instances of things that had gone wrong. "But like all major transit systems everywhere, these things happen," as one investigator, who was leaning toward the theory that weather and maintenance were the factors in the Line 9 case, had told her. "The failsafe systems worked."

True, they work, but not every time, Vera thought.

It was the panic in the drivers' words during those desperate, frantic seconds that told her there was more at play here. Both drivers had been questioned extensively by senior investigators and law enforcement, but Vera needed to speak to them on her own. That's why she'd asked that they meet her privately, outside of an official setting, here at Praça Ramos de Azevedo near the fountain.

She knew them vaguely from department meetings and had a good rapport with them. She gave a wave when they approached. Miguel Vita's hair was tousled, and Marco Mauro had not shaved. Both were on stress leave and appeared to have had sleepless nights.

"Thank you for meeting me," Vera said.

"We've cooperated fully and want assurances," Miguel said.

"This is a conversation only with me, your controller."

The two men traded glances, acknowledging that Vera was the one who had done all she could to help them. They nodded, then over the next several minutes, recounted everything about that day and the events leading up to the near crash.

"Like we said, something bizarre happened," Miguel said. "For those moments, nothing we did worked."

Rubbing the back of his neck, Marco said, "It was as if someone else took over the train."

Their account filled Vera with dread because she had recently learned that in the wake of the deadly crash in Toronto, Canadian investigators had issued a bulletin advising transit systems to monitor software updates and examine any patches *to safeguard against attacks.*

And she knew the recent upgrades to Line 9 had involved software updates.

"What do you think happened, Vera?" Miguel asked.

"I think that what happened on our line could go beyond maintenance or weather issues."

"What do you mean?"

"It could've been a cyber intrusion," she said, biting her lip. "And it's part of something big that is only going to get bigger."

57

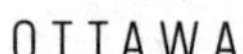

OTTAWA

"In examining the material supplied by Canada, we found that the intruders left a few tiny traces," Jürgen De Jong said from The Hague.

De Jong was an analyst with Europol's European Cybercrime Centre and had joined the search to identify the hackers in the Toronto subway attack.

Today, he was a primary speaker on an international call, coordinated with law enforcement agencies in Canada and the US, where it was still morning. Referring quickly to his notes, he continued.

"They covered their tracks well. But we found bits of code, artifacts unique to a powerful, emerging group—a sprawling web of the best criminal hackers in the world, known as Tarantula."

"We know there's a growing number of dangerous players out there," Claire said from her desk in Ottawa. "But we've seen little intel on this one."

"They've come on like a storm," De Jong said. "We've attempted to track them within the last year, as have our colleagues in other countries."

"That's right," said Rayford Cogan, with the FBI's Cyber Division. "No one was publicly identified as the suspect, but we believe Tarantula committed massive ransomware attacks in Las Vegas six months ago."

Claire nodded.

"That attack stopped two major hotels cold," Cogan continued. "All computers and slot machines and hotel networks went dark. Elevators stopped, room keys failed—everything, and I mean everything, went down. The attackers demanded and got close to fifty million dollars from them."

Another participant appeared. She was from London.

"Again, little was reported, but we believe Tarantula was behind the attacks of several banks in Manchester and Birmingham," said Polly Rowson, with the UK's National Cyber Security Centre.

"How much do we know about Tarantula?" Claire asked.

"BSI's been pulling together recent information," Rowson said. "Over to you, Vivien."

Vivien Schuller worked with Germany's leading cybersecurity agency, BSI.

"We know Tarantula's members are young, phenomenally skilled criminal hackers, predominantly from English-speaking countries, who hang out and scheme on the dark web," she said. "They chat, and brag; groups can buy and sell software, malware, even extort data, hire out developers to build whatever you need, or be contracted for criminal activity."

Claire's eyes widened, and she took notes.

"Members of Tarantula live to orchestrate the biggest attacks causing the most havoc," Schuller continued. "The Toronto tragedy, being the unprecedented, successful hijacking of a major transit system, would be praised as a triumph of legendary scale. Now, we don't yet know which tentacle within Tarantula was behind the Toronto tragedy. But in collaborating with our partners, like the FBI, we've recently come to learn more about the group."

"Yes, this is where things become more troubling," Cogan said. "We know Tarantula has drawn praise from some of the worst cyber gangs in existence, like Ice Wolf."

"Yes, Ice Wolf has been operating for a while," Claire said.

"We believe Tarantula has joined forces with Ice Wolf."

Claire exhaled. "That's not good."

"It gets worse," Cogan said.

"Much worse," Schuller added. "This has caught the attention of hostile nations, who've already been backing Ice Wolf, using them with other criminal groups as a proxy, or tool, to support various penetration tests and attacks on other nations."

"Consider this," Cogan said, "we know hostile nations are using cyber threats against other nations with a mix of strategies. We know they have attempted to employ artificial intelligence and social engineering aimed at infiltrating critical infrastructure with malware. The goal is to lie in wait on those networks, then to unleash unfathomable harm at a time and place of their choosing. Imagine the damage that could befall electric grids, gas pipelines, water treatment plants, hospitals, transportation and telecommunications systems . . ."

"We face incredible battles," Rowson added.

"There are ongoing classified efforts to develop protections," Cogan said. "Technological shields, or keys, to keep systems secure. But bear in mind, we are now facing an unholy alliance of hostile nations using advanced AI, in alliance with cyber terrorists, including those who are younger, faster and more skilled, which makes them chillingly good at what they do."

"Yes," Schuller said, "the Toronto attack was not only a major victory for Tarantula, but it escalates the situation. We are, in fact, facing elevated aspects of state-sponsored cyber war, with time ticking down on us every day before the next event. Of course, we're aware of several recent low-level incidents in Athens, Osaka and Cairo. Things like stuck doors, platform overruns, axel and brake performance. All attributed to mechanical or human error. What's the status of the São Paulo incident?"

"They queried us yesterday," Claire said. "At this point they're looking at maintenance and weather as the cause. But they stress it's early in the investigation."

"Good to know," Cogan said. "In light of Toronto, our job is to track down the players, neutralize them and dismantle their organization. We have a lot of work to do. We're drafting a bulletin on Tarantula to go to cybersecurity agencies throughout the world. We need to keep working on this."

The call ended, leaving Claire uneasy. She gathered her things and said little to colleagues as she exited the boardroom at the Canadian Centre for Cyber Security and returned to her station. At her desk, she reached for her phone. She needed a moment.

Claire looked at the photo of Marissa hugging a white golden puppy at the rescue shelter. She smiled.

You're so smart, and so right, honey. There's always hope.

Claire's computer chimed, and she checked her email. It was an encrypted message from Rayford Cogan. Using the code sent to her by text, she opened the draft of the bulletin. It was good, conveying all the critical information, alerting law enforcement and cybersecurity people around the world.

She sighed. It felt like a lifetime, but it hadn't been much longer than a week since she was first assigned to help on the TTC crash. She thought of the first meeting in Toronto, then flying to Chicago, her meeting with the whistleblower, the logs and threads of data that had helped her and her colleagues around the world gain on the criminals—who knew how to take control of a subway train.

Once more, she looked at the faces of the victims on her screen.

We have to stop their killers.

58

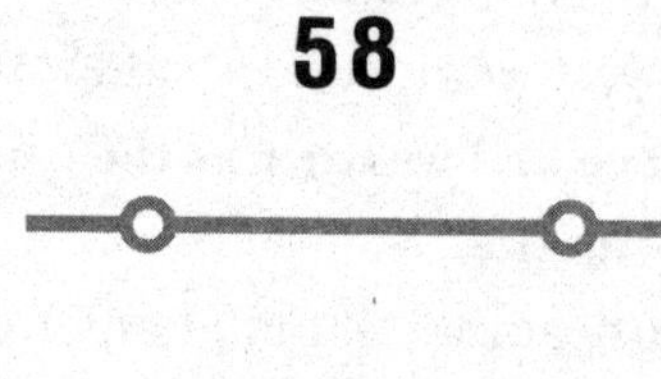

PARIS

That same day, as the bulletin concerning Tarantula was being sent to law enforcement agencies around the world, Constance Renard was wheeling her suitcase across the platform of the Place d'Italie Station of the Paris Metro.

Amid the bustle of commuters, Constance hummed a song to herself. At seventy-two, she bubbled with enthusiasm. She was on her way to visit her baby granddaughter.

Boarding one of the rear cars, Constance sat in a seat, let out a happy breath and reviewed her plan to get off at the busy Gare du Nord for her train to Brussels, where her son's family lived.

Running a bit late, Sebastian Gallet trotted to the train. He was a law student and couldn't afford to miss his lecture. Boarding a midway car crowded with locals, office workers and tourists, he realized he'd have to stand. Gripping a pole, he exhaled, then scrolled through his phone reading messages from his girlfriend. They'd argued the night before.

Further down the platform, Emeline Dromain had memorized a page of dialogue from the script for a big Hollywood film to be shooting in France. Her audition was tomorrow. Getting the small part could lead to big things, her agent had told her. She hoped so. She'd been paying her bills by working at a bistro near Laumière Station.

Emeline boarded at the first car, deftly weaving around people to get a seat up front. As it was a driverless train, her view was unobstructed.

The doors closed, and the train eased out of the station on Line 5. It was one of the lines now undergoing the process of having fully automatic, driverless trains. The upgrading of Line 5 had been running smoothly for months with no incidents.

For years, the Paris Metro, one of the world's largest subway systems, had been transitioning its lines to full automation using advanced signalling networks, making it more efficient. If a problem arose, the driverless train could be remotely controlled by the central command centre.

Gathering speed, the train proceeded north to the next stop on the line, Campo-Formio, a short distance underground from the previous station. Disembarking passengers moved toward the doors, ready to step off as soon as the train came to a stop—but then something unexpected happened.

The train failed to decelerate.

A wave of soft grumbling swept through the cars, and passengers stared up and down the train in frustration. Jaws dropped and eyes widened among those waiting on the platform at Campo-Formio as the train rolled by without stopping.

Inside the train, a stubble-faced man at the door glanced around helplessly, saying, "What the hell?"

Constance raised her head from her phone and looked around, confused. Minutes later, approaching Saint-Marcel Station, again the train failed to stop. People on the platform watched in surprise as it rolled by.

Inside the train, someone shouted, "Why aren't we stopping?"

Sebastian scanned the worried travellers on his crowded car, some speaking with American accents; families of tourists of all ages with their ball caps, T-shirts and backpacks.

"What's happening? Why didn't we stop?"

"This is nuts."

The train continued north. Now it was moving faster as it surfaced aboveground, rising to approach the elevated Gare d'Austerlitz with its translucent roof that allowed natural light. Some riders cried out for the train to stop as it barrelled by the platform where commuters stared in disbelief as it whizzed past yet another station.

Passengers on the train panicked.

"Oh my God! We're going to catch up to the train ahead!"

"Press the emergency stop button!"

A man jabbed the button repeatedly. "Nothing's happening!"

Through the forest of riders, Sebastian noticed the Metro crew member aboard his car was working at a control point attempting to override the auto system. Amid complaints and demands from fearful passengers, Sebastian heard tense dispatches between the crew member and the command centre via a handheld radio.

"Yes! I tried that! Nothing's working! Can't you shut it down from the centre? My God, we've blown by three stations! We're gaining on the car ahead!"

The runaway driverless train was now travelling at nearly three times its average speed. It charged onto the viaduct that crossed the River Seine.

The view of the Seine and Paris strobed through the trusses of the steel framework as the train raced to the next station. As it left the viaduct, entering the curve for Quai de la Rapée, Emeline—seated at the front—screamed at what she saw.

A train was stopped on the track ahead at the platform.

More screams erupted down the cars.

In the rear of the speeding train, Constance, sensing something was terribly wrong, looked at photos of her granddaughter, her son and daughter-in-law, and whispered a prayer, then clenched her eyes shut.

Steadying himself, Sebastian began a message to his girlfriend.

Forgive me. I love you.

At the front, Emeline grasped the tiny cross on the fine chain her mother had given her, which had been blessed at Notre-Dame.

In the seconds that followed, the northbound train rocketed into the rear of the stopped train, which was in the process of loading and offloading passengers. The impact thrust the stationary train forward, while the first car of the moving train wedged under the last car, launching it upward.

The physics of the crash derailed the running train, collapsing it accordion-fashion, hurtling some cars onto the opposing tracks—straight into the path of a southbound driverless train.

59

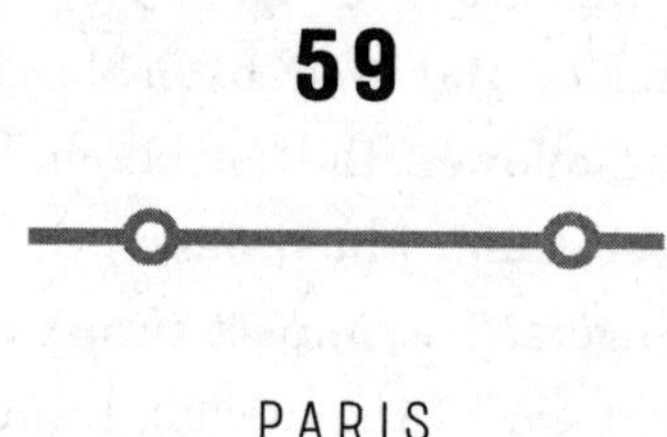

PARIS

The wail of sirens rose and fell with urgency as emergency vehicles fought through the Parisian traffic toward the Quai de la Rapée Metro station. The crash of three subway trains had triggered an immediate response from multiple agencies, and news outlets pulled teams from other stories to dispatch them to the scene. Drones provided live aerial footage of the disaster. Social media exploded as the scope became known across the city, the country, and around the world.

Fire and rail crews in protective gear worked amid the smouldering wreckage to reach those who were trapped. Rescuers, using pry bars, spreaders and hydraulic cutters, sliced through metal to extract victims. Survivors were triaged, with medical personnel first treating those with life-threatening injuries at the scene and then transporting them to hospital.

The dead were covered with tarps.

In a short time, IDs collected with some of the bodies indicated those killed included Constance Renard, aged seventy-two, and Emeline Dromain, aged twenty-eight. But no names were disclosed. Nothing would be released until official confirmations were made.

In some cases, rescue workers had to amputate limbs to free those entwined in the wreckage. They had to sever the lower left leg of Sebastian Gallet, aged twenty-five. Before paramedics transported him, he seized the arm of a police officer near him. Passing in and out of consciousness, Sebastian told him that on his car he had seen American tourists with a child, the crew member trying desperately to stop the train, and that he loved his girlfriend. In the ambulance, with sirens howling, Sebastian died en route to hospital.

"At least ten people are confirmed to have been killed, the number expected to rise, officials are saying," TV reporter Anna Dumas said into the camera, her voice full of emotion. "We know people are rushing here, fearing loved ones may have been on one of the trains."

With the subway cars stacked in a grotesque pyramid behind him, Philippe Morel, a grim-faced national network journalist, noted that—in a bizarre coincidence—the crash site was next to the Institut Médico-Légal de Paris, which housed the morgue, and near a couple of police buildings.

"Amid these horrendous ruins, and across the city, the search for answers begins," Morel said.

The RATP, the authority that operated the Paris Metro, continued taking action by shutting down Line 5 and slowing trains to a crawl on all other lines in the system.

Police also took steps that extended to every level of law enforcement. In a city experienced with orchestrated attacks, French intelligence and every branch of national security turned their full attention to the incident. Government leaders were also immediately briefed.

Across Paris, along the tree-lined streets of Boulevard de la Tour-Maubourg, stood the sprawling stone building of the Secretariat-General for Defence and National Security. The department encompassed the ANSSI, a branch responsible for France's cybersecurity.

Earlier, and within minutes of the crash, Joann Cassin, a senior ANSSI agent, had hurried to the office of her director, Hugo Veil. His door was open, and the three large TV screens on the wall were tuned to live coverage of the tragedy, but he was concentrating on his computer. She knocked on the doorframe.

"Come in," he said, eyes locked on his monitor.

"Sir, we've just now received a bulletin from the international video conference today with Europol, about the cyber intrusion of transit systems. Did we have someone on this call?"

"I'm seeing the bulletin now. Yes, Patrice was on it. He was scheduled to debrief the department when he returned from meetings with defence people at Hexagone Balard."

"Cybercriminals could be behind the Metro crash," she said, watching the TV screens.

"You're right. Hold on," Veil said, then he made several calls—the first to RATP operations to urge shutting down all Metro lines and to demand the command centre check and report any attempts at cyber intrusion. He then tasked his team to prepare for a briefing from Patrice, who had rushed back to the branch. In a few moments, his office was filled with the colleagues he'd summoned.

"Work with RATP to analyze software updates, look at logs, look for back doors and signs of infiltration. Gather more intel from Europol, the Americans and Canadians," Veil directed. "Given what happened in Toronto, we must determine if our event was a technical failure or a criminal act, and if the two events are related."

In embassies across Paris, the Metro collision was being scrutinized. Communication was intense among the security, intelligence and law enforcement channels of several countries.

As the tragedy unfolded, coverage of the news was on all major networks and online platforms with non-stop analysis and debate.

"This could be a signalling issue, a technical breakdown," a transportation expert told a news anchor as footage from the scene replayed in a loop.

"It is more likely a human issue," an official for the subway drivers' union countered. "You know, today's horrible incident evokes the 2019 case when a driverless runaway train missed several stops. Today's tragedy throws into question the safety of the Metro's automated system."

On another network, a transportation security analyst pointed to the recent subway crash in Canada. "My sources are telling me that what happened in Toronto was an unprecedented cyber intrusion, a high-tech hijacking of the train resulting in a crash that left several people dead. Intelligence was recently shared indicating the entity behind it could strike again. I fear this is what we're seeing here in Paris."

On Avenue Gabriel, not far from Champs-Élysées and the Seine, on the upper floor of the US Embassy, several members of the security staff concentrated on details surrounding the Metro crash. They examined every aspect of the incident, collecting and scrutinizing every fragment of intel and data, and searched for any connection, or threats, to the United States and its citizens.

Throughout their investigation they also exchanged information with their counterparts in the British, German, Canadian and other embassies.

FBI agent Noah Bishop, one of the US Embassy's legal attachés, worked with his foreign law enforcement contacts, studying every scrap of data available. Bishop's French police sources had strong—but still unconfirmed—reports that American tourists had been travelling in a car on the northbound runaway train, according to the last words of a fatally injured passenger.

At this stage, confirming and identifying Americans who may have been passengers was a challenge. IDs from the deceased and injured were still being collected. But the urgency increased after Bishop and others at the embassy, and in the US, digested the alert concerning the deadly cyber hijacking in Toronto.

In Paris, analyzing and running checks on intel of recent cyber intrusions and threats, Bishop got a hit arising out of New York. It concerned the abduction of a nine-year-old boy, Dylan Ward, from JFK and the murder of his father Vaughn Ward. Persons of interest sought in the case were Robert Cook, sixty-eight, and Nancy Cook, sixty-seven, of Queens, New York.

Digging deeper into the case, Bishop learned how suspects had hacked into and manipulated JFK's security camera system, which constituted a significant cyber intrusion. Additional intel in the Cooks' background indicated the couple had a strong fascination with global trafficking networks, some with tentacles in Europe.

Then Bishop absorbed the information concerning the murder of Vaughn Ward in upstate New York. Bishop learned how Ward had been an investigative journalist known to break stories about cybersecurity threats and issues.

After going over intel on the Toronto crash and the timeline of events, Bishop looked at the live TV news feeds of today's carnage. His mind hit on an idea rooted in the investigative tenet of leaving no stone unturned.

Consulting his colleagues, he then reached out to police sources on the ground at the scene, then the relevant authorities in Paris. French intelligence had their own drones and video cameras recording the aftermath that were far nearer than the news cameras, which were required to keep a certain distance.

They agreed to share the footage with Bishop and the investigators at the embassy.

Soon the images appeared on Bishop's screen. Subway cars heaved like felled behemoths, or welded in sculptured collision.

Contorted frames, axels broken. Smashed windows and seats ripped away. Debris strewn every which way; tarps indicating deceased riders.

Bishop was told two people, believed to be in their sixties, had been killed in a midway car on the northbound train. It was thought they were American tourists travelling with a child, according to survivors taken to the hospital. Their identities were still unknown.

The footage panned over articles of clothing, shoes, hats, a jacket, all pulled from passengers on impact. Strewn about were laptops, suitcases, travel bags and backpacks.

"Get them to zoom in," Bishop said. "Maybe we can read address tags on some of the items."

The camera got closer, but reading tags was futile—they were all damaged or torn away.

"Wait!" Bishop said.

From one camera angle he saw a small backpack. Dotted with a pattern of gamepads in shades of green.

Bishop checked the JFK case details for Dylan Ward.

He had last been seen with a green backpack with gamepads on it.

60

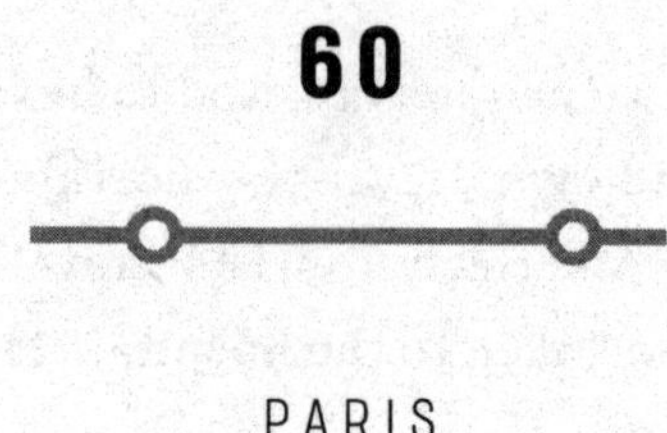

PARIS

Bruno Girard peered over his half-moon tortoiseshell glasses at the TV screens suspended above the assignment desk at *Le Figaro*, one of France's major newspapers.

The veteran editor zeroed in on the comments of an analyst during a live discussion on BFM TV. Citing well-placed sources, the analyst was suggesting today's crash was linked to a recent cyber hijacking and deadly collision of two subway trains in Toronto, and that intelligence was recently shared with other countries to guard against potential strikes.

"*. . . like what we're seeing now in Paris . . .*"

As the discussion continued, Girard, without hesitating, alerted *Le Figaro*'s reporters at the scene of the crash at the Quai de la Rapée Metro station to the analyst's claim.

"Press every official you know to confirm or clarify this information, on or off the record," Girard instructed.

He then reached out to two of the paper's most senior crime reporters and instructed them to work their police sources. Next, he called a reporter on the national security beat, advising her to reach out to her highest contacts for intel.

Soon after, Girard headed to the editor of *Le Figaro*'s international desk, where calls were made and assignments given to the paper's correspondents in Canada, the US and across Europe.

"We're jumping on this information. We're going to own this story," Girard told other editors at the subsequent news meeting. "Yes, we have our cyber and transportation beat reporters covering the driverless automated train issues. But I get the sense, with Toronto and other factors, there's much more to this." He crossed his arms. "And if there's a deeper story behind today's crash, we're going to find it."

After the meeting, he went to the desk of Margaux Fremont, the paper's top breaking-news feature writer.

"I've instructed everyone to file with you first, so you can assemble our piece. We're moving fast on this, Margaux."

Sipping her green tea while reading the wires and consulting social media, Fremont, who'd covered wars and catastrophes around the globe, nodded. She was ready.

It didn't take long before copy began flowing in from reporters covering every angle of the incident. Having pushed their sources hard, they'd submitted key pieces of information. As Fremont worked, Girard, studying the raw copy, made follow-up calls to the journalists. With the major story emerging, he headed to the photo desk, passing critical updates to the paper's photographers at the scene of the crash.

Following instructions, two *Le Figaro* photographers took up separate vantage points from buildings to get an elevated but distant overview of the scene. They used their new 600-mm telephoto lenses with variable zoom range and extreme reach. Focusing on debris, they obtained strong images from varying perspectives. As advised, they closed in on a specific item.

When Girard and other news staff saw the photos, it was clear. *Le Figaro* was on the brink of breaking a world exclusive.

61

BETHEL AREA, UPSTATE NEW YORK

Lottie, the server at the Four Jays Motel & Diner in upstate New York, swiped through her phone as she returned to Jessie and Chelsea's table. "She was at the doctor's office, but I finally got hold of Marleen and she sent three birthday videos."

Sitting across from them, Lottie turned her phone around for the two women, playing the first video.

The radiant face of a little girl appeared.

"That's Marleen's daughter, Cheyenne, turning seven," Lottie said.

Sitting with Cheyenne were three other girls the same age, all talking excitedly at once as the camera panned the table to Cheyenne's dad, who waved, then to two other women.

"Marleen is taking the video," Lottie said.

Jessie caught her breath. *There's Vaughn.*

Lasting no longer than a heartbeat, just beyond the birthday table, the video captured him alone at his booth. He vanished when the perspective shifted before the video ended.

"Now, the next one." Lottie cued and played it.

Cheyenne's face was aglow in the flicker of seven candles on the cake set before her as everyone sang "Happy Birthday."

"There," Chelsea said, pointing to the screen.

A shadow flashed by at the party's edge—a figure approaching Vaughn's table before the camera cut away.

"Is that you, Lottie?" Chelsea asked.

"No, because I brought the cake from the kitchen and stood behind Marleen and sang too."

It was a fleeting image of someone with Vaughn.

"Pause it," Jessie said, then pointed at the blurred image. "Did you serve the person with Vaughn at some point?"

Lottie blinked at the frozen video and tried to remember. "Not really. I came to them with coffee. The new person had their back to me and the man, there, kinda waved, like they didn't want anything."

"Do you recall who or how they paid?"

"They left cash. I'm sorry, I don't remember the second person." Lottie looked disappointed.

"That's okay," Chelsea said, making notes.

The waitress resumed the video, showing Cheyenne blowing out the candles. Soon after, the video ended, and Lottie played the third. Cheyenne opened colourfully wrapped presents to her delight and applause. The camera zoomed in on gifts, a bracelet craft kit, an *Amelia Bedelia* box set, an ankle skip ball, a rainbow T-shirt. To the right of the screen, the camera caught the back of a figure sitting with Vaughn in his booth.

Jessie studied her ex-husband. She knew him well, and she could tell, based on his posture and demeanour, that something was wrong. The camera cut away.

Rose stopped by the table.

"Did it help?"

"Just not enough there," Chelsea said.

Biting her bottom lip, Jessie said, "Can you go back to the first and second videos?"

Lottie replayed them until Jessie had her stop. "There. See? This woman's recording with her phone, too, from a different angle. Who's she? Could we get her video?"

Rose and Lottie exchanged glances. "Marleen will know. I think it's her sister," Rose said, taking out her phone and walking a few feet away. She returned after a few moments and passed the phone to Jessie.

"She'll talk to you."

"Marleen?"

Rose nodded.

Jessie quickly took the phone. "Hi Marleen, this is Jessie Ward."

"Oh my gosh, oh God, I'm so sorry about what's happened to you."

"Thank you. There's one more thing I'm hoping you can do. There are two other women at the party in the video."

"Yes—Felicia, Andrea's mom, and Colleen, my sister."

"Was Colleen also taking a video of the party?"

"She was, yes."

"Do you think we could get her video? It would help if we could look at it as well."

"Yes, but it could take time. After the party she went to New York to fly to Africa, to go on a tour to climb Mount Kilimanjaro. She's a free spirit. She likes adventure."

"Can you reach her and get her to send it?"

"I'll try, but the internet connection where she's going is spotty. With the time difference and everything, it could take a while."

Jessie nodded. "I get it. Please keep me posted, anytime, night or day."

"I will. Anything to help."

"Thank you so much. Thank you." They exchanged contact information.

After the call, Lottie and Rose returned to work, and Jessie and Chelsea sat quietly in their booth, each deep in thought. Chelsea scrolled through her phone, and Jessie peered out the window. She felt they were getting closer to learning who Vaughn had met in this diner before he was killed.

Her phone vibrated with a message from Bobby.

Do you know what's going on in Paris?

Jessie didn't know. But before she could respond, Chelsea gasped.

"What is it?" Jessie said, alarmed.

Chelsea kept reading for a moment, then lifted her gaze from her phone. "A subway train has crashed in Paris with multiple deaths."

Jessie looked at her in shock. "Oh my God."

"There's more," Chelsea said grimly.

"What?" Worry suddenly gripped Jessie.

Chelsea chose her words. "This will be hard. It's all happening now, but from what I read, nothing's confirmed."

"Chelsea, just tell me!"

Swallowing and looking back at her phone, Chelsea took a deep breath. "Okay, our Paris bureau sent this to my editor who forwarded it to me. A story is breaking from a Paris news outlet. Quote, 'Citing sources, *Le Figaro* is suggesting the subway tragedies in Paris and recently in Toronto, the murder of an American journalist and the abduction of his nine-year-old son from JFK in New York might be connected.'"

"What? I don't understand."

"Here." Chelsea turned her phone toward Jessie. "We've used the translation app. *Le Figaro*'s posted article is now in English."

Jessie scrolled through the story concerning the collision of three Paris Metro trains, multiple fatalities, photos of the wreckage.

She kept scrolling until one image emerged on the screen, hitting her hard, nearly knocking her to the floor.

62

BETHEL AREA, UPSTATE NEW YORK

"That's Dylan's backpack!"

Jessie's mouth fell open as she took a shuddery, uneven breath—she went numb, feeling as if she were outside her body.

Staring at the photo, her hands shook with a disconnect between her brain and her vision as she struggled to understand what she was seeing. "This can't be!"

The phone slipped from Jessie's hand to the table.

"It's a speculative piece with unnamed sources," Chelsea said gently, picking up her phone. "Let me see what I can find out."

As Chelsea texted, then made a call, keeping her voice low, Jessie squeezed her eyes shut. A few tears escaped before she opened them and swallowed hard. She had to know more about this crash. Regaining some control, she took out her phone.

Her first call was to FBI Special Agent Jake Garlin.

"Yes," Garlin said, "we're aware of the case in France and reports coming out now."

"Was Dylan in the crash?" Her voice quavered. "There's an image of a backpack. It's Dylan's."

"We don't yet have confirmation that any Americans were involved. We're working with our people there and French authorities." He paused. "The backpack is similar, and it's possible the

Cooks could've fled to Europe. But we've no confirmation on either. We know this is difficult, but please trust that we're working on it."

Jessie hung up and looked at Chelsea, who had ended her call. "The FBI can't confirm anything yet. How about you?"

"Our Paris bureau has learned that before a passenger died on the way to the hospital, he indicated Americans with children were on his car, near where the backpack was found in the wreckage."

"Children?" Jessie's heart leapt. "More than one?"

"One may have been a boy, approximately ten years old."

Jessie raked her fingers through her hair. "I can't stay here. I'm going to Paris. Can you take me back to my hotel in Brooklyn for my things now, then on to JFK?"

"But shouldn't you wait for official confirmation?"

"I can't just sit here, Chelsea. Please, let's go!"

Hurrying back to the Jeep, phone to her ear, Jessie got back to Bobby. The motor roared as Chelsea accelerated along twisting local roads to the highway, and soon Jessie's team in California was on a video call with her.

"I talked to the FBI," Jessie said. "They can't confirm anything."

"This is horrible," Sarita said. "How could the Cooks get to Europe when they're wanted by the FBI?"

"Did they have any details on the child and the backpack?" Dahlia asked.

"Nothing." Jessie's voice broke.

"Did you learn anything upstate?" Dahlia pressed.

"We're close to finding out who Vaughn met at a diner before he was killed."

"How close?"

"We may get some video."

"Really? That's good, Jess!"

"Dahlia, my concern right now is Dylan," Jessie said. "I'm going to Paris."

"Absolutely. Where are you now?"

"We're rushing back to New York so I can get to JFK."

"Jess," Bobby said. "We'll scour the Paris news reports for anything to help."

"I think there's a link to Washington on this," Dahlia said.

"What are you talking about?" Jessie asked.

"Remember Carl Lasker, from MIT and the project—?"

"No—stop. Dahlia, I can't do this now. Dylan could be hurt. He could be *dead.*" Her voice trembled, fading on the last word. It took all Jessie had to hold herself together. "I have to get to my hotel, get my things and get to Paris to find him. I don't care about fucking Carl Lasker, MIT or the fucking project!"

"We understand," Sarita said. "Hang in there, and keep us posted. Don't give up."

An hour later, as Chelsea exceeded the speed limit on the highway, Jessie's thoughts twisted into a whirlwind of fear. The stress of not knowing if Dylan was alive made it hard to breathe as the road rushed under the Jeep. *I can't lose him. I can't.*

She found the story from *Le Figaro* again and zoomed in on the image of the backpack.

Sobbing, she looked out of the window to the forest.

63

SANTA MONICA

Gamepads in shades of green dotted the backpack displayed on the screen in Instinct Nine-99's meeting room.

"My God." Dahlia's attention bounced between the screen and her laptop, where the missing poster the FBI released was on the screen. "It's Dylan's."

"We can't be certain," Bobby said. "The French investigators haven't confirmed any identities. There's got to be others like his out there."

Staring at the image, she shook her head. "Dylan can't be hurt. He just can't be. They've already killed his father. Who's doing this to this family?"

Bobby looked at his notes. "*Le Figaro* cites French security sources saying the crashes in Paris and Toronto may be connected, and there could be ties to Vaughn's murder and Dylan's abduction at JFK." Bobby's keyboard clicked, and several reports on the Toronto subway tragedy appeared on the big screen. "I've been looking at this," he said. "There has been speculation in closed chat rooms within our community that Toronto was a cyber hijacking."

"Really?" Dahlia said. "Does Instinct have contracts with the Toronto system?"

"No," Sarita said, "we have cybersecurity contracts across the US and around the world, but not with the TTC in Canada."

"Yeah," Bobby said, "the rumours in the community said SynerRapid Systems out of Chicago may have left a back door open after a remote software update. It was undetected until hackers moved on it and took control of the train. Apparently international cybersecurity officials suspect Toronto was the work of Tarantula." He paused. "They issued a warning on vulnerabilities to transportation operations hours before the Paris crash—and now it's surfaced in the French media."

"And Vaughn often broke stories on cybersecurity issues," Sarita said. "He'd know about Tarantula."

"Everyone in the industry would be familiar," Dahlia said.

Bobby pulled up a joint alert from the FBI and CISA from months ago that warned about Tarantula, noting that the organization was a cybercriminal group targeting commercial facilities sectors and subsectors. They often bought and sold tools and software on the dark web. They even hired themselves out to work with hostile governments to test and penetrate systems of targeted countries.

Bobby said, "I need to check for any updated alerts on the group."

"Of course, but still . . ." Dahlia cupped her hands to her face. "This would fit."

"What would fit?" Bobby said.

"The guy I was telling you about earlier, Carl Lasker."

"Right. You and Jessie worked on a classified project with him at MIT."

"See," she pointed, "Tarantula buys and sells information for penetration attacks, and Carl works at the DCSA. He has access to Instinct's contracts—your cybersecurity work for government systems which are designed to thwart attacks. Instinct's work would be valuable to Tarantula."

Bobby looked to Sarita, then back to Dahlia and nodded. "You're not wrong."

"As I said," Dahlia looked at her laptop, "I don't trust him. There could be a connection."

"Should we alert the FBI?" Sarita said.

"Yeah," Bobby said, "have them talk to him?"

"I'm not sure. I have no evidence," Dahlia said. "I should go to Virginia, talk to him, feel him out, see what I can learn."

Bobby's laptop pinged with a notification. "Hold on," he said, going to a news story. "*The New York Times*, citing and advancing *Le Figaro*, is quoting its own anonymous sources close to the investigation."

"And?" Dahlia said.

Reading fast, Bobby summarized. "They're reporting fears are growing that an American boy abducted from JFK may be among the victims of the Paris Metro crash."

"No," Sarita said, "this can't be happening."

64

PARIS

The moaning of the injured, IV bags swaying as gurneys were rolled through hallways, the antiseptic smells and non-stop announcements—it all created an air of subdued chaos.

Olivia Barluet and Eric Crouzel, plainclothes officers with the National Police, surveyed the emergency room.

It was evening at the Pitié-Salpêtrière Hospital, one of the largest in Paris, capable of handling mass casualty incidents. In 2015, it had been a lead trauma centre caring for victims of a string of terrorist attacks across the city, which had left more than 130 dead and nearly 400 injured. And years before, it was where Princess Diana had been taken after the deadly car crash.

Now, it was among several hospitals treating those injured in the crash at Quai de la Rapée. Barluet and Crouzel were among various law enforcement teams dispatched to hospitals, assigned to collect statements and the identities of survivors for the investigation.

"We object to police disrupting our work," Dr. Christine Collet told them angrily.

"Doctor, given the belief that this terrible incident could be an intentional attack, we have the authority to proceed," Barluet said.

"And time is against us," Crouzel added.

"What is it you need, *to be precise*?" Collet asked. "We have patients to treat."

"We understand you have received most passengers from the Line 5 train, the striking train?"

"Most, but not all, yes."

"To be precise," Crouzel said, "our investigation is focusing on identifying American tourists."

"Americans?" The doctor gave it thought, blinking quickly. "I want you gowned and masked," she said, waving over a staff member who helped the two officers into hospital clothing. When they were dressed, she beckoned them. "This way."

Walking fast, Dr. Collet weaved through the activity on the ward, leading them downstairs to a lower floor and a labyrinth of halls. She came to a stop at a room and slowly opened the door. Entering, Barluet and Crouzel felt the temperature drop.

Inside were eight raised tables. Atop each was a zipped black polyethylene cadaver bag with a page of information in a protective sleeve of plastic clipped to it. Five of the bags held adults.

Three held the bodies of children.

"The Americans," the doctor said.

On the other side of the city, Joann Cassin, a senior agent with the national cybersecurity agency, worked intensely advising cyber experts for the Paris Metro system. With more security officials briefed on Europol's warning arising from the attack on Toronto's subway system, multiple agencies were deepening their investigations.

"Review your software updates and logs for any signs of infiltration," Cassin advised the analysts for the subway network. "Even if you find nothing, study them again. The attackers are very good at concealment."

Across the country, security forces were on full alert. Every aspect of every network, every system, was being probed for weaknesses and vulnerability. While no clear evidence of a cyberattack on the Metro had surfaced, prosecutors in Paris had opened a national investigation into the incident, suggesting it was damaging and threatening France's fundamental interests.

Building on Europol's warning that indicated the cybercriminal group Tarantula could be a leading suspect, French intelligence worked at connecting the dots. Supporting suspicions the runaway train was in fact a coordinated attack by individuals with a knowledge of the rail system were the threads to Canada, the United States and also potentially Brazil.

The possible link to the cyber intrusion at New York's JFK and the abduction of an American boy, as well as the murder of his father, a journalist who reported on cybersecurity issues, reached into the Paris tragedy.

A backpack consistent with one belonging to the kidnapped boy had been found in the wreckage of Line 5's striking train.

The identification of Americans on that train would be crucial.

At the Pitié-Salpêtrière Hospital, in the room with eight of the fatalities from the crash, Eric Crouzel looked to the doctor.

"How did you identify them as Americans?"

"Nothing is confirmed officially," Dr. Collet said. "That will be the job of the pathologist."

"But we see names, details here." Olivia Barluet leaned close, reading the information on the page.

"As police, you are familiar with initial identification. We worked with the fire brigade, medics, looking at passports, driver's licences, or carte Vitale. In cases of the deceased, pockets, bags and phones were searched. By these means we have strong, unconfirmed indications that they are citizens of the United States."

"Identification can be fabricated or altered," Crouzel said.

"That is for you to determine," Dr. Collet said.

Barluet had leaned down, examining the plastic-covered pages affixed to the bags.

"Eric," she said, "with the adults, we have two with ages consistent."

Staring in his phone, consulting the information provided to French intelligence by the FBI's legal attachés at the US Embassy, Crouzel said, "And the children?"

"One girl. Two boys. One of the boys is consistent."

"Doctor, we will need to photograph some of these victims," Crouzel said.

"I cannot allow this indignity. There are proper procedures."

"And this is one of them. We are conducting an investigation of the utmost importance to the national security of France."

The doctor was silent. She glanced at Barluet, who pointed to the cadaver bags the investigators needed. Taking a moment, the doctor stepped first to the bag holding the body of the boy. Her gloved fingers reached for the tab. Slowly she moved the zipper.

Crouzel had cued up on his phone the photos he already had of Dylan Ward.

Barluet prepared to record the dead child's face.

65

NEW YORK

Chelsea stopped the Jeep in front of the Golden Greenwood Hotel on Fourth Avenue in Brooklyn. "I'll wait in the lobby, then drive you to JFK," she said.

"Okay." Jessie moved to leave, and Chelsea took her hand, her eyes filled with sympathy. "Jessica, I'm so sorry about what's happening."

Jessie nodded. "I know, thank you."

"I'll contact our reporter in Paris, have her meet you, guide you. You won't be alone there. Okay?"

"All right."

Riding in the elevator, Jessie checked her phone for news. Nothing had emerged. She considered some of the new theories Bobby had sent. One noted there was online speculation that the cybercriminal network Tarantula could be behind the Toronto and Paris subway attacks.

Tarantula.

A memory stirred. The diner Vaughn had visited upstate. Rose, the server, had thought she might have seen a word on his laptop. An insect.

A spider.

Spider. Tarantula. Had Vaughn been pursuing a story about Tarantula? Jessie shook her head. She could chase that later.

Right now, Dylan was her priority and she had to get to France as soon as possible.

She reviewed the ticket she'd purchased while Chelsea was driving them back to New York City, relieved she'd had her passport with her. Her flight left in three and a half hours.

In her room, Jessie packed, adrenaline and emotion battling her exhaustion. If she stopped, she'd collapse. She powered through. She'd rest on the flight.

Her phone chimed. It was a message from Marleen, the birthday mom from the diner upstate.

Hi Jessica. I reached my sister Colleen in Tanzania. She says she's trying to send me the video she took but her connection is really weak where she is now. She'll keep trying. Love Marleen.

Jessie thanked her, then went to the in-room safe, entered the security code on its keypad and removed her blue Instinct laptop. After storing it securely, she sat at the desk with the laptop she'd bought in New Jersey.

Logging in, she inserted the green USB flash drive holding the folders from Vaughn's computer. She then opened the app developed by Instinct and resumed trying to open Vaughn's encrypted files.

Images from the birthday videos replayed in her head—the shadowy figure joining Vaughn at his booth in the diner. In desperation, she worked fast, mining the files for any vein—any trail to answers.

Who did you meet? What were you working on. Help me, Vaughn. Who took our son? Please let him be alive.

She'd succeeded in decrypting parts of some files, but most remained secure and unreadable. At this point, she was unable to access much and she didn't want to push it. Partial decryption could result in misinterpretation.

Shutting down her efforts, she went online to check the latest reports out of Paris. The news videos and photos of the crash were horrific. Some were from the earlier crash in Canada. More US outlets continued repeating the fears that the Paris and Toronto subway tragedies, and a near collision that had taken place in São Paulo, were linked to cybercriminals, the killing of an American journalist and the kidnapping of his son in New York.

She took a breath. Time was slipping away. She looked at her watch. She should meet Chelsea. She was just standing to collect her things when her phone rang.

"Jessica Ward?" It was a familiar voice.

"Yes?"

"It's Garlin, we have an update from Paris."

Her stomach knotted, but his neutral tone betrayed nothing. The room shifted. *This is it.*

"You still there?" Garlin asked.

"Yes." Squeezing her phone, needing to steady herself, she sat on the bed. "Yes, I'm here." She gripped her knee, rocking gently, ready.

"Your son, Dylan, was not involved in the Paris Metro crash."

A sensation rippled through her almost lifting her into the air. She started shaking, sobbing quietly, a hand covering her mouth. "You're certain?" she whispered in between cries.

"Yes. Based on preliminary identification, and the photos of the victims we've seen, we can confirm that there were American citizens among the deceased and injured."

"Oh no."

"However, the ages, the races, the physical attributes are inconsistent with our case. The only consistent factor was the backpack associated with one of the children being the same model and colour as your son's backpack."

"This is so horrible."

"Yes." Garlin paused. "I will add, as is often the case, speculation and conspiracies on all the incidents are rampant. But the fact is, as you know, we cannot rule out a connection between your case, Toronto and now Paris."

"Yes, but Agent Garlin, where is Dylan? Where are the Cooks?"

"Apart from his abduction," Garlin said, "we have no evidence he's been harmed. I assure you, hundreds of investigators everywhere are leaving no stone unturned to reunite you with your son."

After Garlin's call, Jessie's fingers trembled as she managed to alert Chelsea to the news, then cancel her flight. Overcome, the weight of her exhaustion forced her into bed.

It's not Dylan.

Sobbing, she realized that it would soon be nine days since his abduction.

Will I ever see him again?

As she fell asleep, images tormented her: Vaughn's car pulled from the lake, the horrific crash scenes in Paris and Toronto.

Dylan at LAX, smiling at her one last time.

66

MARYLAND

On I-95, about thirty miles northeast of Washington, DC, a white SUV drifted across the lane markings, weaving through the southbound lanes. As Maryland state trooper Paul Reed watched, his pulse quickened. He ensured his dashboard-mounted video camera was recording, then hit his emergency lights and siren. Accelerating, he closed in on the vehicle, pulling it over on the right shoulder near Route 100.

After notifying dispatch of his location and the stopped vehicle, Reed approached the driver's side of the SUV. He gestured to the driver, and the window lowered to a white male in his mid-sixties.

"Sir, could you shut your car off and place both hands on top of the wheel?"

The man complied. He seemed calm. Reed glanced at the passenger, a white female, mid-sixties, who looked concerned.

"Ma'am, could you place your palms on the dash?"

She hesitated. "But why, Officer?"

"Please, ma'am."

Reed's nose twitched slightly while surveying the interior. Blankets and luggage were piled in the back, but there were no other occupants. He didn't pick up any signs of alcohol.

"Sir, could you slowly provide me with your licence, registration and proof of insurance?"

Reed observed the driver as he shifted to get his wallet, then reached into a compartment for the other records.

"Have you consumed any alcohol or substances today?"

"Only a cheeseburger and coffee at the Denny's a ways back," the man said, passing the information to Reed. His hands and voice were steady. "I don't think I was speeding."

"You were weaving." Reed examined the licence.

"Oh Lord, I told him to stop for a rest," the woman said. "It's been a long drive from New York City for him, and he gets drowsy after he eats."

"I wasn't drowsy."

"Then why are we in this situation?"

Reed glanced at them, then walked to his cruiser where he entered the information into his system, which ran checks for expired licences, suspended driving privileges, stolen vehicles and outstanding warrants or alerts.

It didn't take long.

No hits. No wants. No warrants.

Reed began the paperwork on his system, then went back to the driver, returning his information along with a ticket.

"You crossed without signalling. This can be dangerous. I'm citing you for a lane violation," Reed said. "I advise you to take a break at the next stop and have a coffee. It'll be safer for you and everybody else on the road."

Then he gave them a wave and went back to his car.

For the next hour, he patrolled traffic along the busy north-south corridor until his shift ended. He clocked out at the Waterloo Barrack, got into his Dodge pickup truck and headed home, kneading the back of his neck.

He was coming off two twelve-hour shifts and starting his three-day weekend. He had court duty next week, then he'd be on a training course. Things were good, he thought—reflecting on his life as he drove. He was coming up on three years of patrol duty. In a couple of weeks, he'd put in his application for detective. It was only a step in the process, but his hope was to make it into the Criminal Investigation Bureau, maybe get assigned to Homicide or the Cold Case Unit.

Listening to "Take Me Home, Country Roads" by John Denver, he counted himself fortunate because he didn't live far, having inherited his uncle's place in Highland Park—what some called horse country. It was a small ranch house on a couple of pretty acres along Mink Hollow Road near the Patuxent River.

Wheeling into the driveway, he parked next to his wife's Chevrolet Blazer and went into the house, where Lynn was in the kitchen making dinner.

"Hi," she said, "we're having spaghetti. How did it go today?"

"Same old, same old, up and down the interstate."

She leaned into him as he kissed her cheek.

"And how was your day? You run all your errands?"

She stopped slicing mushrooms and looked at him. "I almost got killed."

"What happened?"

"I was driving down to Laurel, to that shoe store I like. I'm on 95 and this guy cuts me right off. He's got four freaking lanes and he cut so close. I swear, I thought he was going to graze me. I had to slam on the brakes."

"You should've called it in."

"Yeah, I was going to." She smiled. "But then a couple of big rigs came up on either side, close. I had to slow down and I lost him." She waved her hand then resumed slicing the mushrooms. "I don't have to tell *you*, but people drive like idiots."

Reed stood there, thinking for a moment before heading outside to his wife's car. He returned and logged into his computer just as Lynn joined him.

"What're you doing?"

"I put those dashboard cameras in the truck and the Blazer for this sort of thing."

After inserting the tiny memory card into his computer's adapter, his fingers moved over his keyboard, mouse clicking. In seconds, he was retrieving dashcam footage.

"About what time today did it happen?"

"Maybe two-ish, two thirty?"

Reed played the footage from the Blazer. Streets, mall parking lots and traffic blurred as he sped through images, eyeing the date and time stamp to pinpoint the incident.

He arrived at a segment of multi-lane freeway traffic.

"What color was the car?"

"White."

"Do you know the make, model?"

Lynn shook her head. "It was a white SUV."

Mindful of the time on the video, he zipped through it. Something large, white and very near flashed.

"There!" Lynn said. "That's it."

Reed reversed the segment, replaying in slow motion the white SUV cutting off his wife.

"Man," he said, "I would have so written this guy up."

"Well, it's over with," Lynn said as hissing and the rattling lid of a pot boiling over pulled her back into the kitchen.

Studying the footage, Reed zoomed in, getting a clear image of the vehicle. A Toyota RAV4. He went closer. An XLE Hybrid. He got the plate.

New Jersey.

He picked up his phone and called dispatch on the non-emergency line.

"Joy Singer."

"Hi, Joy. Paul Reed, Waterloo Barrack. I need a favour."

"What's up?"

"Can you run an out-of-state plate check for me?"

"Go ahead."

Reed heard the rapid-fire clicking of Singer's keyboard as she keyed in the New Jersey plate.

"Here we go." Singer recited the information for a Ford F-150 pickup truck.

"That's not right." Reed's brow creased. "Looks like we may have stolen plates on a ghost car."

"What else you got?"

"Hold on."

Reed studied the white RAV, spotting a Statue of Liberty decal on the low right corner of the rear window and a cracked left taillight. He recited the details to Joy.

"Can you run those against any alerts and BOLOs?"

"Stand by."

Reed knew the automatic licence plate readers used throughout Maryland, and I-95, could sometimes miss a plate. Could be lighting, sun glare, dirt on the plate or on the camera lens. The plate could be obstructed for any number of reasons. Also, traffic cameras along I-95 in Maryland only provided real-time live feeds to monitor traffic conditions. They didn't record.

"Oh boy," Singer said. "Coming up all cherries, Paul."

"What do we have?"

"NCIC and other databases show intense interest to locate a white 2024 RAV4 XLE Hybrid, with holdback details a Statue of Liberty decal on right rear window and a broken left rear taillight."

"Really?"

"The RAV4 is sought in the abduction of a boy from JFK about a week ago, which may be tied to criminals hacking into subway systems in France and Canada to hijack and crash trains. Vehicle may also be linked to a homicide in upstate New York. So far, no stops and no location of the vehicle."

"Damn." Reed tried to get a better image of whoever was inside the RAV, but glare prevented a clear picture.

"What is it?" Lynn, a towel in her hands, looked over his shoulder at the screen.

He searched news headlines and photos to show her. "That's the car that cut you off today. Look at this."

Lynn covered her mouth with her hand.

"Joy," Reed said into his phone, "we spotted the suspect vehicle a few hours ago. Southbound on 95, heading to Washington, DC. I'll send you a photo."

67

NEW YORK

Jessie woke before sunrise, beads of sweat rolling down her cheeks, sheets twisted from fitful sleep. Rubbing her temples, raking her fingers through her frazzled hair, she faced what was now the tenth day of Dylan being missing.

Sorting her thoughts, she clung to the relief that he had not been involved in the Paris crash. Her heart went out to all those who were, but until she held her son again, every breath was torture.

In the dim light, she glanced at the room's desk and her laptop.

Yesterday, she had spent long hours painstakingly attempting to decrypt Vaughn's files. Success had come in frustrating bursts of partial revelations, like a note on the story he'd been investigating: *I'll meet with . . . take me into the network . . .*

Who was he meeting? she wondered. *What network?*

She believed she was getting closer to identifying his source, convinced it had to be the person he'd met at the diner just before he was murdered. The birthday videos could help, but there was still no word on receiving them.

Then, after many attempts, Jessie had a breakthrough. She succeeded in partially opening an encrypted file labelled "Thoughts."

It appeared to be his journal. The text was garbled, but the first few fragments she managed to access stunned her.

I should never have done . . . what I did to Jess . . . I regret . . .

"Regret what?" she whispered to herself. "What did you do, Vaughn?"

Jessie got out of bed, showered, dressed, made hotel room coffee and ate a stale bagel before settling back to work at her laptop. She looked for updates and found none. She checked for progress on the video from Africa. Nothing.

Taking a breath, she resumed her efforts to decrypt Vaughn's files. Little by little, revelations emerged like scattered pieces of a puzzle.

. . . could get me access to group . . . dark web chatter . . . attacks . . .

A chill coiled up her spine.

Attacks? Like in Paris? Toronto? Who could get him access? Vaughn knew a lot of people, including people from Harvard and MIT. Dahlia has tried to reach everyone we knew back then.

Jessie glanced to the in-room safe where she stored the blue laptop. If Vaughn had been pursuing hackers, and anything tied to Instinct's work, she was certain he would have told her.

She jumped when her phone rang.

"Jessie," Chelsea said. "The Cooks' SUV was spotted yesterday!"

"Oh my God! Where?"

"On I-95 near Washington, DC."

"What about Dylan?

"They don't know if he was in the car."

"Did they arrest anyone?"

"I see no details. Look, the *Daily News* just put up a story and a picture."

Fingers flying on her keyboard, Jessie found it.

SUV wanted in JFK kidnap spotted near DC

Jessie's hand covered her mouth as she began reading:

Investigators released this photo and updated details of a vehicle tied to the kidnapping of a 9-year-old California boy at JFK.

"We're asking for the public's assistance locating this vehicle and its occupants," an FBI spokesperson said.

The car, a white 2024 RAV4 XLE Hybrid, with New Jersey license plate number . . . rear window decal and damaged taillight . . .

68

LOS ANGELES, EN ROUTE TO WASHINGTON, DC

The twinkling lights of Greater Los Angeles faded in the predawn as Dahlia's early morning flight climbed over Southern California.

Holding onto the armrest, her pulse steady, a growing certainty settled in her bones.

The moment she'd learned the Cooks' SUV had been spotted on the Maryland Interstate, she'd felt it. The FBI photos confirmed what her gut had already told her—the RAV4 was heading for the Washington, DC, area, and that had to mean it was headed for Carl Lasker.

But she had to prove what she knew.

Working at the Defense Counterintelligence and Security Agency, Carl had access to the kind of classified information that cybercriminals like Tarantula wanted.

She scrolled through her phone, frustrated by how it had taken Carl so long to answer her repeated messages, pleading for help for Jessie.

Been busy. Sorry. Terrible what's happened to Jessica. Wish I could help.

That was it.

He hadn't responded to Dahlia's follow-up pleas.

And she'd made it clear to Bobby and Sarita that all the other people she'd reached out to had offered help or given advice or compassion. But not Carl. A college colleague's husband had been murdered, her son abducted, and the best Carl could do was a cold shrug. Anyone would think it was as if he were distancing himself from events.

Anyone would think that something's not right here.

Putting all of these aspects together with the sudden sighting of the SUV was enough to convince Dahlia now was the time to get on the earliest flight possible.

While boarding, she had let Bobby and Sarita know of her plan. Then she'd texted Jessie.

Later, as the jetliner levelled, Dahlia looked at the news stories coming out of Toronto, Paris and São Paulo, then the story on the sighting of the wanted vehicle. She studied the dashcam photo of the white RAV4 headed for the DC area, wondering where the Cooks and Dylan were now.

69

MARYLAND

Staring at the flat tire on the right front of her Subaru, Kim Reeves cursed to herself, again.

Why today of all days?

She could change it herself, but she'd just gotten a manicure for the job interview she had in a few hours. She still had to pick up her business suit from the cleaners. Instead, she was stuck in the busy parking lot of a shopping centre in Hillandale, northeast of Washington, DC, near the Beltway.

Leaning against her car, she looked at the tire. She could hear the voice of her late dad, a mechanic.

Come on, Kimmie, you've changed flats before. Do it just like I showed you.

She raked her teeth over her bottom lip. But she'd already called Triple A and they were on the way. The app said that they'd arrive in fifteen minutes. She sipped her Starbucks while scrolling on her phone. A big story was trending on her social media feeds but—

"I don't want to!"

Before she read further, Kim's head snapped up from her phone at the loud protest of a child nearby. Surveying the parking lot with cars coming and going, she searched for the source.

"No, I don't like this!"

This time it sounded like the child was frightened, rather than misbehaving. Kim's curiosity sharpened to concern as she scanned the lot. She spotted shoppers headed to a car, but they were too far away. Then—there. A row over, just above the beds of a couple of pickup trucks.

A man and a woman, in their sixties or seventies, she guessed, wearing surgical masks, had gotten out of a car. At the edge of one of the pickup trucks, Kim had a partial view of the child who was with them and also wearing a mask.

What's going on there?

Careful not to be obvious, Kim navigated around parked vehicles to get closer. The child appeared to be a boy about ten, wearing jeans, a hoodie and running shoes.

"We'll take you to the bathroom, get you a drink, then get back on the highway," the woman told the boy, pulling his hood over his head.

"Let's go," the man said.

"When will I get to see my family?"

Kim's mouth opened slightly. *What? What's that mean?* She watched the trio head into the shopping centre, then glanced at their car, a white Toyota RAV4 with New Jersey plates. She was processing what she'd witnessed when her phone chimed, indicating the Triple A truck had arrived.

Seeing it in the lot, she waved it over to her Subaru, then went to the technician. He confirmed her identification and membership, then set out assessing her car, the area and the condition of Kim's spare. As he began loosening the lug nuts on the flat, Kim looked at her watch. She would need to rush getting her suit and cleaning up before her interview, which was for a position that meant the world to her—assistant director of a large child care centre in Silver Spring. Kim knew she was qualified, but in many ways this was personal. Ever since her little sister was struck and killed by a car over twenty years ago, Kim had been devoted to being a protector of children.

The technician finished, got her to sign off on a service receipt, then left.

". . . keep your voice down . . ."

Kim looked to see the couple and boy returning to the white SUV.

Something's up with them.

Again, she found a vantage point, only now she cued her phone to record.

Not my business, but this is weird.

The woman was carrying a takeout bag of fast food. The boy had a drink in his hand and was grumbling in low tones. The man glanced around to be sure no one was in earshot. He didn't see Kim, who was close and near the rear of a van.

"We'll be there soon, don't worry," the woman said.

At that point Kim noticed that the boy had pulled down his mask to drink before getting into the SUV.

After watching them drive off, Kim checked to make sure she'd recorded the scene. Behind the wheel of her car, before leaving, she checked her social media feed.

One item trending concerned a car spotted in Maryland that was wanted in a kidnapping at JFK airport in New York.

A white Toyota RAV4.

70

NEW YORK

Let him be okay.

The rear of the white Toyota SUV filling Jessie's laptop screen became increasingly grainy as she enlarged the image in the *Daily News* story.

It was the closest frame the dashcam video had captured on I-95 in Maryland. A few quick key taps and she continued zooming in, desperately attempting to see if Dylan was inside.

And that he's alive.

But the vehicle's rear glass reflected the sun, obscuring the interior. The side mirror, the one Jessie could see, offered nothing. She examined reports in other news outlets, searching for more clarity—*anything to help*. But each story used the same image released by police, and all she could think of was how the Cooks could be affiliated with international human trafficking.

Oh God, what's happening in that car?

She called Garlin but got no response. She tried Chelsea again. *Nothing new,* Chelsea texted back. *But we're hearing there might be a news conference later.*

Jessie had resumed working when her phone buzzed with a text from Dahlia.

Jess, remember me talking about Carl from MIT? Jessie cursed and lowered her phone. *Why is she so fixated on Carl?* Shaking her head, Jessie resumed reading the message. *Now at DCSA, with access to your contracts. Got no proof yet, but with this news that the Cooks' car has been spotted headed for DC, my gut tells me there could be a connection to Carl. Got to be 100% certain before we tell police. Flying to DC now to check myself. Arrive in five hours. Will keep you posted. Stay strong.*

Jessie caught her breath.

What the—?

Dahlia was flying to Washington, DC, to talk to Carl Lasker. She really thought this nightmare could be linked to him and Instinct's work.

I can't believe it. No, it can't be us. Because if it's us, it means—no it can't be us . . .

Her stomach clenched as she shifted her thoughts.

She still hadn't heard from Marleen. She texted Bobby to see if there was any way he could help get the birthday video from her sister.

Tell you what, Bobby typed back, *give us the contact info and we'll see what we can do to help get the videos for us to review.*

Jessie had just sent him Marleen's phone number with her thanks when a message from Special Agent Jake Garlin came through.

Are you good for a video call ASAP.

Yes.

Within seconds, Garlin's face appeared on her screen.

"We need your help with a break in the case." His voice, which was normally professionally neutral with her, now held an underlying current of urgency—even a tinge of emotion.

"A new video has been sent to the FBI. It comes out of a shopping centre parking lot in Hillandale, Maryland, near Washington, DC."

Jessie's breathing quickened.

"Our people have authenticated it. It's not a hoax and has not been manipulated. We believe it shows your son, Dylan. We'd like your unofficial verification, to assist us before we release it. It's a short clip, the sound is low, so boost your volume." Garlin looked directly at Jessie. "Are you ready?"

She gripped both knees. "Ready."

The video came to life and played on Jessie's screen, showing a boy about Dylan's size walking through a parking lot with two older people. All three were wearing face masks. The woman held a takeout bag. The boy had a drink.

But Jessie knew—even with his mask, she already knew.

As they neared a white Toyota RAV4, the boy tugged his mask down to drink and . . . Jessie's heart nearly burst from her chest.

"It's Dylan! Oh God!" Reflexively she reached for her screen. "It's him! Yes, it's him! His voice, his walk. It's my son! He looks okay—how long ago? Did you arrest them?"

"Jessie," Garlin said. "This is where we're at. The good part is the video is a few hours old. We've not located the vehicle, yet."

"You've got to find them!"

"We're gaining on them. We're going to release this video with a public appeal. Bear with us."

Nodding with both hands on her mouth, trying to keep herself together, Jessie surveyed the room as if the earth were shaking under her. "I'm going to find him!"

"Jessie, you have to hold tight, let us do our job."

"I have to go!"

Jessie slammed down the lid of her laptop. Adrenaline pumping through her, she grabbed her phone to determine the fastest way to travel to Washington, DC, at this time of day. She made an urgent request for a car, then she removed the blue laptop from the safe. Taking up her things as if her room were on fire, she ran to the elevator, jabbing the button.

After snapping at the clerk to rush her checkout, she was relieved her summoned car was waiting out front. In minutes, the driver was expertly navigating traffic, motivated by the enormous cash tip she'd promised.

As they crossed the Brooklyn Bridge, Jessie reread Dahlia's text. Could her friend be right about Carl Lasker? Yes, he'd been a kind of self-contained genius at MIT; yes, he'd also been strange and untrustworthy. He *would* have access to Instinct's classified contracts. And the Cooks appeared to be headed for Washington . . .

Still, that proved nothing.

They made good time cutting across Midtown to Penn Station. As the car came to a halt, Jessie thrust cash at the driver, then rushed into the Moynihan Train Hall where she bought a ticket for the high-speed express train, which departed New York for Washington nearly every hour.

It seemed like a lifetime, even though it was about forty minutes, until Jessie had settled into the window seat of Amtrak's Acela train. Her phone assured her this was the fastest way at this time. It would get her to DC's Union Station in about three hours.

As the train began rolling out of Penn, her thoughts clawed back to the video Garlin had showed her.

Dylan's alive.

Her heart slammed against her ribs. All she could think of was her son.

"I'm coming for you, sweetie," she said softly.

71

WASHINGTON, DC

The shop was sandwiched between a nail salon and tax services office in a strip mall along Pennsylvania Avenue in Southeast DC. Scissor-style security gates were mounted inside the store window and door, which issued a toned chime when Carl Lasker entered.

To the left, he saw a countertop with a skyline of computer towers. Below, shelves were packed with hardware, cables and other components.

He noticed the dome cameras in the ceiling.

To the right, shelves with more components under screens listing services and fees. He saw an area highlighting drones and drone repairs. A glass case displayed new laptops and equipment. It was near the cash where a woman in her twenties, sitting on a stool, looked up from her phone.

"Can I help you?"

"I'd like to see Rod Tate."

"And you are?"

"Carl Lasker."

His name grabbed her attention, as if she'd heard something she shouldn't have heard.

"Is he expecting you?"

"I need to see him, now."

Assessing Carl, the woman blinked a few times before deciding on how to respond. "One moment," she said before going to the back, closing the door behind her.

Carl worked at keeping calm. Tate had told him never to visit his shop, but pressure was mounting. He felt like a clock was ticking, and he wasn't sure how much more he could take. It was why he'd booked off work early to drive here, to set things right.

The woman returned. "He's on a call, Mr. Lasker. Have a seat. He won't be long."

Taking one of the two empty chairs near a potted palm, Carl's nerves got the better of him. To soothe them, he bounced his right leg slightly. Scrolling through his phone, he inventoried his growing fears.

The news reports of Jessica Ward's case alarmed him with the speculation of ties to her work at Instinct, the recent subway attacks, her husband's murder, her son's abduction.

And now the suspects' car is heading to the DC area.

Then there was Dahlia Wynn, freaking him out with her relentless requests for his help, pressing him on his job at the DCSA, his access to contracts and information.

He rubbed his chin. *What does Dahlia know?*

The payments had stopped far short of what he was owed. He was a long way from being free and clear of everything.

"Mr. Lasker? He'll see you now. This way."

The woman led him through the back, passing workstations holding several machines in stages of repair. Another dome camera above them. Tools, computers and parts were stacked and stored everywhere. A male, barely out of his teens, dressed in jeans and a T-shirt, was hunched over a motherboard. He shot Lasker a glance. The acrid smell of burnt plastic floated from a corner where a girl in a white hoodie, about the same age as the boy, worked a soldering iron, which hissed and crackled. She looked at Carl, threw a glance to the boy, then back at Carl.

The door to an office was open. Inside, Tate swayed in a high-back chair with a phone to his ear, waving Carl in.

He took a seat across the desk, and the woman left, shutting the door.

"Yeah, he's here. I'll get back to you." Tate finished his call, tossed his phone on his desk, propped his elbows on it, dragged his hands over his face and then looked at Carl. "Big mistake coming here."

"I have concerns."

"I'm sure you do."

"I kept my end of the deal," Carl said, then voiced his suspicions and fears about being implicated in current news reports concerning Dylan Ward's abduction. "I want my money, and I want out. Now, Tate."

"So," Tate said, "you think my clients used your information and are somehow behind all of these events you're talking about?"

"I don't know what you, or your clients, have done with the information I gave you. I don't want any part of it. Give me my money, we're finished."

Tate let a long moment go by. "You can't undo what you've done."

"Maybe not, but you know what I can do? I can report it."

"*Report what?* You have no proof, no evidence of anything, other than what you did."

"I'll turn myself in, help with an investigation."

Tate smiled. "What, go to the FBI? You can't be serious, Carl?"

"I'll get a plea deal."

"A plea deal?" Tate shook his head, chuckling. "There won't be any deal. You'd face charges of espionage, treason, violation of security of information acts, conspiracy. You'd never get out of prison. Your family would be shamed, ostracized. Everything you love would be destroyed."

Carl took a moment, digesting his situation.

"Are you feeling the gravity here, Carl?"

Carl shut his eyes slowly in acknowledgement.

"Now," Tate said, "as it happens, I was going to contact you with a proposal to address all of your concerns."

"What're you talking about?"

"Would you like to be finally paid in full and be done with our transaction?"

They both knew the answer.

"While you were waiting out front, I spoke with my clients. They said that if you can complete one more task, you'll be paid in full and all this goes away like it never happened. Simple as that."

"What task?"

"A small task to be done tomorrow."

"What if I refuse?"

"Do you have a choice, Carl?"

At that moment the burner phone which Tate had given Carl months before, at the beginning of their business, vibrated.

"Take a look," Tate said.

Carl saw that $25,000 had been deposited into the offshore account. His eyes flicked to Tate.

"That's an act of good faith on the part of the clients," Tate said. "The remainder owed to you will be paid after you complete the task."

"I need to know more before I agree."

Tate opened a desk drawer and gave Carl another phone. "You'll get more information tonight on this."

Carl looked at it.

"Just think," Tate said. "You're less than twenty-four hours away from your big payout, freedom from worry and security for your family."

Carl's stomach tightened.

"You should leave now," Tate said, "before the traffic back to Stafford gets worse."

72

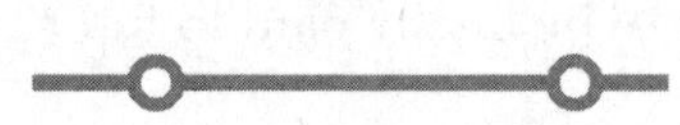

OTTAWA

At the Canadian Centre for Cyber Security, Claire Brenner tapped her pen rapidly on the conference room table as she studied the large wall-mounted screen.

Her colleagues in the room stirred in their chairs as the latest video call with international law enforcement and cybersecurity agencies progressed.

In the wake of Toronto and Paris, the intelligence sharing moved with professional, urgent calm against a rising death toll as Claire summarized the newest development.

"Over the last thirty-six hours"—Claire straightened, consulting the notes on her laptop—"we've worked with our Brazilian friends probing the near collision in São Paulo."

There came a soft sweeping noise as her colleague slid a physical file folder to her. Claire opened it, glanced at the pages, nodded, continued.

"We now believe São Paulo was a case of cyber intrusion orchestrated by Tarantula." Blinking several times in concentration, she went on. "Much of the groundwork had been done by us, and our colleagues in Europe and the US, enabling us to make a precise examination of São Paulo."

In scrutinizing all aspects with the engineers and experts in Brazil, studying logs, data, diagnostics and other matters, it was confirmed that a recent software upgrade to the modules had resulted in a back-door opening. The upgrade and system were not built by SynerRapid Systems, but it was similar. And it had been exploited by skilled cybercriminals whose signature matched Tarantula's.

"Fortunately, in this case, at the last moment the failsafe systems thwarted the attempt to collide the hijacked trains," Claire said, still tapping her pen.

A moment of dread fell upon the meeting in the face of three significant incidents of cyber hijacking of major mass transit systems on three continents. It left the officials on the call from around the world to fall into a murmur of individual conversations, for they were now confronted with a challenge—informing their respective government leaders at the highest level of the severe risk of further attacks.

They all knew that it would lead to discussions of the potential security measures, including the possible shutting down of transit systems and the deployment of special cyber-hunting units. Such steps, with their heavy social, financial and psychological impacts, would have political ramifications and overtones of "giving in to terrorists."

Consequently, Claire knew that any action would take time.

Still tapping her pen, breathing evenly, she wondered when and where the next attack would be.

She glanced at the clock on the wall, watching time tick down.

73

EN ROUTE TO WASHINGTON, DC

Trees blurred by Jessie's window.

Her train was over halfway to Washington, DC. As it rocked and swayed, she struggled against picturing Dylan in every horrific scenario. A thread of icy sweat slithered down her back as she willed the train to go faster.

In the time since it had left Penn Station, she'd worked on her laptop, eyes locked on the screen checking for updates, finding nothing. Now, as they crossed into Maryland from Delaware, her screen chimed with an incoming video call. She put in her headphones and angled her laptop to ensure a degree of privacy, then answered. Bobby and Sarita appeared.

"The Amtrak app says you're nearly there," Bobby said.

Cranking her volume, her voice low, Jessie said, "I am."

"Anything at your end?" Bobby asked.

"Supposed to be a police press conference coming, and I'm still working on Vaughn's files. You guys have anything?"

"We've made headway on the birthday video," Sarita said.

"Really?"

"We contacted everyone," Bobby said. "The travelling sister saved it on her phone's internal memory. We tracked down her group's guides in Tanzania. We're arranging with them to transfer the video to a computer, compress the file and transmit with Starlink or OneWeb for us to grab."

"Good work."

"It'll still take time, given where they are," Bobby said.

"But hopefully we'll find out who Vaughn met with," Sarita said. "And hopefully, it will lead us to Dylan."

"We did some poking around," Bobby said, "and this guy Dahlia is chasing, this Carl Lasker, is like a ghost."

"He doesn't have an online presence," Sarita said.

"Probably keeps a low profile for security reasons if he's at the DCSA," Jessie said. "I haven't looked yet, but check our contracts with the agency."

"I did," Bobby said. "I found a number and email address for him. Reached out with a routine admin question. He hasn't answered. Dahlia could be onto something."

"Maybe she'll be able to tell you more, Jessie," Sarita said. "Her flight landed at Dulles over ninety minutes ago."

After her call ended, she resumed skimming Vaughan's files.

. . . friend would meet from time to time . . . some years back assigned to a conference in Athens . . . good conversations . . . knowledgeable . . . could be valuable source?? . . .

At a loss as to why this was in his personal file and not his story research file, Jessie continued.

. . . met again more recently . . . source claims connex to dark web actors . . . can take me deeper inside . . . key for the story . . . ?? keep checking . . . poss link to classified government cyber project done years ago??? . . .

A classified project done years ago?

Jessie scrolled through garbled passages until she came to another semi-clear segment.

. . . things bad at home with Jess . . . we're stressed . . . accuses me . . . I travel too much . . . work too much . . . . . . we argue too much . . .

Dylan hears, sees . . . we're falling apart . . . can't live together . . . I need to move out . . . started divorce proceedings . . .

Tears rolled down Jessie's face as she kept reading.

. . . been on my own . . . alone . . . aching for my son . . . it was after . . . I was . . . hurting . . . alone . . . the person I was with last night . . . the morning after . . . I can't find the words . . . what have I done? . . . Last night . . . it's not who I am . . . it was a mistake . . .

Who was his mistake?

She paused to collect herself, thinking back to what Chelsea had told her—how Vaughn had confided in her at the bar, had appeared regretful and wanted to reconcile.

The train swayed, jolting Jessie from her thoughts, and she continued working decrypting another short passage from Vaughn's last journal entry.

. . . need to connect dots . . . it's coming together . . . something big, dangerous . . . maybe coordinated attacks? . . . source has more details . . . will meet upstate . . . could be huge . . .

Could be huge . . . meet a source upstate . . .

A recollection niggled at Jessie. There was media speculation that the criminal group Tarantula was behind the cyber hijackings of the subways in Toronto and Paris. Yes, something else pinged: Rose at the diner saying she'd glimpsed the word "spider," or something like that, on Vaughn's computer. But Jessie's thoughts slipped away.

Swallowing hard, she was fighting waves of emotion to process and find meaning in what she'd uncovered. She tried to understand why, in his last days, Vaughn had blended his thoughts and story research. At that moment, a notification on her laptop signalled a live news conference was in progress.

She opened up the link to see the NYPD's chief of detectives, with other officials, assembled at a podium next to a large monitor.

"We'd like to thank private citizens who've stepped forward in this case to provide what, as you will see momentarily, is critical information," said the chief. *"We're also thankful to the Maryland State Police, Montgomery County Police Department, Prince George's County, the FBI and so many other agencies for their assistance.*

"Several hours ago, earlier today at a mall parking lot in Hillandale, Maryland, northeast of Washington, DC . . ."

He went on with a summary. Jessie moaned softly as the video of Dylan played in slow motion—the same video Garlin from the FBI had shown her. Aching for Dylan, she gripped the sides of her laptop. As the chief indicated the Cooks—*"who are persons of interest"*—were believed to be in the area, he made a public appeal for more help locating them.

Jessie turned, touching her fingers to the window as the train rolled into the greater metro area of DC.

He's somewhere out there.

The chief and other officials took several questions before the news conference ended. The train slowed as it began lumbering deeper into DC, and Jessie got a new message, this time from Dahlia.

Just got into Washington, Jess. Where are you?

About twenty minutes from Union.

Let's meet in the lobby of the Hilton, it's a short walk.

Yes.

I saw the news conference, Dahlia said, *everything's pointing to DC—deepening my suspicions of Carl Lasker.*

74

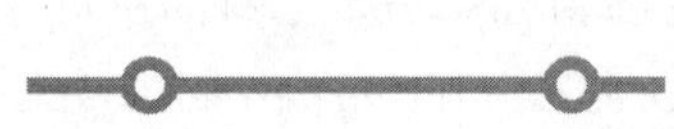

WASHINGTON, DC

Jessie covered the few blocks from Union Station to the Hilton in minutes.

Sweeping into the elegant lobby with its four-storey atrium and welcoming atmosphere, she scanned the reception and seating areas.

"Jessie!"

She turned to see Dahlia, and the two women hugged.

"Thank you, thank you for flying here!"

Dahlia tightened her hold, then pulled back to look at her. Exchanging teary smiles, they silently acknowledged the events that had unfolded since they were last together in Jessie's home in Santa Monica. Then Dahlia nodded to the restaurant. "Do you need a drink? Something to eat?"

"I'm good."

"Want to talk for a bit, then, right here?"

Jessie nodded, setting her bags next to her as they sat on the plush sofa. "Dahlia, did you see him in the video in the parking lot?"

"Yes, thank heaven, he looked okay."

"Thank God. And maybe you're right about Carl."

"But I don't want to alert the police yet."

Jessie stared at her. "Why not? We're talking about my son, about Vaughn's murder, and if you think Carl Lasker—"

Dahlia lifted her palm. “That’s just it, Jess. I have no proof he’s involved, just a lot of circumstances. Before I make an accusation that I can’t take back, I have to be sure. That’s why I’m here. And with everything that’s happened, I think I’m getting closer.”

“Do you know where he lives?”

“No, he hasn’t responded to my messages, and I can’t locate him. Listen . . .” Dahlia took in the large area, the glass-walled elevators looking into the atrium, and the ambient noise, but dropped her voice anyway. “I’ve been pushing hard on all my colleagues, our old MIT people, people I know in the community, pushing really hard, and I’ve learned a little more about him.”

Jessie listened.

“Remember how he gambled in school?”

“Yes, on sports.”

“Rumour is Carl developed an addiction over the years and now has run up huge gambling debts.”

“And you think it’s a factor in all of this?”

“Not conclusively. There are a lot of dots to connect. But gambling debts would make him vulnerable in his job at the DCSA, where he has access to Instinct’s work.”

“Yes.”

“And Bobby and Sarita have said your team is developing advanced cybersecurity technology for the government. I mean, come on. Professor Jackson thought your work was brilliant. You were the star. Everyone knew that, including Carl.”

Jessie shook her head. “But I haven’t received a ransom, anything. Instinct’s work is secure with me. I don’t understand any of this.”

“You told us you’ve been working on decrypting Vaughn’s files. Have they revealed anything, like who he met near Bethel—before he was, you know?”

“We’re working on getting video of his meeting upstate.”

“That’s good. That will help.”

"And I've only been able to retrieve fragments of his files. We know Vaughn was investigating a story, something he thought was big. He referred to a classified government project. Maybe it was Gold Arrow Horizon, and Vaughn didn't know it. He referred to 'attacks,' and now we see cyber infiltration of the Toronto and Paris subways. Could Vaughn have been on the trail of the attackers? Maybe his story involved Carl? What I don't get . . ." Jessie's voice trailed away before it broke, but she kept going, shaking her head with tears in her eyes. "What I don't understand is why he was murdered and why Dylan was taken by two senior citizens with some sort of ties to human trafficking."

Dahlia passed her a tissue, touched her hand, then said, "Let's go upstairs to work out a plan, all right?"

Jessie nodded.

"Let's get you a room. I've already checked in."

75

WASHINGTON, DC

Jessie got a room a few doors from Dahlia's.

Before they regrouped, Jessie needed a few minutes alone. Sorting her emotions, she called her mother in California.

"Oh, Ms. Ward," Allie Peña answered. "We're praying for you and Dylan."

"Thank you, Allie. Can you put me through to my mother?"

"Of course, but first I have to tell you something. Unfortunately, yesterday, a resident, Mr. Hartley, tried telling her he'd seen your case on the news."

"Oh no." Jessie's stomach dropped.

"Our staff intervened, explaining to her that he was talking about a movie. She seemed to accept it."

"Good, thank you."

"I'll put you through now."

A click, then her mother came on the line.

"Hi honey. Are you coming over today?"

"I'm sorry, Mom, I'm still out of town on business."

"It's been a long time."

"I know, I'm sorry. How are you?"

"A little sad."

"Why?"

"I haven't seen Dylan in so long, I bet he's grown."

Jessie stifled a sob before saying, "He has."

"I can't wait to see you all again. Honey, promise me you won't work so hard."

"I promise."

Hanging up, Jessie choked back tears, then swiped through pictures of Dylan until Dahlia came to her room.

They ordered chicken sandwiches and strong coffee from room service. Then, setting to work, they monitored TV news reports, online news outlets and social media for any new sightings of Dylan and the Cooks. They continued reaching out to people they knew. Building on the Hillandale video, Jessie was unyielding in her pursuit of Carl Lasker's address—desperate to talk to him, either to remove suspicion or lead her to Dylan.

Hours later, Jessie turned to Dahlia. "I know things haven't been easy for you lately, Dahlia. Thank you for dropping everything to be by my side."

Dahlia squeezed her hand. "We've known each other so many years."

"Yes, it's been a long time."

"I've always admired you, Jessie, for what you've achieved. Envied you a little for what you have. You're the best of us. How could I not help?"

"Thank you," Jessie whispered.

Dahlia went back to her laptop but a few moments later lifted her head. "Jessie, Instinct's contract concerns advanced tech, and that falls under the DCSA?"

"Yes, but the specifics are classified."

"But Carl would know, and he'd know more about it than most people."

"Yes, most likely," Jessie said.

"So, it could be a factor, right?"

Jessie took a breath, then opened up about Instinct's work. "The contract is advanced technology using AI, arising out of early concepts from Gold Arrow Horizon. Remember the idea of an eternal key that could serve as an impenetrable shield against all cyber intrusions?"

"I remember you coming up with this years ago," Dahlia said. "Jackson loved it."

"That's what we developed for the US government."

"But, Jess, if criminal groups got their hands on your work and offered it to a hostile state to reverse-engineer, or to wield as a weapon, they'd be invincible."

"Conceivably."

"And maybe that's the story Vaughn was going to break."

Jessie was silent.

"It's just a theory, Jess. Connecting dots. But see how all these elements point to Carl?" Dahlia counted the points she made on her fingers. "One, we worked together on the MIT project so he knows your concepts. Two, he knows about you and Instinct. Three, he's rumoured to have gambling debts."

"You're right," Jessie said.

Dahlia's computer pinged, and she looked at it. "Oh boy, I just got something, Jess. A guy here in DC, who might have seen Carl recently, said he was acting very strange, nervous. My guy is former National Security. He says he'll try to find out more and will meet me tomorrow morning."

"We'll go together."

"Hang on." Dahlia reread the message, then said, "I think seeing you with me might make my guy nervous."

Jessie thought, then nodded in agreement.

Then Dahlia asked, "Have you got any leads on your front?"

Jessie consulted her screen.

"Yes, maybe. The DCSA's in Quantico, so I'd been checking towns in Virginia nearby where he might live, like Woodbridge, Triangle, Fredericksburg, Dumfries and other places."

"And?"

"I also asked some of our MIT friends I kept in touch with to check his wife's social media, track her down. Apparently she uses her maiden name online. Vanessa Stroud. And a friend of a friend helped me get an address."

Jessie turned her laptop around. Looking at it, Dahlia nodded.

"Why don't you go to Virginia tomorrow morning and I'll meet my guy in town. Separately, we'll cover more ground faster. Then we can compare notes."

"All right." Jessie paused. "Dahlia, what if we're completely wrong?"

"What do you mean?" Dahlia asked.

"We're chasing shadows." Jessie cast her arm to the window and the city. "Searching for a needle in a haystack. The Cooks must've seen the news reports, the video. What if they've driven a thousand miles away? What it they—?"

Dahlia took Jessie's hands firmly in hers. "You're exhausted. You're going through hell. We have to believe what we're doing is right. We can't lose faith." She searched Jessie's eyes.

"You know," Jessie said, "when Vaughn and I separated, he met someone."

"What do you mean?" Dahlia tilted her head slightly.

"It was in his journal I decrypted. He called it a mistake, said he wanted us to reconcile, wanted us to be a family again."

Blinking back tears, Dahlia said, "Oh Jessie."

"It's why I've been refusing to accept that these horrible things—his murder, Dylan's abduction—are about our work. Because I know that if it's true, then it's my fault—I created

Instinct, I developed the key, I pushed Vaughn away. It's my fault, and it's cost me everything!" Jessie sobbed as Dahlia held her for a long time, until Dahlia pulled away and looked into her eyes.

"Get some sleep. Don't lose hope. Do not give up."

Jessie nodded.

Later, as she lay in bed, she gazed out at the lights of the city, gleaming and sparkling like a never-ending galaxy.

Ten days, it's been ten days, she thought before she faded into sleep, wondering where Dylan was.

Will I ever see you again?

76

MARYLAND

The next morning, far from his mother's hotel, Dylan Ward woke up hungry, his cheeks stiff with dried tear tracks after crying himself to sleep.

Like he'd done every night.

Because something was really wrong.

The two weirdos who'd taken him were liars, tricking people at the airport to think they were his grandma and grandpa. They'd rushed him to the subway, making him wear a mask, warning him not to talk to anyone because it was dangerous. Then they'd got on another train, then got in a car and drove and drove.

"Why are you doing this?" he'd cried. "You're not my grandma and grandpa!"

"That's right. I'm Mary," the woman said. "And he's Joseph."

"Son, do you know what great book those names are from?" Joseph asked while they drove.

"No, and I'm not your son."

"No?" the woman said. "Goodness, what do they teach children in school these days?"

"Please take me back! Why are you doing this?"

"We are your special guardians," Mary said.

"What?"

"We've rescued you," Joseph said. "Bad people are following us, so we have to be careful."

"I want my dad, my mom, my grandma and grandpa!"

"Son, we'll take you to your real family as soon as it's safe."

"I don't like this! Let me go! Take me back!"

"Dylan," the woman's voice was soft, singsong, "it'll all be over when it's safe, and it will be better for you, sweetheart."

"You have to believe us," Joseph said. "We're protecting you. We're not going to hurt you."

Dylan didn't know how many days it had been now. He'd lost count of them driving and driving, sleeping in the car. They always locked the doors from the inside so he couldn't ever get out. Most of the time he had to go to the bathroom in bushes at the side of the road with Joseph standing near. Sometimes, a gas station. They made him wear a mask if they took him out of the car.

He hated this. He just wanted to be with his family.

Mary and Joseph hadn't hurt him. In some ways they were nice, making sure he had his favourite food, like Twinkies, chicken nuggets or crunchy peanut butter and blueberry jam on white bread with chocolate milk.

But they'd taken his phone, his watch, his Switch, everything, so he couldn't call his grandparents, his dad or his mom. They gave him this little yellow puzzle game, Spaceracer. It wasn't connected to anything and was so boring. They also gave him a bunch of comic books, *Spider-Man* and *Iron Man*.

But Mary and Joseph scared him because, even though they were always smiling at him, with toothy smiles, their eyes were wide, glazy, like zombie people in movies. Dylan thought there was something sad about them, something not quite right, and it terrified him.

They kept telling him that maybe it would all be over soon. Dylan was starting to believe that maybe it would. Because today, when he woke up, pushed himself out of the sleeping bag and blankets in the car, and poked his head up to look at the window, he saw Mary, and she waved for him to get out.

Trying the door, he was surprised. It was unlocked. He gazed around to see the car was parked in a big empty storage place that seemed abandoned. Getting out, he heard cooing above him and flapping wings. He saw birds perched on rafters, then smelled bird poop, mixed with an earthy, wood odour. Mary was sitting on an office chair, an extension cord snaking from an outlet to a heater, its fan droning. Abandoned office furniture was stacked nearby, in what was otherwise a big deserted warehouse building.

He walked over to Mary. Her face was in her phone. "Good morning, sunshine," she said, looking up and smiling that freako smile at him. "It's a blessed day. I think today's the day."

Dylan stared at her. "I'm hungry."

"Joseph went to get some food. He should be back soon."

"I have to pee."

She swivelled her chair and pointed. "See, by those huge storage containers, there's a porta-potty."

Dylan hesitated. Was she actually letting him walk off alone? He glanced around at the enormity of the building.

"It's okay, hon, we're all locked in solid here. We're safe. Go ahead."

He walked off, holding his breath from the foul air, glancing up at the birds and around at all the discarded office stuff, wondering what this place was.

The porta-potty smelled so bad. It had cobwebs in the corners, bugs crawling on the floor, the walls, the ceiling.

When he finished and stepped out, he noticed that Mary couldn't see him. Were they really locked in this big place? Maybe there was a way out? His pulse kicked up, and he scouted the building, moving quietly between rows of towering storage containers and shelves.

There was no way Mary could see him as he moved toward a far wall. He was startled by two rats running along the floor's edge.

But he kept going, coming to a window. Slowly he pushed a box under it, then carefully climbed up. He found a lever and latch. He pulled, but it was rusted, stuck. Grunting, he pulled again.

It wouldn't budge.

He glanced to where Mary was, but he couldn't see or hear her.

Dylan couldn't believe it. He was completely alone here. If today was the day, then he had to get away.

Using both hands, he hooked a finger in the latch loop and nearly hung from it, using his weight. His finger went numb before the latch slid open with a crisp, echoing snap.

The window was hinged at the top. With a couple of hard shoves, he got the steel frame to move. The window creaked, reluctantly opening wide enough for Dylan to peer down.

It wasn't a big drop, and the ground looked grassy. His heart was pounding. He hefted himself over the frame, hung down and dropped as the window slammed.

"Dylan!" Mary shouted after him.

He stood and ran into the woods.

77

WASHINGTON, DC

The sign over the shop said "EL Brille Computer Solutions."

Studying it, Dahlia drummed her fingers on the steering wheel. She'd made good time this morning from the hotel, after seeing Jessie off in her rental. Jessie had left early to hunt for Carl Lasker in Virginia.

Dahlia was tense, having trouble keeping her patience. She'd demanded the rep at the rental car place expedite the inspection, agreement and handover, so she could get moving. It was the eleventh day of the search, and time was ticking. Dahlia knew they were close.

This has to work.

The guy she needed to see was a former NSA comms expert. She checked her phone, then entered the store. A chime sounded. She scanned the shelves of computer components, the dome cameras in the ceiling. She stepped up to the glass case displaying new laptops, near the cash, where a young woman on a stool greeted her.

"Good morning. May I help you?"

"I'm here to see Mr. Tate."

"Your name?"

"He'll know. He's expecting me. Tell him I'm here."

Assessing Dahlia, the younger woman sent a text.

Seconds later, the phone pinged with a response. Reading it, the employee then looked at Dahlia. "This way, please."

They passed by workstations where two technicians were busy making repairs, then to Tate's office.

"Have a seat," Tate said from behind his desk as soon as his employee had left. "I believe it was Prague, wasn't it?"

Dahlia ignored him and remained standing.

He stiffened. "Suit yourself."

"Where's Carl Lasker?"

"I don't know."

"I think you do," Dahlia said. "And now's the time to tell me."

She swiped through her phone, then turned it to Tate.

He looked at the screen, the blood drained from his face and recognition dawned. He met Dahlia's eyes.

"Do you understand now?" she asked.

Tate's Adam's apple rose then fell.

Dahlia leaned closer to him and said, "Tell me what I need to know because we don't have time to waste."

78

GREATER WASHINGTON

Everything in Carl Lasker's life was hanging by a thread.

He took another hit of coffee as he progressed on I-95, north toward DC. The pressure was intense, but if he could just hold on and do this one thing, he'd be free and clear.

He needed to get this over with.

Then he'd go to the ball game this afternoon with Greg. The Mets were in town, he'd relax, and everything would be all right.

He adjusted his grip on the steering wheel. *Just be cool.*

Yes, he'd face criminal charges for what he'd done; and with the recent news reports, sightings of the boy, the subway attacks, he could be further implicated. And being contacted by Dahlia, his old classmate from MIT, unnerved him.

Does she know how much I'm involved?

He glanced at the console of his Rogue and the newest burner Tate had given him.

Look at the positives, he told himself as he got off the Beltway, then onto the scenic Baltimore–Washington Parkway. The new payment of $25,000 had gone through, which was a huge plus.

And like Tate said, he was so close to being paid in full—"*freedom from worry, and security for your family.*"

All he had to do was this one task.

His knuckles whitened on the wheel. The problem was he didn't know what the task was.

This morning, he'd been told to drive to a destination, then wait for further instructions. He'd been assured it wouldn't take long and he'd make it to Nationals Park in time for the game.

He glanced at his GPS. He was approaching his destination—near Laurel, Maryland.

79

VIRGINIA

Standing at the door of Carl Lasker's house, Jessie rang the bell. After a few seconds, she heard someone approaching from inside. She steeled herself, preparing to confront Carl or a family member.

Maybe Dylan.

She took a quick breath as the door opened to a man in his early seventies wearing a plaid shirt, jeans, glasses and a short beard.

"Yes?"

"Hello. Could you help me? I'm looking for Carl Lasker."

Making a curious assessment of Jessie, the man shook his head. "He doesn't live here."

She checked her phone and the house number at the door. "This is 267 Walnut Meadow Lane?"

"It is, but he doesn't live here."

Jessie's heart sank, and the man moved to shut the door when a woman called out from behind him.

"Who is it?"

The man paused to respond over his shoulder.

"Someone looking for Lasker!"

"They moved," the voice called back.

"Oh," Jessie said. "Do you have his new address?"

The man turned back to Jessie as a rosy-cheeked woman in her sixties appeared beside him.

"Hi," the woman said. "The Laskers moved a year ago. We're renting from the new owners. Who are you?"

"I'm an old school friend of Carl's. I was passing through, and I guess I don't have his new address."

"I do, dear." She left and Jessie heard a table drawer open. "We still get their mail. One sec."

"Stafford? Isn't it?" The man scratched his beard.

"Yes. Here it is." The woman opened a small address book, turning it to Jessie, who lifted her phone.

"Would it be okay if I took a picture of it?"

"Sure."

"Always with the phones," the man grumbled. "Folks don't write things down anymore."

"Thank you, you've been so helpful," Jessie said after she'd taken the photo.

In the car, she entered the address into her GPS, and twenty minutes later, after following directions out of Fredericksburg to Stafford, she arrived in front of a two-storey brick house with a double garage and a Ford Explorer in the driveway.

She took a moment to check her phone. Nothing new from Dahlia, or California. No news, or police updates. The silence after the Hillandale sighting fuelled her fears.

She took a breath, walked up the path to the house and rang the bell.

The woman who answered was about Jessie's age and had pretty features. "Yes?"

"Hi." Jessie returned her smile. "Does Carl Lasker live here?"

"Who are you?" the woman asked, her smile fading, her face tightening slightly.

"I'm sorry. I'm Jessica Ward," Jessie said apologetically. "Does Carl live here? Could I speak with him?"

A storm gathered behind the woman's eyes, a swirl of puzzlement, shock, then a sudden realization. "You've been in the news." She covered her mouth with her hands. "Oh my God! Your son's missing—your husband was killed." She stared. "I'm so sorry."

Jessie nodded. "Are you Carl's wife, Vanessa?"

The woman pressed her lips together. "Yes. But why are you here?"

"I think Carl can help me." Jessie glanced beyond Vanessa's shoulder. "Is he home?"

"No, he isn't."

"Can you tell me where he is?"

"I don't know how he can help you, or why you're here."

"We went to MIT together," Jessie said. "We had some of the same classes, same professors."

Vanessa frowned in disbelief. "But Carl said he didn't know you."

"We worked on a classified government project together."

"You *worked* together?"

"Did he ever talk about me or my company, Instinct Nine-99?"

"No, I told you," Vanessa said. "No."

Jessie's heart raced. "Has he been following the news about my son?"

"We watched a recent report but—"

"Does he know Robert and Nancy Cook?"

"No, I don't think—"

"Does he still gamble?"

Vanessa's eyes widened in shock. "What? How did—?"

"Does he have a gambling problem?"

Vanessa blinked back tears. "Why are you asking these things? I want you to leave!"

Jessie put her hand on the front door, stopping Carl's wife from shutting it.

"Vanessa, please help me. My son is missing. Carl may be able to help me find him." She paused. "Does Carl have an addiction?

Was there a sudden influx of money recently? Has he been secretive about things the last couple months or so?"

Unease and concern webbed across Vanessa's face. "I don't know what's happening."

"Where is he? Can you call him now?"

Vanessa hesitated. "You're scaring me."

"Just call him! Please!"

Reluctantly, Vanessa pulled her phone out of her back pocket and dialled, holding the phone to her ear. Jessie could hear the phone ringing—agonizing seconds passing with no connection.

"He's not answering," Vanessa said, looking at Jessie. The call went to voicemail. "Call me. It's urgent. Call me now."

"Thank you," Jessie said as Vanessa hung up. "Can you track his phone, his laptop, his car?"

Vanessa shook her head. "He disabled all of that stuff for his job."

"And you don't know where he is?"

Vanessa lifted a hand to her temple. "He said he went to do more freelance work before going to the Nationals baseball game this afternoon."

"Where? What is the work?"

"He couldn't tell me. He said he was bound by an NDA."

Jessie thought for a moment. "You said he was going to a game today. Do you know where his seat is?"

"He's meeting Greg, my cousin's husband who has season tickets. He wrote it down somewhere on our calendar."

"Can you get it please? Maybe I'll catch him at the game."

Vanessa stepped away, then came back seconds later with a slip of notepaper, handing it to Jessie. She took in the details under the note's butterfly graphic, nodding.

"I think it starts around one."

"Thank you," Jessie said. "Let me give you my number. Please, Vanessa, if you have any information, please call me."

"I know Carl's been—we've had problems." Vanessa hugged herself while she cried. "I don't know what's happening with him, with us." Tears rolled down her face. "You have to believe me. Please understand, this is so hard for me."

Her words hit a nerve in Jessie.

"This is hard for *you*?" Vaughn's murder and Dylan's abduction could be tied to subway tragedies in Toronto and Paris. Whatever empathy she'd had for Vanessa vanished in a blinding white flash of anger. "I have to *believe* you? This is *hard* for you?"

Maybe it was eleven days of anguish, horror and exhaustion, but Jessie's hazy restraint evaporated in an explosion of fury.

"Dylan!" she screamed, shouldering past Vanessa into the Lasker home, rushing through the living room. "Dylan!"

"What're you doing?" Vanessa shrieked, chasing after her.

Jessie hurried through the kitchen, the study, the laundry room, the bathroom, dining room, every room on the main floor, looking everywhere, calling for her son. She flew downstairs to the basement, checking storage and utility rooms.

"Dylan!"

Jessie thumped upstairs to the bedrooms with Vanessa behind her.

"Stop this! Get out of my house!"

Jessie searched, room after room, opening closets, checking under beds, before coming to a room with a closed door.

"Dylan!" She opened it, fighting off Vanessa's futile attempt to pull her back.

"Mom!" A girl almost Dylan's age, her eyes wide, was curled up on the bed, terrified.

Jessie checked under her bed, checked her closet, finding nothing.

"Get out!" Vanessa screamed. "Get out now, or I'll call the police!"

Breathing hard, Jessie gave Vanessa one last look, then marched out of her home and got into her rental car, leaving a long strip of rubber as it roared down the street.

She didn't drive far before pulling into the parking lot of a McDonald's and sobbing behind the wheel.

80

MARYLAND

Dylan ran as fast as he could, Mary's voice fading behind him as he raced deeper into the woods, the blood rush deafening in his ears. Branches tugging and slapping him, he stumbled at times over the uneven ground. Frantic, his terrified senses peaking at a level he'd never experienced, he searched, thinking he had to find a house, a person, anyone.

He was free. This was his chance to get away.

Eyes wide, ears pricked, he kept going, brambles scraping and snagging him, gasping until . . .

Until.

He stopped cold to listen.

He heard a voice—*far off.*

Then a bark.

Dylan's breathing whimpered, his hope soared.

His salvation was somewhere through the forest. Far away, but close enough to hear—a person with a dog.

People with dogs were friendly. He saw them all the time in California, smiling and waving. Friendly people with friendly dogs.

He continued running, this time with determined focus, running toward the sound, scanning the woods, until he heard the voice again. Then, like a distant star, he glimpsed a faraway flash of colour, a tiny patch and another bark.

"Help!" Dylan's cry had escaped him before he realized it. Gasping, panting, he smashed through the low branches, a glimpse of a path ahead. But the ground grew more treacherous, the brush denser, and he lost his footing and fell.

Breathing hard, he pressed his palms into the earth.

Drawing up his knees to stand, his eyes found a pair of shoes in front of him. He gazed up to the pants, a swinging 7-Eleven tote bag and Joseph's face smiling down at him.

"Hi there, son."

81

VIRGINIA

Static crackling from the nearby drive-thru speaker wrenched Jessie from her anguish.

Take-out orders from customers in cars echoed across the parking lot, where she took a breath to collect herself.

Keep it together.

Forget what just happened with Vanessa Lasker. Focus on what you know.

She texted Dahlia.

Went to Carl's home. He's not there. Wife says he'll be at the ball game this aft. I have his seat #. Will search for him there. Heading back to DC. You get anything?

A few seconds later, Dahlia responded.

I'm following a lead on where he may be going right now in the DC area. If I strike out, maybe we'll chase him down at the game together. Let's keep following the plan—we must be getting close, Jess.

I'm praying, Jessie texted back.

As she headed north on I-95, a flicker of remorse for her actions at the Lasker family home niggled at her, but she shoved it away, knowing she had done what any mother would do. But as the miles rolled by, questions flashed like road signs. *What if it's all a case of circumstance and Carl has nothing to do with Dylan's disappearance? What if we're wrong?*

Jessie searched ahead for answers.

Yes, but I won't know until I find Carl, Dylan or the Cooks. I have to keep going.

Her phone rang. It was Bobby. She answered with hands-free.

"Jess, we've got the upstate birthday video—sending it now."

She tightened her hold on the wheel, checking traffic lanes.

"Hang on, I gotta find a spot to pull over."

82

MARYLAND

"Now *that* was a close call," Joseph chuckled upon returning with Dylan to the warehouse.

"Thank heaven." Mary clasped her hands together. "I thought we were locked in here. Goodness, I don't know how he got out."

"All of it, divine intervention, I'd say. A sign."

Joseph winked at Dylan while unpacking the tote bag on the large desk serving as their table. He placed egg salad sandwiches, potato chips, apples, sliced celery and carrots, fruit pies, cookies, chocolate milk and sodas on the table.

Staring at nothing, Dylan's eyes glistened.

"You have to eat, sweetheart." Mary began unwrapping the sandwiches and opening a chip bag then a milk carton for him.

"Son, we understand running off like that. Lord knows, this adventure has been a lot to take in." Joseph scrolled through his phone after biting into his sandwich. "The good news is today truly is the day."

"Please eat, Dylan," Mary said. "I know you're hungry."

His eyes flicked to her, then to Joseph. He didn't move or speak.

"Leave him be to sort it all out," Joseph said. "He'll eat when he's ready."

The rafters were rattled by breezes fingering through the old building as Mary and Joseph ate. Occasionally, Joseph glanced lovingly at his wife. This mission had been an ordeal for them, but it was the right thing to do, given her condition. Some years ago, long after they were told they could never have children, she had created a fantasy to deal with her unhappiness. She believed they'd had a son and that he was dead—or at times, she thought he'd been abducted. Therapy had worked, but only temporarily. Ultimately, she retreated into the delusion, to cope with her unfulfilled desire to be a mother.

She seemed to find comfort online, learning about stolen children, trafficked children, children taken in every horrible situation imaginable. Joseph had a neighbourhood kid show him how to get on the dark web, where they saw sickening videos. They also saw videos of brave groups around the world, regular people like them, who rescued children in planned missions. People with all kinds of skills teamed up to embark on righteous operations to save children.

The more they studied and watched, the angrier they became. They were determined to take part in a rescue mission. They submitted all the required information—their photos, bios, location, everything—to several different groups.

It was a happy day when they were contacted and informed that they'd been selected for a mission to rescue a boy from traffickers pretending to be his family. They would be delivering him to others who would return him safely to his true, loving family. The rescue would take place at JFK before the evil traffickers, posing as his grandparents, collected him from one flight and then flew off with him on another, overseas where he'd be sold.

The rescue and recovery network—"the angels," his wife called them—was vast. Dozens of people were involved from around the world. People who seemed to know a lot about everything. Every aspect was prearranged by those on the rescue team, under the direction of various leaders. Joseph and Mary, as rescuers, were given detailed instructions on what to do every step of the way, with secret help at every turn. It was critical to borrow a vehicle; new plates were supplied; they ceased all social media activity. On rescue day, they went from JFK to Penn Station, then the train to Secaucus, to where the car had been moved. Security cameras had been manipulated or obscured. Most important, they were advised that the boy would be frightened, even resistant to rescue. There would be news reports, allegations, accusations, but they were to ignore them because the news media, most police and other officials were part of the vast, clandestine network of evildoers and traffickers who would attempt to thwart them and cover it up.

Joseph looked again at Mary. The mission had helped her. She was happy. He looked back at his phone, the one the rescue team had assigned to them, marvelling at how organized the group was. Later, they'd receive post-mission instructions on how to return to life.

His phone buzzed with an update.

Today was the day.

He turned to Dylan and smiled. The boy was eating heartily now.

Suddenly, there was a sound from outside. All three of them turned to the building's main doors. Their attention had been pulled to an approaching vehicle.

The car stopped outside.

A moment later, a large door to the building creaked open, allowing in a diffusion of sunlight, silhouette and shadow, as someone stepped inside.

Joseph caught his breath, looked to Mary.

"It's happening!" she said.

They both looked at Dylan. Then Joseph spoke.

"Today's going to be a glorious day!"

83

VIRGINIA

Jessie signalled and used the exit at Woodbridge.

Finding a safe spot, she pulled over to the shoulder and turned on her hazard lights.

"Have we still got you?" Bobby asked.

She picked up her phone.

"Yes."

"Okay, one of the tour guides in Tanzania sent us the birthday video from the sister's phone. It took several attempts and there were delays, but they transmitted it using a satellite internet service. I've sent it to you. Did you get it?"

She checked her phone. "No. I don't see anything."

"Hold on."

A long moment passed, but then the message came through. A few seconds later, the video loaded.

"Got it."

She touched the arrow to start it. Instantly, the footage took her to the Four Jays Motel & Diner in upstate New York and the birthday party.

Here was seven-year-old Cheyenne—joyous, with three little friends, all thrilled in animated chatter. At the table with them:

three adults. Not in the video was Cheyenne's aunt Colleen, who was recording it.

Jessie caught her breath.

"Are you seeing it all right?"

"Yes."

There, at the edge of the frame, in a corner booth was Vaughn alone, looking out the window. Light flickered in the foreground from candles on the cake.

Then the singing of "Happy Birthday."

A shadow brushed the background and the camera's angle caught the back of a person joining Vaughn. In the foreground, gifts were presented, the camera shifting as each was opened, displayed and cheered. A different angle captured Vaughn's booth, the fervour drawing brief attention from his mystery guest, who turned.

"Oh my God!"

Jessie's heart stopped as she gazed at Carl Lasker, her former classmate, slightly aged by time.

"Yep, it's him," Bobby said. "We used old MIT photos in your office and ran them through a facial app to be sure."

Jessie went numb and hung up. *Carl was Vaughn's source, the last person to be with him before he was murdered?* She blinked, staring at the screen. Dahlia was right.

Checking her mirror, Jessie eased back onto the road and resumed driving. She had to get to the baseball game, had to find Carl.

Right now, he was her only hope of finding Dylan—a hope that was held by the thinnest of threads.

84

MARYLAND

Carson Blake looked up from his laptop and reached down, massaging the shoulders of the dog at his feet. “What’s up, Bear? You’re all clingy, buddy.”

“Something in the woods spooked him when I took him out earlier.” Nora, Carson’s younger sister, was at his bedroom doorway, peeling an orange.

“Like what? A squirrel?”

“Dunno. I thought I heard something near the old asylum complex. Like a kid’s scream. Maybe a screech. It was far off.”

“An owl.” Carson shrugged. “Or kids messing around.”

“Yeah, but when we hear kids, there’s usually laughing. With this, the tone was, like, panicked, and Bear picked up on it.”

“Panicked?”

“Yeah, and it’s bugging me. What if someone was, like, screaming for help? I thought it was a joke.” She swallowed, looking concerned. “But Carson, what if maybe somebody got hurt?”

Carson closed his laptop. “Let’s check it out.”

“Seriously?”

“No school today. Mom’s gone to work. I got nothing going on. Let’s go.”

A few minutes later, Carson and Nora crossed the street with Bear. They entered the woods near their home, cutting into the overgrown path that led to the abandoned asylum. It had been shut down decades ago, and since then it was rumoured to be used for rituals, or was haunted.

Nora, who'd just turned thirteen, never ventured in there alone and was glad to be with Carson. He was seventeen and her protector.

Bear's collar jingled as they progressed into the forest. He was a black and tan German shepherd they'd had since he was a pup. At the moment, the way he was panting, Bear seemed happy to be with them.

"So where were you guys, when you heard it?" Carson asked.

Nora pointed to a thick grove.

It took them a few minutes to reach it, with Bear barking a confirmation.

"Hello! Anyone there?" Carson called out.

Bear barked.

Nothing but birdsong.

Through the trees they glimpsed part of the deserted complex. "Let's go that way," Carson said.

Bear got a little ahead of them, then circled a spot wagging his tail and barking for them to catch up.

Nora got there first. "What is it, Bear?"

He moved his snout toward the ground, and she glimpsed a flash of bright yellow. Parting a tangle of thick underbrush, she saw the object, about the size of a candy bar. It looked out of place, and she picked it up and handed it to Carson.

"Spaceracer," he said. "A little kid's game."

"What do you think?" Nora asked.

"I don't know." Carson slipped the game in his pocket and looked through the trees to the building nearby. "I think we should look in there."

It was an abandoned warehouse. Last year Carson would hang out there and drink beer with high school pals for something to do. Bear led them to the front, where a chain and padlock still secured the big doors. Carson lifted the lock to study it. His brow creased.

"What is it?" Nora asked.

The silver lock was new. "This used to be an old, rusted lock, like the chain." He looked at his younger sister. "Someone's been here recently."

"Who?" Nora looked around, saw nothing and no one.

"Hello!" Carson called, and Bear barked.

A long moment passed; the only response was the breeze in the treetops, and Bear's panting.

"Maybe we should leave," Nora said.

"Let's go in."

"But it's all locked up, Carson."

"This way, c'mon." Carson, with Bear, led Nora along the front to a corner where he began pulling at some loose weather-worn wooden slats. "Deke Haskell showed me this back in the day." He grunted, pulling until the slats creaked and he managed to pivot them enough to create a triangular opening.

"Let's go."

"Carson, I'm scared."

"But what if someone needs help? You said you heard a kid crying."

"Let's just call the police and wait outside."

"No, let's go in and check."

Nora hesitated.

"It'll be okay," he said. "I promise."

Nora took a breath, nodded, and they stepped inside. After adjusting their eyes to the light, Carson found a broken metal chair leg on the floor. He picked it up and held it up to assure his sister. It would serve as a weapon if they needed it.

They stirred dust as they emerged from the corner, navigating around tall storage racks to the main area where Bear was barking.

They stopped in their tracks.

"What the—?" Carson said.

In the distance, looking out of place, stood a late-model white SUV. Bear trotted over to it.

"I don't like this," Nora said.

"Yeah, it's weird," Carson said, tightening his hold on the chair leg and motioning for Nora to stay behind him as they approached.

Bear had disappeared around the side of the SUV and barked again. Near the front, a few yards away, chairs were positioned around a desk with an assortment of food, drinks and wrappers, as if someone's picnic had been interrupted.

Carson and Nora neared the car. Bear was out of sight, but his barking was more insistent, drawing them around it to the other side.

Legs and feet were the first things they saw.

A man and a woman were sitting on the ground, their backs against the car. In that moment, it appeared they were resting. The man was slumped, his chin on his chest. Then Carson saw his temple, which had a bloodied mush of brains visible from a hole. The woman was leaning against the man, part of her face missing. Blood—in clumps and strings of it—laced the car door behind them, pooled on the ground, drenching their clothing.

Nora's scream vibrated throughout the building. Pigeons fluttered hysterically and Bear barked and barked.

Somehow, Carson got his sister away from the bodies to a chair at the table. Somehow, he got out his phone and called 911. Somehow, he was able to answer the emergency operator's questions.

"I want to report a double murder at the old asylum on Appletree Lane! In the warehouse!"

Staying on the line with the operator, who'd dispatched resources, Carson saw Bear disappear next to a couple of large storage containers. He continued barking intensely. While answering more questions from the operator, Carson withdrew the child's game from his pocket, describing it to the operator.

At that moment, he walked around a storage container and froze.

"No, not another one!"

The operator asked Carson to repeat himself.

"There's another body! Three murder victims here!"

85

WASHINGTON, DC

"You were right about Carl!" Jessie voice-texted Dahlia while heading back to DC. "We got video of him meeting Vaughn before he was killed. I'm sending it to you now."

Knuckles whitening on the wheel, she accelerated, weaving around slower vehicles but carefully heeding directions from her GPS, getting in the lanes to take her to the ball park.

She'd gone to a couple of Dodgers games in Los Angeles, so she knew there were steps to take in advance. Using hands-free commands, she bought a ticket. Thankfully, today's game against the Mets was not sold out. Still, things could fill up fast, and parking was limited, so she used an app to reserve a space on a private lot three blocks from the stadium, relieved to get one of the few remaining spots.

It wasn't long before she reached Southeast Washington, and as she got near the Navy Yard, the traffic slowed. But Nationals Park was in view, things kept crawling, and soon she arrived at her lot, parking in her reserved space.

Jessie had also checked the policy that basically restricted fans from carrying computer bags with them. It made her anxious about securing Instinct's blue laptop. Time was ticking.

She bit her bottom lip.

I have no choice.

Taking care that no one was near, she slid the blue laptop out of its bag, went to the back seat and folded the backrest down. The side upholstery seam had a hidden zipper. She opened it and slid the laptop into the back where it vanished between the backrest foam and the cover. She rezipped it and repositioned the backrest. Then she left her other computer bags on the floor, crammed under the driver's seat, purposely allowing a strap to be visible. If a thief broke into her car, that was the bait.

She locked up and hurried to the stadium, joining the flow of other people moving toward it, the roar of the crowd and announcements over the public address system growing louder as she got nearer.

Entering at Center Field Gate, she joined fans who were wearing Nationals jerseys, T-shirts and caps. Vendors called out offering souvenirs and food. The carnival atmosphere whirled. Each time she saw a boy Dylan's age, she studied his face. She did the same with men who resembled Carl Lasker, or older people who looked like the Cooks. The aroma of popcorn and hotdogs, the sound of thudding music, and mounting excitement filled the air.

Not caring about where her seat was actually located, Jessie found a woman wearing a jacket labelled "ASK ME." Jessie showed her the details of Carl's seat and sought directions.

"That's upper deck, right above us. Section 311, gallery level, behind home plate." She pointed. "You want to take those stairs to the third level."

Manoeuvring around the slow movers, Jessie ascended the stairs. At different points, she glimpsed the beautiful brilliant green of the vast baseball field, the stands curving in majesty. With the New York Mets in town, attendance approached the stadium's capacity of more than forty thousand.

Breathing hard, she reached level three.

Gripping a railing, she stepped into Carl's section searching for the correct row and seat. The air thundered with cheers for a successful double play by the home team. Fireworks bloomed on the screen of the big scoreboard as Jessie came to the two seats for Carl and Greg.

They were empty.

Her heart sank. Vanessa Lasker had lied about her husband being at the game with his in-law.

She looked at the people sitting next to the seats. A woman in her twenties, sunglasses and a Nationals cap, ponytail. She was with a man in his twenties—cap, sunglasses, arms sleeved in tattoos.

"Excuse me!" Jessie raised her voice.

The woman turned to Jessie, cupping her hand to her ear.

Jessie leaned down. "Excuse me! Do you know the guy who sits here? He has season tickets?"

The ponytail swung as she shook her head, then leaned over to her male friend, saying something in his ear. He shrugged, then pointed to the older woman and man seated one row below the two empty seats. Jessie took a step down.

"Excuse me," she said, asking the same of the older couple, explaining that she was with friends and supposed to meet the guy with season tickets for the seats behind them but didn't know him.

The woman had pink hair; the man had a patch over one eye. The couple consulted each other after Jessie's question.

"The guy's name is Greg," the eyepatch man said.

"He comes to most games," the woman said. "Friendly, likes to chat. Lives in Virginia."

"Fredericksburg," the man said.

"Is he here today?"

"We haven't seen him yet," the woman said.

"So sorry. One sec, could you help me?" Thinking fast, she cued up the video from the diner showing Carl. Freezing the frame on his face, she enlarged it and turned her phone. "Have you seen this man here today? He's my college friend—should be with Greg."

The couple stared at the image before they shook their heads. Thanking them, Jesse retreated to the small tables next to the concession stand and the aroma of popcorn and hotdogs.

Nerves strained, she stood at the railing. Based on what she'd learned, it seemed Vanessa had been telling the truth about Carl's in-law, Greg, who had season tickets for the empty seats she was watching. Fredericksburg wasn't far from Stafford. It seemed plausible.

So where are they?

Jessie texted Dahlia.

I'm at the game. Carl's not here. What do you have?

Lowering her phone, Jessie—her nerves tingling—paced, thinking this was not good. Her phone vibrated with Dahlia's response.

I'm following up on where he may have gone before the game. Be with you soon. Send me your location in the stadium.

Jessie sent Dahlia a pin just as the crowd roared in response to another big play. She looked at the scoreboard, rubbing her temples as the seconds ticked by.

86

UNITED STATES/CANADA/EUROPE

Twenty-five miles northeast of where Jessie was keeping vigil in Nationals Park, thirteen-year-old Nora was in the back of an ambulance outside the storage building of the abandoned asylum complex, struggling to calm down. The paramedics hesitated then allowed Bear to be with her. The dog's presence was calming.

Her brother, Carson, was in the back of a patrol car, giving an account to the sheriff's deputies, who'd called their mother at work.

Police radios crackled with dispatches, emergency lights flashed, and sirens wailed as investigators from a range of agencies responded to the call.

Yellow tape sealed the area, grid searches with canine units were launched, drones deployed, a canvass organized. Forensic experts suited up in hooded coveralls, opening the doors to enter the building as news crews descended on the scene. A command post was set up and jurisdiction sorted as it soon became clear that these three suspicious deaths were part of something bigger.

The vehicle in the building was a white 2024 Toyota RAV4 XLE Hybrid. When Maryland investigators ran its New Jersey plates, VIN and other descriptors, it lit up the databases. The plates were stolen, but other details confirmed the vehicle was wanted in connection with the kidnapping of a nine-year-old boy from JFK, which might be tied to his father's homicide and the cyber hijacking of subway systems in Canada, Brazil and France.

Updated alerts went out to the law enforcement organizations across the country and in Canada, Europe and South America, all working together in the ongoing, exhaustive investigation. This development boosted the momentum of the detectives, analysts and agents.

In Ottawa, Claire Brenner was at her desk, working at dissecting Tarantula's trail to help thwart any more potential intrusions. Inquiring about the identities of the victims in Maryland, she was told they hadn't yet been confirmed.

Claire prayed for the kidnapped boy.

In New York, FBI Special Agent Jake Garlin, and NYPD Detective Mario Lugano, welcomed the news that the Cooks' SUV had been located. Garlin was on the phone to agents who were on the ground at the abandoned asylum.

"A bad scene out there," Garlin told Lugano. "Too early to determine exactly what they have. We got to hang tough."

Garlin and Lugano returned to studying the various reports that had been started at the outset of Dylan's abduction and whose findings concerned the analysis of every aspect of the case.

Across the Atlantic in Paris, prosecutors had opened a national investigation into the deadly crash at the Quai de la Rapée Metro station. The day before Carson and Nora Blake discovered the Cook's SUV in Maryland, French investigators had had a break of their own.

At Charles de Gaulle Airport, in a preboarding area for a flight to Istanbul, a retired French detective overheard a fragment of conversation leaking from the earphones of a fellow passenger, just as he was slipping them in.

It was in a Slavic language he understood.

"*. . . your work on the Metro was unbelievable . . . more spectacular than Toronto . . .*"

The young man sitting with his back to the retired detective responded, "*The spider strikes again . . . soon we'll have what we need to make everyone shake in their boots . . .*"

Concerned by what he'd heard, the old detective got up, pretending to stretch his legs. He dropped his trash in a bin, all while assessing the young traveller. In his mid-twenties, tattoos on his neck and hands, concentrating on his laptop, earphones in place. He gave the old detective a bad feeling. Not wanting to let it go, he strolled off and casually alerted airport security.

During boarding, the desk agent feigned a problem with the traveller's boarding pass and passport. Denying him boarding, the agent advised the traveller to step aside where he was quickly escorted to a room by three security officers.

His fingerprints were scanned into a mobile reader. A search of his bag, which had a hidden compartment, uncovered four different passports from former Soviet republics, each with his photo, each with an alias. He was immediately arrested for questioning.

Now, as Jessie kept watch for Carl Lasker at Nationals Park, and police processed the scene at the abandoned asylum in Maryland, the suspect in Paris facing his second day of questioning.

His name: Dmitri Semyon Vampa, aged twenty-six, nationality unknown.

He was being held in Paris at the headquarters of the Direction Générale de la Sécurité Intérieure, the DGSI. He was in a secure high-level interview room with cameras and a recording system. He was wearing inmate coveralls, seated at a plain table, his wrists handcuffed to an anchor bolted to the tabletop.

Seated across from him were Klara Boche and Renaud Durand, agents from the Counterterrorism Division. On a chair nearby was a court-approved translator.

Time was running out for Vampa to be held before having access to a lawyer.

This was day two of long hours of questioning.

Vampa was exhausted and hungry.

A tray of fresh bread, sliced sausage and cheese was on a table in the corner. Wisps of the spices in the sausage, the bread, wafted over to Vampa.

"It took some doing," Boche said, "but our cyber experts found incriminating information in your laptop, maps of the subway systems in Toronto and Paris."

"Your spider tattoo," Durand said, "is a stylized tarantula, indicating you're a full-fledged member."

"Dmitri, the death toll in Paris has risen to fourteen," Boche said. "You'll be spending the rest of your life in prison."

Vampa's stomach growled.

"If you cooperate, the prosecution may lessen your conditions. It could mean the difference between having a spacious cell to yourself or a cramped cell with a beast as a cellmate. Day in and day out. Let that sink in," Durand said, helping himself to bread, cheese and sausage, fashioning a sandwich, eating it in front of Vampa. "Oh, this is good." Durand savoured every small bite as he chewed.

"Admit your actions," Boche said. "Unburden your soul, tell us what we need to know. How big is your faction of Tarantula? Who and where are all the players?"

Vampa looked at his reflection in the one-way mirror.

In the room, observing from the other side, from embassies in Paris, were investigators from the FBI, the RCMP and European police agencies.

"What did you mean?" Durand brushed crumbs from his hands. "That was so good . . . Now tell us, what did you mean when you said to your friend—who has been arrested in Turkey, by the way and is likely to flip on you—when you said, 'The spider strikes again, soon we'll have what we need to make everyone shake in their boots'? What did you mean by that?"

A knock sounded at the door and an officer entered, placing a file folder on the table before the agents. They opened it to find photos of the Cooks, Dylan Ward, Vaughn Ward and a white Toyota SUV.

Boche showed them to Vampa, studying his reaction, a near-imperceptible flinch.

"Do you know this couple?" She tapped the faces of the Cooks. "Are they part of Tarantula?"

Vampa was silent.

Boche continued. "We know you were involved in Paris. We know you were involved in Toronto, and likely São Paulo."

Vampa looked at her impassively.

"What was your role in the operation at JFK? Does Tarantula have any connections with any US government security agency? Any US cybersecurity company?"

Vampa still said nothing, as if aware that the correct amount of time would soon pass and then he could have a lawyer.

Durand put his big palms on the table, his chair scraping loudly as he pushed it back to stand. He drew his face within inches of Vampa's so he could smell the sausage on his breath.

"We can place you in a cell tonight with unpleasant company, Dmitri," Durand said.

"Tell us what we need to know," Boche said.

"Is another attack coming?"

Vampa looked into Durand's face and remained silent.

87

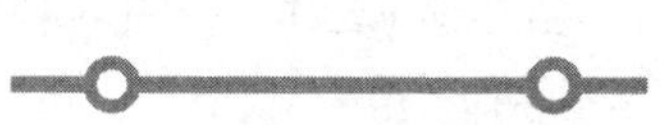

WASHINGTON, DC

Inning after inning passed, and Jessie struggled against a sense of futility. Impervious to the rollercoaster emotions of the crowd, she kept watch from the railing near the concession stand, eyeing every person moving about the section. She grew familiar with those coming and going as her helplessness deepened

The seats for Carl and his in-law remained empty, and she hadn't heard from Dahlia.

Another deafening roar from the crowd sent Jessie's memory back years to the time she and Vaughn had taken Dylan to a Dodgers game. Dylan was glowing, wishing he could catch a foul ball, as Vaughn explained the rules to him.

They'd been a happy family. But now they were broken, and she was trapped in a nightmare.

Why did Carl go to New York to meet with Vaughn? Could they have known each other from Vaughn's time at Harvard and Carl's time at MIT? Was he Vaughn's source, or did he kill Vaughn to stop him from reporting something he'd uncovered about Tarantula? Why did the Cooks take Dylan? Why is Dahlia convinced Carl is involved? Please, don't let it be connected to Instinct's work. Because if it is, oh God, no, because if it is, then Vaughn's murder, Dylan's abduction, the subway tragedies—everything would be my fault!

The stadium erupted in wild applause; the Nationals had made an outstanding play, coming from behind as the game was winding down.

But Jessie was indifferent. She couldn't believe that Carl was a no-show. All she could do now was hope that Dahlia had found him.

Jessie's phone vibrated in her hand.

It wasn't Dahlia, or Bobby and Sarita, or the police.

It was breaking news story from *The Washington Post* with the headline:

3 bodies discovered with SUV wanted in boy's JFK abduction

Jessie's breath caught in her throat, gripping the railing as she read the short item.

The report stated that police were at the scene of a shuttered asylum complex in a wooded area near Laurel, Maryland. The discovery indicated links to recent subway tragedies, according to a source who could not be named. Two of the deceased, whose identities were unconfirmed, were believed to be an older couple sought in the abduction aspect of the case. The article ended with a line saying no information was known about the third body at this time.

Jessie gasped, looking at the news photo accompanying the story.

It was grainy, shot from long distance, taking the reader deeper into the crime scene. The doors to a warehouse were open, and forensic investigators in coveralls worked near a white Toyota SUV, its New Jersey plate identical to that used by the Cooks'. Next to it, on the ground, a crime scene tech was bent over bright yellow tarps.

Those tarps were covering the dead.

"Dylan!" Jessie's scream was drowned out by the explosive roar of the crowd. Knees buckling, she steadied herself on the railing, choking back sobs. "Oh God, please no!"

The big-screen scoreboard animated with fireworks, then the words "Nats! Nats! Nats!" as fans joined in with the full-throttle chanting.

Her fingers trembling, Jessie sent the story with a message to Dahlia.

I need you here. Where are you?

In a panicked blur, she sent the *Post* story to Garlin at the FBI, to Bobby and Sarita in California and to Chelsea at *Veritas Sola*, pleading for help. Wiping her tears, she battled to stay strong, to get to Laurel and find her son—*to hold my sweet boy again.*

Her phone vibrated and rang.

"Oh God, Dahlia! Did you see? Oh God—he's—"

"Jessie no! Listen he's not—" The crowd booming, Jessie covered one ear and moved away from the stands, past the concession and nearer to the bathrooms, where it was quieter.

"What?"

"Can you hear what I said?"

"Say it again!"

"*Dylan's alive!*"

"He's alive?"

"Something was happening after I pursued Carl this morning, and they contacted me."

"Who contacted you?"

"Tarantula, the people with Tarantula."

"What?

"They want all of Instinct's work, your new technology."

"But—"

"Jessie, they have Dylan!"

88

WASHINGTON, DC

"Mom."

Oh God!

Dylan appeared on Jessie's phone.

"Dylan, honey, are you all right?"

Heart swelling, fingertips trembling, hovering over the screen.

Moments ago, Dahlia had said Tarantula would contact Jessie with a video call, proving they had Dylan. And here he was—alive and so close, yet so far—with rings under his eyes, his voice quivering.

"Those people at the airport weren't Grandma and Grandpa. Somebody got shot. They covered my eyes. Mom, where are you? I'm so scared."

Jessie wanted to reach into her phone and pull him to her, but she had to be sure. Knowing what was possible with AI manipulation, she had to be certain she was talking to her son. Scrutinizing the background, the little of it she could see, revealed nothing. Examining his face, searching for Vaughn's features, listening to the boy's voice, she had to remove any doubt it was Dylan.

"Yes, honey, I want to get you, more than anything, but . . ." She swallowed hard. "Honey, can you tell me our secret words?"

Dylan blinked and he said nothing. Seconds swept by, the stadium echoing, the public address system booming as the game neared the end. That's when Dylan started singing the theme to a cartoon show, a song about living in a pineapple under the sea.

His weak, timid voice lifted Jessie's heart. This was her son.

"Oh honey, where are you?"

Dylan vanished.

Her screen went black. "Dylan! Come back! Dylan!" she shouted at her phone.

From the abyss of her screen came an ominous robotic speaker, whose words were altered through a voice changer.

"Listen carefully. We will exchange the boy for the technology Instinct is developing for the government." The speaker paused, letting Jessie digest the demand. "Your husband said you always travel with it."

Jessie went cold. She was listening to the voice of Dylan's abductor—and Vaughn's killer. The menacing voice was deep, with a slow, commanding cadence. "Get it and proceed to the Metro, the Navy Yard–Ballpark Station. Purchase a Metro SmarTrip day pass. Get on the platform and await instructions."

The call ended.

Jessie rushed to join the flood of fans cascading down the stairs, level by level, jostling to get by.

"Hey, lady!"

"Excuse me, excuse me," she said as she left the stadium and began running to the parking lot. Breathing hard, she unlocked her car and looked around. There were no obvious signs of a break-in. Fishing the blue laptop from its concealed spot, she also got her computer bags from under the seat.

Quickly, carefully, she stored the laptop in one bag and her new laptop in another, slung them over her shoulder, locked the car and hurried to the Metro.

She was slowed by the clog of fans entering the Navy Yard–Ballpark station.

"Hey what's going on with all the cops?" someone complained.

"It's the DC National Guard," a man said. "Extra security popped up. Must be a threat. Wasn't like this before the game. They're even doing random bag checks, slowing things."

Craning her neck, Jessie glimpsed armed guardsmen in camouflage scattered across the station, and her pulse thudded wildly. It would take too long to explain her situation to them. The people who had Dylan could escape. Her breath came fast, every nerve ending was fraying.

No. I can't be stopped. Not now.

Tightening her grip on her bags, scanning the crowd, she came to where people were being pulled aside for spot checks: a couple with a stroller and big bags; two young women with large mountain-climber backpacks. As guardsmen probed their belongings, Jessie manoeuvred deftly between them in a line that appeared to be flowing by. Thankfully, she passed through without being selected to have her bags checked.

From that point, she did her best to thread her way to a machine, where she purchased her SmarTrip card. She hurried through the turnstile, bypassed more guardsmen, got to the escalator and then the platform. Blending in with the people crowding it, awaiting instructions, she was taking in the arching waffle ceiling, a hallmark of the Metro system, when her phone vibrated. She inserted earphones to hear clearly.

Bobby and Sarita appeared on her phone screen; concern carved in their faces.

"Jess, we saw the news story—we've got something critical about who Vaughn met at the diner—"

"I know—it's Carl. He's with Tarantula. They have Dylan."

"No, wait—they have Dylan?" Sarita said. "No, Jess, it wasn't—"

At that moment of confusion an urgent beep tone sounded. Jessie had an incoming call.

"I have to keep the line clear—"

Bobby said, "Jess, wait, it's not—"

"I have to keep the line clear. I have to go."

Not hearing what Bobby and Sarita were saying, Jessie took the call from a blocked number.

"Listen carefully." The foreboding voice filled her earphones. "Get on the very next train northbound for Greenbelt. You must board on the third car and ride in the middle of the car. Do not fail, if you want to see your son again."

In less than a minute, the platform edge lights flashed, signalling the arrival of a train. Soon after, the train emerged, easing into the station. Jessie bumped other people, positioning herself to get into the third car. She stayed in the middle, shouldering and elbowing her way to a seat near the doors, drawing dirty looks.

She stared at her phone, awaiting instructions, glimpsing views of the buildings of the Navy Yard as well as the Anacostia River before the train descended underground toward the downtown core. The train's interior lights reflected on the windows as it rolled through the tunnels to a series of stops. First Waterfront, next was L'Enfant Plaza, then came Archives, the short trips punctuated with announcements.

For about ten minutes, Jessie was welded to her phone, relieved internet connectivity was good on the Metro. She grew increasingly desperate for instructions, as the train approached Gallery Place Station.

Her phone rang, and the deep voice spoke.

"Leave the Instinct computer under the seat at the final moment before you step off. Do not look at or engage anyone. Leave the train immediately, and get to the upper level in time to catch the next Red Line train bound for Shady Grove, arriving soon. Board on the second car."

As Jessie's train slowed, she shifted the computer bags to her feet on the floor.

"Do you understand your instructions?"

"Yes. I understand."

She jammed one bag, as deep under her seat as possible, blocking it with the other as the train slowed and people collected around her and at the doors.

The doors opened. Jessie picked up her other bag and shoved her way onto the platform. With garbled announcements echoing, she navigated the crush of passengers, locating the escalators leading up to the Red Line trains.

On the escalators, most people kept to the right. She rushed up the moving stairs, bumping arms and bags.

On the upper level, Jessie looked up at a digital sign.

RED LINE TO SHADY GROVE ARRIVING IN 1 MINUTE

She got to the platform just as the edge lights flashed, indicating the train was arriving in seconds. Gliding into the station, the train's doors hissed open and passengers spilled out. Jessie aligned with the second car, working her way between bunches of boarding passengers, finding a seat as the train lurched forward for the long ride to Shady Grove.

89

WASHINGTON, DC

Her chin trembling, Jessie squeezed her eyes shut to stay in control during the short tunnel trip to the next stop.

Metro Center, a transfer station with vast platforms and throngs of commuters.

Time is slipping away.

It took less than a minute to load and unload riders at Metro Center. Doors closed and the train moved on, arriving at Farragut North where the process was repeated.

As the train pulled away from the station, Jessie battled to breathe, eyes on her phone, checking her earphones when she got a call. The menacing voice ordered her to "Exit the train at Woodley Park–Zoo/Adams Morgan."

Another short trip, through the tunnels under the city, to Dupont Circle, with Jessie studying the faces of the people settling in her car.

Within seconds after departing Dupont, Jessie, her nerves tingling, thought only of Dylan. A few minutes later, as the train slowed, she caught her breath when her tormentor called again.

"Exit here," the deep voice ordered, "then immediately reboard on the fourth car of this train. Look to the rear."

She rushed down the platform, pinballing off commuters entering and exiting the train at Woodley Park–Zoo/Adams Morgan.

Stepping into the fourth car, working her way around a long-haired tattooed guy with a bicycle, she was stuck behind an older man with a cane, who was slow to lower himself into a seat. Then she was blocked by a wall of boisterous teenaged girls, tourists speaking . . . *what, Japanese?* Parting the all-girl cluster, she reached the back.

Jessie froze.

"Mom!"

Alone in a seat by the window, hoodie on his lap, was her son.

"Oh God, Dylan!" She flew to him, half sobbing, half laughing, crushing him into her arms, kissing his face, stroking his hair, breathing him in, feeling whole again, feeling alive.

He blinked at her, crying softly, trying to smile.

"Oh, honey, it's really you!"

Yes, he was thinner, haggard, but something was different. Something was—*where are his hands?* She followed his gaze to the hoodie covering his lap. She lifted it, and the metal glinted in the car's interior light.

Dylan's wrist was handcuffed to his seat frame.

"God, no!"

The doors whooshed closed.

The train pulled out of the station.

90

WASHINGTON, DC

Fear coiled up Jessie's spine.

She pulled at Dylan's handcuffs, tried sliding them from the frame, looked in her bag for something to insert in the keyhole.

Nothing worked.

It was useless.

I'm running out of time—before they open the Instinct bag!

She pushed through the teenaged girls to the bicycle man.

"Can you help me?"

He tugged out his earphones.

"Help me, my son's handcuffed to his seat!"

"He's handcuffed? You serious?"

She pointed to the storage bag attached to his bike's frame.

"You must have tools or something in there."

"Yeah, but I don't think I have anything that'll work. He's handcuffed? Let me see this."

He stepped around the girls, then lowered himself in front of Dylan.

"Wow, little dude. How'd this happen?" Then he looked around. "This a prank to go viral?"

"No! Help me!"

"All right, calm down. Have you got the key?"

"No, I don't!"

"Weird. Who did this?" Grasping the cuffs, the man pulled and twisted. When that failed, he grunted, forcing his weight on the seat frame attempting to get enough slack to somehow slide the cuff out.

"No dice," he said. "Was he fooling around with them?"

Jessie called 911, fighting to stay calm, her voice shaky.

"My son is handcuffed to the seat of a Metro train on the Shady Grove Red Line."

The emergency operator collected Jessie's information then advised, "We'll inform the train operator to hold at your next stop, Cleveland Park. Firefighters are on the way to free your son."

Thanking the emergency dispatcher, and the bicycle man, Jessie heaved a sigh of relief and sat with Dylan, calming him.

"When we get off this train, we'll tell the police everything. It'll be over soon, okay?"

She felt him nodding against her as she hugged him, then her phone vibrated and rang. Bobby was calling. She replaced her earphones.

"Jessie!" His tone urgent. "It's not Carl with Vaughn in the video from the diner! It was manipulated."

"Manipulated?"

"My friend from Stanford is an expert who's been helping us. It's not Carl! She says it's Dahlia!"

Dahlia!

Stunned, another video from the diner appeared on Jessie's phone screen. Bobby had sent a clip showing Vaughn with Dahlia, who could be seen when she turned to the camera.

"Oh my God!" Jessie said under her breath, her body going cold.

"Listen to me," Bobby said, "the video was somehow intercepted when it was being sent from Tanzania. Sally thinks people from the dark web did a sloppy rush job to manipulate it with AI. She unmasked it for us."

"Bobby, I can't believe this."

"It's why Dahlia arrived in LA to help you, then rushed to DC," he said. "Jessie, she's with Tarantula!"

"Okay, listen Bobby," Jessie said. "I've got Dylan back and he's okay, he's good!"

"You've got him back!" She heard Bobby shout "She's got Dylan" to Sarita, who cheered. "That so freakin' great, Jess!"

"We're on the Metro. As soon as we get off, we're going to tell the FBI—" Jessie was interrupted by shouting from the passengers.

"Hey! Stop!"

"What the hell?"

The train had blazed passed Cleveland Park Station without stopping. She glimpsed the shocked faces of commuters on the platform as the train raced by with a gust of wind in its wake. A frightened rider in her car said, "Tell the driver to stop!"

Jessie sensed the train gaining speed. At that moment she received another call from the ominous voice. She answered.

"You have your son," the voice said, "but it's not over."

"I know it's you, Dahlia."

Silence followed.

"Why, Dahlia? Why hurt innocent people? Why hurt us?"

Another silence before the robotic voice continued. "Vaughn was mine when I met him. You took him away, had a life together, had everything that I dreamed of. My life was broken promises and betrayals. The more I failed, the more I realized how you and Vaughn had taken everything from me."

"I don't understand. How can that be?"

"I was broken, I drifted in darkness, took my skills to where I had control, where I was welcomed. The people with Tarantula have never lied, never betrayed me. I rose in the ranks. We knew, I knew, you'd developed the eternal key—and now we have it."

The deep threatening voice of her friend filling Jessie's head was surreal.

As the train neared Van Ness–UDC Station, passengers yelled for it to slow for the stop.

Dahlia continued. "Vaughn was working on a story to take down Tarantula. He reached out to me, not knowing I was a member. You were separated, and I sensed Vaughn had come back to me. I fell for him all over again, offered to be his source—not to help, but to learn what he knew. After we had one night together, he told me being with me was a mistake." Dahlia scoffed. "*A mistake!* He wanted to be with you and your boy. So he discarded me. Again."

The train swayed, speeding to the next station. Jessie looked at Dylan, still handcuffed to the seat frame. "Dahlia please, you have to stop this."

"Tarantula proved its power with Toronto, Paris and São Paulo. But to seize control of any system and be invincible, we needed Instinct's key. I could've stolen your laptop at any time, but I worked with Tarantula, channelling my vengeance, orchestrating spectacular attacks, like this one. The artistry of it. The late great Professor Jackson would've been impressed. Now you will know my pain, seeing everything you loved destroyed."

"Dahlia, no!"

But she was gone.

The train blew past the next station, and the passengers screamed. Some were calling 911. One person slammed down on the emergency intercom button to tell the train operator to stop.

Up front, in the cab, operator Chad Ryan was assailed by passengers pressing the call buttons in every car. His control panel lights were strobing. Nothing he did had any effect.

"We've got a system failure!" Ryan pleaded over his radio for help from the Metro's Rail Operations Control Center.

Across the city, in an eleven-storey building in Southwest Washington, traffic controller Tom Harris scanned his console with disbelief.

"A failure?" Harris said.

Like most systems across the country and around the world, the Metro's Red Line was running under Automatic Train Operation. The driver could override the automated system to take control manually in an emergency—*like now*.

But nothing Ryan did was working.

"Affirmative! We have a system failure!" Ryan repeated.

"I don't see it." Puzzled, Harris searched his console. "All my readings show you are operating normally."

"We just blew through two stops and we're accelerating! I tried bypassing ATO, switching to manual, it didn't work!"

"The brakes?"

"They won't respond!"

"Kill power to the motor."

"Tried it! Nothing!"

"Hang on, I'll cut the power at my end."

Two seconds passed.

"Done! Are you decelerating?"

"No! We're accelerating! We're coming to another stop! We're minutes away from gaining on the train ahead of us!"

In seconds, pulse jumping, Harris put out a system-wide alert for a runaway train on the northbound Red Line to Shady Grove.

The slower train was minutes ahead of Ryan's and pulling out of Bethesda Station. Harris ordered the driver to override ATO.

"Go manual, accelerate now! Do not stop at Medical, proceed fast to the Grosvenor–Strathmore pocket."

Meanwhile, the runaway train's wheels screeched, it rocked wildly with passengers hanging onto poles, gripping their seats or holding each other as it tore past Tenleytown–AU Station.

"Mom, I'm scared."

Jessie pulled Dylan tight to her, angry at what Dahlia had unleashed.

Fight back. Don't go down without a fight.

At the control centre, Harris had only minutes to get the other trains safely out of the way. He then radioed the driver of the next northbound train, which was departing Grosvenor–Strathmore, and issued similar commands.

"Accelerate. Do not stop at North Bethesda, proceed to Twinbrook and use the crossover."

In car four of the runaway train, Jessie's mind raced, her heart raging as the seconds slipped by. She let go of Dylan, reached into her bag and withdrew a metallic blue laptop.

Instinct's laptop.

The laptop she'd bought in New Jersey for everyday use was blue too. That was the one she'd left on the subway for Tarantula. She knew she'd taken a huge risk. Soon they'd find out she hadn't given them what they wanted—but she had only minutes to live with her choice.

If there was anything in this world that would help her, it was Instinct's work.

The tunnel tracks clicked with the rhythm of machine-gun fire as the train blurred past Friendship Heights Station, where panicked travellers on the platform fled for safety.

In the control centre, looking further along the line, Harris saw the last train in play was now leaving Rockville for Shady Grove. Shady Grove was a terminal station with multiple tracks to get that last train out of the way.

Harris issued an order for the operator.

"After you unload at Shady, move clear onto another track in the trainyard."

Jessie took a deep breath. Steadying herself against the train's jouncing, she fired up her machine and initiated the verification process.

With Dylan handcuffed to a hijacked train, speeding headlong to their deaths, she concentrated with every fibre of her being.

Fingers blurring over her keys, she drew upon every iota of her work, her research, her intelligence, to think like Dahlia and her band of cybercriminals.

For years, Jessie had developed the technology with the power to thwart a cyberattack. She was skilled in the knowledge of track modules, sensors, relays and remote software upgrades.

In the control centre, Tom Harris savoured a degree of cautious relief, having set in motion actions to divert trains along the line. He hadn't noticed supervisors and other senior controllers, who'd heeded his alert, had also taken steps. Platforms were being evacuated; emergency services and area hospitals were alerted. As the minutes swept by, Harris and other officials at the centre struggled to stop the runaway train.

On the Red Line, the train had now reached a breakneck speed of 100 miles per hour as it emerged from the tunnel, bursting past Grosvenor–Strathmore, whizzing by natural green spaces and suburbs.

Jessie saw none of it as she worked.

At the control centre, technicians and traffic officials frantically tried every avenue possible to stop the train.

It was futile.

In minutes, the train shot past other stations—North Bethesda, Twinbrook and Rockville—then the control centre was alerted to the unthinkable.

After the last train stopped and unloaded its passengers at Shady Grove, it had shut down, unresponsive to any commands, either manually or from the control centre. The platform had been cleared, but the empty stationary train was immovable—and it was sitting in the path of the oncoming train, which was now barrelling along at 112 miles per hour.

Passenger cries inside the speeding train all but drowned out Chad Ryan's warning through the public address.

"Brace for impact!"

He was staring at a photo of his wife and daughter.

In the fourth car, Jessie held steady against the jostling. Concentrating with all she had, she found a back door into the Metro system, certain she'd followed Tarantula's path through a recent remote software upgrade.

Immediately she started work on undoing everything that Dahlia and Tarantula had wrought on the system.

At the control centre, excited shouts from a technician reached Tom Harris.

"We got it, Tom! We've released the brakes!"

Harris radioed Ryan. Ryan's control flashed, followed by deafening screeching and metallic scraping as the brakes engaged. Sparks sprayed from the wheels, then there was smoke and an acrid burning smell as passengers were tossed and jolted, the train rumbling and bumping as it ground on the tracks, sliding toward the train ahead. The rear of the stationary train ahead grew larger before Ryan's widened eyes as his own train slowed, vibrating to a halt just a foot away. Smoke enveloped the train, accompanied by a hissing. Every car fell silent before the passengers exploded with joyous cheering.

Jessie crushed Dylan to her and sobbed.

EPILOGUE

The laptop Jessie left on the subway had a built-in tracking app, but it was disabled by the person who'd taken it.

However, Jessie had put the PC in the Instinct bag she'd used to carry the company's blue computer. The bag had several tracking devices concealed in the fabric, which enabled police to locate and arrest Dahlia and the other members of Tarantula working with her.

In France, aided by his lawyer—who'd secured the prosecutor's promise of a solitary prison cell—Dmitri Semyon Vampa cooperated. His information led investigators to identify members of Tarantula who were behind the deadly attacks in Paris, Toronto, São Paulo and Washington, DC; Dylan's abduction at JFK; and Vaughn's murder in New York. Officials moved quickly, making arrests across Europe, in South America, Canada and the US, as they dismantled the cybercriminal network. The suspects faced multiple murder and terrorism charges and life sentences.

Investigators had determined that it was Dahlia, who now was facing life in prison, who had guided Tarantula's assassins to murder Vaughn—an act she'd witnessed. They'd also uncovered how, with help from Tarantula, Dahlia had lured Carl Lasker to the abandoned asylum where she murdered him and the Cooks.

Through her attorneys, Dahlia attempted to reach out to Jessie, but Jessie refused the contact. The two would never speak again.

As more became known, Tarantula was global news for weeks. Journalists in several countries dug deep, piecing together solid accounts. But none surpassed the depth of the multi-part series produced by *Veritas Sola*. Chelsea Webber, backed by Rich Lafont—who'd assembled a reporting team—worked with Jessie. With Bobby's help, they decrypted all of Vaughn's notes.

The team drew upon interviews with Jessie, Bobby, Sarita, former MIT classmates, law enforcement agencies around the world and court records filed in several countries.

The extensive articles covered all aspects of the case, including how Tarantula's members had used anti-trafficking sites to search for, then lure, mislead and recruit the Cooks for what the older couple had believed was a righteous rescue operation of Dylan at JFK. Guided by Dahlia's knowledge of and involvement with Project Gold Arrow Horizon at MIT, Tarantula had also sought out, targeted and manipulated Carl Lasker. The group's members worked methodically, carrying out Dahlia's vengeful plan to secure the eternal key, which had culminated in the murders of Lasker, the Cooks and Vaughn. It was a vainglorious, vile series of acts orchestrated by Dahlia to prove her skills surpassed Jessie's.

The stories were heart-wrenching and at times haunting—especially the reporting on Vaughn's murder, given that each report published by *Veritas Sola* also carried Vaughn's byline.

"Our way of honouring him and his work," Rich Lafont told Jessie.

Studying Tarantula's tactics and methods, and drawing upon Instinct's technological advances, experts around the world had moved fast to strengthen cybersecurity.

In Washington, DC, lessons were learned—building upon those from earlier disasters, like the deadly 2009 Red Line crash near

Fort Totten. ATO was not to blame in that case. Still, Tarantula's attack had challenged officials to make the system safer.

In Ottawa, Canada, at the Communications Security Establishment, Claire Brenner was promoted for her work after the Toronto tragedy to lead the effort to enhance protection against cyberattacks.

Claire learned of her new position the day her family went to the rescue shelter to get the white golden retriever puppy Marissa adored. *It's time for us to start a new chapter*, Claire thought the next day after they'd planted a dogwood tree in the backyard in memory of Max.

In Washington, DC, in the immediate aftermath of events, Dylan was assessed by doctors, including being treated by a psychiatrist specializing in trauma. It would take time for the young boy to process all that he'd been through, the doctor told Jessie, advising her to arrange treatment for him when they returned home.

Before they left the hospital, Dylan told his mother that he felt like "something more real and hugely bad was coming."

That was when the psychiatrist worked with Jessie to tell Dylan that his father had been killed and there was going to be a memorial service for him. The boy was devastated and confused, breaking into sobs. But he endured, deciding that he wanted to go with his mother to New York for his dad's funeral service.

The psychiatrist told Dylan that it had to be his choice to go. He guided him on what he might see, hear; how people would be acting around him; and that it was okay to cry, or not to cry, or to ask any questions or take a break.

At the service, Miller and Lillian looked older, more fragile, but their pained faces brightened at seeing and holding Dylan. Comforted by his presence, they clung to him the way shipwrecked survivors hold onto wreckage in a seething ocean.

They accepted Jessie's embrace, yet during the service, as she mourned Vaughn, there were moments she sensed an undertone of blame directed at her. Or maybe it was just a reflection of her own guilt.

Maybe it was fallout from the trauma she would carry for the rest of her days, she thought, staring at Dylan, then at the clouds on their flight home.

In California, upon arriving at LAX with Dylan, Jessie took no questions but read a statement to the news people waiting for them, thanking everyone for their help.

Bobby and Sarita were there to take them home to Santa Monica. A few days later, Jessie took Dylan to the Palm Breeze Valley Senior Living Center to see his grandmother. Upon seeing them, some staff and residents applauded.

When they stepped into Florence's room, her eyes grew wide and she smiled, lifting her arms to hug her grandson.

"Oh, it's been so long, honey. Where have you been?"

"I've been away, Grandma."

Dylan glanced at his mom, who nodded.

"But now I'm back."

"Oh honey," Florence said. "I'm so happy."

Watching them, Jessie blinked back tears. Her family had been reunited to carry on with their lives, and to find hope again.

By knowing the Mother
   one knows her children
By knowing her children
   one comes to know her
Such is their unity
   that one does not exist without the other
. . .
Stay with the Mother, shut the mouth, close the gates
   and you are never in trouble

—Lao Tzu, *Tao Te Ching*, translated by John Minford

ACKNOWLEDGEMENTS

AND A PERSONAL NOTE

First off, my apologies if you've read this on your subway commute.

I make no claim to possessing knowledge of transportation, computer engineering, criminal investigations or any aspects of these fields. My apologies to the experts among you for errors that would cause you to say, "That's just plain wrong."

I get it.

In my effort to give this "what if" scenario a ring of truth, I studied reports on incidents made public by investigative agencies around the world. I also wanted to encompass the all-too-real threat of cybercriminals and advances being made in technology every day.

Above all, *One Second Away* is fiction, drawn in my imagination where I exercised creative licence and took liberties with technical realities, jurisdiction and the investigative process to present a drama concerning flawed human beings facing their worst fears.

Writing is a solitary job, but in shaping and getting this book to you, I benefitted from the hard work and support of many people.

My thanks to my wife, Barbara, and to Wendy Dudley for their invaluable help improving the tale.

Thanks to Laura and Michael.

My thanks to the brilliant Amy Moore-Benson and the stellar team at CookeMcDermid Literary Management in Toronto. Also to the extraordinary Lorella Belli and the outstanding team at LBLA in London.

My thanks to Bhavna Chauhan, fantastic associate publisher at Doubleday Canada, and to Amy Black, the wonderful publisher at Doubleday Canada and VP, Penguin Random House Canada. My thanks to the entire gang at PRH in Toronto and around the world.

It seems like the idea for this tale, and its evolution into the book you now have, came so long ago. While the bulk of it was drafted at my desk at home, the story never left me. In the months it took to complete, parts of it were written in New York City, Toronto, Halifax and Nashville, on trains (yes on trains), planes, in airports and hotels.

The final product is a culmination of the hard work and generosity of too many people for me to thank individually. People in editorial, narration, production, marketing, sales, distribution; librarians, booksellers and the people who hand deliver it to your address.

It brings me to what I believe is the most critical part of the entire enterprise: you, the reader. Those of you familiar with my stories are aware that this part has become something of a credo for me, one that bears repeating with each book.

Thank you for your time, for without you, the story remains an untold tale. Thank you for setting your life on pause and taking the journey. I appreciate my audience around the world and those who've been with me since the beginning who keep in touch. Thank you all for your kind words. I hope you enjoyed the ride and will check out my earlier books while watching for new ones.

Feel free to send me a note. I enjoy hearing from you. I have been known to participate in virtual book club discussions of my books. The best way to actually reach me is an email through my website. While it may take some time, I try to respond to all messages.

Rick Mofina

www.rickmofina.com
Instagram: @rickmofina
Facebook: rickmofina
X: @rickmofina
Bluesky: @rickmofina.bsky.social

Michael Mofina

RICK MOFINA is a *USA Today*, *Globe and Mail*, and *Toronto Star* bestselling author of more than thirty crime fiction thrillers that have been published in nearly thirty countries. A former journalist, he has interviewed murderers on death row, flown over Los Angeles with the LAPD and patrolled with the Royal Canadian Mounted Police near the Arctic. He has also reported from the Caribbean, Africa, Kuwait and Qatar. He is a two-time winner of the Crime Writers of Canada Award of Excellence, a Barry Award winner, and a multiple finalist for the International Thriller Writers Awards and the Shamus Award, presented by the Private Eye Writers of America. *Library Journal* calls him "one of the best thriller writers in the business."